THE CROMWELL FILE

THE CROMWELL FILE

William Harrington

ST. MARTIN'S PRESS | NEW YORK

Design by Philip Denlinger

Library of Congress Cataloging-in-Publication Data

Harrington, William, 1931–
The Cromwell file.

I. Title.
PS3558.A63C76 1986   813'.54   85–25083
ISBN 0-312-17648-1

First Edition

10 9 8 7 6 5 4 3 2 1

To LES FITCH,
who showed us that courage
is more than just a word.

AUTHOR'S NOTE

ONCE UPON a time it was sufficient to use the word "novel" on the jacket of a book to notify all readers that the book was a work of fiction. Of late, the word alone is apparently insufficient to convey the idea. Let me emphasize, then, that this is a work of fiction. The events described in this story never happened—and, indeed, let us fervently hope that nothing like them ever does happen. I have tried to avoid using the name of any real person or business as the name of a person or business that does evil or embarrassing things in this story; and if by chance it has worked out otherwise, it is coincidence.

THE CROMWELL FILE

1

AS A ROMAN, Dr. Clara Babila Giardini had found it difficult to accustom herself to the early hours and to the unending busyness of Milan. Impatiently, she tossed her cigarette from the window of her car to the pavement of the Corso Magenta. With the sun just lifting itself ponderously into a purple sky and the pigeons hardly off their overnight roosts, traffic was already heavy, the city was already noisy, and already she was late for work. She had only a few hours before they would begin to admit the tourists to the refectory, and by then most of her day's work must be done.

She turned off the Corso at last and headed her Fiat into a reserved space: one of the few parking places available under the walls of the monastery of Santa Maria delle Grazie. She parked, locked the car, and entered the monastery grounds, into a half-quiet refuge where wet gray mist still lay over the grass and shrubbery and seemed to muffle the sounds spilling in from behind her. The soles of her loose sandles slapped the stone floor of the cloister, echoing noisily: the only noise inside the walls.

Dr. Giardini had been forty-one years old for just one week. Her face was lined, though—some said by her dissolute way of life, including her fondness for strong, unfiltered cigarettes and harsh Spanish brandies. She was a blonde by virtue of chemicals applied monthly by the alchemists of a Milanese hairdresser's shop, so her hair was coarse. Her figure suggested that she ate well, though in truth she was solid, hard, not plump.

By preference she would have been wearing on this warm spring morning a pair of softly faded, and probably tight, blue jeans and a summer-weight knit shirt. Her dark-blue skirt and white, mannish shirt were a concession to the Church. She had made concessions, and the Church had made concessions. She was the best in the world at what she did; to have her for this work, the authorities of the Church had overlooked her vigorous amorality and her want of formal churchly piety.

She entered the refectory and switched on the lights. The great painting appeared: *The Last Supper,* by Leonardo da Vinci—what was left of it after five centuries of neglect, vandalism in the name of restoration, and the assaults of history and nature. The painting glowed in the shadowless glare of a dozen floodlights. It shone behind its scaffold and behind the banks of sensors that recorded the temperature, humidity, level of pollution, expansion and contraction in the wall, and vibration.

She walked toward the painting in the early morning silence before the intrusion of the first tourists, moved as always by how genius endured, moved also by religious inspiration, which had rarely touched her life before she received the commission to restore *The Last Supper.* She grabbed a steel brace and swung herself upward onto the scaffold. She climbed with abrupt, confident agility and for a moment stood facing the figure of Matthew.

She was proud of what she had accomplished with Matthew. Before her work, past restorers had made him a static figure, leaning toward Thaddeus and Simon for no particular reason. Restored as Leonardo had painted him, his mouth was open, talking excitedly. She had restored an element of the tense drama of the painting.

Moving to her microscope—not just a tube full of lenses but a complex machine mounted for a month now before the figure of Judas—she began again to examine the flaking pigment, glue, and wax that comprised the ravaged surface of the painting. Peering at the work she had done yesterday on the figure's right wrist, at the edge of the sleeve, she was satisfied and knew she could move along to another square centimeter.

She had restored the hand of Judas, the one clutching his silver, and it had emerged from under the damage of centuries, as had the face of Matthew and the food on some of the plates on the Passover Supper table. It was as if layers of mud and dust had been removed. The restored parts of the painting were bright in contrast to the unrestored portions.

Through the microscope she examined a centimeter of the edge between the blue sleeve and the wrist. She dipped a brush into a bottle of the special solvent developed for this work after months of study and experimentation. Gently she touched the surface of the painting with the solvent, then bending close watched it soften decades-old—centuries-old—overpainting, varnish, glue, and dirt. Quickly, before the solvent could reach the pigments of Leonardo, she blotted. Her blotting paper came away with a muddy gum. She repeated the process. Less came away. She continued. A tiny fragment of the surface, a few flakes of blue paint covering an area no more than an eighth the size of a postage stamp, gradually emerged and glowed with something that must have been very much like the original color.

But she had to be careful. Leonardo's paint was exceedingly delicate and had been flaking away from the primer and the plaster for five hundred years. If a flake fell away it could not be restored, and that much more of the painting would be lost.

Much of *The Last Supper* was in fact lost forever, but Dr. Giardini meant to show the world as much as was humanly possible of what had led the High Renaissance to proclaim it its finest work of art.

"Ah, good morning, Dr. Giardini!"

Fra Vittorio had entered the refectory and approached without her hearing his footsteps. He carried two cups of coffee. She swung around and dropped down from the scaffolding, amused to see the friar turn away his eyes as her skirt flew up for an instant.

Fra Vittorio looked up at the painting as they sipped the steaming coffee. Though she shared coffee with him often in the cloister or on a bench in the garden, he rarely came in, protesting that the work was so slow that he would rather see it only at long intervals, so as to be surprised and pleased each time at the progress he could perceive.

"Ah, Judas," he said. "I thought you might leave the dirt on him."

"A special challenge, Judas," she said. "We have Leonardo's drawing for Judas, you know. The painting differs so much that almost certainly it has been overpainted. It will be interesting to see if we can clean off a later artist's changes and learn how Leonardo painted him."

Fra Vittorio glanced up again. "How he saw Christ . . ." he murmured. "That's what I pray we will be spared to see: how he saw Christ."

"Christ will be last," said Dr. Giardini. "I will use everything we have learned from all the rest of the work. Only when I have learned everything I possibly can will I touch the face of Christ." She looked up. "That is the supreme challenge."

When she was alone again in the refectory, Dr. Giardini climbed the scaffolding once more and stood in the center to stare at the damaged outline of the face of Christ, wondering for the ten-thousandth time how much she would be able to achieve with it. It would be the challenge by which everything else she had done would be judged. Seven years of work . . . How many more? Maybe seven more. She—

For the barest instant she was conscious of a shock. Before she could form a thought, the face and figure of Christ burst from the wall and threw her backward off the scaffold. In the last moment of her life she realized that the wall and the painting were dissolving in blast and fire. As she landed hard on her back on the floor of the collapsing refectory she knew she was being buried in the dust of *The Last Supper*.

2

THE WINDOWS of their meeting room in the Hôtel Crillon overlooked the Place de la Concorde. Major Duncan Glynbourne found it ironic that this conference should be meeting in a chamber overlooking a square so named. He was a student of history, however, and quickly remembered facts that canceled the irony: that hardly fifty yards from the façade of the Hôtel Crillon had stood the guillotine that sliced through the neck of Louis XVI; that within view of these windows had stood another that did the same to his unhappy queen, Marie Antoinette, as well as to Danton, Robespierre, Jeanne du Barry, and Charlotte Corday, to name only a few; and that the square had been renamed by the Directory in hope of cleansing it of a part, at least, of its bloody reputation. It was the Place de la Concorde now, but it had been the Place de la Révolution, the site of the most grisly scenes of the Terror. It was too much, Major Glynbourne supposed, to imagine that the organizers of this police conference against terror had been so imaginative as to choose the Hôtel Crillon for the fact that citizens had stood at these very windows and watched terror at its supreme moment.

Officially, the invitations to the conference had come from Interpol and had been directed to the Interpol National Central Bureau in each country—Great Britain, France, Italy, Spain, Portugal, Germany, Belgium, The Netherlands, Switzerland, and Austria. It was

5

unthinkable, though, that Interpol had chosen the Hôtel Crillon. That impecunious organization would never have held a meeting in such a setting. The Dutchman Theodorus Companjen, representing the executive committee of Interpol and now acting as chairman of the conference, lived in St. Cloud, but likely as not this meeting was the occasion of his first visit to central Paris in six months. He was the typical Interpol file clerk, a dedicated man, meticulous beyond the edge of dullness, and if it had been up to him, probably the conference would have met in the gray-steel-and-plastic Interpol offices in St. Cloud.

More likely the Hôtel Crillon had been selected by the spare young Frenchman, the chain-smoking André Bonnac, and likely his government was paying the cost. Officially, Bonnac was a major in DGSE— Direction Générale de Sécurité Extérieure, military security—but almost certainly, in Glynbourne's judgment, he was also an agent of GIGN, which the French still liked to pretend did not exist. Bonnac was a professional security agent: prosaic, proletarian, highly competent, efficient, and—in all likelihood—entirely ruthless.

They had worked together before, five years ago. Bonnac had identified himself then as an inspector with Sûreté Générale, but Glynbourne had developed a strong suspicion that he was really an agent of the now abolished SDECE, the Service de Documentation Extérieure et de Contre-Espionage, and specifically of Service 5, known as Action Service, which specialized in the quick and brutal elimination of threats to the Gaullist régime. On that occasion, just as Scotland Yard was about to arrest the Syrian, Haddad, he had somehow managed to cross the Channel back to France, where Sûreté shortly reported he had been found dead. Glynbourne had always believed Bonnac had kidnapped him in London, taken him back to France, and killed him there, which would have been characteristic of Action Service; and he had not forgotten the resentment he had felt then, not only that such a decision had been taken and carried out, but also that it had been done without consulting a cooperating agency.

If the suspicion was correct and Bonnac had been with Action Service, then logically he would now be a member of GIGN, Groupe d'Intervention de la Gendarmerie Nationale, France's crack new anti-terrorist unit.

Glynbourne had a similar suspicion about Karl Schuman, the late-middle-aged German whose credentials identified him as an agent of BFV, Bundesamt für Verfassenschutz, the Federal Republic's domes-tic counter-espionage and anti-terrorist office; but SIS files contained a report to the effect that Schuman was probably actually an agent of BND, Bundesnachtrichtendienst, the old Gehlen organization, the Federal Republic's military intelligence service.

There was no question about the Spanish representative. Colonel Adolfo Martinez. He was from CESID, Centro Superior de Informa-ción de la Defensa.

The conference, then, was a strange mix of representatives from the civilian police agencies to which the invitations had been sent and men from military intelligence or special paramilitary counter-terrorist agencies. Half the governments represented had not sent represen-tatives from their national central bureaus.

Major Duncan Glynbourne himself was from Group Four of Secret Intelligence Service, special anti-terrorist section with powers con-ferred directly from the prime minister.

Italy, on the other hand, had chosen a conspicuously civilian po-lice official—Galeazzo Castellano, former prefect of Milan, now sec-ond- or third-ranking officer of SISDE (Servizio Informazioni Sicurezza Demacratico), and significantly not an officer of SISMI, the Italian Military Security Service.

Finally, among the more prominent conferees—among, that is, the ones that Glynbourne recognized or on whom he had been briefed before he left London—was the observer from the Vatican, Monsignor Charles Maurice de Périgord, the man to whom Glyn-bourne was instructed to look for a signal about a later meeting. There was an odd bird! How did you define him?

It occurred to Glynbourne as he shifted his eyes to the cassocked monsignor that the man's illustrious ancestor may well have been one of those Frenchmen who stood at these windows and watched the slaughter on the Place de la Révolution, for his grandfather's grandfather had been the illegitimate child of the notorious alliance between Charles Maurice de Talleyrand-Périgord, Bishop of Autun, Prince of Benevento, Napoleon's foreign minister, French representative at the Congress of Vienna, et cetera, et cetera, and Dorothée, Princess of Courland, Duchess of Dino, the pretty young wife of Talleyrand's nephew. His heavy-lidded eyes and the worldly smile on his wide mouth gave the monsignor a resemblance to Talleyrand that was not imaginary. Handed a powdered wig, the monsignor could have stood at the window and, looking down, given a start to the ghosts that must prowl the pavement below.

He held a special position in the Church, though exactly how it might be defined was a mystery except to observers skilled in decoding the circumlocutions so beloved of the Vatican. He seemed to have no connection with the Vatican Central Vigilance Office, the two-hundred-man papal security force. Formally, as nearly as one could tell, he was assigned to the Administration of the Patrimony of the Apostolic See. Specifically, he was attached to the Extraordinary Section, which meant that he should have been chiefly concerned with the Church's investments. That was too simple. It was also understood that he did not report to the cardinal-president of the Administration, but directly to the Sosituto, the deputy to the Papal Secretary of State.

If his place in the organization had been purposefully made obscure the better to mask his function, that goal had not been achieved. Most of these conferees well understood that Monsignor de Périgord was the chief of a small, select, and secret group of young priests assembled after the 1981 attempt on the life of the pope and charged with the responsibility of working with all national police and intelligence forces to "frustrate the purposes of those who would physically and criminally assault His Holiness, any of his Pontifical Family, or the holy relics and treasures of the Apostolic See."

This was not the first time Major Glynbourne had seen Charles Maurice de Périgord. He had encountered him twice, ten or fifteen years ago, when the now-monsignor was an acknowledged agent of the SDECE. Glynbourne had heard, about 1968, that Périgord had entered the Church, and he had lost track of him until 1981, when he learned that Monsignor de Périgord was—to put it simply and to use a title he would have denied—the new Vatican intelligence chief.

Castellano was about to speak. It was Italy that had suffered most from the new terrorism, including the outrage that was the genesis of this conference, the destruction of *The Last Supper*. Glynbourne had dined with him last evening. In Italy, Castellano said, the original sense of shock had metamorphosed into a foul, sullen national mood that could have long-range political consequences. That was necessarily one of Castellano's concerns. Editorials in Rome and Milan had suggested that only a more disciplined nation could preserve the pride and character of Italy—meaning of course a nation ordered more nearly as it had been by Mussolini.

Galeazzo Castellano was a handsome, sturdy, fifty-five-year-old Milanese: white-haired, with a neatly trimmed white mustache, dressed in a dark-blue pinstriped suit beautifully tailored with a typical Italian flair. He seated half-glasses on his nose and stared at his notes as he began to speak, in English:

"The reports on which I base my remarks this morning are in the process of being translated into French and English. Copies will be provided in the language of your choice. Our investigation has, as you already know, produced clear evidence that the destruction of *The Last Supper*, together with the refectory and much of the Church of Santa Maria delle Grazie, is the work of the terrorist our friend Major Glynbourne has named Oliver Cromwell."

"Oliver Cromwell? *Ich verstehe nicht. Was bedeutet das?*" said Kriminalinspektor Hildebrand, the Austrian.

"A whimsy," explained Glynbourne. "Cromwell's troops destroyed many beautiful treasures of religious art in churches all over England. Our new terrorist seems to make a point of attacking churches containing venerated objects of our Christian heritage. So . . . Oliver Cromwell. For a code name, it does as well as any."

"One man . . ." said Colonel Martinez.

Castellano nodded. "The explosive was plastique, C-4, once more a very large amount of it, though this time the terrorist attempted to throw the force of the explosion against the wall by loading the far side of the van with sandbags. The detonation was caused by a radio signal. Once again, the detonator was a simple device, obtainable anywhere—a radio-controlled garage-door opener."

"Ah?"

"A very common device in America," said Castellano, nodding to the Belgian. "In Europe they are not so common, but not rare. You can buy one in a dozen stores in Milan, perhaps in a score of them in Paris."

"It's a rather bulky thing to use for the purpose," said Bonnac.

Castellano nodded. "Of course, the electronic components are removed from the metal or plastic case in which the device is normally seen on the ceiling of a garage. Ordinarily, the device requires a bit of antenna, which we believe was afforded by a length of wire we found still taped across a bit of the body of the van. The range . . . well, it can vary. The person who sent the signal that detonated the bomb may have been a hundred meters away, or as far as two kilometers. Two people were with the van when the explosion occurred—a young man inside and a young woman just outside. Both were killed instantly, of course."

"Precisely the same as occurred at Assisi," said Monsignor Périgord.

Castellano nodded. "Except that this time the evil purpose was accomplished."

"The damage to Santa Chiara should have been enough to satisfy anyone's purpose," said the monsignor sadly.

"Except that almost certainly the target was San Francesco," said Castellano. He referred to the Basilica of St. Francis of Assisi, which Italian police assumed had been the target of the bombers, who damaged the nearby Basilica of St. Clare only when they found they could not drive their van of explosives close enough to the Basilica of St. Francis to bring down the structure.

"All very amateurish," said Bonnac. "Crude, in fact. Although not, of course, amateurish at all in one respect. I think we may assume it is the intention of Oliver Cromwell to kill his assistants in the explosion. It is most likely that in each instance they are the only members of his conspiracy who could identify him. Incidentally, have you identified this latest pair?"

"Only one," said Castellano. "The woman. She was a Milanese, named Margherita Catania. Twenty-one years old. The daughter of a watch repairman. She had a police record: minor problems with narcotics, two arrests for prostitution, one for her participation in a riot."

"And what of the CPCI?" Bonnac asked. He turned to the Belgian, who seemed about to ask, and explained—"Crociata Populare Contro Imperialismo—People's Anti-Imperialist Crusade."

"More and more I am of the opinion," said Castellano, "that it is a myth. Margherita Catania, from all we know of her, seems an unlikely terrorist, unlikely to have adhered to any political philosophy. I am more inclined to believe Oliver Cromwell hired her for money."

"The one you were able to . . . reassemble sufficiently to identify after the bombing at Assisi," said Monsignor Périgord, "seems more likely to have been a hireling than a fanatic."

"Yes," agreed Castellano.

"It is not certain, then," said Colonel Martinez, "that the horror perpetrated in Toledo was the work of your man Oliver Cromwell. There was no van. The explosives were carried into the cathedral in a tourist's shoulder bag—"

"But the 'tourist' died in the explosion," interrupted Bonnac. "The explosive was plastique, and the detonator was activated by a little radio receiver. The shoulder strap of the bag contained the antenna wire. Once more a young woman died—"

"And so did the El Grecos," said the Spanish colonel bitterly. "With many other beautiful things."

"I should like," said Monsignor Périgord in unaccented English, "to count the cost in human life. Then let us think of the other costs." He glanced around the table. "In the destruction of *The Last*

Supper, we count, I believe, four—Dr. Giardini, the unfortunate roofer, and the two bombers. At Santa Chiara in Assisi, six were killed, were they not? The young priest, the two American tourists, the fruit vendor, and, again, two bombers. In Toledo, only one, the young woman who carried the bomb into the sacristy."

"I believe you are driving at a point, Monsignor Périgord," said Major Glynbourne. "I see it myself, and I hope you make it forcefully."

The monsignor bestowed a cool, measured smile on Glynbourne, along with a faint nod. "It would almost seem," he said, "that Oliver Cromwell makes it a point to murder his bomb-carriers and to avoid to some extent the slaughter of innocent bystanders. Consider. He detonated the bomb beside Santa Chiara during the noon hour when the church was closed. He destroyed *The Last Supper* early in the morning, when only the restorer was in the refectory. The bomb in Toledo—if it was his work—went off when the young woman with the bomb was alone in the sacristy. Consider what would have happened if he had set off the bomb in the refectory or at Santa Chiara when the tourists were inside. Also, ordinarily the sacristy at Toledo would have been crowded with tourists."

"Unless," said Colonel Martinez, "it is a matter of coincidence, then Oliver Cromwell was within the cathedral when he detonated the bomb. How else could he have known when no one but his bomb-carrier was in the sacristy?"

"But who," objected Kriminalinspektor Schuman, "are these fools who carry his bombs and die in his explosions? Do they know what is going to happen to them?"

"One more question unanswered," said Bonnac.

"Besides the cost in human life," said Monsignor Périgord with the air of a man who has not allowed his chain of thought to be interrupted, "at Assisi we lost the priceless Crucifix of San Damiano, preeminent among the relics and works destroyed in the collapse of the Basilica of Santa Chiara. I do not even mention the crushing of the body relics of the saint herself. At Toledo we lost, among other treasures, precious works by the revered El Greco. And finally, tragically, we have lost Christendom's greatest treasure of art, *The Last Supper*. All these in the past eight months. One trembles to think of what may be next."

"And that, Monsignor, is why we are here," said Bonnac.

Monsignor Périgord nodded. "I'm afraid I have interrupted Signore Castellano's description of what the investigation has so far produced."

Castellano glanced at his notes. "There is not much more, I am afraid. The van was purchased two days before the crime, by the young woman. It was old and battered. She paid cash. No one seems to have seen it parked anywhere, so we suppose it was put in a garage somewhere and the explosives loaded into it there. Once again, it is much the same way things were done in Assisi. The van there had been bought in Perugia. It, too, was old and rusty."

"Where do they get such quantities of plastique?" asked Schuman.

"The answer to that is the key to the investigation," said Bonnac. "A very limited number of sources are available. In any event, that Monsieur Cromwell has so much at his disposal proves he is no amateur, no stupid fanatic. No. He is a professional, in the employ of one of the very few organizations that could supply him with so much plastique."

"Wilson is supposed to have supplied Qadaffi with twenty *tons* of it," said Schuman.

"Which," said Bonnac, "Colonel Qadaffi does not hand out to any fool who thinks he wants to blow up something—any more than does the KGB. Anyone who relies on those sources for their plastique does their work."

"The telephone calls . . ." suggested the Belgian.

"We received one after Santa Chiara and one after Santa Maria delle Grazie," said Castellano. "Only the second used the term CPCI. Of course, you will remember we received a similar call in Florence and one in Pisa, but nothing happened."

"We received no call at all in Toledo," said Colonel Martinez.

"In each instance, however," observed Monsignor Périgord, "the bombing or the threat involved a cherished treasure of the Church."

"There can be no question, I think," said Bonnac firmly, "but that this new outbreak of terrorism is directed at the Catholic Church. Personally, I relate all of it directly to the 1981 attempt on the life of His Holiness. It is all of one, and the motive behind it is brutally simple."

"Whether or not I agree," said Major Glynbourne, "that tells us little about how to cope with it. My hope in coming to this conference is that we will find a means of preventing further outrages."

The conference might have continued for two days, or three; the call had not specified its length. By four o'clock, only an hour into the afternoon after the break for lunch, it seemed to wind down of its own weight; everyone had said everything, and it was plain nothing more was to be accomplished. The meeting adjourned with little achieved other than a hearty promise on the part of all the conferees that they would report often and in detail to each other, and as they reluctantly separated there was among them a palpable sense of unease and dissatisfaction.

With the sole exception of the conferee from The Netherlands, on whose part it was probably only an unconscious omission, all the conferees made a point of saying a personal good-bye to the observer from the Vatican—some of them, as Glynbourne understood, with the expectation of hearing an important word from him; others with no such expectation. Monsignor Périgord spoke quietly with each, receiving each into an implied intimate perimeter that seemed to emanate from his cassock, for a few words in private. In his almost whispered conversation with three men, he extended a confidential invitation to dinner. It was thus that the three of them arrived, within a few minutes of each other, at about half-past eight, at a house on the Faubourg St. Honoré—Duncan Glynbourne, André Bonnac, and Galeazzo Castellano.

The monsignor offered no explanation for the house. He received

them in a small room off the center hallway, a study or library lined
with glass-fronted bookcases filled with leather-bound books. The
walls were covered with red silk. The furniture—several chairs, a set-
tee, a low table—were Louis XV. A dozen fresh red roses were arranged in a crystal vase on the table. A bar was set up on another
table: glasses, a bucket of ice, a seltzer bottle, Beefeaters, Stolichnaya,
Glenfiddich, Cinzano, as well as some crisp biscuit and three small
cheeses. A little houseboy in a white jacket—perhaps a Vietnamese—
stood by the bar and poured drinks.

Monsignor Périgord wore his black cassock, a gold pectoral cross, a
red zucchetto. "I have acquired," he said, speaking English, "a taste
for American martinis. Do you know them? You pour a splash of dry
vermouth over ice, then fill the glass with gin. I warn you, though,
they must be what causes Americans to cast their votes for such men
as Gerald Ford and, uh, well . . . Nixon, Carter, and Reagan." He
smiled. "On the other hand, what do we French drink to have produced Mitterand?"

"Calvados," said Bonnac, nodding at the monsignor and conceding
a faint, humorless smile. He had lit a Gauloise without inquiring if
smoking were acceptable in this house and had found on the low
table, by the roses, a small glass ashtray, which he now cupped in his
left hand. He held his cigarette in his mouth to leave his right hand
for the glass of vermouth he had accepted. The flesh of his face was
drawn down over a long, pointed jaw and was rough with whiskers
that had reappeared within hours after he had shaved for a second
time that day. He wore rimless octagonal eyeglasses. His double-
breasted gray suit hung stiffly on his long frame. "*Quel dommage.*"

Major Glynbourne sipped gratefully from a glass of Glenfiddich. It
was always difficult to find a decent whisky in France, except by paying exorbitantly, and he welcomed the honest astringent taste of a
good Scots whisky, a relief from the fruity fumes of French spirits. He
was a spare, solemn man, with a tanned and deeply pitted face, cool
hard-blue eyes, a narrow mouth. His voice marked him. Once heard,
it was never forgotten; it was like the trained voice of a Shakespearean

actor: low, carefully used, authoritative, often suggesting more calm
self-confidence than he actually felt. He wore his graying hair short,
almost bristly. His black pin-striped suit, from a Savile Row tailor, fit
with smooth precision on a trim, erect body.

Castellano drank vodka. He stood a little apart from the other
three, observing, and wondered if either Monsignor Périgord or Duncan Glynbourne had noticed what he had when he shook hands with
André Bonnac: that the Frenchman was armed with a small automatic inside his ill-cut gray suit.

"I would like to confirm something," said Major Glynbourne,
moving closer to the others and lowering his voice so that the houseboy might not hear. "Is it certain that Ink has been terminated?"

Bonnac nodded.

"I'm afraid I don't understand the reference," said Castellano.

"I'm sorry," said the monsignor. "SISDE has probably had no occasion to learn of Ink. I'm sure SISMI knows of her." He glanced for
a quick moment at the faces of each of the others. "Each of you has
your government's highest clearance, and each government has given
the most emphatic assurance of your discretion. I see no reason for
any information to be withheld from any member of this committee,
wherever it originated, whatever its significance."

"Irena Nikolayevna Khurkov," interjected Bonnac, "was one of
those many Russians who come to the West, ostensibly as clerical
employees of the various Soviet embassies and missions, actually as
KGB agents. She served in Paris the past three years. Two weeks ago
she was recalled to Moscow and given a lethal injection."

"Strangled," said Monsignor Périgord.

"An injection," Bonnac insisted.

The monsignor settled a calm, heavy-lidded gaze on Bonnac. "In-
jected with sodium pentothal during interrogation. Strangled when
the interrogation was over."

"I stand corrected," said Bonnac dryly. "Anyway, no one need be
concerned about her interrogation. She was carefully handled here
and knew nothing we didn't want her to know. Moscow has recalled

two other agents, obviously out of fear she compromised them. But she didn't."

"Strangled . . ." mused Glynbourne in his deep, rolling voice. "Ghastly way—"

"I only regret I could not do it myself," said Bonnac blandly.

"That bad?" asked the monsignor, regarding the Frenchman with mock insouciance.

Bonnac's eyes narrowed behind his frameless glasses. His lips whitened. "I should like to know what she told them after they drugged her," he said. "If it was what I hope, perhaps she at last earned the money we paid her."

"Then *you*—" gasped Castellano.

"Of course," said Bonnac coldly.

From the moment he was given the assignment, Glynbourne had wondered if his government had not made an error in appointing him to work with GIGN. In his frame of reference, murder was still a crime. He glanced at Monsignor Périgord and wondered how *he* felt. He decided he would never find out if he had to read the monsignor's thoughts from his face. Perhaps he had learned at the Vatican—it was said they all did—to let his moods and expressions communicate only what he wanted the world to see. He would have liked to know, anyway, how the monsignor reacted to the fact that Bonnac was undoubtedly more interested in killing the bomber than in capturing him.

A little later the houseboy opened the double doors between the study and an intimate dining room furnished in the same style. They dined over a round table, on courses of fish, then of meat, with wines appropriate to each course, all attentively served by the houseboy and a maid.

With the two servants constantly moving in and out of the room, they kept their conversation light, of politics and personalities, battles and wars, art and music, history and philosophy. Glynbourne was pleased to see how well each of these men acquitted himself in such wide-ranging talk. Even Bonnac proved to know something of music, a little of art, and a good deal more of the shakers and movers abroad in the world now and over the last decade.

When coffee and brandy were brought to the table, Monsignor Périgord told the houseboy to leave them; the gentlemen would serve themselves and would not require his services further.

"Well, gentlemen," said the monsignor then. "We constitute, as your governments told you we would, an ad hoc committee. We are the members. I trust our purpose and the extent of our authority are completely understood."

"I should like to hear a statement of that," said Glynbourne. "It would be unfortunate if there were any misunderstanding."

"It would indeed," said the monsignor. "Our purpose, Major Glynbourne, is to protect the cherished works of Western civilization from terrorist attack and destruction. To do that, we are authorized to take extraordinary measures if necessary. Your governments will support us. The Church will, to the extent of its influence and authority, support us as well."

"And how do we define the term 'extraordinary measures,' Monsignor?"

"It may be necessary," explained Castellano, "to adopt extra-judicial methods."

"Meaning murder," said Glynbourne.

"Prime Minister Thatcher," said Monsignor Périgord quietly, "was most specific in explaining your situation to us. You have all the authority you need, special authority not normally granted even to MI6. On the other hand, we understand the limitations."

"I cannot," said Glynbourne solemnly, "participate in an extra-judicial execution."

The monsignor nodded heavily, his eyes fixed on a nut he was cracking with a silver nutcracker. "Mrs. Thatcher was most emphatic," he said, "that if Oliver Cromwell is apprehended on British soil, processes of British law must be allowed to take their course."

"On the other hand," said Bonnac, "we were given an assurance that if the man is encountered elsewhere and it is the judgment of the rest of us that he must be nullified, you will not interfere. I for one would like to hear your personal confirmation of that assurance."

"You have it," said Glynbourne. "I will act according to my instructions."

"More is at stake," said Castellano, "than monuments or artifacts, more even than the human lives that have been lost in these outrages. The destruction of *The Last Supper* has produced an alarming public mood in Italy—"

"And in France," said Bonnac.

"In all of Europe, to some degree and another, as I understand," said Castellano. "And in America as well. It is no exaggeration to say that these bombings could constitute a threat to democracy."

"Which is probably the motive behind them," said Bonnac.

"There are," said Monsignor Périgord, "relatively few personalities whose assassinations would have produced such a sense of shock and horror as the destruction of *The Last Supper* . . . and of course to a lesser extent the destruction of Santa Chiara and that of the sacristy in Toledo. And what is next? St. Peter's? The *Pietà* again? Notre Dame? Chartres? Westminster Abbey? Canterbury? Sainte Chapelle? St. Mark's? Whose death would so much outrage the world as the destruction of one of those? For the most part, we can protect men and women." He shook his head. "We cannot protect all the beautiful and holy things in the world."

"The prime minister was entirely clear about the authority granted," said Glynbourne, his thoughts never having abandoned his original question. "And I did accept it." He reached for the bottle and poured a splash of cognac into his glass. He nodded. "I did accept it. Though I must tell you, I was a bit surprised the assignment came to me."

"You wonder why you were chosen," said the monsignor. "The prime minister told us a good deal about you. You are known to your government as a shrewd and dogged investigator. That is the kind of man we need. We have no idea who Oliver Cromwell may be. We must find out."

"Really, you might have found a better-qualified man," said Glynbourne. "I am not a linguist, for one thing. I learned to speak German when I was serving with the Army of the Rhine. My French and Italian are . . . schoolboy."

"Once we knew something about you, we asked specifically for you," said Monsignor Périgord. "If you don't mind my saying so, Major, loyalties within the British intelligence services have sometimes been more directed toward the social class and university background out of which your agents are recruited than toward serving your country. We did not want to have to deal with some of the amoral eccentrics your universities have sent into MI6."

"The Cantabridgians," said Glynbourne. "All that's behind us. Our recruiting is far more careful now. You no longer get in just through Old Boy connections."

"Yes," said the monsignor. "You are evidence of that, I suppose. You're certainly not of the Old Boy network. Your father is a dispensing chemist, I believe. A shop in Kensington? And, uh, your late wife was quarter owner of a fine-woolens shop in the Burlington Arcade. Prime Minister Thatcher mentioned that you even go to church now and again—an unusual habit for a man pursuing a career in SIS." The monsignor smiled. "Since our task is to preserve treasures of the Christian heritage, I was not unhappy to learn you are a Christian—Anglican though it is."

"How did you choose *me*, then?" Bonnac asked with a shallow laugh. "I'm no Christian."

"No," said the monsignor. "You are an atheist. Other than that, and the fact that you remain unmarried, outwardly your background is surprisingly similar to Major Glynbourne's. You seem to acknowledge only one loyalty, Monsieur Bonnac: to the French state. You have no wife or children and no faith, and your only political philosophy seems to be your intensely personal dislike for communism. You come highly recommended, Monsieur. No man, we are told, knows more about fighting terrorism."

"So *you* chose us," said Glynbourne. "You chose—"

"Actually," the monsignor interrupted, "the impetus for a joint effort involving several nations came from the Italian government and from Cardinal Alberti. I was assigned responsibilities early in the process, as was Signore Castellano."

"The Spanish also have suffered," said Bonnac. "Actually, of course, France has not, not yet, nor has England."

"Spain was not invited to send a representative," said Monsignor Périgord. "Nor was the Federal Republic. Signore Castellano and I were not satisfied that either of those governments could . . ." He turned to Castellano. "How shall I say it?"

"Be trusted," said the Italian. "In any event, we have here the talents we need. It would serve no purpose to extend the membership of this committee."

"And the conference today was . . . ?"

"A gesture. And a cover," said Castellano.

"In any event," continued the monsignor, "for better or worse, here we are. You represent the most effective police and security agencies in Western Europe: SIS Group Four for England, SISDE for Italy, and GIGN for France."

"Do not omit yourself, Monsignor," said Bonnac. "We haven't a name for your organization, but we see its work."

"A few priests trying to cope with a special manifestation of evil in the world," said Monsignor Périgord with a self-deprecating shrug.

Bonnac and Castellano chuckled. Bonnac lifted his brandy in salute to the monsignor.

"And now," said the monsignor. "What do we know and what can we do?"

"Since Monsieur Bonnac and I are new to this investigation," said Glynbourne, "we can only work with the facts we have been given. Are there others?"

"I should like," said Castellano, "for you to accompany me to Milan and Assisi, to see for yourself the situs of each crime and the physical evidence. You may see something we have not yet noticed."

"For myself," said Bonnac, "I propose to come to Milan, to talk with the family and friends of the late Margherita Catania. I seem to have a facility for inspiring people to recall facts they neglected to recall when first interrogated. Is that agreeable to you, Signore? Will you provide a man to work with me?"

Castellano nodded. "Gladly."

"Can we meet again, say in a week?" asked the monsignor. "Shall we say in Rome?"

Castellano remained with Monsignor Périgord after Glynbourne and Bonnac had gone out to find a taxi. The monsignor poured fresh coffee for them both.

"*Il segugio ed il carnefice,*" said Castellano, nodding toward the door through which the Englishman and the Frenchman had just left. The bloodhound and the executioner.

3

DURING THE EVENING when the ad hoc committee first met in the house on the Faubourg St. Honoré, the man the committee had elected to call Oliver Cromwell dined on lobster with his mother at Wheeler's Sovereign in Mayfair, then returned her to their flat in Audley Street. A little later he went out again, for a champagne supper with a young Haitian dancer who was celebrating her one-hundredth performance in *Cats*. The next afternoon, which found Major Duncan Glynbourne, André Bonnac, and Galeazzo Castellano on a flight to Milan, and Monsignor Charles Maurice de Périgord on a flight to Rome, Oliver Cromwell went running in Hyde Park.

His name was David Tomas Betancourt. He was twenty-eight years old, an Argentine national, the son of the late Vice Admiral Hector Andrées Betancourt and Laura Nicolson Betancourt, the mother with whom he shared the Audley Street flat. David wore a light-blue velour Dior running suit, with white-and-blue running shoes; he had just completed a circuit of the park and of Kensington Gardens and was running across one of the central paths toward the Serpentine and The Pergola, where he meant to sit down and drink a bottle of Perrier water and then a whisky.

Betancourt was six-feet-one and perfectly configured for his height. His shoulders were broad, his hips narrow, and under his running suit his body was hard muscled and sleek. His unruly blond hair flipped as he ran, and he slapped at it often. His face was flushed and gleamed with perspiration. His eyes were blue. Young women smiled at him as he ran by. He was not surprised. He was accustomed to thinking of himself as an exceptionally handsome young man. Girls who learned he was an Argentine rarely failed to express surprise. They asked him to speak a sentence or two of Spanish to prove himself. Expecting an Argentine to look like Rudolph Valentino or Lupe Velez, they found it hard to believe that this long-jawed blond with pink cheeks was a Spanish-speaking South American.

He trotted over the bridge at last and turned into the park restaurant and bar. In the bar, in the bright sunlight that burst through the glass roof and walls, he grinned at the waitress, who knew him well, and ordered what he wanted with a friendly gesture and no words.

An odd coincidence occurred. Wiping the perspiration from his forehead with a paper napkin, still heaving gently from the exertion of his run, David chanced to allow his eyes to meet those of a pretty, brown-haired girl sitting with another girl at a table across the room. He discovered she was staring with interest. He could have smiled in return. If later he had been asked why he didn't, he could not have answered. Instead, he returned her solemn stare with a stare of his own, fixing her with his cool, pale-blue eyes. The girl was intrigued, yet frightened. She smiled nervously and turned away. Their eyes did not meet again, and they would never see each other again. Her name was Betty, daughter of Major Duncan Glynbourne.

When David left The Pergola, he walked back across the park to Park Lane, across the lane at Grosvenor Gate, and returned to his flat. His mother was there. He embraced her, made a joke about the program she was watching on the telly, and went to his room to change. He put on black jeans, a cotton-knit turtleneck, and a yellow nylon windbreaker against the rain suggested by the gray clouds that were hurrying across the restless sky. Then he went out again, walking east in Mayfair to Regent Street and across into Soho. In Soho he crossed to Dean and Firth and Greek Streets, into the area of sex shops and strip theaters.

It was not by chance that he entered this neighborhood. Indeed, he had walked in these streets so often in the past few days that his presence was remarked by certain people, on whose part some curiosity had arisen as to just who he was, this well-built blond young man in sunglasses and black clothes, who yesterday had engaged the Pakistani clerk in a sex shop in a conversation about his homeland and the day before had paused to chat with a prostitute who accosted him, inquiring about her family origins. One man had guessed that the young man was looking for a very special girl, for very special requirements, and hoped to offer him a teen-aged virgin who had just become available. Two other men had concluded he was a journalist and had ordered their employees not to talk to him.

At half past three David crossed Dean Street to the entrance of a tiny theater. It was open from noon, as he knew, and operated with girls who came in off the street, stripped on its little stage, then hurried away to do the same in other, similar theaters nearby. They did it all afternoon and until long after midnight, circulating from one tawdry little theater to another, stripping repeatedly, picking up a few quid each time. Most of the girls also worked as hookers on the street, dodging the coppers and offering themselves as opportunity arose, particularly to men with briefcases or cameras.

He paid three pounds to be admitted and went inside the dark, smoky room where no more than two dozen men sat hunched over their cigarettes in the two rows of seats closest to the stage and stared silently at a black girl lying naked on her back on a sort of table slanted toward the seats, spreading her legs in a wide V.

David knew these places and was not surprised at what this one offered. There was no pretense to dancing. Each young woman came on stage to a spatter of applause from one or two patrons, took off her clothes quickly and spent some ten minutes displaying herself naked, posturing awkwardly to show her private parts as openly as possible to her critical, unsmiling audience. Most of the girls were bored and saw no reason not to let the men know it. Two or three of them taunted the audience from the stage. ("It's more than you could handle, grandpa." "Whatsa matter, fellas? 'Fraid you might show how much you like it?") As each girl left the stage, half a dozen men applauded, and the rest looked down to their newspapers as the house lights came up for the five-minute interval before the next performer came on.

David had not thought to bring in a newspaper, and while the curtain was closed he sat with nothing to do but study the men around him. Most of them were apparently businessmen—some with flat leather briefcases on their laps. Only a few were not wearing neckties. The man to his left asked for a light, and David told him he did not have a match or lighter.

He sat through performances by seven young women. Not one of them was white. They were Asian and African, with skins that ran from glossy-chocolate-brown to dusty near-white. All of them spoke London street English without the trace of an accent that might have suggested this was anything but their first and only language. All of them stripped out of their street clothes: tight, short skirts, vinyl boots, and thin satin blouses that clung to the contours of their breasts. For the most part, they were one more unanticipated result of Britain's long-time liberal policy of unrestricted immigration from the former empire, but some of them were the daughters of refugees.

He became intrigued with the seventh girl who stripped. Her performance was the same—she lay on her back on the slanted table and spread her legs as far as she could, showing herself to the intent stares of men leaning forward for the closest possible look—but she stared blankly at the ceiling, as if pretending they weren't there. He let himself imagine he saw a little reluctance, some vestige perhaps of a sense of self-abnegation in putting herself so rudely on display. She was, judging from appearance, a Pakistani. Her skin was that dusty, tea-with-milk color he identified with the Pakistanis. She was taller than the others, her body more taut and slender. She wore no makeup and none of the cheap jewelry affected by the others. As her ten minutes ran on, he convinced himself she was miserable in this public show of her raw nakedness. The girl might be just what he was looking for.

David left the theater just before she finished her performance. He stationed himself on the street—still in bright sunlight—just outside the theater and waited for her to come out and hurry toward another performance a few streets away.

"Hello, there."

She stopped, cocking her head and openly judging him. For a moment she stood alert, as if she needed to ward off some threat; then she relaxed a bit and nodded. "Hello, handsome," she said.

He nodded toward the theater. "I just watched you in there."

"I saw you."

"You're the only one that interested me. Are you available?"

She raised her chin, and he saw something flicker in her deep brown eyes—his imagination, which seemed to be stimulated by this girl, said it was a painful surrender to reality. Her answer sounded like nothing his imagination suggested. "Like for what?" she asked in a crisp, high voice.

"Well, not a quickie," he said. "The night."

"All night?" she asked. ("All noight?") "That's worth a hundred."

"You promise it'll be worth a hundred?" he asked.

"Well . . . Nothing kinky. Straight and French. That's all. I mean, you know, no ropes or 'cuffs, nothing like that."

David grinned. "What's your name?"

"Barbie."

"Okay, I'll tell you what, Barbie. Let's have dinner. You know Angelo's? Say ten o'clock. Here's twenty to show I'm serious. If you do a good job, it won't count against your hundred."

"'Ow you know I won't . . . skip?"

"You live around here, don't you?" he asked. He didn't wait for her answer. "I'd see you around sooner or later. Be on time now. My name's Fritz, and I don't like waiting."

She was waiting when he pushed his way down the stairs into the cellar dining rooms of the restaurant. He wore an English-tailored dark-blue suit, white shirt, a narrow blue-and-red-striped necktie, and black Gucci loafers. She had not changed and was still dressed in her short red skirt, boots, and shiny white blouse. In fact, he suspected she had stripped in some small theater not more than fifteen minutes ago. She was waiting at his table, one of two in a candlelit alcove behind an arch of old pink brick.

"What's your name?" he asked as he sat down with her.

"Barbie," she said. "I already told you."

"'T isn't, of course," he said.

She lowered her eyes. "It's what I call myself," she said defensively.

"I am Friederich Reitlinger," he said. "I'm German, from Frankfurt. My company makes surgical instruments, and I sell them here in England. Now, once again, your real name is . . . ?"

"Sohaila," she said quietly. "Sohaila Mohmand."

"Ah," he said. "Sohaila." He savored the name on his tongue. "Sohaila. Much nicer than Barbie. You are . . . Pakistani?"

She shrugged. "My father and mother are Pakistani. I was brought here, I mean to London, when I was four years old, and I've lived here all my life, in Soho or Camden Town. I've never seen Pakistan and don't want to. I don't speak Urdu. I'm not a Muslim. You can call me Pakistani if you want. The English do."

"The English," he said, nodding, drawing in breath. "For them to call you English, you have to have been here since the Conquest. They lump everyone else . . . Well, you remember their old saying—'The niggers begin at Calais.'"

"I've been called that as well," she said.

"They don't call *me* that," said David, "even though I'm a foreigner and so fall within the definition. Actually, because I'm as white as the whitest of them and speak their language as well as they do, they don't call me anything; but I've heard Germans called Krauts and Nazis. Nazis, can you imagine! Forty years after the war!"

"The war," she said. "Yes. The 1940's war, the one you all think about all the time." She sighed and looked away, at a couple being seated at a table across the room: both well dressed, the woman in gleaming silk. "Politics . . ."

David ordered a dinner of veal with pasta, accompanied by a bottle of Chianti. Sohaila said she had never eaten anything like it before. Her mother, she said, cooked only simple Pakistani meals at home. She had never learned to cook English. The family rarely ate out, but when they did they ate in one of the Pakistani restaurants in Soho.

She was an only child. Her mother had given birth to a son in Pakistan, but the child had died. Her father, she said, blamed the government of India for the death of his son. When David asked what India had done to be blamed, Sohaila shook her head and said she did not know for sure. David asked her where in Pakistan her family had come from. The eastern part, she said. Bangladesh? She nodded. David said he would like to meet her father. Take a bus ride, then, she said. He was a fare collector on a London Transit bus. David judged he had asked enough questions and dropped the subject of her family.

He had booked a room in a small, cheap hotel in Bayswater. He took her there a little after midnight. Sohaila was a complaisant bed partner, glad to have the money apparently and willing to please him to earn it. He made a point of treating her gently, with respect even. In the morning she told him he had surprised her. He was the first man ever to take her to dinner and one of the very few ever to engage her in conversation and take an interest in what she said. He surprised her again. He told her he would like to see her again and made a date for three nights later.

At eleven the next morning David kept an appointment at the Monmouth Street offices of Trafalgar Trading Company, Limited. He took the automatic lift to the third floor and emerged in a blank, orange-and-white reception room. The equally blank eighteen-year-old receptionist gave his name to someone nearer the executive suite, and after a moment he was welcomed by Nina Blankenship, personal and confidential secretary to Malcolm Worth, vice-president for continental operations.

Worth received him in a designer-created but spartan office, with windows overlooking chimney pots and tarred roofs. The office was decorated with framed prints of prominent advertisements and corporate logos of some of the companies whose products and services were marketed through Trafalgar Trading: Aquascutum, Renault, Lever Brothers, Seagram's, Gillette, Philips. In the furniture, vinyl substituted for leather, veneer for solid wood, nylon for wool, plastic for stainless steel . . . and so on. Ceiling lights burned down from tracks on all of this, laying more emphasis on it than David supposed any of it deserved.

Malcolm Worth was a tall man, ravaged by time or misfortune. His skin was pitted, his hair splotched unevenly with gray, his clothes old and thoughtlessly worn. Though he did not smoke, his face had the drawn, lined, sallow look of the heavy smoker. He welcomed David Betancourt with a warm handshake and pushed him toward a chair.

"I have three thousand pounds for you," Worth said. "May I assume that will cover you for a while?"

"I paid a Pakistani prostitute a hundred twenty last night, plus twenty-five to dine her," said David.

"Thirty-one hundred forty-five, then," said Worth. "I assume it was business."

David allowed himself a little smile. "Sometimes," he said, "business and pleasure are not entirely separable."

Worth did not smile as he made a note. "You have an unlimited expense account," he said.

"I will be seeing her again in a few days. That may be enough to find out if the money is well spent. If it is, she may require more."

Worth nodded. "The three thousand will be deposited to your account at Westminster Bank. You may pick up, say, five hundred cash on your way out. Make out an expense voucher of some sort."

"What word?"

"None. I will acknowledge to you, David, it was a triumph. At their meeting in Paris, they were compelled to admit they had no idea who destroyed their ugly old painting. Or why. They've given you a name, though. Oliver Cromwell. Does that mean anything to you?"

David winced. He nodded. "I understand the allusion."

"Now, then," said Worth. "I suppose the Pakistani prostitute represents a forward step. Anything further to report?"

"I can report," said David with a sigh, "that if this proves to be another false start, General Sekhar may elude us."

Worth shook his head firmly. "No, David," he said. "If your Pakistani girl does not lead you to the Bihari Committee, you will have to work out another way to solve the problem. General Sekhar is not to escape us."

"He is important, then. I didn't understand he was so important."

"He is immensely important," said Worth.

"You don't have his schedule yet?"

"We will provide it when it is available. I am sure it will afford you more than one opportunity. Just be sure you are ready. The Commonwealth Defence Conference opens in three weeks."

"You have the plastique?"

"No, not yet. Bringing it into England is not so easy. It might be well if you had an alternative ready."

"Malcolm," said David firmly. "I am employed as an expert with explosives. I don't know how else I would do it. If you want the general shot, or whatever, you had better have an alternative of your own: a man who can do it."

"The plastique will be provided," said Worth.

"I will find the Biharis," David promised.

The next day, in a busy hardware on High Holborn Street, he picked up his electronic garage-door opener. He liked this one. It used its radio frequency as a carrier for an audio frequency that the owner could choose and set in by flipping some small switches in the box. The receiver would activate the electric motor and open or close the garage door only when it picked up a signal on the correct frequency, carrying the correct audio tone. The idea was that the garage door should not be opened by stray radio signals, from someone else's device, or from some maladjusted communications transmitter. At the workbench in his bedroom, David removed the little receiver from the opener mechanism, substituted a battery for the transformer and rectifier meant to power it from house current, and wired a small bulb onto the relay circuit that was designed to close the switch between the power line and the motor. He went bird watching then, in Hyde Park. He mounted the receiver in a crotch in a tree and walked away from it, looking back at it from time to time through his binoculars and pressing the button on the little transmitter. The bulb glowed each time.

He shopped for a van. He had decided this time to rent the van. He found what he wanted. He would return when he needed the little vehicle.

On Friday night he kept his appointment with Sohaila. He went to see her strip. She saw him standing along the wall to the left of the stage—that night all the seats were filled, many with loud bully-boys from the provinces—and he was compelled to shoulder his way to a standing place close enough to the stage for her to see him. She nodded solemnly at him. He was half sorry he had come in. He imagined it was more difficult for her to perform with him watching.

He had told her he wanted to see one of the Pakistani restaurants where her father and mother might eat. She took him across Shaftesbury Avenue, to a cluttered little foodshop called New Lahore. In a back room there were half a dozen tables. The air was heavy with the odor of deep frying and spice-laden steam. They sat down, and the waiter came. He bowed to Sohaila. He knew her. He spoke quietly to her, and she responded. She ordered. The waiter assumed David would not know how.

There was no wine, no alcohol of any kind. Nor was water offered, only little bowls of strong tea. Dark-skinned men sat at three of the other tables, talking quietly in a language of which he could not understand a word. Wisps of smoke wafted through from the kitchen.

"Is your father a Bihari?" David asked Sohaila. He used a low voice. He did not want anyone to hear the question.

"What d'*you* know 'bout the Biharis?" she asked.

"They are the people who remained loyal to Pakistan in the 1971 war that resulted in the formation of Bangladesh," he said. "Many are refugees. Many lost their homes. Many still live in detention camps in Bangladesh, in squalor and misery." He nodded. "I've read about it."

"My father is a Bihari," she said. "And my mother. We were driven from our home, made refugees. My brother died. I can remember that. My father's business was burned. The ruins were seized and turned over to an Awami. Awamis were the ones that wanted the separation, you know. Still, we were luckier than most. My father carried a bit of gold money, and we were able to get to England. I've got cousins in the camps. I had cousins that starved."

"I would like to meet your father."

"Why?"

"There is a possibility we may be able to do a service for the Biharis."

She shrugged. The waiter approached with two bowls of hot, spiced chicken soup. That was followed by *kofta kari*, a large dish filled with beef meatballs stuffed with almonds, and *hari chatni pollau*, a dish of rice and potatoes flavored with mint and ginger and *ghee*. The waiter brought a platter of curried birds, perhaps partridges, a bowl of yogurt, and a salad.

"I told him you are a rich man and can afford a complete meal," Sohaila said. "This is the way Pakistanis eat if they can: lots of heavy food."

"I wish your father were here to share it," said David.

"He would be grateful," she said solemnly.

They lingered over the meal. It was the only way to cope with it. At the end, the waiter brought *kheer*, a milk-rice pudding and the only dish David did not really care for. He paid in cash.

They walked back across Shaftesbury Avenue, supposing it would be easier to find a taxi there. He did not care, actually, if they found a cab immediately. He was in a mood for a walk through the seamy, gaudy-lighted streets, maybe to find a table in a bar and have a drink before they left for Bayswater. He took Sohaila's hand. He made a joke about the amount of food they had eaten, and she laughed.

At the corner of Frith and Old Compton Streets, a man stepped out of a doorway and fell in step behind them. Suddenly alert, David crossed the street and reversed course to test him. The man kept up, a dozen paces behind. He was small, dark skinned, wearing a worn, unclean, double-breasted gray suit, with a white shirt buttoned to the throat and no necktie. After two blocks, David stopped and turned to confront him.

The man stopped. He tipped his head to one side: a beckoning gesture; and before David could speak or stop her, Sohaila stepped away from him and over to the man. For a moment they talked, the man obviously demanding, brooking no argument, she shaking her head and gesturing with her hands. She shrugged and returned to David.

"He wants the hundred pounds," she said.

"Tell him to fuck off."

"No. He might hurt you. He'll hurt me for sure."

"So," said David, his calm restored. "So that's how it is?"

"Wha'd you expect?" she asked plaintively.

David looked at the man, who stood with his hips cocked, his chin lofted, returning David's stare with scorn and hostility. His mustache was lopsided, and stray whiskers grew from his cheeks and jaws, inch-long strands of black hair against his cocoa-colored skin. If ever David had seen dissolute cruelty on a man's face, he saw it there.

"Here's the hundred," David said to Sohaila, digging the notes from his pocket and handing them to her. "Do you get to keep any?"

"He'll give something to my father tomorrow," she said.

She went to the man and handed over the notes. The man counted them, then turned on his heels and walked away.

"What's his name?" David asked.

"Sjarif," she said.

"Your father. . . ?"

"He'd kill 'im if he dared."

*   *   *

Malcolm Worth had let David get by with his statement that he knew nothing but explosives. He knew well enough, though, that David Betancourt had formerly held a commission as a captain in the Argentine army, had studied at Sandhurst, and had trained with the Coldstream Guards. He knew explosives, that was certain; but he knew other weapons as well. He had killed an IRA irregular in Belfast, with his Wembley revolver—a shot through the throat, they said. He had been taught many other ways of killing a man.

Saturday afternoon he bought a knife. Not any knife would do. He purchased a Sabatier at Harrod's: a vegetable knife with a five-inch blade. At home in the bathroom he wrapped the handle with sticking plaster—adhesive tape—to be sure it would not slip, even in a hand damp with sweat.

He dined with his mother and afterward walked with her to the Grosvenor Street flat where she would spend the evening at bridge with three of her friends.

He returned to their flat, and when he went out again he carried not only the knife, tucked in the waistband of his trousers and hidden by his jacket, but also a Walther automatic, equipped with sound suppressor, in a shoulder holster. He was dressed in a dark-gray suit, made for him in Paris by a tailor who understood how to cut a jacket to hide a weapon in a shoulder holster, and he carried a cheap vinyl-and-nylon airline bag marked with the logo of Sabena.

He returned to Bayswater, not to the hotel where he had spent two nights with Sohaila, but to another one, engaged a room in his own name, and told the clerk he would be going out but would return after midnight.

"Roight. And good hunting, guv. If your luck's not good, I can p'raps arrange a little something for you."

"I'll keep that in mind."

In the shabby room with the sagging bed, he opened the airline bag and took out a jar of makeup. He spread his face and neck, his hands and arms, with the colored cream, darkening his pale complexion, giving himself a Mediterranean tan. He settled a dark wig on his head and stared at himself in the mirror. Satisfied, he removed the wig and put it inside his jacket, on the opposite side from the pistol. When he went downstairs again and passed the clerk at the desk, it was obvious the man did not notice his darkened complexion. The change was not, in fact, dramatic. On the street, out of the clerk's, out of anyone's, sight, he pressed the wig into place on his head again. Then he hailed a cab.

He had the cab drop him at the Lexington Palace Hotel, and again he walked into Soho. He stayed away from the strip joints where he knew Sohaila worked. His disguise was not so good that she would not have known him. He walked, stopping in two bars for whiskies. He browsed through sex shops. He stood outside clubs and theaters, scanning the posters. He began to think he would not find his man tonight and would have to try again, maybe on Monday, when at last he spotted him.

Sjarif was still wearing his stained and rumpled gray suit. He stood in the brightly lighted passageway in front of Raymond's Revuebar, and when David saw him he was touching the elbow of a man who was unmistakably American, engaging him in urgent conversation. The American was confused and anxious to be rid of the dark, threatening little pimp, and he kept shaking his head while Sjarif persisted.

David crossed the street. He stood at the posters for Raymond's and mimed curiosity and indecision. Sjarif took the bait.

"Hey, you want see *good* show? Good show? None dis stuff. Dog and pony. What you like. Private show. Okay?"

David frowned as if surprised and skeptical. "*Donde?*" he asked.

Sjarif frowned. "Uh . . . uh, *cerca,*" he said. "*Si!* Near. *Cerca. Muchachas,* huh? *Desnudas.* Naked, huh? *Desnudas. Y putas. Putas!* Whores. You want? Cheap. Cheap. Ten pounds. Uh . . . *barato!* Hey! *Muy bueno! Muy bueno, amigo!*"

"*Puedo sacar fotographias?*" David asked.

"Uh . . . Take pictures? *Si. Si!* Sure! *Muy bueno!*"

David mimed hesitation. Then he nodded. "Okay," he said. "Uh
. . . *diez* pounds," he added, raising a cautioning finger.

"Ten pounds! Good! *Bueno! Si, diez. Diez* pounds."

Sjarif gestured, and David followed him out of the bright lights and
along the shadowed street. He pulled the knife from under his jacket
and slipped it up his right sleeve. Sjarif led him around two corners
and into a short, dark street a little apart from the activity of Soho. He
stopped before a scarred green door and took a key from his pocket.

"*Teatro*," he grunted.

David nodded.

Sjarif opened the door and gestured that David should precede him
into the darkness of a narrow hallway. David shook his head and
pointed—he would follow. Sjarif shrugged and led the way. David
lowered his arm and let the knife fall into his hand.

"Sjarif."

The man spun around, grabbing inside the double-breasted gray
jacket for something: a knife of his own or a pistol. David was ready,
and he was quick. He whipped the five-inch blade into Sjarif's throat
and nearly lifted him from the floor with it, jerking him back and
forth to cut whatever the blade reached. Sjarif went limp and sagged
against the wall. David pulled the blade out and thrust it in again.
Then he did it a third time. Sjarif gurgled for a moment, then was
silent.

David listened and peered into the darkness. He knelt beside Sjarif
and felt inside his jacket. He felt a sap, a blackjack, what Sjarif had
been reaching for. He reached into his pockets and pulled out a wad
of notes. It was well to take those; it would make the death look like
robbery. He looked outside and saw no one on the street. He stepped
out and pushed the door shut with the tip of his knife.

On the street, as he walked away, he wrapped the blade of his knife
in his handkerchief and held it by the blade as he stripped off the
tape. The knife was clean of fingerprints—he was sure of that—and
he tossed it almost casually into the gutter.

He walked out onto Piccadilly Circus and down into the Underground station. In the men's room he shoved the dark wig into a trash receptacle, and he wiped off most of the makeup with wet paper towels. It was David in his usual manifestation who boarded a train on the Bakerloo line and rode to Charing Cross. He drank a whisky in the bar of the Charing Cross Hotel before he caught a cab for his hotsheet hotel in Bayswater.

"Bad hunting, sir?" the desk man asked with a smirk.

"To the contrary," David said. "Hunting was excellent tonight."

4

"DAVID! David Betancourt! My God!"

"Emily?"

She had just stepped out of Fortnum & Mason and stood in the late-afternoon sunshine, blonde and exquisitely beautiful, tall, with those long, sleek legs that seemed to characterize American women. She was dressed in emerald-green silk that clung to her indecently, a dress designed for her no doubt: made to appear modest on casual glance but to reveal every curve and plane of her body to the respectfully appreciative.

She spoke to the doorman. "Oh, no cab after all, thank you." Then to David—"My *God*, David, I had no *idea* you were in London. Are you in the phone book?"

"Under my mother's name," he said.

"Oh, yes." Her face fell. "I read about your father, David. I am terribly sorry. I didn't know where to reach you to say so."

"I've been here, actually," he said. "I was here, with my mother, when it happened. We haven't been back. In fact, you know, we can't go back."

"I thought they said you could."

He shook his head. "They lie."

She shook her head. "Oh, David." She reached for his hands and took them in hers. "Anyway, you look so good! We must . . . We've

39

got to get together. There's so much to talk about! So many things have happened."

"How is Frank?"

She turned down the corners of her mouth and managed somehow to smile with her eyes at the same time. "Haven't seen him for six months. I'm Emily Bacon again, got my maiden name back. And you? You're not married?"

"No."

"Then we must . . . I mean . . . You know. What the hell? We were awfully good friends. Aren't we still?"

David smiled. He decided he was glad to see her. His first reaction had been dismay, but after a minute he decided it was good to see Emily, that she was still the girl he remembered: an odd mixture of extroverted, girlish innocence and polished sophistication, the result perhaps of educating a girl at the best schools in America while insulating her from realities she was only to see through a train window or read of in the pages of *The New York Times*. Anyway, they shared good memories. He was ready to touch that kind of innocence once more.

"What are you doing, David?" she asked ingenuously.

"I'm with an export-import firm," he said. "You know. If you speak four or five languages and have to make a prosaic living, you can hardly avoid a trading company."

She laughed. "But is it good for you?"

That was a typical Emily Bacon question. He smiled and shrugged. "Where are you staying, Emily? How long are you here?"

"At the Ritz," she said. "And . . . Well, I don't know. I have no particular reason to go home. My divorce is still considered a scandal. I mean, it is to my parents' friends. And to them, that's what counts. Are you free for dinner, David?"

"I'm afraid not," he said. "I wish I were. Tomorrow—"

"Tomorrow night?"

"Yes. Say, eight? I'll call for you."

Her sunshiny American smile broke across her face. "Oh, marvelous! Eight. I'll be ready."

He could not have dined with Emily that evening because it was the occasion at last for him to meet Mikhal Mohmand, Sohaila's father. He had been on Piccadilly, in fact, on his way to the New Lahore food shop and restaurant, to speak with the proprietor, to be certain a table would be saved and to arrange for a complete meal, as Sohaila had put it—everything her father would enjoy. He ordered all the dishes he had been served before, plus curried mutton and shish kebab, with plenty of yogurt and salad and dried fruits. He left with the proprietor a fifty-pound note as an earnest against the preparation of a special meal, with an engraved business card: FRIEDERICH H. REITLINGER, REPRESENTING GEBHART UND WEIBEL, U.G., FRANKFURT.

When he returned in the evening, the father and daughter were already at their table, sipping from small bowls of strong tea. Sohaila was not wearing her usual short skirt and revealing satin blouse but a loose blue-and-white cotton dress. Mikhal Mohmand was a man of fifty years, as David judged him. His beard was iron-gray. His dark eyes were nearly hidden under heavy brows and in a maze of thick wrinkles in his brown skin. He wore a blue-green, pin-striped, double-breasted suit with a wrinkled white shirt buttoned tightly against his throat, and a brimless, high-crowned black hat of knit wool embroidered with curls and loops of colored threads.

After the few minutes given over to greeting, followed by another few minutes of awkward reticence as David tried to draw him out, Mikhal Mohmand proved willing to talk; in fact he proved garrulous.

"My daughter is not religious, Mr. Reitlinger," he said. "But in this country, what can I do? She has said that, if I attempt to impose the way of God on her, she will walk away from my doorstep. In this country, she could. In this country . . ." He shrugged. "You know what she is."

"We aren't here to gab about me," said Sohaila.

"Under God's law, she would be stoned," said Mikhal.

Sohaila laughed. "I get stoned sometimes here," she said.

Her father ignored her joke. "Have you heard of the law of 1979?" he asked David. "Under the Islamic law of Pakistan, she would be spared stoning, actually, because she is not a Muslim. As an infidel, she would be whipped only, a hundred stripes. It is Islamic law, restored in Pakistan."

David could not be certain if the grave words were meant to be taken literally or if the Pakistani was preaching a fatherly sermon to his rebellious daughter. Mikhal Mohmand spoke blandly, without emotion, in the tone of a man simply telling facts. His English was accented, but the accent was soft, and he was entirely understandable.

"What he calls law!" laughed Sohaila. "Law! What kind of law would whip somebody for fucking?"

"She would be seated at a post," said Mikhal, ignoring her words, "and bound to it. Her back would be bared. No more. The decencies are observed. And she would receive one hundred stripes."

"For each offense?" David asked.

"After one such whipping," said Mikhal soberly, "it is unlikely there would be a second offense."

"And what about 'im, then?" Sohaila asked irritably. "He's been with me twice."

"Mr. Reitlinger has committed no offense," said Mikhal. "You are a harlot."

David was not unhappy with the course of this conversation. It afforded him a chance to guide Mikhal Mohmand's thoughts toward a helpful conclusion, a step in the chain of logic he hoped would prepare Mikhal for the proposition he wanted ultimately to make.

"And you took the money gladly enough. What Sjarif gave you," grumbled Sohaila. "You're no better than me."

"A man is entitled to what his daughter earns by harlotry," said Mikhal loftily.

"Sjarif . . ." said David quietly.

"He's dead," said Sohaila.

"I know," said David solemnly, fixing his calm blue eyes on hers. The understanding came to her gradually. The newspapers had not yet reported the death of Sjarif; the identity of the dead man found Saturday night had not yet been released, if indeed the police knew it; even on the streets, very few who knew a dead man had been found knew who he was. How then could Fritz know? She read the truth in his eyes; and he read understanding in hers, watching it grow from a quick little suspicion to knowledge, a certainty. Her jaw trembled, and she licked her lips. He showed her a trace of a smile, and he nodded.

"What is this?" Mikhal asked. "Sjarif . . . dead? God be praised!" He lowered his eyes and muttered. "God is good, God is merciful, praised be the name of God."

"Praised be the name of Fritz," murmured Sohaila quietly.

David reached for her hand under the table, took it, and squeezed it.

"What?" asked Mikhal.

Sohaila leaned across the table, to speak quietly in her father's ear. "*Fritz* killed him, not your stupid Allah," she whispered.

"If this is true, then you are an agent of God, Mr. Reitlinger," said Mikhal. "Sjarif . . ." He jerked his head to one side, and if they had been outdoors he would have spat, David guessed. "He was a Hindu."

"I won't claim I'm an agent of God," said David, settling a steady gaze into Mikhal's eyes. "I will claim your friendship. I will claim your trust."

Mikhal Mohmand nodded. "Indeed." He turned to Sohaila. "You are to honor this man and keep his trust."

Holding Sohaila's hand, David felt her tremble. She glanced up, then lowered her eyes. "I think I'd be afraid not to," she whispered.

"You are a Bihari," David said to Mikhal.

"Sohaila tells me you know about the Biharis."

"Yes. I know what the Indians did to you."

"Treacherous . . ." said Mikhal through clenched teeth. "Spiteful. Surely they are of the Devil."

"You know the name Lal Nath Sekhar?" David asked.

Mikhal Mohmand stiffened. He looked up at the waiter, who had just arrived with platters of shish kebab and curried lamb. "He asks if we know the name Lal Nath Sekhar," he said with a bitter laugh.

The waiter nodded. "Only too well," he muttered.

"He led the Hindu armies into East Pakistan in 1971," said Mikhal. "The butcher!"

"He is the Indian minister of defence now," said David. "He will be in London in two weeks, for the Commonwealth Defence Conference."

"If only . . ." sighed Mikhal, shaking his head.

"If only what?"

Mikhal Mohmand glanced around the room and lowered his voice. "Like Sjarif," he said.

"Is that just talk?" David asked coldly. "Or would you help do it, if you could?"

"If he has his way, Nina Stepanova, a joint Chinese-Indian force will intervene in Afghanistan."

"Is this certain?" asked the woman, who was ostensibly Malcolm Worth's secretary, known in London as Nina Blankenship.

"It is not certain, of course. But the likelihood is great. That is why—"

"I understand," she said. "If Lal Nath Sekhar achieves his purpose of a military alliance between India and China, intervention in Afghanistan is not the only mischief that might result."

They sat in Malcolm Worth's private office. He was out. He had in fact been dismissed and had left the building.

Nina Stepanova Samusev smoked a short, fat cigarette, drawing the thick smoke deeply into her lungs. She was forty years old, and in her fifteen years in London the style she had adopted to be Nina Blankenship had become her own. She wore black slacks, a gray blouse, and a gray cable-knit sweater. Her straight blonde hair was cut short, but she let it lie in bangs over her forehead to her eyebrows. Her face was lined around her eyes and mouth: a face that suggested an intense and perceptive cynicism.

They spoke Russian. She welcomed the occasional opportunity to use it; sometimes she suspected she was losing her ability to converse in her native tongue, so infrequently could she do it.

Vasili Ivanovich Litvinko smoked too and sipped at the tea she had brewed on the hotplate in the outer office. "Has he made the contact with the Bihari Committee?" he asked.

"Not with a committee, apparently," she said. "With a bitter individual he thinks will serve the purpose."

"He must understand," said Litvinko, "that identification is essential. It must appear that the Biharis assassinated General Sekhar for their own reasons."

"It will be understood," said Nina Samusev dryly, "that the man they now call Oliver Cromwell was the assassin."

"Exactly," said Litvinko. "And that is why the Bihari connection is so very important. He did well in Italy. He established identification with the so-called People's Anti-Imperialist Crusade, as he was ordered to do. But in Spain he failed to make the required identification with the Basque nationalists. Here he must not fail. His work must always be associated with some squalid little gang of fanatics. That is essential."

"He understands. He has been instructed."

"By Worth?"

"Yes."

"It may be time, Nina Stepanova, to let him make contact a step higher. Who do you suppose he thinks you are?"

"Malcolm Worth's subordinate, certainly," she said. "He understands fully that Trafalgar Trading Company is ours, but I imagine he still believes Worth is in command here."

"He knows enough already to jeopardize you," said Litvinko. "If

Trafalgar Trading Company is compromised, I don't think you'll survive."

"I plan to," she said coldly.

"Of course. I mean as an effective agent in London. My point is
that it may be wise for you to take over responsibility for Mr. David
Tomas Betancourt."

She nodded. "Very well. I do have a problem, though. He is an
expensive young man. He lives well on what we allow him, and there
has been inquiry."

"I am aware of how much he costs," said Litvinko. "I accept responsibility for that. Keep him on a short rein, though, Nina Stepanova. Let him believe you are under severe pressure to limit the
expenditure."

She smiled. "Very well. And thank you. I will feel more comfortable about Oliver Cromwell now."

Emily Bacon stretched. She lay on the great brass bed in her room
at the Ritz, comfortably satisfied. She was nude except for her stockings and a garter belt, and she had turned on her back to smoke a
cigarette. David lay beside her, also nude, also on his back, staring
with idle curiosity at the elaborate chandelier on the bedroom ceiling.
He did not smoke, and he did not like the harsh stench of burned
tobacco on a woman, but he chose not to make an issue. She was,
after all, a North American woman, and if he told her he did not like
the stink she was making, she might tell him to go to the devil.

Anyway, why say anything negative? He couldn't have been more
fortunate than to have encountered Emily on Piccadilly the other
day. She was intelligent, witty, sympathetic—indeed, solicitous—and
a most pleasant companion. Besides, she was quite wealthy and had
insisted on paying the dinner check.

"David."

"Mmm?"

"Do you have a car?"

"No."

"If I rent one, will you drive me up to Cambridge? I haven't been back."

"Sure, if we can find a day when I can," he said.

They had met at Cambridge, when he was a student at Trinity College and she at Girton College.

She had known him a year, almost, before she learned he was an Argentine. In his late 'teens, David let people suppose he was English, and there was nothing about him that suggested he was not. His English was as good as anyone's; he had, in fact, learned English and French before he learned Spanish—English from his mother and a nanny, French from his father and a tutor. His first school was the English school in Buenos Aires, where the children of the international community were taught in English and studied Spanish as a second language. He spent summers in England, where the Betancourts always kept a flat, and from London his parents took him often to the Continent, where they encouraged him to learn a bit of German and Italian. He learned more from the children in his school in Buenos Aires: the sons and daughters of diplomats and businessmen from all the European countries and from North America. From Cambridge, that year when Emily first knew him, he went home on holiday to a flat in Kensington Palace Gardens, or to her family's home in Kent. He did not go to Argentina. When Emily learned, finally, of his nationality and chided him for denying it, he had grinned and shrugged and said he owed no allegiance to Maria Estela Perón. Later, when the military assumed control of Argentina, he was more willing to acknowledge it. His father was one of the leading men of the military government.

"That was a good time, wasn't it?" she said. "I mean, when we were at Cambridge." She blew smoke toward the ceiling. "Happy years."

"Sure. Good years."

"I should have married you instead of Frank."

"I'm afraid it wouldn't have been possible. My father was indulgent about some things, but he wouldn't have been about that."

"He had arranged a marriage for you."

"Yes."

She crushed the cigarette in the ashtray on the bedside table. She turned on her side, to face him. "Tell me about it, David," she said urgently. "Tell me what happened to you. So much has happened, I know. You've more than matured. You—"

"Why don't I just make up a lot of lies?" he suggested with a little smile. "I used to tell you lots of lies."

She kissed his neck. "I told you lots, too. Did I tell you I was a virgin?"

"No. You didn't tell me that. To the contrary, I remember you said to me, 'I love to ball.' It was the first time I'd heard the word used that way. I wasn't sure if you really meant what I thought you meant."

"I guess I told Frank I was a virgin. The damn fool believed it, I think."

"No, he didn't."

"You talked about me!" she protested, laughing.

"All the time."

Emily's face clouded. "Please tell me what happened, David," she said seriously. "I read so much in the newspapers. Was it true?"

"I don't know what papers you read."

"Never mind. When you left Cambridge, you went to Sandhurst. Frank couldn't believe it. He saw you once, in uniform. He said the uniform had been tailored to you and you carried yourself like a professional soldier. With a swagger stick under your arm, he said!"

"My father was an admiral, you know," said David. "A political admiral but nevertheless an admiral. For me to have the political career he wanted for me, he thought it necessary for me to have an army commission. He arranged for me to be commissioned a captain in the Argentine army and to go to Sandhurst to learn a little something about being an officer. I didn't graduate, of course. I just studied there, as a lot of young officers from foreign armies do. But I took it all quite seriously. I didn't want to be just an ornamental officer."

"But when Frank saw you, you were with a British regiment."

"Yes. I was attached to the Coldstream Guards so I could take further training with the Guards officers. President Galtieri wanted his army officers to learn something of counter-insurgency tactics."

Emily got up. There was champagne on ice in a bucket by the bed, and she poured two more glasses. "And your father arranged a marriage for you, too," she said.

"Maria."

"Was she beautiful, David?"

He nodded. "She was an angel. I had known her since we were children. Maria de Monroy y de Córdoba. My father was descended from a French family—one that I could contact now if I wanted to. Her family on both sides were pure Spanish. They are very proud of it and very Catholic. They were our neighbors, both in the city and the country. Her father and mine agreed that Maria and I should marry. He wrote me a letter and told me. I went home. I hadn't seen her for two years, and she was my fiancée. She was happy with the arrangement. She had expected her family to arrange a marriage, and when they settled on me, I suspect she was relieved."

"And you, David? Were you happy?"

He sipped champagne. "Well . . . Why not? She was beautiful. She was educated and intelligent. She was an heiress. She was complaisant." He grinned. "And if she had said she was a virgin—which was something she would never have said; it was assumed—it would have been no lie."

"Did you fall in love with her?"

He inhaled deeply. "Yes. I did," he said quietly.

Emily sighed. "Oh, God, David . . ." she whispered.

He slackened as he released his deep breath. "We were to have been married in June. I was to be posted to Paris, to the office of the military attaché in the Argentine embassy. We were going to live in Paris, then, maybe later . . . London."

"But—"

"But my grandmother Nicolson died. My mother hurried back here, and I came with her. We went down to Kent for the funeral. It was there, on the afternoon of the funeral, that we got the news that President Galtieri had ordered the invasion of the Malvinas. We came back to London. There were of course no flights from England to Argentina. We planned to fly to Paris, knowing we could easily fly on from there to Buenos Aires. But I was a captain in the Argentine army. We were visited by agents of British intelligence, and they impounded our passports. I was lucky I was not interned."

"And the war went badly for you," said Emily quietly.

"*Life* went badly. We were cut on the streets. Lifelong friends. My mother's family, even. They would turn away from us, would not speak."

"Oh, David!"

"We had no direct word from Argentina. All we knew was what we read in the papers or what we saw on the telly. My father . . . Well, I've said he was a political admiral. He was a brilliant man and a good man, really, but he had no idea of naval strategy or tactics. Neither, for that matter, did many of his officers; they were most of them political. He didn't know what to do with the old cruiser, and neither did they."

"The *General Belgrano*," she said.

David nodded. "It was the biggest ship in the Argentine navy, escorted by two destroyers. They made a little task force. For a while, all they did was cruise up and down the southern coast. The navy was criticized. It wasn't doing much to support the troops ashore on the Malvinas. So . . . finally my father ordered the *General Belgrano* to steam toward the islands."

"And it was torpedoed."

"The British had declared a two-hundred-mile exclusion zone around the Malvinas," David continued. "The *Belgrano* was thirty-five miles outside the zone when it was torpedoed."

"Then your father wasn't—"

He shrugged and interrupted. "What difference? The whole operation was a debacle. The cruiser was lost doing nothing, only making a little show of steaming toward the islands. It never even fired its guns.

What was worse, the two destroyers ran away, leaving the crew of the *Belgrano* to drown."

"Most were rescued," said Emily.

"More than three hundred died," said David. "Including the sons of powerful people. That was the beginning of my father's downfall. Not long after that the British landed troops on the Malvinas, and the navy was unable to do anything to support our forces. The navy couldn't even evacuate our little army. Argentina was made a great, tragic joke—the posturing dagos who'd tweaked the nose of the British lion and got a good, well-deserved clawing for their trouble."

"Your president was a fool, David."

"Ah, but he was the president. He was an army man, and so were the others of the junta. They needed a scapegoat. It was convenient to blame the navy for the defeat of the armed forces of Argentina. It was convenient to blame Admiral Betancourt. Besides, there were lots of old political scores to be settled."

Emily put her glass aside and stroked David's cheek. "The newspapers said—"

"The Argentine papers—publishing of course what the government dictated—said the navy had failed, not only because of the incompetence of its admirals but also because Admiral Betancourt had made himself a rich man out of navy funds. The junta sacked him and ordered him to go to our country place and stay there until they decided what to do about him. A Perónista mob—*descamisados*—burned our home in Buenos Aires, and the next day a squad of policemen arrived at our country place. They said they were there to protect the admiral."

"Our papers said he was under house arrest."

"A vicious euphemism," said David bitterly. "We don't know exactly what happened. The police outside said they heard shots in the house. When they went in, he was dead. He had shot my sister. She was dead. He had shot Maria, who unhappily had come to the house to offer sympathy. She died in a hospital before the night was over. He had shot his favorite dog. Finally, he shot himself. He had tried to set the house on fire, too. The police put it out. This is what we were told later, in a report sent to us by the government."

Emily wiped the corners of his eyes with the tips of her fingers, coming away with his tears.

He drew a breath and went on. "My mother and I first learned of all this from the London newspapers, then from the telly. I was on the street. I saw the headline on the *Evening Standard*—'Argie Admiral's Pistol Orgy!'" He paused and nodded. "That's what it said," he whispered.

She drew his head down on her shoulder and stopped him. "I'm sorry I asked you about it, David," she murmured as she bent over to nuzzle him. "I'm sorry to have made you go through it all."

"Oh, there's more," he said. He left his head on her shoulder but turned it a little so he could talk. "They bankrupted us. Everything in Argentina was seized. They called the seizures recovery of funds he had embezzled, or fines for old offenses they conveniently remembered. My mother was left with almost nothing. There was a small account in the Bank of Scotland. The flat in Kensington was heavily mortgaged, and we couldn't afford to keep it. We moved to where we are now, in Audley Street. I sold a Monet my father had inherited and brought to England. My mother's family helped for a while—somewhat grudgingly, actually—until I could find employment. Life turned a little sour, Emily."

"I would have helped, if I'd known," she said simply.

"Not many did," said David. "We weren't welcome anymore, in places where we'd gone all our lives. Even people who meant to be sympathetic couldn't be. I mean, my father's death was a part of their triumph. His final insanity proved what they had said all along—that decent English farmers in the Falklands couldn't be left to the mercy of spics. You know the English. 'The niggers begin at Calais.' Suddenly they remembered we were niggers."

"David . . ."

He pulled away from her and sat erect. He reached for the champagne bottle. "Sorry, Emily," he said, forcing a smile. "I'm a man without a country now. There's not a nation on earth that I owe allegiance to, and you'd be surprised how liberating that is."

"Your passport?"

"Oh, Argentine still. The new government—I mean, the one that replaced the junta—invited my mother and me to Wilton Crescent—to the embassy, you understand—and assured us we are respected citizens. They want us to come home. I'm still an officer in the army and can have an honorable career." He shook his head. "I don't trust them. And my mother would never think of going back. She's never been sure the Argentines aren't in fact spics."

Emily responded to his ambiguous little smile, herself smiling uncertainly. "I think you're exaggerating now," she said.

"You want to hear the supreme irony?" David asked. "If my mother has always suspected Latin Americans are a little stupid, emotionally unstable, and maybe racially inferior, my father never had the least doubt about it. He held the Argentines in complete contempt. French was his first language. He never thought of himself as Argentine; no, he was a European, a Frenchman, living like a colonist in a primitive country where money was to be made. I have no doubt he stole as much as they said he did. And more. And there are still scores to be settled in Buenos Aires. I will never go back."

"Would you like to come to the States?" she asked.

He chuckled. "Typical Yankee," he said. "All problems can be solved for anyone who can just take up residence in the States."

"You could leave behind some of your problems," she said.

"Well, maybe . . . sometime. After I've made some money." He smiled, this time genuinely. "Make enough money to set myself up well in the States . . . Well, maybe, Emily. Maybe."

5

GALEAZZO CASTELLANO grabbed the handle of the huge switch and gave it an upward push. The cavernous warehouse filled with glaring light. He stepped through the little door and turned to welcome Major Duncan Glynbourne with a quick courtly bow. Glynbourne entered the brightly lighted silence, conscious of the arrhythmic clacks of their heels as they walked out of step across the concrete floor.

"As well as we could," said Castellano, gesturing with a hand toward the ordered display that filled the center of the floor.

They had, in a grotesque sense, recreated the scene of the explosion at Santa Maria delle Grazie. A yellow line painted across the floor was meant to represent the plane of the wall of the refectory. A dozen heaps of shattered bricks and stones were arranged on the far side of that line. On the near side lay pieces of the Volkswagen van that had carried the explosives—all laid out in order: wheels at the four corners, engine block at the rear, fragments of the body in their approximate positions, shreds of the seats, part of the steering wheel, shards of glass. On tables to the side were more grisly exhibits—shreds of clothing stained brown with blood. On still another table were tiny fragments identified with some degree of credulity as bits of the bomb.

Castellano knelt beside some of the stones. "Notice," he said, pointing.

Bits of metal had been driven into some of these stones by the force of the explosion. Others were stained with blood.

"And look at this," said Castellano. He picked up a hunk of stone the size of a fist and handed it to Glynbourne. A bit of steel the size of a fingernail was driven into the stone, but under it was wedged a tiny yellow fragment of something that had the distinct appearance of bone.

"Human?" Glynbourne asked.

"Yes. We had another fragment like it and let the technicians separate it from the stone and steel for microscopic examination. It is human bone. The woman, Margherita Catania, was standing outside the van when the explosion went off. She was between the van and the wall, in other words."

"And the man was inside?"

"Yes. Some of the steel fragments over there have bloodstains on what was clearly the inside of the body of the van."

What the Italian technicians had identified as bomb parts was a little arrangement of electronic components, some of them still soldered to tiny fragments of burned and shattered circuit board. Fortunately, as Castellano pointed out, there was a corner fragment with a number on it, and two intact transistors. Glynbourne recognized a small screw with a plastic cap threaded on it as probably one of the terminals from a large dry cell. A length of wire attached to the screw had made it possible to find.

"We have had excellent cooperation from an American corporation named Tandy," said Castellano. "While I was in Paris, they flew a man to Milan at their own expense. He identified these scraps as the parts of a Tandy-manufactured garage-door opener. He confirmed our expectations, in other words. The device could have been sold under a variety of brand names—Sears, Roebuck and Radio Shack, among others. They are imported from the States in large numbers, by every nation in Europe."

The two men wandered along the edge of the array of torn steel van parts.

"There's the wire I mentioned in Paris," said Castellano, pointing out a length of thin, insulated wire taped to a piece of the van body with white surgical tape. "An extension of the antenna, we assume. We had our people do some tests on the range of these little transmitters and receivers. They are capable of picking up signals from as far as two or three kilometers—even more in ideal conditions. Actually, you wouldn't want one to do that. The householder driving up his street wants to open his garage door from fifty meters away, not more. Otherwise, stray signals will open it. So you keep your antenna wire short. On the other hand, the device is not reliable from more than fifty meters unless you supplement the antenna. I would judge that Oliver Cromwell adds antenna wire to his and sets off his explosions from some distance, from as far away as he can view the site through binoculars. So he tapes wire on the body of the van, to extend his antenna."

"One has to give the man a degree of credit," said Glynbourne. "Grudgingly, of course. Except for the plastique and the detonator, everything he uses is garden-variety stuff that he can pick up anywhere without causing anyone to take particular note."

"That is why," said Castellano, "it is essential to find out who is supplying his C-4 plastique."

The litter of blood-stained clothing scraps was laid out on two tables and arranged in order. At one end of each table were bits of shoe materials—leather and rubber. At the opposite ends were shreds of fabric that seemed to have been a shirt and a blouse. The man had been wearing a leather belt. The woman had been wearing a brassiere. Both of them had worn blue-denim jeans, hers well faded and soft, his more nearly new and still dark blue.

"Nothing unusual, I'm afraid," said Castellano. "Nothing that identifies the man."

To one side of the woman's table was a small vinyl-and-nylon shoulder bag, with the contents spread out around it. She had been carrying cigarettes—Pall Malls—and a lighter, a linen handkerchief, a bus ticket, a few thousand lire.

Glynbourne picked up the shoulder bag. Except for the broken strap and some bloodstains on the gray vinyl, it was intact. He opened it.

"There's an odor . . ." he said quietly. He handed the bag to Castellano. "Did you notice?"

Castellano sniffed. "Cheap perfume," he said.

"To the contrary," said Glynbourne, sniffing again. "Actually, it has the odor of a rather fine English scent called Stephanotis." He smiled shyly. "I'm not an expert. A lady of my acquaintance indulges herself with it." He reached for the handkerchief. "Oh, God! This has been *drenched* in it. Is it imported? Is it available in Italy, do you know? Can you have that checked?"

Castellano nodded. "I will have the handkerchief enclosed in a plastic envelope and carried to some shops."

"Good," said Glynbourne. He glanced around. "I'm afraid for the moment that's all I have to contribute—the possibility that the young woman somehow got her hands on a flask of a characteristically English flower scent."

"Then you will wish to see the bodies, of course."

Glynbourne drew breath. "I don't, actually, but I suppose I must."

They were conducted into the cold-storage vault by a white-jacketed technician, who donned a heavy, sheepskin-lined coat and recommended that they do the same. The young woman smiled coquettishly at Glynbourne as he struggled to pull the heavy coat on over his jacket. She was amused but probably was also acknowledging, as perceptive women often did, that she saw something intriguing about him, something beyond the fact that he was a trim, erect, rather good-looking man—perhaps how his narrowed blue eyes seemed ironically to communicate a philosophical detachment in contrast to the solemnity of his general bearing and expression. She laughed and reached to help him with the coat.

Although the vault was equipped with drawers for the cold storage of bodies, the pieces gathered up from the rubble of the refectory remained on two zinc-topped tables under a glaring light in the center of the room. And they *were* pieces, not intact cadavers. In neither case was there enough to gain any real impression of how these two people had looked, or even to tell on quick observation which was the man and which the woman. Like their clothes in the warehouse, they were laid out in an order approximating the correct positions of the identifiable parts—fragments of skull and jawbone at one end of each table, toes at the other, the intermediate parts between. Bones were visible, with shreds and scraps of frozen skin and flesh still attached.

"This is Margherita Catania," said Castellano, nodding at the display on the table nearer the door. "We were able to get fingerprints, you understand, and so have no doubt whatever as to her identity. The man's fingerprints . . ." He shrugged. "Not on register anywhere. He was younger than she, maybe only seventeen or so."

"The ink marks?" Glynbourne asked. He had noticed that each human fragment was numbered with black ink.

"They match photographs that were taken of all these parts as they were found. Also, they match a chart of the area. Her left arm was found on the walkway around the dome of the church."

"What's that on the hand?"

"Uh . . . *cerotto*. Americans call it a Band-Aid."

"A sticking plaster," said Glynbourne, leaning closer and peering intently at the flesh-colored adhesive tape affixed to the waxy, dead flesh of half a hand. "Have you peeled this back? Do you know what's under it?"

"*Un taglio*," said the young woman, the technician.

"A cut," said Castellano.

"New? Uh . . . *nuovo?*"

"*Sì*," she said.

"A distinctive shape, that plaster," said Glynbourne. "Looks very much like what in England we call Airstrip. See, it has small perforations, so air can penetrate to the skin. Most others you'll see, such as American ones, aren't cut with those rounded ends—not like that, anyway. What's more, the gauze on an Airstrip doesn't extend to the edges of the plaster, as it does on an American one. Airstrip is quite distinctive, as these things go. If you could have a photograph of that shown to some chemists in Milan ... . Of course, Airstrip plasters may be imported and may be common in Italy."

André Bonnac pinched his cigarette between his lips as he sucked hard on it and pulled smoke deep into himself. He sat in a high-backed wooden booth in a *taverna*, in deep shadow and all but out of sight to the Milanese industrial workers, who drank and laughed at nearby tables. Before him on the scarred table was the greasy plate from which he had eaten a cold sausage, a slice of cheese, some black olives, and a hunk of bread. A third of his liter of wine remained in the bottle.

His patience was at an end. Basilio Ciano, the investigator assigned to him by Galeazzo Castellano, had been gone too long. If Ciano could not find Farinacci, then he was supposed to return here, not leave Bonnac sitting two hours, eating greasy food and drinking sour red wine.

Ciano had made it plain enough that he did not welcome the intervention of a French investigator. To the contrary, he saw it as a humiliating concession. On the other hand, he was an SISMI man, an agent of another of the effective old military information services that had been abolished in the recent fad for more complete democracy. Basilio Ciano was older than Bonnac by at least ten years. He was experienced. He could teach even Bonnac something about counter-terrorist tactics, and Bonnac had been studying him with interest.

It was past ten o'clock. The crowd in the *taverna* had begun to thin. Those who remained were gradually slipping into a wine-sodden torpor. These working people did not keep late-night hours.

Ciano arrived. Bonnac, though irritated, had never really believed he wouldn't. Farinacci, stumbling as though drunk, but more likely weak with fear, was with him.

"*Le presento il Signor Farinacci,*" said Ciano.

Bonnac's Italian was weak, but he knew it was stronger than

Farinacci's French, which was probably nonexistent. They would speak Italian. *"Molto lieto,"* he said.

Farinacci was a young man, no more than twenty-five, if indeed that. He was effeminately handsome, as Bonnac judged him—with heavy-lidded eyes that by their very shape suggested insouciance and arrogance. He wore tight black pants, a white knit shirt, a black-nylon jacket. He was afraid, though. Whether he knew who Ciano was, he was afraid of him. Ciano had defined himself with brutal clarity.

Bonnac slid out of the booth. He indicated with a gesture that Farinacci was to sit by him, against the wall. The young man slid in.

Ciano slid in on the other side, across the table. He was a bigger man than Farinacci, bigger in fact than Bonnac. He wore a black suit over a worn white shirt and knit black necktie. His long, lined face spoke weariness, cynicism, impatience. His right cheek was made sinister by a deep white scar.

Bonnac, without a word and with bland expression, slapped a photograph on the table in front of Farinacci. It was a police picture of Margherita Catania.

Farinacci looked at the picture for a moment, then turned his heavy-lidded eyes on Bonnac and shrugged.

Bonnac struck with his elbow, digging hard and deep into the soft hypochondrium just below Farinacci's lowest rib. Farinacci gasped and bent forward in pain. Bonnac chopped him across the nose. Farinacci's nose broke and began to bleed. Bonnac stared at him coldly, his eyes half obscured by glittering reflections in his rimless octagonal spectacles, and he tapped on the photograph.

Farinacci clutched his abdomen. "Catania . . ." he grunted. A small trickle of blood ran over his upper lips and into his mouth. "Margherita Catania."

"Ah," said Bonnac. "You know her?"

"I never denied it," gasped Farinacci. "I told the police everything I know about her."

"They already knew a lot about her," said Bonnac. "They had a dossier on her. But *we* know nothing. You must tell us all about her."

Farinacci bent forward, clutching his abdomen, letting the blood from his nose run over his lips and onto his chin. "What do you want to know?"

"Everything. We know nothing," insisted Bonnac.

"I slept with her. A few times," said Farinacci. "Only a few times. She was . . . *insaziabile*."

Bonnac shrugged.

"I . . ." The young man stopped and licked his lips. "I admitted to the police I slept with her three nights before she was killed. What more do I know?"

"Perhaps something," said Bonnac quietly. "You tell us."

Farinacci swallowed. He shook his head. "Nothing . . ."

Bonnac sighed. He clenched his right fist at his left shoulder and fixed his eyes on Farinacci's ribs, as though he were about to strike again.

"*No!* No, wait! I . . . What do you want to know?"

"What do you have to tell us?"

"I had nothing to do with the bombing," said Farinacci breathlessly, lifting his hand in a gesture of swearing.

Bonnac shrugged. "So. All right. We didn't ask about that. Tell us about Margherita Catania."

"She was *pazza*." Mad. "She sniffed cocaine. She took pills. Didn't the autopsy show that?" Farinacci studied Bonnac's face and saw—or thought he saw—annoyance. He hurried on. "She was pregnant once and went to Switzerland for an abortion. She was . . . very political, too. She didn't like the way things are. She would read the newspapers and become shrill about things she read. That's why . . ." He stopped.

Bonnac was lighting a cigarette, and he paused with the lighter in his hand and the cigarette in his mouth. He fastened a cold, anticipating gaze on Farinacci.

"I told the police I'd never heard of the Crociati until I heard the name on television after the bombing," said Farinacci. "But—"

"*Les Croisés*," said Ciano. The Crusaders.

"She was one of them," said Farinacci.

Bonnac lighted his cigarette. He said nothing to prompt Farinacci. He just kept on listening, with almost no change of expression.

"I am not one," said Farinacci. "I know nothing of them. Almost nothing. Only what *she* said. She talked about them. In bed. It was difficult to know if she was telling the truth. A lot of it was . . . was *raving*. They were going to change the world. They were going to make a woman pope. After all, the Holy Mother of God was a woman. Pope Miriam. She talked about Pope Miriam. A Jewish girl, like the Mother of God. Margherita was . . . *pazza*, like I said. She bragged of the big things she did."

Bonnac smoked and listened.

"She told me they killed a man. For no good reason. Just to show they could."

Farinacci stopped. He picked up a greasy, crumpled paper napkin from the table and wiped the blood from his nose, mouth, and chin. Ciano opened his mouth to speak, but Bonnac raised his chin abruptly and glared at him. Ciano waited then, with Bonnac. Farinacci glanced from one to the other.

"I don't know any others," he said. "I swear to you I don't. She . . ." His eyes widened as he watched Bonnac crush his half-smoked cigarette. "I . . . Wait! Wait. There is one. Gottardi. I'm not sure. She mentioned him. He may not be . . . In the name of God, whatever you do, don't tell him—"

Bonnac shook his head. "No, of course not. Would you care to finish the wine?"

The three men walked together—Castellano leading the way, Bonnac, for once uneasy about his cigarette and looking for somewhere to dispose of the butt, and Glynbourne calmly glancing around, taking in all the impressions he could collect.

"That he lives here is a measure of his standing," said Castellano. "Even prominent cardinals have difficulty renting quarters within the walls."

The immense bulk of St. Peter's Basilica loomed over them, dominating, solid, secure—although on the south walls a spidery framework of steel scaffolding and a dozen half-busy, gesticulating *sampietrini* evidenced the prosaic work of maintenance that preservation of the famous fabric constantly required. In the yellow light of a midafternoon sun, the shadows lay dark among the varied buildings. A small automobile sped across the square ahead of them, and Glynbourne was amused to find that here, inside the walls of the Vatican City, a prominent place had to be given to such secular objects as three petrol pumps.

Castellano led them to a large wooden door. He rang the bell, and the door was opened by a burly man in a blue suit. Castellano introduced himself and said he had an appointment with Monsignor de Périgord. The burly man nodded and gestured toward the narrow door of a small elevator.

They emerged on the third floor of the building to find the monsignor waiting for them.

His apartment seemed to consist of four public rooms, arranged around the central hall where the lift opened. Through open doors they could see into a cluttered office where four telephones sat on a desk covered with files and loose papers, into a sitting room furnished with chairs and a sofa covered with pale-yellow silk, into a formal dining room that would seat eight guests, and finally into a small chapel. The hall itself and all the rooms but the chapel had uncarpeted white-marble floors, high, arched ceilings, and walls painted a yellow-toned white. A profusion of green plants grew in tubs and baskets in every room, lush from the sunlight that filled these rooms through their wide windows. Paintings, mostly from the Renaissance but a few very modern, hung on the walls, and sculptured busts and figures in marble and bronze stood on pedestals.

Monsignor Périgord led them into his sitting room. "Gentlemen," he said. "Wine?" Without waiting for an answer, he rang a small silver bell. A young nun in a white habit and white rubber-soled sneakers appeared, and he spoke quietly to her, to one side, telling her what to bring.

"We may thank God," said Castellano when they were seated, "that Oliver Cromwell has attempted nothing more since we last met."

"We may well thank God," said the monsignor, "since I understand we ourselves have achieved little."

They spoke English, as a courtesy to Glynbourne, whose German was fluent but whose Italian and French were only serviceable.

"Very little, I should say," said Castellano. "Yet it may be significant."

"It may not have been entirely fanciful," said Glynbourne, "to call our terrorist by the English name of Oliver Cromwell."

"An English connection?" asked the monsignor.

"A possible English connection," said Glynbourne. "We noted the odor of an English scent called Stephanotis in the shoulder bag Margherita Catania carried to her death. When we examined the personal effects the police had taken from her quarters, we found a tiny flask of that scent. Only one Milanese shop stocks Stephanotis, and it is so unusual an item for them that they were able to tell us they had not sold a flask of it in more than twelve months."

"Which suggests, of course," said the monsignor, "that—"

"That she received it from an English friend," said Glynbourne. "And none of her known friends was English."

"A slender lead, Major Glynbourne," said the monsignor.

"Coupled with another," said the major. "The young woman had suffered a small cut on her hand within a day or so of her death. That cut was dressed with an English sticking plaster of a kind that is not often seen in Italy."

"Suggestive," said the monsignor.

"It doesn't prove anything," said Glynbourne, "but it suggests a lead for the investigation."

"Yes. Indeed it does," said the monsignor.

The young nun returned, carrying a silver tray on which there were two heavy, cut-glass flasks, one of brandy, one of cool white wine, with glasses. A white cheese and several big yellow apples lay on a plate on the tray. She placed the tray on a low table in the center of the room and silently retreated.

Monsignor Périgord poured wine for Castellano and himself, brandy for Glynbourne and Bonnac. "I understand," he said as he replaced the stopper in one of the flasks, "that the Crociata Populare turns out to be real."

"Real," said Bonnac. "Insignificant to our investigation, but real."

"Insignificant?" asked the monsignor. "I understood—"

"They were Milanese," said Bonnac, "and there were only six of them. Of the six, only two really were capable of doing any mischief. The rest were poseurs, playing at being wild revolutionaries—good for declaring principles, writing proclamations. The other two didn't trust them and didn't tell them what they were doing. Sometimes they let them run errands. The two dangerous ones were Margherita Catania and Bruno Gottardi."

"Farinacci?" asked the monsignor.

Bonnac sipped brandy and shook his head. "He wasn't a member. The Catania woman was a nymphomaniac. He was one of the young studs she kept at her disposal."

"Oliver Cromwell," said Castellano, "contacted the Crociati through Guido Messe, one of the philosophical members. Messe had been a member of the Red Brigade but was thrown out for cowardice and doctrinal unorthodoxy. Messe never saw Cromwell. Cromwell telephoned him."

"And Messe put him in touch with Catania after only a telephone conversation?" the monsignor asked skeptically.

"He represented himself as having a quantity of plastique to sell," said Castellano. "Messe carried that word to Gottardi and Catania, and Catania kept an appointment with Cromwell."

"Was Gottardi the man killed in the explosion?"

"No. That was a very young man, another one of Margherita Catania's studs."

"Where is Gottardi now?" the monsignor asked.

"Dead," said Castellano.

"How so?"

"Reverend Father, I don't think you want to know," said Castellano.

"I accept my share of responsibility," said Monsignor Périgord. "I will hear whatever I should hear."

"Gottardi," said Bonnac, "was a co-conspirator. Nevertheless, he was insignificant to the investigation. He never saw Oliver Cromwell, never spoke with him, had no idea who he was or where he came from. That was by his own choice, as much as by Cromwell's. Gottardi was a tough, dangerous man, with an obsession for self-preservation. If Cromwell had turned out to be a police informer, he could not have named Gottardi."

"What was his role?" asked the monsignor.

"He encouraged Margherita Catania to go through with the bombing—not that she needed much encouragement. He made the call afterward, claiming credit for the Crociata Populare."

"Which, incidentally, terrified the philosophical members," said Castellano. "Messe, for example, literally trembled when we questioned him."

"Are you arresting the philosophical members?" the monsignor asked.

"No," said Castellano. "They are badly frightened. We'll let them remain so."

"Then with the deaths of Gottardi and Catania, the organization is. . . ?"

"Dead," said Castellano.

"Actually, it is the death of *three* members that killed the CPCI," said Bonnac. "In the past there was another dangerous member, named Loffredo. He was an oaf. He blew himself up with his own bomb."

"Seven months ago," said the monsignor. "In Turin."

"Yes. That's the one," said Castellano. "He was a member of the Crociata."

"They killed two people before the bombing of *The Last Supper*," said Bonnac. "One murder was political: the Milanese policeman, Novari. For the other . . ." He shook his head and smiled at the monsignor. "It was Gottardi who killed Tiengo."

"Tiengo! Of the Red Brigade?"

"Revenge," said Bonnac. "He blamed Tiengo for his expulsion from the Red Brigade. They expelled him for refusing to accept discipline, to take orders. Tiengo, though, added that he was a coward. Gottardi killed him."

"You learned all this most efficiently," remarked Glynbourne. "I mean, after all, the Italian authorities have been working on these matters for months."

"Vigorous interrogation," said Bonnac dryly. "My speciality."

"And did Signore Gottardi die of 'vigorous interrogation'?" Glynbourne asked with lifted brows and an air of innocent curiosity.

Bonnac looked at Monsignor Périgord and shrugged.

"Tell us," said the monsignor.

Castellano spoke. "Monsieur Bonnac and one of my most trusted agents reached the conclusion that the nullification of Gottardi was absolutely necessary, taking all factors into consideration. When the interrogation was finished, they disposed of him."

"It was not—how shall we say?—a collegial decision," said Glynbourne.

"Your conscience is clear then," said Bonnac blandly.

Glynbourne met Bonnac's cold eyes with a glance equally cold. "We may, I suppose, put it that way," he said.

Monsignor Périgord reached for the heavy flask and poured himself another glass of the crisp, cold white wine. "Oliver Cromwell," he said. "Incidentally, Major Glynbourne, I like your name for our terrorist. I think we know something about him now. I can perhaps contribute something to our stock of knowledge."

The monsignor passed the brandy flask to Bonnac, whose glass was empty.

"I sent a young man to Madrid," said the monsignor. "He spent two days with the CESID, reviewing the evidence accumulated about the Toledo bombing. I need hardly say that the pattern was the same. You know that. The young woman who carried the bomb was a Basque nationalist. The explosive was C-4 plastique. The detonator was triggered by a short-range radio signal. And so forth. All very much the same pattern. But with a difference."

Monsignor Périgord paused and took a small sip of his wine.

"We might assume," he went on, "that the explosions at Assisi and Milan were the work of an imaginative amateur. The technique looks crude. All he seems to have done in those cases was to set off a very large quantity of plastique, as much as he could get, one supposes. Professional demolition experts have a phrase for that technique— 'Shoot hard and wish it well.' But that is not what he did at Toledo. The amount of plastique used was precisely measured. He meant to damage the treasures in the sacristy, not to bring down the building. Also, as we have noted, he seems always to want to avoid killing a large number of people—which he would surely have done if he had set off a big explosion in the sacristy. At Toledo he used a measured charge, enough explosive to accomplish his purpose and no more."

"You are saying he knew how much to use," said Bonnac.

The monsignor nodded. "And because the explosion in Toledo was so much smaller, the remains of the bomb are much more instructive. We can see, for example, that his detonator was a Potapava Karandash. Bits of the steel jacket were found driven into the young woman's body."

"The latest and the best," said Bonnac.

"The Karandash—you know, of course, that the word means 'pencil' in Russian— is manufactured only in the Soviet Union," said the monsignor. "That is not, however, a suggestive fact, since in the past five years the KGB has supplied thousands of them to various Arab and Palestinian organizations and probably to others as well. The Israelis among others have captured entire cases of them—"

"And use them," interrupted Glynbourne. "The damn things turn up—"

The monsignor nodded. "They've turned up all over the world."

"Blowing the hands off amateurs who didn't know how to use them," said Bonnac. "Oliver Cromwell was either damn lucky or he's no amateur."

"He is no amateur," said the monsignor. "He knows how to use explosives. I have asked a dozen agencies, including the CIA, to review their files on professional bombers, known or suspected. So far they've turned up nothing. Every one they know can be accounted for, one way or another. They're dead, they're in prison, and so forth. We may hear something yet, but for the moment I suggest we are looking for a renegade demolitions expert."

"Unless he's from the East," said Glynbourne.

"Unless," conceded the monsignor. "In the meantime, I suggest you ask your respective governments to check their files for men trained by their military for demolitions work—and subsequently separated. Do we have somewhere an embittered former army explosives expert, turned terrorist?"

"I suggest something more," said Glynbourne. "What we know suggests we are not dealing with a grubby fanatic. This man has money and uses it. He is fluent in Italian and apparently also in Spanish. I should imagine he is attractive to young women. We are perhaps seeking a rather good-looking man, probably well educated, certainly intelligent, either an engineer who has learned the use of explosives as a civilian or a soldier, and . . . What more? Oh, yes—the Stephanotis. Where did Margherita Catania get *that*? If from Oliver Cromwell, then he's been in England for more than just a brief visit. Your casual tourist is hardly likely to come across a scent like Stephanotis. It's an English taste. I hope you don't think I put too much emphasis on it—"

Monsignor Périgord smiled slightly, and gestured for the major to continue.

6

LOUNGING COMFORTABLY in a corner of the couch in Malcolm Worth's office, Nina Stepanova Samusev—Blankenship—clutched at the left shoulder of her sweater with her right hand and rested her chin on her arm. Her hair fell across her eyebrows, and she looked at David Betancourt with narrowed, appraising eyes. It was difficult not to admire the young man more than was rational. Again—she had done it many times before—she speculated on what it might be like to lie in bed with him.

His own thoughts were not dissimilar. She had about her an air of sensuality that suggested a sexually vigorous woman. Except for the stench of cigarette smoke in her hair and clothes, she attracted him. She might be a very interesting experience—far more so, now that he knew it was she, and not Malcolm Worth, who was the agent in charge here.

She disciplined her thoughts. "The plastique is available to you," she said. "In the garage on New North Road. Twenty kilograms. Enough to blast out a city block."

"The Karandashi?" he asked.

"Six of them," she said. "They are here, in the office."

"I'll take two with me," he said. "Don't touch the others unless you know how to use them. I mean that seriously. Don't allow anyone to touch them who doesn't know exactly how to use them."

"Such are my orders," she said.

"Now," said David. "The Savoy. That is out of the question. The only place where the blast would be effective and certain is in the court between the hotel and the theater, and security will be tight there. I looked at the area. Even a Mercedes limousine is examined if it lingers there. If I knew precisely the moment when Sekhar is coming out and could have a Mercedes or Rolls ready to move in . . ." He sighed and shook his head. "But if they are mounting any security on him at all, they will stop traffic from entering at that moment."

"You may have to vary your technique, David," she said.

"If you mean try to shoot him or something like that, find someone else. I told Malcolm—I am employed to do what I do; I won't even attempt another method."

She ignored the challenge to discipline. "We wouldn't let you try another method," she said. "For all other methods, you are an amateur, and Lal Nath Sekhar is too important to be left to an amateur. I am suggesting, though, that you may have to deliver your explosive charge into his presence by means other than a motor vehicle."

"Maybe in a briefcase," he said sarcastically. "During a session of the conference. Under the table. That's how they assassinated Hitler in July of 1944, you will remember. Very effective," he sneered.

Nina smiled. "I am not that old, David. I don't remember. But I am sure you will find something effective."

"We can't get close to him," said David. "We don't have a Colonel Stauffenberg to carry the bomb to his side. I may not be able to get the charge closer than ten yards. So I'm going to blast a crater in London that will make the English think the V-2s are coming in again."

"On the Strand?"

"No. It's got to be where he stops and gets out of a car. A restaurant. A visit to . . . I need his schedule."

"As soon as possible," she said.

"Consider," said David to Mikhal Mohmand. "If India and China form an alliance and choose to intervene in Afghanistan—where will

their armies have to move? Across Pakistan. Suppose they use intervention in Afghanistan only as a rationalization for an armed incur-
sion into your country? What happened in East Pakistan could
happen in the west."

Mikhal Mohmand, dressed in his uniform as a fare collector on a
London bus, sipped from a mug of hot tea. "Afghanistan," he said
quietly. "I am beginning to understand whose interests you represent,
Mr. Reitlinger."

"My interests and yours coincide," said David. "That's why I
sought you out."

"Why did you choose me in particular?"

"You are a Bihari," said David. "You have lost much at the hands
of the Indians. You have reason to hate them, so you can understand
the importance of what I am proposing to do."

Mikhal Mohmand nodded. "Do you know what it does to a man,
Mr. Reitlinger, to lose his only son and to see his daughter become an
infidel and a harlot? Every day she shows herself naked to any man
who will pay money, and every night she lies in bed with whatever
man will pay her price. And she mocks me when I—"

"I know," said David. "I don't know whom you should hate most,
the Indians for what they did to you or the English for what they've
made of your daughter."

"Sekhar," muttered Mikhal. "I used to dream of killing him. At
first I was grateful to the English. They gave us refuge. And
then . . ." He shrugged. "If I had a son again, it would be the same
with him as it is with her. She is what this country, this city, has
made of her. It has overpowered me in my efforts to save her."

David nodded sympathetically.

They sat once again in the New Lahore food shop, in early evening. Mikhal glanced around. "There are other Biharis in London,"
he said. "We have a committee, in fact."

"I know you do."

"I shall consult with the committee."

"If you do, we are finished," said David bluntly. "Every additional person who learns of our plans makes the idea more dangerous. And less likely to succeed."

Mikhal Mohmand stroked his beard. "If you were a police agent—"

"If I were a police agent, I wouldn't have killed Sjarif."

"True . . . True."

"Your Bihari committee is not the subject of elaborate police plots to trap you," said David. "The police don't care about you. You haven't done anything."

"We've had no opportunity."

"You have it now."

"God be praised," murmured Mikhal. "To have vengeance against that Hindu butcher . . . But I . . . I have no driving license."

David smiled. "If you are stopped by the police, your want of a driving license will be a very small worry indeed."

"You don't yet know where I will have to drive?"

"Not yet. When I know, we'll rehearse. All I need to know is, are you committed? If not, say so now, so I can look for someone else."

Mikhal Mohmand nodded firmly. "I am committed," he said simply.

The Potapava Karandash is a steel cylinder about a centimeter in diameter and some twelve centimeters long. It is, in other words, about the size of a ballpoint pen. Each end is covered by a small plastic cap held in place only by friction. When one of these caps is pulled off, it exposes a threaded sleeve around the end of the cylinder and a small hole in the tip. When a wire is inserted in the hole and the sleeve is twisted clockwise, two tiny teeth inside the cylinder close on the wire and grip it tightly. The teeth are also electrodes. When wires are in place in both ends and an electrical circuit is closed across them, the Karandash explodes with a quick, white-hot shock, acting as a detonator for the larger charge into which it is inserted.

The Karandash is a stable and trustworthy detonator, perfectly safe for the professional who knows how to use it. It has, however, a devilish defect that has injured and killed at least a score of amateurs.

The smudged little instruction card packed in each carton of Karandashi is in Russian. It is infrequently seen anyway, as operators rarely receive a whole carton. The trained operator, or one following the instructions, strips off precisely one centimeter of insulation and inserts his wire in the hole just to the limit of the insulation. Then he turns the sleeve and so fastens the wire securely in place. The untrained operator pokes the wire into the hole as far as it will go. When he does that, the sharp tip of the wire often penetrates the soft plastic container that holds the liquid explosive. The corrosive and unstable compound leaks out into the cylinder and begins to oxidize and to combine with the iron and copper it touches, growing hot and more unstable—until a fatal level of instability is reached and the Karandash explodes prematurely. The process takes a few minutes, and sometimes by then the unskilled operator has inserted the Karandash into the main charge. Even if he has not, the Karandash itself may blow off his hand.

David knew the idiosyncrasies of the Karandash, as anyone did who'd had counter-insurgency training. He carried the two he had taken from the offices of Trafalgar Trading Company to a chair along the Serpentine in Hyde Park. There he sat in the sunshine, and within the view of anyone who was curious enough to watch him, he inserted the wires in the two steel pencils. With the wires in place, he put the Karandashi in the greasy paper bag in which he had carried two Wimpy burgers into the park. He dropped the bag in a nearby trash container and sat down again, fifty yards away, to watch and wait. When, thirty minutes later, the Karandashi had not exploded, he retrieved them from the trash.

He had known they were safe. But why take chances?

On Thursday he drove Emily to Cambridge in a Jaguar she had rented. She brought a picnic basket packed for her by Fortnum & Mason, complete with iced champagne in a covered plastic bucket. Emily wore a long, full, multicolored skirt and a loose white blouse—

picnic clothes, as she said—and was full of happy chatter. She told him she had been invited to spend the weekend in Scotland, visiting the family of a friend she had encountered in London, but she wouldn't go if David had something more interesting to offer. He said he couldn't offer anything at all this weekend or the early part of next week; his company was pressing him to finalize two important sales.

They ate their picnic on the Backs, sitting on a bench near King's Bridge. Afterward, they crossed the bridge and strolled among the colleges.

"Oh, my God, David! Look!" Emily cried as they turned into Trumpington Street. "Isn't that Sedgwick?"

The man approaching them was in fact John Sedgwick, a professor whose lectures on twentieth-century art had fascinated both of them during their student years. Occasionally they had been invited to his house, usually for tea, once for cocktails. He had been and apparently still was a bluff, florid, abrupt man, a little past sixty years of age now.

"Professor Sedgwick! Do you remember us? I'm Emily Bacon. And this is David Betancourt."

"Emily. Hmm? Well, my recollection is a little vague, but I believe I do recall you. And Betancourt. Yes. I remember you. Argentine, right?"

"Yes," said David. "It's good to see you, Professor."

"Back in England, are you? Visit?"

"I live in London."

"Ah, good. Where were you during the nastiness over the Falklands?"

"In London. I was a captain in the Argentine forces, actually; but I was in England for my grandmother's funeral when the war broke out, and I couldn't go back."

"Well. P'raps that was good luck for you, Betancourt. It was a bad business. Manifestation of the Latin American mentality, I thought. Maybe you wouldn't agree. I had to be happy, though, with the way it came out; and I hope the lesson was learned."

"David's father was killed in the war, Professor," interjected Emily.

"Oh. Sorry to hear that. My sympathy." The professor frowned with concentration. "Don't I remember that your mother was English, Betancourt? It was your father who was Argentine, wasn't it? You spoke English like an Englishman and fit in very nicely here, as I recall. Going to seek English citizenship, since you live in this country?"

"Perhaps," said David.

"Suggest you do. You qualify, I should think."

The encounter turned David inward. His mood darkened. He was less responsive to Emily's uninhibited talk. For a while she was subdued herself and respected the barrier he had put around himself; but on the drive back to London her sense of fun and whimsy overcame her patience. She pulled her skirt up around her hips, exposing all of her long sleek legs and her little white panties. When his eyes rose from her hips to her face, she was grinning. He grinned and reached to stroke her legs.

"You're sure we can't do something interesting this weekend?" she asked. "I haven't accepted the invitation to Scotland. And next week—"

"Next week," he interrupted, "is going to be a tough week for me. Company directors' meeting coming up. I've got to close a couple of deals on the weekend or early in the week, or my sales report is going to suggest a cut in my salary."

"What do you sell, David?" she asked, leaning into the corner between the car door and the back of her seat, tugging on her skirt and keeping it high.

"Don't you know?"

"No, I don't."

He smiled. "Spirits mostly," he said. "Gin and whisky on the Continent. Brandy and vodka in the U.K. Then, of course, some wine and champagne. I visit the big distributors."

"Could you sell in the States?"

He shrugged. "Except that I'd be cutting in on other men's territories."

"Well, it's an interesting idea, don't you think? I have a feeling you'd be happier living somewhere besides England. Anyway, when will I see you again?"

"I'll call you as soon as I have a day or an evening free," he said. "Before next weekend, anyway."

Late Friday afternoon he stood in the back of the little theater and watched Sohaila strip, conscious more than ever that the spectacle was afflicted with an overpowering monotony that she and the other girls could not have overcome even if they had tried. Sohaila was pretty, though, in spite of the ugliness of what she did and where she did it. Her dark body was lithe; and even as she lay on her back, spreading her legs and displaying her shiny inner flesh, she moved with an unconscious grace that was totally absent in all the others.

They sat down for a whisky in a Soho bar.

"My father forgot to ask you something," she said. "Actually, he didn't forget; he couldn't find words to ask and still keep his dignity."

"He wants money," said David.

"Yes. And why not? Aren't *you* being paid?" ("Pied," she pronounced it.)

David rubbed his chin and affected a severe look. "He told me he is committed. Are you telling me he is not committed unless he is paid?"

"I didn't say that. He's grateful to you, about Sjarif. And so am I. But he's poor, Fritz. He's fifty years old, and he doesn't have nothing. If he lost his job, he'd be on the dole. What's more, all these Africans coming in are threatening jobs like his. He—"

"How much does he want?"

"A thousand pounds."

David raised his chin. "So. A thousand pounds will reinforce his devotion to the Bihari cause, will it?"

"You can be sure he wouldn't be involved in your scheme if it wasn't for the Bihari cause. My father's not a murderer. People besides Lal Nath Sekhar are probably going to be killed."

"I want to know something, Sohaila. How many people know what we are going to do?"

"My father's told nob'dy," she said. "Not even my mother."

"And you?"

"I 'aven't told nob'dy. You can be sure of that."

"There are just three of us, then."

"Two of you," she said. "You and my father."

"No," said David. "Three of us. Three of us know, and three of us have to take part. We're going to need you, Sohaila. Your father will drive the van. You must arm the charge."

"No. I don't want nothin' to do with it, nothin' more than I have to do with it now. Understand, Fritz, I'm not a Bihari. I don't give a damn about what goes on on the other side of the world, or how many was killed by the Hindus fifteen years ago, and I'm not going to kill somebody 'ere because of it. If my father thinks it's what he has to do, I won't argue with him, but I don't have to be a part of it. I don't see no profit for me in it."

David threw a deep breath. "Sohaila," he said. "If you don't go along and help, I will not pay your father his thousand pounds. If you do, I will pay him a thousand and you a thousand, and you can tell him or not, as you choose, about your thousand."

"But—"

"Let me finish. There's a better reason for your going. The job takes three people: one to drive the van, one to arm the charge at the last minute, and one to send the signal that sets it off. If it's done by two people, it's much more dangerous. When we rehearse the thing, you'll see why it takes three. And I don't want to trust anybody else."

"It's not supposed to be dangerous," she said.

"A thing like this can't be done without *some* risk, obviously. But we do it so as to minimize the risk. That takes three people. With two only, it's much more dangerous."

"Get another Bihari fanatic," she said sullenly, tossing back her whisky.

"*You* get me one," he said. "One you trust. One you can trust not to talk some day."

"Why do *I* have to trust him? It's you and my father that has to trust him."

"You're a part of this thing, Sohaila. You've helped already. You brought your father and me together. You know what we're doing. If your father and I are caught, you'll go to jail too, just like we will. Or, if long after I'm gone, some other Bihari talks—"

"We made a big mistake in getting mixed up with you," she said.

"No. Your father will have his revenge on the Indian general he calls a butcher, he'll have struck a blow for the Biharis, and each of you will be a thousand pounds richer."

Sohaila closed her eyes and sighed. "How many people are going to get killed, Fritz?" she asked quietly.

David summoned the waiter to bring them more whisky. "Lal Nath Sekhar," he said. "Probably a bodyguard or two. Hindus. Maybe an English policeman or two, if they get too close. I hope not."

"Bystanders?"

He shook his head. "General Sekhar is a nabob. They'll keep people away from him."

She raised her solemn dark eyes to touch his. "You're sure my father won't get hurt? And I won't?"

"I am going to teach you exactly what to do," said David. "We'll do it over and over, until you can't possibly make a mistake."

On Saturday he met Malcolm Worth in a Fleet Street pub, where he found him sipping from a pint of lager and scanning a newspaper.

"We've got a bit of information for you," Worth said quietly. "Westminster Abbey. Lal Nath Sekhar is going to Westminster Abbey. Wednesday morning."

David shook his head. "We don't want to commit genocide," he said.

"It'll be all right," said Worth. "They're going to take him through early in the morning, before the place is opened to tourists."

"A private visit," said David. "The Abbey . . ." He frowned and nodded. "Is damaging the Abbey a part of the assignment?"

"The people we work for don't care how much the Abbey is damaged. Though I must say *I'm* curious. How much damage do you think you'll do?"

"Sekhar will go in through the west door," said David. "I'll have to place the charge on the street there, just in front. It's going to damage the façade severely, you can be sure of that. A lot of stained glass is going to be shattered."

"The building won't come down?"

"No. Nothing so dramatic as that."

"What they want, David, is the death of Sekhar," said Worth grimly. "Nina says the opportunity to damage the Abbey is a little bonus for you—a chance at last to do something to hurt your friends the English."

David ignored that. "You have the hour?" he asked. "I need more information than just that he's coming to the Abbey on Wednesday morning."

"We will have it. You can call. It's one of *my* people, actually, that's come up with this one. For years it's been a poor contact, and now suddenly he's made himself worth everything we ever paid him or did for him."

"I need two thousand pounds, Malcolm. Cash. Small bills."

"The Biharis?"

"Something to fortify their principles."

Worth lifted his pint of beer. "You'll have it."

"I'm going to want something for myself as well."

"You've gone through the three thousand I gave you?"

"No. That's maintenance, a salary so to speak. This is a fee."

A fleck of foam clung to Worth's upper lip. "That'll be tough. We don't have unlimited funds, you know."

David leaned back and smiled faintly. "I was surprised to learn you work for Nina."

"You know who she is?" Worth asked.

David shook his head.

"She's Russian. KGB. I'm English. She's been my contact for ten years. She runs us, David. You understand what that means?"

"How do you retire, Malcolm? Someday I'm going to want to."

"They don't give money away. They're very tight. My retirement will be Trafalgar Trading Company. It's a success, you know—makes a legitimate profit. I'd cultivate my sales contacts if I were you. Your retirement may well be a job as a salesman for the company."

"Tell her I want ten thousand pounds for Lal Nath Sekhar."

"I'll tell her. And you won't get it."

The Commonwealth Defence Conference opened with a dinner on Sunday evening. It was to continue through Thursday. The movements of the delegates, except for the sessions themselves, would not be the subject of prior public announcement.

The canons of the Abbey were not, perhaps, the most security-conscious men in London; and perhaps the protection of Lal Nath Sekhar had not been much emphasized among them. In any event, through one of them who talked to a teacher in Westminster School, Malcolm Worth was able to give David a precise Wednesday-morning schedule for the Indian. He would leave the Savoy Hotel at 8:45 A.M. He was expected at the Abbey at 9:00, which would give him forty or forty-five minutes to tour the Abbey before it was opened to tourists at 10:00. He was to be met in the west door by the dean, who would conduct him on the tour. Leaving the Abbey a minute or two before 10:00, he would be driven on to the Wednesday-morning session of the conference.

On Monday afternoon, David rented the van. It was old and rusted, and the man who rented it was careless. David wore the dark

wig he had used the night he killed Sjarif, but with a darker makeup.
The suit he chose for the occasion was black and worn, almost thread-
bare. He carried a driving license in the name of Henry Dillard. It
showed a Camden Town address.

"I'll take it for a week, mate," he told the man in the rental agency.

"Where will it be going?"

"Just around town. I've got a window-washing service, and my regular van has a broken axle. I need a van for the week, during repair."

"I'll have to have a deposit."

"I expected that. How much?"

"Well, uh, say two hundred."

David sighed heavily as though surprised by the amount. "All right,
then," he said. "You can take the week's rent out of it when I return
it."

He drove to the garage on New North Road. The plastique was
there, packed as Nina had told him in splattered gallon paint cans. He
installed a cutoff switch in the van's ignition system. Then he went
over the van with a cloth, wiping his fingerprints from every surface
he had touched. Thereafter he would not touch it without gloves.

He took the underground to Whitechapel and had two small plastic
signs made—DILLARD WINDOW WASHERS SERVICE. These, too, he
would not touch with his bare hands.

Tuesday was for rehearsal. Mikhal Mohmand called his supervisor
at London Transport to say he was sick and would not be at work as a
fare collector either Tuesday or Wednesday. The three of them—
David, Mikhal, and Sohaila—rode the Underground to New North
Street early in the morning. David rubbed the signs around on the
dusty, gritty garage floor until they were dirty and scratched, then he
mounted them on the sides of the little blue van. By ten o'clock the
van was on the streets, Mikhal practicing at shifting the gears and
guiding the rattling little vehicle around Islington. Shortly he was
confident, and David was confident of him. David ordered him then
to drive south through Pinsbury and The City, to cross the river into

Southwark. He had him drive to Waterloo Station and from there across the Westminster Bridge to Parliament Square, Victoria Street, and the Abbey. They returned to Waterloo Station, and Mikhal drove the trip again, timing it. David had him make the trip four more times.

Finally, David showed Mikhal how to operate the pull-rod he had installed under the steering column—a length of stiff wire attached to a switch between the coil and distributor. Pulling the thin rod disabled the van's ignition. Pushing it restored it.

They drove back to New North Street.

Sohaila wore a pair of violet corduroy slacks, with a yellow blouse and a flowered scarf tied around her neck. She squatted beside the van, on the garage floor, where David had laid out his plastique and the detonators on the clean smooth surface of vinyl trash bags. Mikhal stood above them, watching intently.

"This is the explosive," David said to them, putting his hand on the soft C-4, bundled in one-kilogram brown-paper packages. He ripped the paper back from one package, exposing the puttylike substance. "It's perfectly safe to handle and transport. I mean, I could light this paper with a match, and the plastique would not go off. It takes a small explosion to set it off. That is the purpose of the detonators."

He carried once again a Wimpy bag, with two egg Wimpies in it. The Potapava Karandashi were wrapped in a wad of paper napkins, in the bag with the sandwiches. He took out the napkins and unwrapped the detonators.

"Here's the dangerous part," he said. "See the wires? Touch the ends of those to the terminals of a battery, or to any other electrical source providing at least six volts, and the sensitive explosive inside these pencils will go off. There's the batteries. To be sure, I've got two of them. Also, we've got two detonators. When the time comes, the current from those batteries goes through those wires. The detonator pencils will be in the plastique—"

He pressed one end of one of the Karandashi into the uncovered plastique. The thin steel cylinder and its bottom wire slid into the explosive with little resistance, until nothing but the top end and two wires protruded above the plastique. Then he repeated the process with the second Karandash. He pushed the package aside.

"All right," he said. "See, it's not sensitive. It didn't object to having the two pencils pushed into it. But it will object strongly to having those pencils explode inside it. Now. Between the batteries and the pencils we need a switch. That's this . . ."

The circuit board and relay switch of the garage-door opener were powered by a third cell. The whole was taped firmly to a length of board with white sticking plaster.

"This is a switch attached to a radio receiver. When the proper signal is received, the switch closes. We set off the explosion with a radio signal, which we send when you have moved to a safe distance. This"—he picked up the little plastic-cased transmitter with which a householder would open a garage door—"is the transmitter that sends the proper radio signal. When I press the button on this box, it transmits the signal, and the detonators are fired."

He pressed the button, and the relay closed decisively, with a sharp click.

"All right?" he asked. "You understand? Now. The little transmitter operates on one radio frequency. What is more, it transmits an audio-frequency signal, carried on the radio frequency. Only this one or another one exactly like it can set off the explosion. But there are thousands of these in the world. That's why we will not attach the wires until the last minute. It's a remote chance but still possible that somewhere between here and the Abbey someone might transmit a signal that would set off the explosion. To avoid that chance, we don't connect the wires until the last possible minute."

"When, exactly?" asked Sohaila.

"When the limousine pulls up in front of the Abbey," said David. "Not before. As long as you're in the van, apparently working to get it started, the police won't interfere; they won't try to get in the back and see what's there. When the limousine arrives, Sekhar's bodyguards will get out first and look around. They'll talk to the police. That's going to take two or three minutes, which is plenty of time for you to arm the bomb and walk away. At that point, with Sekhar present, the police will be watching him, not you. Even if they see you walk away, the explosion will shortly take all their attention. I'll be watching through a telephoto lens. When I see Sekhar get out of the limousine, I'll detonate the bomb. You'll be far enough away to be safe. I'll be able to see you, too, and I'll wait until you're far enough away. You simply walk down into Westminster Station and board the first train you can."

"What if the police say they want to get in and see what we have in the van?" asked Mikhal.

"Then you push your rod to reconnect the ignition, start the engine and say, 'Look. How fortunate. I can drive away.' All they want is for you to get away from there. They'll be uncomfortable about having a disabled van close to where Sekhar's limousine is going to stop, but if they hear your starter grinding away and think you can't start the engine, they're very unlikely to give you any trouble. Anyway, remember we're going to time this so you will be there only five minutes or less before the limousine pulls up. The important thing is not to abandon the van until Sekhar's limousine is there. If you walk away too soon, that will raise a suspicion, and the police will check to see what's in the van. What's more, they might come after you."

"There is risk," said Sohaila. "If we make any mistake, we will—"

"For once," said her father solemnly, "remember the words of the Prophet. 'God obliges no man to more than He has given him ability to perform.' Our work is blessed. We go to do justice."

At 8:15, David climbed out of the van at Waterloo Station. After a short final word with Mikhal and Sohaila, he entered the station and boarded a train on the Bakerloo Line. After a quick run across the river, he transferred at Charing Cross to a train on the Circle Line and came up to the street at Westminster Station. He walked across Great George Street and south along the fence around the Parliament buildings, then across the Abbey grounds to Victoria Street, where he crossed over and walked a short distance into Tothill Street. There, by Central Hall, and some two hundred yards distant, he had a view of the Abbey towers and the forecourt where Defence Minister Lal Nath Sekhar had to walk from his car, through the gap in the wrought-iron fence, and past the Abbey bookshop to the west door.

David was dressed as a tourist, in a brown tweed jacket, a tweed cap, worn corduroy slacks. He carried a Pentax camera and a leather binoculars case. The transmitter that would send the signal to detonate the plastique was in the binoculars case.

He was in place and watching the street at 8:50.

Mikhal Mohmand drove away from Waterloo Station shortly after David left the van. Traffic was heavy, and for a few minutes he believed he would not reach the Abbey before nine. When finally he could turn into Westminster Bridge, he was distressed to find traffic was blocked entirely; but it began to move shortly, and with relief he drove across and made his turn into Victoria Street.

Sohaila, in the back, held a pair of wires in nervous, sweating hands. David had so rigged the connections that all she had to do was squeeze an alligator clip that was soldered to each wire from the receiver and let the clip clamp shut on the twisted-together wires from the two detonator pencils. It was simpler than simple, but he had made her try it ten times last night.

The neat brown-paper packages of plastique were stacked and bound together with heavy surgical tape. The detonator wires that she held in her hands protruded from the one package David had torn open. The radio receiver and the batteries were taped to a board and the board taped to the floor of the van. An antenna wire, similarly attached to the body, ran up the wall and across the ceiling.

Sohaila looked at her watch. It was 8:56 when her father cut off the engine by pulling on the wire under the steering wheel. She leaned over the seat and watched as he guided the little blue van to a stop in a parking place at the curb just outside the wrought-iron fence before the Abbey.

Her father began his charade. Mumbling and cursing, he turned the engine over and over with the starter. It ground and whined, but of course it would not start. She knelt by the big package of plastique and with trembling hands clipped the wires from the radio receiver to the wires from the detonators.

8:56—David watches through the telephoto lens on his Pentax. Everything now depends on Mikhal Mohmand's acting. A policeman walks up to the van. David cannot see Mikhal, but he must be for the moment effective, because the policeman walks away. (Keep grinding the starter, man! Run down the battery.)

8:57—A second police officer approaches the van. He stands by the driver's door, gesticulating, obviously ordering Mikhal Mohmand to move his vehicle. After a moment he begins to speak into the small radio clipped to his lapel. No sign of the limousine from the Savoy.

8:58—Sohaila—a splash of color in her violet corduroy slacks and bright yellow blouse—emerges from the doors at the rear of the van. If she has done her job, the bomb is armed. She walks to the side of the van where the second police officer is still speaking sternly to her father. (All right. Careful, Sohaila.) The policeman is distracted and pauses to look at her. No black limousine in sight.

8:59—Two more police officers arrive. They make no move to look inside the rear of the van. If they do, they will understand the situation immediately and will move quickly to disarm the charge. David unzips the binoculars case and puts his finger near the button on the transmitter. No black limousine. (Can Malcolm Worth's canon have been wrong? No. Why else so many policemen on the scene?)

9:00—Sohaila edges her way to the back of the truck and steps a few paces away from it. (No, Sohaila! Don't lose your nerve now!) Three policemen are clustered before the van, talking. They do not look excited. No limousine.

9:01—The door opens on the right side of the van. Mikhal steps out. (No, damn it! Not yet!) A policeman stops Mikhal and begins talking to him. David fastens the camera to his eye and watches closely. Mikhal's arms are moving. The talk is heated.

9:02—Mikhal spins away from the policeman talking to him and walks rapidly toward the back of the van. (No, you fool!) Sohaila falls in beside him, and they hurry east, striding along the wrought-iron fence. (No! No! No!) The policeman trots after them, an arm raised, yelling. Two others jerk open the back doors of the van. David's hand is already inside the binoculars case, his finger on the button on the transmitter. (Damn!) He presses.

Westminster Abbey disappears behind the fire and smoke and dust of the explosion. A police car and a black Rolls limousine careen into Tothill Street and speed past David, who has been staggered by the force of the blast and has fallen to his knees on the pavement.

7

IT WAS quite unbelievable. The horror of the thing was beyond experience. Major Duncan Glynbourne arrived at the Abbey twenty minutes after the blast.

Westminster Abbey. The fabric stood at least, but the west face was scarred and broken. All the glass was gone, leaving the façade starkly gaping, burned out inside. Ornate stonework that had stood for centuries had toppled to the forecourt pavement. The Abbey bookshop was gone entirely, as was the Jerusalem Chamber and much of the Deanery—blown in and collapsed. The stonework above the clock in the north tower had fallen, stripping the face from the clock. The west door was gone, and the interior of the Abbey was exposed to the street. Dust still rolled from that gaping door.

Every window was gone from the north façade of Westminster School, and the corner adjoining the Abbey had toppled in. Thankfully the school was closed for the summer holidays.

A gaping crater stood open in the street. Scraps of twisted sheet steel, the wreckage of vehicles, police cars and others, hung from the face of the Abbey and the walls of the school. Fragments of the column of the Westminster School monument had been thrown across the street like logs from a felled tree. Rubble was strewn everywhere. Windows were blown out of buildings for hundreds of yards around.

Emergency vehicles streamed into Victoria Street and Great Smith

Street, their pulsing horns howling an arrythmic beat, blue lights blinking dimly in the bright morning sunlight. Their crews huddled in tight clusters around the fallen and twisted bodies that lay in the rubble and on the lawn of the Abbey grounds. Vehicles moved out with the injured. A hundred officers, some on horseback, struggled to keep the area closed, to hold back the crowds, who pressed from every quarter.

Major Glynbourne had been called off the tennis court and had taken a few more minutes to reach the scene than he would have wished. He ordered his driver to head the Jaguar to the curb on Tothill Street, and he confronted a uniformed police officer immediately and offered his credentials.

"Superintendent Grimsby is in charge, sir," the officer said. "I'll advise him you're here."

"Thank you," said Glynbourne. "Be so good as to keep an eye on the car, will you?"

Glynbourne was dressed in a gray tweed jacket and black trousers, with an Irish tweed walking hat. The sergeant major, his driver and assistant, wore brown tweeds. Sergeant Major Bryan Tate was armed with a police Walther under the jacket of his ill-cut suit. Glynbourne never carried a weapon. They walked among the emergency vehicles, toward the crater and the west front of the Abbey.

Detective Superintendent Ronald Grimsby of Scotland Yard was easy enough to find. He was standing by a communications van drawn up almost to the edge of the crater, receiving word from a stream of officers who hurried to him, and giving orders they scurried off to carry out. He was a slight man, anything but prepossessing, pallid, bespectacled, with a harried air that was justified this morning but was characteristic of him even in easier hours.

"Ah," he said. "SIS. I expected you."

"Carry on, Superintendent," said Glynbourne. "We'll hear what you can tell us when you have a moment."

"I'll take a moment now," said Superintendent Grimsby. "We seem to have eight dead, about a dozen seriously injured, half a dozen more not so seriously. The damage . . . Well, you can see. The dean is in serious condition. He was behind the door, about to step out, when the blast occurred. Door blew in on him. We've lost four officers. We have bodies of two Asians we think were the ones who delivered the bomb. We have two bodies we haven't identified yet. As for motive, we have to assume it was an attempt to assassinate the Indian defence minister, General Lal Nath Sekhar, who was due here for a private tour of the Abbey but fortunately was a little late."

"Yes. He has gone on to the conference," said Glynbourne.

"If indeed our two dead Asians are the bombers, they seem to have set their timer badly," said the superintendent. "Not only did they fail to assassinate the defence minister, but they neglected to allow themselves enough time to escape."

"I am going to guess, Superintendent, that the bomb was not detonated by a timer," said Glynbourne. "If you can find enough to look at, I think you will find it was set off by a radio signal. We should do whatever we can to find a man who was watching this area through binoculars, from two or three hundred yards away."

"Then our two dead Asians are not the people who delivered the bomb."

"I am afraid they probably are," said Glynbourne. "The only two people who could identify the man who sent the signal. May I see the remains, please?"

The superintendent stayed beside his communications van. He assigned a detective to show Glynbourne and Sergeant Major Tate the two bodies.

They lay unmoved about fifty feet from the edge of the crater—the man on the pavement, the woman sprawled over the broken wrought-iron fence and partly in the grass. The bodies were intact, though their blood stained the pavement and the ground. The man was bearded and dressed in workingman's clothes and looked late middle-aged. The woman was much younger. They had died of the effects of the blast—from the impact of debris driven into their bodies by its force. The young woman's head was almost severed from her body by a shred of steel that had hit her like shrapnel. She was dressed in violet-colored corduroy slacks. Only a few bloody scraps remained of what must have been a yellow blouse that the blast had torn from her, and she lay on her back with her breasts bare in the sunlight. Her eyes were open, and her stare seemed impossibly fixed: straight into the morning sun, as if when life left her she had deferred the darkness for a final instant by fixing on the brightest light she could find.

"I wonder if he made love to her," said Sergeant Major Tate. He was a bulky man with a red walrus mustache. He walked with a limp, his reminder of a much less violent blast in Belfast four years ago. "She was a pretty lass."

"We must place priority on finding out who they were," said Glynbourne to the Scotland Yard detective. "My guess is that they are Biharis. My guess also is that Lal Nath Sekhar has been extraordinarily lucky. The man who meant to kill him this morning does not often fail."

Major Glynbourne and Sergeant Major Tate entered the Abbey. They did not expect to learn anything there, but they went in anyway, drawn by their apprehension about what they would see. They found the nave filled with dust and the floor littered with glass, burying the memorial stone to Sir Winston Churchill and the tomb of the Unknown Warrior under a multicolored, glittering layer. Wreckage of the wooden door and the wooden entryway was scattered halfway down the nave, and hundreds of chairs had been swept into heaps by the force of the blast.

"Sir?" A canon approached, his footsteps crunching glass.

"Glynbourne, Secret Intelligence Service."

"Ah. It's a horror, isn't it?" said the canon.

"The vaulting?" asked Glynbourne. "The structure?"

"Sound, apparently. It's amazingly strong. Look above you. The great west window. The glass of course is gone. But not the stone. It's fifteenth-century, that. The glass was eighteenth. It can be replaced. But the stone, the marvelous, irreplaceable, delicate framework of stone . . . It stands. At least for now. God be thanked for that."

"It's a happy circumstance that we can find something to be thankful for," said Glynbourne.

From his office window, the major had a view of some Mayfair rooftops, then of Hyde Park, from Marble Arch to the Albert Memorial. His office was not to his taste, being modern functional, with much vinyl and veneer; it depressed him, and he was glad his work kept him away from it most of the time. He stood at his window—he had never liked to sit behind a desk; to do so had an irrational symbolic significance to him.

Major Duncan Glynbourne was the son and grandson of dispensing chemists who kept a shop in Kensington, selling prescription drugs, medicinal soaps, deodorants, and toothbrushes. His father had intended that he should follow in the family business and had expected him to begin life serving quietly behind the counter, attending to the needs of fusty ladies shopping for mid-Victorian nostrums for their attacks of the vapors. His grim, willful mother—a woman he had found it difficult to love in spite of what she did for him—had entertained other ideas. She had bullied his father into borrowing money to send young Duncan to Gordonstoun, the school in Scotland where Prince Philip and Prince Charles were educated. In nine spartan years there he had learned two lessons above all others: that he was irremediably middle class, but that in spite of that he was not suited for the shop.

At the urging of a master at Gordonstoun, he had sat for the examinations for Sandhurst, had passed brilliantly and gone there, and instead of a clerk in a chemist's shop had become a trim, crisp, dutiful subaltern in a tank regiment of the Army of the Rhine. By 1972 he had attained the rank of captain. When Brigadier Fulham was transferred to command of SIS Group Four in 1975, he asked for Captain Glynbourne—to keep his tennis partner as he said.

Actually, of course, the brigadier had a better reason. Glynbourne was by then already doing counter-terrorist work in Germany, in fact had been doing little else since the murder of the Israeli athletes at the

Munich Olympics. He had never liked the work: it gave him the aspect of a civil servant and denied him the identification he had sought in a military career; but he brought to it the characteristics by which he was known and for which he was valued—his logical mind and a quiet tenacity in investigation. He despaired now of ever serving in uniform again.

"Thank you, Agnes," he said distractedly. The young secretary had brought in their tea. As she went out, he walked to the tray, where it sat on the wide steel windowsill with the louvered vents for the air-conditioning system and lifted the pot to pour. "So, Sergeant Major," he said. "Why don't you be first. Tell Superintendent and me what you've learned."

Detective Superintendent Grimsby accepted a cup of tea and raised his eyes expectantly to Sergeant Major Tate.

The sergeant major, too, took a cup of tea and balanced it precariously on his knees while he referred to a small notebook. "The subjects were Mikhal Mohmand and his daughter Sohaila Mohmand," he said. "Both East Pakistanis. Immigrated in 1972. The man was fifty-one. The gel"—he glanced up—"was eighteen. The man was a fare collector for the London Transit System. She"—he looked up again, this time touching his big red mustache and frowning—"was a prostitute. They are survived by a woman of forty-two, the wife and mother. The woman received in this afternoon's mail an envelope containing two thousand pounds in notes of assorted denomination."

"There's a touch," said the superintendent.

"The gel," the sergeant major continued, "was the subject of a police investigation a little more than two weeks ago. An Indian named Jawaharlal Sjarif, who was her pimp, was murdered in Soho. All the gels known to be attached to him were investigated, but none of them were suspects, actually. I have the impression little attention was given to Sohaila Mohmand."

"How was this Sjarif killed?" asked Major Glynbourne.

"Professionally, I'd say," said the sergeant major. "With a knife, thrust upward into his throat with considerable force. The weapon was thrown away. It was a new knife, handle wrapped in sticking plaster. Unlikely a gel did it. Anyway, Sjarif was involved in activities besides pimping, including the sale of narcotics in a petty way. It's supposed one of his business associates relieved the world of him."

"Any political connections?" asked Major Glynbourne.

"If so, Scotland Yard doesn't know of them."

"Let's pursue that," said Major Glynbourne. "Let's see what we can find out about this Sjarif."

"Yes, sir. As to the Mohmands, father and daughter, they were Biharis, as you expected. Anyway, the man was. They lived in Camden Town. Wasn't possible to question his wife, the gel's mother, really. Neighbors said they'd seen no strangers near the flat lately, nothing unusual in the man's conduct. The gel rarely came there. I'm afraid, sir, that's about all I've got."

"A good day's work, Sergeant Major. Superintendent?"

"The explosive was C-4 plastique," said Superintendent Grimsby. "Some forty or fifty pounds of it. It was brought up in a window-washer's van that supposedly stalled in front of the Abbey just a few minutes before it went off. The two Asians were inside. They tried to run away but didn't make it far enough before the explosion. So far as the detonator is concerned"—he shrugged and shook his head—"we've found nothing."

"May I ask you to keep looking, Superintendent," said Major Glynbourne.

"We will, of course," said the superintendent. "We have people literally sifting the better part of a ton of debris."

"Electronic components," said Major Glynbourne. "No matter how small a fragment. A few bits may be enough to identify the radio receiver that triggered the detonator."

"Could enough pieces to make an identification actually have survived a blast that strong?" asked the superintendent.

"They did in Milan," said Major Glynbourne. "This charge was heavier than that one, but . . . Just set aside, please, anything that might be an electronic component."

The superintendent nodded. "Yes . . . And when we learn the bomb was set off by a radio signal, what do we know, Major?"

"That very likely the explosion was the work of the same man who destroyed *The Last Supper*, Superintendent. That should be enough to inspire us to extraordinary effort, even if the damage to the Abbey didn't. Should it not?"

Friday morning, Sergeant Major Tate walked into the New Lahore food shop. The shop was open. In the little restaurant behind, the chairs were piled on the tables. He inquired first of an elderly, white-bearded man who seemed to be selling an assortment of dried weeds from little baskets. The old man professed to understand little English, to know nothing. The sergeant major persisted, and the old man began to nod, asked for patience with a gesture of his palsied hand, and disappeared somewhere in the rear of the shop. A younger man emerged, one with a black beard. He said his name was Ahmed Yayah and that he spoke English, as his father did not.

"Mikhal Mohmand," said the sergeant major. "He ate dinner here, with a European. About two weeks ago."

The man nodded. "Friederich Reitlinger. A German. From Frankfurt. He ate here twice and returned to take tea one afternoon. I have his card."

"Can you describe him?"

Ahmed Yayah shrugged. "A good-looking young man. Blond. Tall. His waiter was Ali, both evenings. He can tell you more. I will summon him."

The waiter, Ali, sat down at one of the tables with Sergeant Major Tate.

Ahmed Yayah joined them. "You are investigating the explosion," he said.

"Yes."

"They talked about Lal Nath Sekhar," said the waiter breathlessly.
"They sat here. I heard them. Reitlinger caused their deaths, I think."
"We are Biharis," said Ahmed Yayah. "Do you know what that
means? Our people were slaughtered. Many die even today in the
concentration camps of Bangladesh. Our homes were stolen. Our
businesses. We were driven out naked. This man Reitlinger. Who
knows why *he* wanted to kill the butcher Sekhar? Instead, he killed
Mikhal Mohmand. A fine man."
"And his daughter," said the sergeant major.
Ahmed Yayah shrugged. "A whore."
"If you suspected all this, why didn't you call the police?" asked the
sergeant major a little impatiently.
"We knew you would come."

About the same time, a policewoman, Alice Stevenson, was ques-
tioning the girls at the strip theater.
"She'd got 'erself a connection, it looked like," a black girl said.
"Good lookin' 'e was, too! Blond. Athletic-type build. Had money.
Bought her dinner before they went to a hotel."
"Did you ever hear him speak?"
The girl shrugged. "A word or two. If you want to know about an
accent, 'e didn't have one. Spoke the Queen's English."
"What did she call him?"
"Fritz."
The young man who sold tickets and admitted men to the theater
said he remembered Sohaila's man well. "Anglo. Pretty." He nodded.
"Good. Big. Tall."
"I don't know," said another young woman, a small, pretty Pales-
tinian. "There was something threatening about him. I thought once
he'd done us a big favor. Now I'm not so sure."
"What favor?"
The young woman sighed. "Well. It's only a guess, but I had the
idea maybe he was the one that killed Sjarif."

*   *   *

They heard, eventually, about the dinner at Ricardo's. Friday evening the sergeant major called there. The proprietor, dressed in a black tie and preparing to receive his patrons, spoke as he took calls to book tables.

"If the man thought he was keeping an incognito, he made a big mistake," the man said. "Take myself. I should hardly have remembered him. But he brought a known prostitute in here. There is hardly anywhere he could have gone in this neighborhood that *she* would not have been recognized. I didn't know her name, but I knew what she was. I actually considered refusing them a table that night. But she behaved. And he—Well, he knew food and wine, ordered well, ate well. Paid cash. I took him for a young businessman who had arranged something very nice for his evening in London."

"A foreigner?" asked the sergeant major.

"Well, if his name suggests his nationality, a German, I should think. Uh . . . See, here's his name. He booked the table in person, not by telephone. Friederich Reitlinger."

"Accent?"

"None whatever. Good public-school English."

At noon on Sunday a meeting assembled in a small conference room one floor below Major Glynbourne's office. The room was soundproof. No windows, no telephone. One wall was covered by a large, slick-surfaced white board on which a marker pen could be used to write and diagram. No notes were ever brought into the room, and none were taken there. No paper came in, and none went out. Briefings were from memory, and conferees were expected to remember what was said. When a meeting broke up, the white board was cleaned by the conferees themselves, with a wet cloth.

Major Glynbourne presided from a chair in the center of the table, facing the white board. To his left were Colonel Harcourt and Captain Fenwick of Group Four. To his right was Superintendent

Grimsby. Sergeant Major Tate sat across the table, where he could handily rise to write on the board.

"For the moment," said Major Glynbourne, "I should rather we didn't call our bomber by the name Oliver Cromwell. Although circumstantial evidence certainly suggests he is, we have no solid evidence that the man who detonated the bomb before Westminster Abbey is the same man who set off the explosion that destroyed *The Last Supper*; and if we assume he is, we may lead ourselves off in the wrong direction. May we, therefore, for the moment call him what he called himself, that is, Friederich Reitlinger?"

The others nodded, and the major continued, speaking in his characteristic throaty voice. "Reitlinger left a business card at the New Lahore restaurant indicating he was affiliated with a Frankfurt firm named Gebhart und Weibel. The firm exists. Friederich H. Reitlinger does not. We have checked with the Federal Republic. Both the BFV and the BND assure us that Gebhart und Weibel is an honest business, not a front for anything. No one, however, has ever heard of Friederich Reitlinger. Interpol has nothing on that name. We have checked with Immigration. No Friederich Reitlinger—"

"Then it's an alias," said Colonel Harcourt firmly, apparently satisfied and anxious to move on. The colonel was a handsome retired Guards officer, long-faced, pink, peering over half-glasses.

"What is more," said Major Glynbourne, "the business card he offered at the New Lahore was not printed in the Federal Republic. That was easy enough to establish. The paper, the thermographic process used to print the card—that is, the type of resin in the ink—are characteristic of work done in this country, or in Canada or the States. Nothing like it in Germany."

"So what do we know about Reitlinger?" asked Colonel Harcourt.

"That he is a rather handsome, blond young man who speaks unaccented English, dresses well, and has impeccable manners. He dined twice at the New Lahore, once with Sohaila Mohmand, then with her and her father. He returned once more, to drink tea with the father. On the second occasion, when he was with both father and daughter, they were overheard to use the name Lal Nath Sekhar. Also, Reitlinger dined once with Sohaila at Ricardo's. He used her services as a prostitute at least twice, perhaps more.

"He did not encounter her by chance," the major continued. "Our evidence of the following is a little less certain than the evidence of what I've so far told you, but it appears he spent some time in the Soho area, looking for Biharis, before he found Sohaila Mohmand, who led him to her father. We have inquired of Asians working in the neighborhood, and several believe they remember a man matching Reitlinger's description as the man who engaged them in apparently casual conversation about the injustices done the Biharis by the Indian armed forces in 1971."

"Which brings us to the subject of motive, I should think," said Colonel Harcourt. "Are we to believe that—"

"If you will excuse me, sir," said Major Glynbourne. "I should like, if you don't mind, to report a few more facts before we talk about possible motive and other speculative topics."

The colonel nodded.

"Sohaila Mohmand," said the major, "was in thrall, as I believe the term is, to a pimp, a certain Jawaharlal Sjarif, an Indian national resident in London since 1966. Sjarif ran four girls, it seems. The usual thing: dominated them by threat of violence. He traded in narcotics in a small way. He seems also to have been a common mugger. Ten days before the blast at the Abbey, Sjarif was murdered. The other girls on his string suspected Reitlinger had done them a favor. They kept quiet about it, of course. All we know about it for the moment is that it seems to have been done in a cool, professional manner. Sjarif had lots of enemies, but his death, coming when it did, has the look of Reitlinger ridding himself of an obstacle."

"So where are we now, Major?"

"We continue sifting the blast debris. So far, we've learned nothing very helpful, wouldn't you say, Superintendent? And we continue to circulate in Soho and Camden Town. So far we haven't found another Reitlinger card, nor have we found the print shop that made the one we have. We're checking every hotel. We are going to show about one of those wretched drawings police artists make."

"At the moment, if I may summarize, we have no more idea who the bomber is than we had on Wednesday morning," said the colonel. "Is that unfair?"

"Not entirely," said the major calmly. "We do have a physical description. We know something of the man's habits. But we have no idea who he is, I certainly grant you."

"His motive, then," said the colonel. "Why did this man want to assassinate the Indian defence minister?"

"One is compelled to the conclusion that he is a professional," said Major Glynbourne. "One supposes he works for money."

"Indeed, yes," said Colonel Harcourt.

"Let us for the moment put aside our resolve not to assume Friederich Reitlinger is Oliver Cromwell," suggested Captain Fenwick. "Then we are brought to the question, Who would have motive to destroy *The Last Supper*, attempt to destroy the Basilica of St. Francis at Assisi, destroy some treasured El Grecos and other works in Toledo, and now attempt to assassinate Lal Nath Sekhar? It is perfectly obvious who has such a complicated motive, is it not?"

"You are about to mention the KGB," said Colonel Harcourt. "I do object to using the KGB as a bogeyman, the explanation for every misfortune that befalls. We have gone from the Cheka, to the NKVD, to the MVD, to the KGB, using all of them as a convenience when we are unable to catch a crook."

"Some of us," said Captain Fenwick coldly, "have had direct personal experience of the KGB."

"Whilst others," said the colonel loftily, "have spent their time fighting back against the nastiness of the Stern Gang, then the PLO, the IRA in its various manifestations, Colonel Qadaffi, the Ayatollahs, the Islamic Jihad . . . Would you care to name others, Captain? I am sure we can come up with half a dozen other despicable enemies of everything civilized men hold dear. I am unwilling simply to assume it is the KGB, and not one of these others or some new one, who is behind Oliver Cromwell and Friederich Reitlinger."

"Let me outline a scenario for you, sir," said Captain Fenwick calmly. His background was like Glynbourne's: a pubkeeper's son sent to Charterhouse, then to Sandhurst, followed by a stint in the SAS— Special Air Services— and transfer to Group Four as a tough, angry man, capable of doing whatever a difficult assignment might require. He had a brittle personality and was at no pains to avoid clashes with men of the colonel's very different background. "The Polish pope has attracted a certain following in Eastern Europe. He's like Mary, Queen of Scots—a lot of mature men who should know better focus on him their hope to be rid of governments they don't like. To some extent, he encourages them. The KGB tried once to kill him. He—"

"Really, Fenwick!"

Captain Fenwick raised a hand. "Oh, I know. You are going to tell me the Bulgarians acted on their own, without KGB prompting. The best evidence of that, I should think, is the fact that the attempt was crude, was botched, and would in any event have succeeded only in creating a powerful martyr. Suppose, on the other hand, the KGB wanted to send Karol Wojtyla a signal: You are not safe, nothing tangible that you cherish is safe, and if you continue to encourage dissidence in our territories, we will apply growing pressure to you. That would explain the destruction of treasures of Christian art and architecture, together with some holy relics. It's a message to the pope. To the Church. More than that, it's a message to the world: You can't protect anything from us. We are your future."

"Rather dramatic, don't you think?" said the colonel. "And they employ one man, Oliver Cromwell, to send this message?"

"Initially. And so long as he is effective."

"Then how does the attempt on the life of Lal Nath Sekhar fit into your scenario?"

"It is just possible," said Captain Fenwick, "that the Abbey was the real target and the Indian was just a bonus. On the other hand, I suggest that motivation for the assassination of Lal Nath Sekhar is easier to understand than motivation for the other crimes. I suggest the Soviet leadership would take desperate measures to prevent the initiation of a military alliance between China and India."

"And this makes Oliver Cromwell—"

"A hired assassin," said Captain Fenwick. "An embittered young man. An intelligent young man filled with hate. If we could guess why, we could identify him."

"I believe," said Major Glynbourne, "that we are looking for a mercenary terrorist."

"There's a new phrase," said Colonel Harcourt.

"But not a new concept," said the major. "However much they may have hated Lal Nath Sekhar, the Mohmands—or, for that matter, any other Biharis resident in England—could not have attempted the assassination by this means. It required money, explosives, expertise. The latter they may conceivably have had. The other two . . ." He paused, shrugged. "The man we call Friederich Reitlinger, or Oliver Cromwell, was supplied with money and the necessary materials by someone other than the poor Biharis."

"If I may say so, sir," said Sergeant Major Tate. "It has been my impression of the Biharis that, on the whole, they would not take part in such a crime. If the Mohmands were not the only Biharis involved in this, I would judge that very few others were."

"Reinforcing our suspicion that an organization such as the KGB is behind the crime," said Major Glynbourne.

"And the supposition that Reitlinger-Cromwell is a mercenary," said the superintendent.

"I shall advise the other agencies involved," said Major Glynbourne. "It is their supposition that Cromwell is a mercenary. The task of finding him may be considerably simplified if we can have confidence in that supposition."

At four o'clock on Sunday afternoon, Brigadier Fulham and Major Glynbourne mounted the steps at Number 10 Downing Street. The prime minister was punctual about her appointments, and they were admitted to her office only two minutes past the exact time.

"Your daughter, Major?" asked Mrs. Thatcher.

"Still in remission, Prime Minister. Thank you for asking."

She closed her eyes for a moment. "If there is any way we can help . . . You understand, I am sure, that you have our constant prayers and hopes."

"Thank you. She has the best of care and simply lives each day that's given her."

The prime minister nodded and sighed. "Well. Turning to business. Was it Oliver Cromwell?"

"We believe so, Prime Minister," said the brigadier—a tall, gray man, thin to the point of emaciation, who tried unsuccessfully to keep his lips so stretched when he spoke that he did not reveal a set of ravaged, crooked teeth.

"Who is safe? What is safe?"

"Nothing. No one."

"One can look at it in a number of ways," she said. "One can say, for example, that such incidents, and the losses attendant on them, are simply the cost of living in a violent world and being, or trying to be, a force for decency and order. I could take the attitude that we lose eight lives—it will probably be nine before the day is over, since one more policeman is likely to die yet today—and the west face of Westminster Abbey as a part of the cost of trying to preserve civilization against the barbarians. I am not willing, however, gentlemen, to be quite so philosophical."

"Nor am I, Prime Minister," said Brigadier Fulham.

"I cannot," she went on, "when I face questions in the House, reply that I have authorized Group Four simply to kill Oliver Cromwell and his co-conspirators, whoever they are and wherever you find them. I cannot give you written authority to do so."

"We quite understand."

"I assume, Brigadier," she said, "that Major Glynbourne has been

relieved of all other responsibilities and is giving his entire attention to
this matter."

"Exactly so, ma'am. And he has extraordinary authority to call for
assistance from any agency whatever."

"Use my name, Major, if you must," she said. "Understand that
the Government place full confidence in you. It is within the scope of
your authority to act in whatever way you shall find most appropriate
to eliminate this danger. I will defend you in whatever you do, assuming—" She paused and smiled faintly. "Assuming only that you do
not use worse judgment than I can possibly imagine your using."

"I believe I understand," said Glynbourne.

"In brief, Major, the restrictions formerly stated are removed."

"We quite understand."

The Prime Minister closed her eyes. "No question will be raised
about whatever measures you elect to take. You know your business.
Do it, Major. I may not even want to know what you do."

"My regret . . ." He frowned, rubbed his mouth with the back of
his hand to cover the moment of emotion that had threatened to
choke his voice, and drew a deep breath. "My regret is that the task
will be so demanding of my time, require so much travel. I'm afraid
you and Katrina will see little of me for a while."

"We'll miss you, Daddy." His daughter smiled. "Obviously, others
have learned at last what we always knew about you: that you are the
best they have. But we will miss you."

He would miss her, too—only his thought was not of missing her
the next few weeks or whatever time it took to run down Oliver Cromwell, but of how very much he would miss her when he had lost her,
which he knew he was bound to do all too soon. He had considered
asking for an extended leave of absence from the service, so he could
spend all his time with her as long as she lived. Her doctors had
protested. It would signal her that he believed her death imminent,
and that was a signal they did not want her to see.

She was nineteen. She had always been pretty, since she was a child; but the delicacy that had come with her illness had robbed her beauty of the robust nature that had characterized it before and rendered it ethereal. The disease had been in remission eight months now. Her hair had grown back, long and fine, though a lighter brown than it had been before. She was able to go out. She went to the parks with her friends, to enjoy the sunshine, and they took her to the cinema once a week, which she loved. Before the remission was established, she had spent a great deal of time in hospital, then confined to the flat. She was so much better now that it was easy for all three of them to deceive themselves into supposing the disease was conquered. They knew better. Her mother had lived nineteen months after the doctors had announced remission.

"I should hate to be Oliver Cromwell," said Katrina softly, in her odd little German accent. "With Major Duncan Glynbourne on his trail, his days are numbered."

Katrina lived with them, as Betty's companion, so Betty would never be left alone. She was the daughter of an officer of the Bundeswehr; her family and the Glynbournes had been neighbors during the major's service with the Army of the Rhine; and the two girls, in spite of five years' difference in their ages, had become the closest of friends. After Glynbourne's transfer back to England, the girls had corresponded constantly and exchanged visits every summer. Two years ago Katrina had come to London as an au pair girl, to live with a family on York Terrace, and had telephoned Betty Glynbourne within hours of her arrival. She had been shocked at what she learned and deeply distressed to have to write back to her parents that Mrs. Glynbourne was dying of cancer and that early symptoms of the same disease had been found in Betty, too. She had spent as much time with Betty as she could during her year as an au pair; and, when that year was over, Katrina had proposed she return to London after a short visit home, to move in with the Glynbournes and stay as long as Betty needed a companion. She had arrived a year ago, just after the major's wife died and just before Betty's first experience of chemotherapy.

Katrina was a mature young woman, blond, with a sleek, taut figure. She carried herself with the confident natural elegance of movement and posture that had characterized Betty, too, before the onset of the disease. She tended to be quiet. She had a peculiar, illogical sense of humor that manifested itself in occasional soft-spoken observations that the major often carried to his work and quoted to people perceptive enough to understand them.

His relationship with Katrina had developed into something none of them had anticipated, though it had been perhaps almost inevitable. They had not yet been quite able to tell Betty that they would marry as soon as they felt they could. They were not confident of how she would accept it. Besides, as they saw it, they must first travel to Hamburg together and face Katrina's parents with their surprising announcement; and since the two of them would not leave Betty at the same time, the journey had been postponed until she was strong enough to go—or until something bad happened.

What neither of them suspected was that Betty was observant enough to have seen them fall in love. It would have taken more subtlety than either of them possessed to conceal it. Betty knew they slipped back and forth between each other's rooms as often as they could, when they supposed she was asleep. She understood that they would marry as soon as they could—and she perfectly well understood what they were waiting for.

8

EMILY FAVORED emerald-green iridescent in silken fabrics. This morning, Saturday, she wore a tiny bikini, shining green, as they strolled along the beach not long after sunrise, hours before the crowds would come. It was cool yet, and the world was wet: the air wet with sea mist, the beach wet from the receding tide, the trees dripping with dew. She wore a white terry-cloth coat over her bikini, but it was open, showing off her solid breasts hanging in the two connected green slings of the bra. It was perhaps her long, sleek American legs that most attracted the glances of the few men who were out on the sand this early. She walked lightly, as if her legs did not really impose her weight on the sand under her feet. Her graceful carriage was in contrast to her direct American speech and manners, which sometimes amused David and at other times annoyed him.

"Thank God for this week, and God save me from East Lothian," she said. "May he save me from the 'Mac-Fairrr-sons,'" she added, mimicking the pronunciation given their name by her host and hostess of two weekends ago. "David, you are the most resourceful man I have ever known."

"A half dozen bottles of fine champagne brandy will unlock many doors," he said insouciantly.

They had left London ten days ago—the day after the explosion at Westminster Abbey—driving south in a Ford Granada she had rented, carrying in the boot the case of brandy he would share among hotel managers who gave them the kind of rooms they wanted, as they had left London without bookings. They took rooms at an inn in Winchester for two nights, without giving away any brandy; and finally, last Saturday, one of his telephone calls got them a seafront booking. They were at Sandown, on the southern shore of the Isle of Wight where, for half a dozen bottles, the manager had manipulated his bookings and had been able to give them a room with bath for a week. On Monday they would move on to St. Helier, to spend another week on the Island of Jersey, where the manager of the beach hotel had been happy to accept the remaining half dozen bottles and find a room for his friend Mr. Betancourt.

It had been a splendid week. They had of course surrendered the Ford at Southhampton, and on the island they had rented bicycles with which they had toured from Totland to Benbridge, from Cowes to St. Catherine's point. They were taken for newlyweds, and they looked the part: young and healthy and exuberant.

David had stopped shaving. Already he had grown the beginnings of a handsome blond beard, which Emily alternately liked and disliked. Coming out of a shop yesterday, after ten minutes' separation from him, she'd had difficulty recognizing him, she said—what with the beard and his sunglasses and cap. He was amused. He spent some time judging the beard in mirrors and in the bathroom trimming its edges with a wet razor.

"You must have had a big success, to follow up your busy week with two weeks' vacation," she had suggested on their first day.

"Not entirely," he had said. "I needed to get away from it, to think about it."

He didn't seem to spend much time thinking about his business, she observed. He had been a little moody at the beginning. He read the newspapers with care, and watched the news on the telly. On the beach he sometimes stared out to sea and appeared to be absorbed in some compelling play of thought and imagination; but he had responded to her teasing and her erotic advances; and by now he was as bright and amusing as ever she had seen him.

"The history of this place!" she said to him as they walked along the beach, letting the waves wash up over their feet. "Imagine being here seventy-five years or so ago, when the fleet was reviewed every year at Spithead. What a sight it must have been! The Spanish Armada fought out there, right off these beaches. From the island, people could see the fleets banging away at each other with their big old guns."

"I'm afraid," he said dryly, "I have developed a bit of distaste for the glories of British arms."

"I'm sorry, David."

"Don't be. We've been propagandized all our lives. Drake and Nelson and Wellington are supposed to be the world's heroes, not just England's—because they fought for right and justice and civilization. Who commanded the Armada? Do you even know? The Duke of Medina Sedonia. Ever hear of him?"

"Yes, David. I know the name well. I was a history major, remember?"

"Oh, yes."

A gull wheeled in out of the mist and settled in the water's edge ahead of them, squawking a complaint. It pecked at the sand for a moment, then strutted along ahead of them, being raucous.

"American Anglophobes called the English 'perfidious.' Did you know that?" Emily asked.

"We traveled in high circles in London," David said, his thoughts having run away from hers. "Embassy parties. Openings. Balls. Clubs. When my father came to London, he would have more invitations than he could answer. The president of Argentina didn't visit England, but Admiral Betancourt did. When my mother and I were here without him, sometimes we had to check with the embassy protocol officer before deciding which invitations to accept."

David kicked idly at the sand as he walked, his head down, a faint smile on his face. His talk was reminiscent, not bitter.

"When the war came . . . Well, it was awkward. Even today, it's awkward. Can the Duchess of Kent receive the widow of Admiral Hector Betancourt? Should she invite him to her reception for the opening of the ballet season? And what of the son, the captain in the Argentine army? Should he be asked to the regimental dinners he always attended before?"

"How did *you* handle it, David?"

"Once the war was over, and after observing what is called a decent period of mourning for my father, we went where we'd always gone— unless it required an invitation we didn't receive. Of course, we received fewer and fewer. We still go to embassy receptions occasionally. The Argentine embassy continues to pretend that we are distinguished citizens only temporarily absent from Buenos Aires. I can on occasion, if it's required, trick myself out in white tie, with my medals. I decline to wear my dress uniform, but I still have it."

"You have medals, David?"

"In ornamental armies, everyone has medals," he said. "In spic armies, everyone has gaudy medals."

The sun, slowly whitening and burning through the thinning mist, warmed Emily, and she shed her jacket and folded it to carry on her hip. "It's something I just can't imagine," she said. "I mean, you a soldier."

"Our English friends saw me once, not just as a soldier, but maybe as a spy," he said.

"They suspected you?" she asked. "An Argentine spy? During the war?"

He shook his head. "No. An English spy. Later."

"David . . ."

"It's the truth," he said.

It was the truth, and he proceeded to tell her. It was in 1983. The war was over. He and his mother were invited to a reception at the Mexican embassy. They arrived, and his mother was immediately swept into the company of a dozen ladies anxious, first, to express their sympathy, next to hear anything she might be willing to tell them about the dramatic death of her husband, daughter, and prospective daughter-in-law. He was formally dressed, with his two jeweled medals pinned to his breast; with a glass of champagne in his hand, he found himself standing momentarily alone beside a white marble fireplace, under a portrait painting of a Mexican statesman he did not recognize. He had turned to squint at the little plate on the gilded frame when a man spoke to him from behind.

"Betancourt, isn't it?"

"Yes. I do beg your pardon—"

"Fogg," said the man. "Bill Fogg. Don't be embarrassed if you don't remember me. I've seen you, you've been pointed out to me, but I can't say we've been introduced. Sandhurst, you understand. The Coldstream, later."

Fogg was a little older than David but was, like himself, a handsome blond young man. His eyes were pale blue and sharp, but they were, as David would remember them, the least communicative eyes he had ever seen: not cold, perhaps, but totally unmoving.

"Sorry about the way things happened for you, Betancourt," Fogg said. "My sympathy."

"Thank you," said David.

"Understand you feel you can't go back," said Fogg. "To Argentina, I mean."

"In any event," said David, "I am not at all sure I want to go back."

"No. I can understand that. On the other hand, suppose you had a reason to go back. Your government says it would welcome you."

"Would it?"

"It would, yes."

"You seem to know a good deal about my situation," said David. "At least as much as I do. Maybe more."

"That's my business, Betancourt. You've had army training. You know what DI5 is."

David nodded.

"We wouldn't ask you to act against your own country. On the other hand, an Argentine army captain, serving at home or in an embassy in some other country's capital, as was planned for you, could do some very useful things for us. We would make it well worth your while, of course."

"I had supposed DI5 was more subtle," said David.

"Depends on the circumstances," said Fogg.

"How I am supposed to answer?"

"Express an interest. Or no interest."

"The Argentine army," said David, "just took a humiliating defeat, which it tries to rationalize by blaming my father. I somehow doubt that I would find a promising career in it. Anyway, I don't like the way the army sustains its political power."

"That's nothing new, Betancourt."

"It would be to me. No, Fogg. I am not averse to being of some service to England, if I can—particularly if I decide to apply for permanent residence status here—but I am not going back to Argentina within the foreseeable future and especially I am not going to serve in the Argentine army."

"But if we call on you for some service in the course of your civilian career. . . ?"

"I will probably perform it," said David.

"But, of course, they haven't called on me," he said to Emily. "I don't know how I'd react if they did."

"I'd hope you'd take an assignment," she said. "That is, I hope you would if it didn't involve any danger. You can't live all your life as a man without a country. Either you're Argentine or you're not; either you're English or you're not."

David squatted, picked up a pink shell and examined it, then tossed it into the surf.

"You could become American," she said. "I could arrange that. A private bill, a grant of citizenship direct from the Congress."

"Purchased for a price?" he asked.

"Of course. When you're from Massachusetts, it's easy to own a congressman or two. We trade in them, like any other commodity that's on the market."

"How very cynical," said David.

"I am not talking to an idealist," she said.

"Only the very rich or the very poor can afford idealism," said David.

After dinner in their hotel in St. Helier, on Jersey, they undressed in their room and at midnight sat in the chairs on their balcony overlooking the beach and the sea—he in his slingshot underpants, she naked. The Normandy coast was ten miles to the east and dimly visible as a gray line on the moonlit sea. St. Helier was silent at midnight. Faint lights blinked in French villages. Their chairs were side by side, and he held Emily's hand.

"I'm going to say it, David, even if you never say anything like it to me. I'm going to take the chance."

"Emily—"

"I love you, David. I wish I'd never known any other man but you."

"Emily. I am an evil man."

She fell silent for a long moment, then asked, "What is that supposed to mean?"

"You don't know me," he said. "You knew me seven years ago, and now we've met again. I'm not a schoolboy any more, Emily. Five years ago I killed a man."

"David!"

"Oh, in the line of duty, of course. I was with the Coldstream Guards in Northern Ireland. A part of my training. Some Irish thugs charged us in the street. We had to fire. My aim was better than others', I guess. Or maybe more determined, more angry. I can't tell you; I'm not sure. They withheld my name. They didn't want it known that the Argentine captain, supposedly just an observer, had shot a man dead. I saw the funeral, on the telly. I saw his wife and children."

"Wasn't your fault, David!" Emily protested.

"Depending on how you rationalize," he said. "I'm not quite sure. Maybe I shot the man because I wanted to."

"It doesn't make you evil," she said. "And I don't give a damn anyway."

"The English did. It demonstrated to them something they had suspected all along: that a spic couldn't control himself, could never be the cool, controlled, professional officer the British army so obsessively admires. From that night on, I was never again really one of them. After that, they tolerated me: a political officer from an ornamental army, never quite to be trusted. The man I shot might have killed one of them. That's what he wanted to do. But the superior Brits wouldn't have shot him, or so they supposed. I think what they imagined was that they would simply have faced him down, that he would have dropped his gun and surrendered in the face of their calm and courage. I denied them the opportunity to demonstrate that."

"David, really," said Emily. "That's irrational."

"Precisely."

"David . . . Oh, God! I love you! You're not an evil man. Let me help you."

When he telephoned Nina, she told him she did not want to see him at the office, that he must meet her at lunch in a small French restaurant on Theobald's Road.

"You look older," she said of his beard. "And the spectacles?"

"I've worn contact lenses for years," he said. "Without them, I need glasses."

The beard was long enough now to be shaped a bit, and he wore it full on his cheeks and trimmed into the beginning of a point at his chin. His eyeglasses covered his face from his brows to the top of the beard; they were shaped like airmen's sunglasses and were colored with a faint pink tint in the glass to cut reflections. His hair was longer, too, and he wore a brown-tweed jacket and dark-brown slacks. He had put a tweed hat on the extra chair, with his leather briefcase.

"It really is effective, David," she said. "What's the fashionable term? A new persona?"

"I exposed the other one rather widely," he said.

"Yes. I'm afraid if you walked through Soho wearing your old face, you'd be picked up instantly. I was a bit surprised at how accurate the descriptions are. And have you seen the drawing?"

"All those look alike," he said. "But there are people who would recognize me. Even with the beard, I am not taking strolls in London for a while."

"It was a good idea to get out of town for two weeks," she said. "I wish you had let us know where you were going, though."

"Considering how badly the thing went, I wasn't sure you would care where I'd gone."

Nina smiled. "In that respect, I have a surprise for you, David. The attempted assassination of Lal Nath Sekhar turned out to be just as good for our purposes as the effected assassination would have been. We are not at all unhappy with the results."

"Frightened him?"

"So much so that he abruptly ceased to press the Chinese connection with his government. The Indian Defence Ministry asked to be thoroughly briefed on the investigation by DI5. They understood as well as DI5 did that the two Biharis could not have acted alone, that someone with resources was behind the bombing. That was enough. Lal Nath Sekhar got the message."

The restaurant was attractive, light, and airy inside large windows that opened on the sunshiny street. When David arrived, Nina had already drunk a glass of wine from the bottle that rested in a silver bucket beside the table, and she had herself poured for him before the waiter could come. Now she again took the bottle in hand and refilled their glasses.

"Did you suppose you were in our bad graces?" she asked.

"My Biharis lost their nerve at the last minute," he said.

"You asked too much of them," she said.

He nodded. "It all depended too much on fine timing. On the

other hand, killing a man is different from knocking down a building. The man, unhappily, has the ability to move. In one minute—even less—he would have been there."

"Yes. But it's water under the bridge, as the English say. What are your plans, David?"

"Am I unemployed?" he asked.

"I have no further assignment for you at the moment."

"'At the moment,'" he repeated. "Then your answer is yes. I am unemployed."

"You are employed," she said, "as a sales representative of Trafalgar Trading Company."

"And how am I expected to live? On my commissions?"

"Why not? I live on the salary I am paid as a secretary to Malcolm Worth."

"And on the satisfaction you take in serving your country," he said. "My commissions are not supplemented in that way."

She raised her glass. "You sent through Malcolm a demand for a large bonus for the Abbey explosion. You will agree, I suppose, it is not due, since the Indian did not die?"

"What difference, since the purpose was accomplished?"

"The Indian lost his nerve," said Nina. "A bit of luck. We might have achieved that by sending him a threatening letter—at the cost of a postage stamp."

"I've done damn good work for you."

"I'm not complaining of your work, but let's look at your record. You have undertaken four projects. The one in Milan was a complete success. In Assisi you blew up a minor church, not the basilica. In Toledo you failed to establish the Basque connection, which we had told you was essential. In London you damaged the Abbey and failed to kill Lal Nath Sekhar. You have been successful one time out of four, David. I am not complaining, but your record does not put you in a position to make demands. It does not put you in a position to demand we support you in luxury."

"I have an idea. A spectacular project."

"Your assignment now," said Nina firmly, "is to build credibility into your cover. Get out and sell some wine and spirits. Earn some commissions. You might be surprised how much money you can make."

"Not enough to live on," he said angrily. "Anyway, I'm not a god-damn salesman, as you well know."

"Then take some money from the American girl. Her family is quite wealthy."

"Well, thank you, Nina. Thank you so much. In the meantime, the rent is due on the flat."

The French immigration officer glanced twice at David and twice at his passport photo.

"Barbe nouvelle," grunted David. A new beard.

The officer nodded, stamped the visa, and handed back the pass-port. As David had expected, the new beard made no difference. Im-migration officers everywhere were accustomed to the appearance and disappearance of beards and mustaches; they made their identifica-tion—if indeed they bothered to make any at all—from the eyes chiefly. For that reason, David had taken off his spectacles as he left the plane.

He glanced at the smudged visa stamped in his passport. French officialdom had admitted Mr. Roger Duncan McConnell, of Chi-cago, as a tourist for a short stay.

He had two telephone calls to make and stepped immediately to a kiosk.

First he phoned the Soviet Embassy. The voice on the line, at first friendly, turned cold when he asked for Olshanskii and said Coun-selor Olshanskii was out of town. "Ah," said David. *"Dites-lui que Monsieur Leonard a téléphoné. Dites-lui me rappeler."*

The second call was to the offices of Groupe d'Intervention de la Gendarmerie Nationale. Colonel Cau was not available, but the next man down the line came on the telephone when word was passed that *"le fils de l'amiral est à l'appareil."*

"Captain Betancourt. Is it you?"

"Yes. Hello, Major. You are probably busy, so just let me tell you I would like to draw another hundred thousand."

For a moment the line was silent. Then—"Very well, Captain. I guess that can be arranged."

"As before."

"Very well. You'll have the money in London day after tomorrow. In pounds?"

"Please."

"All right. You'll have it. But remember this, Captain: your credit here will not extend much further. There is not much money left in the account, and you are not the only one with a claim against it."

"Understood. I hope I won't have to call on you again. On the other hand, maybe I can do something for you sometime."

"Personally, I would like to see you, Captain Betancourt. Anytime. Professionally, I hope I don't hear from you again."

David chuckled. "Actually, I suspect the business relationship has been more pleasant than a personal one would be. More productive of mutual benefit anyway. Nevertheless, thank you, Major Bonnac. I shall try not to have to call on you again."

"*Zdravsvitye, Josef Vladimirovich*," David said quietly to the man who stood uncertainly before him.

"Betancourt?"

"*Syegodya horoshaya pogoda.*" It's a nice day.

"Speak French, David. This is Paris. Anyway, your Russian accent is execrable."

"Well, I'm working on it. Sit down, Josef," said David. "It is good to see you."

They were in the park on the north side of the Champs Elysées, David wearing eyeglasses and tweed hat, and licking a vanilla ice-cream cone he had picked up at the nearby pavilion, Josef Olshanskii rigid and erect, dressed in a black suit, black tie, and white shirt, carrying a worn black briefcase.

The Russian sat down beside David on the iron bench. "You were not to call me. Not in any circumstances," he said gruffly.

"If circumstances required it, you said," David argued. "You didn't say in *no* circumstance. Anyway, if you meant that I should never call you, why did you give me the code?"

Josef Olshanskii, as David knew, was not humorless; neither was he the formidably tense man he was trying to mime. He allowed a little smile to soften his long, strong-jawed face.

"They are not very good, your London crowd," said David.

"The ones you've met, you mean," said Olshanskii dryly. "Even them you probably underestimate."

"You haven't met them, have you? You work through a contact."

Olshanskii shrugged. "You know better than to ask."

"Yes," David agreed, nodding amiably. "But now I'm going to ask you to overrule them."

"In what way? And why?"

"I want one of two things, Josef. I want a new assignment—and I have an important one in mind. Or I want to retire, with a couple of hundred thousand English pounds compensation for what I've done for you."

"Which of the two do you prefer?" Olshanskii asked.

"I want the assignment. If, after you've considered the proposition I've come to Paris to make, you don't want to give me the assignment, then I want retirement. What I don't want, Josef—won't accept, in fact—is to be kept dangling on a string by Nina."

"She respects you," said Olshanskii. "I have even been told she's developed an attraction for you."

David laughed. "I think not."

Olshanskii allowed himself a broader smile. "Perhaps not. But what is the problem between you and Nina Stepanova?"

"It was disingenuous of you, Josef, to let me suppose I was working for Malcolm Worth."

"Who did you expect to be working for?"

"Not for an underling's underling."

"That's what I am," said Olshanskii. "An underling's underling. And so is the man I work for. Who do you think you're entitled to report to?"

"All right," said David. He sucked the tip off his ice cream. "I responded to Malcolm Worth's approach exactly as you asked me to. We've carried out four projects. I haven't been paid much."

"None of us are. Money is always in short supply."

"Suppose I want to quit," said David.

"You have a position with Trafalgar Trading Company," said Olshanskii.

"Yes. So I understand. And that's it?"

"You've done well. I can put through a request for more."

"Maybe I'll get a medal," said David.

Olshanskii did not respond. He watched a Frenchwoman herd three small children past. One of the little girls yelled something incomprehensible to him, and he nodded and smiled. It was late afternoon. The sun was low, throwing long shadows through the chestnut trees. The heavy traffic on the Champs Elysées sped through the deep shadow of the Grand Palais. David watched a mini-skirted girl leading a dog. She stopped a short distance from them and raised a dark-colored handkerchief to her face. It was an awkward movement, not a natural wiping of her nose, and David was alerted. He kept an eye on her as she walked on east, until he saw her stop for a moment at a black Citroen parked in the access road a hundred meters away.

"Suppose I carry off a very big job for you," said David.

"What kind of job?"

"On October fifteenth," said David, "a monument will be dedicated in Notre Dame. Have you read about this?"

Olshanskii shook his head.

"It is a monument to allied intelligence agents who died in Gestapo prisons in the 1940s—chiefly British agents. The British will be represented at the ceremony by the Prince and Princess of Wales. I think I know how I can get enough plastique into the cathedral to—"

"David! What conceivable advantage to us could there be in the assassination of the Prince of Wales?"

"Hear me out. Suppose the blast were set off by the Irish Republican Army."

David paused and nibbled a corner from his cone, while Olshanskii frowned and pondered.

"What would the British do?" David asked rhetorically.

"We'd find out if they've any guts left," said Olshanskii.

"Remember what the Austrian government did in 1914? Could the British do any less? Their public opinion would drive them to military action. They'd send an expeditionary force into Ireland. I have little doubt of it."

"Yes. Possibly they would. And? What are you suggesting would follow?"

"When the Brits made war over the Malvinas," said David grimly, "no one came to the side of Argentina but a few banana republics. But suppose crack British regiments were making bloody war in Ireland. The American Irish would go berserk! The Atlantic Alliance would be strained to the breaking point. What's more, think of what the British would have to pull out of their NATO force to sustain a war in Ireland. They—"

"You are betraying your enthusiasm, David," said Olshanskii dryly. "There is no certainty that any of this would happen. Indeed, I think it all very unlikely. When the IRA killed Mountbatten—"

"The English played their game of being little tin gentlemen," said David scornfully. "This would be different. It's not just the prince who is attending the ceremony, remember. The princess will be there, too."

"Yes . . . Yes. But to go to war with Ireland! The idea is insane."

"Exactly," said David. "The death of the Prince and Princess of Wales would drive them insane."

"Well . . . You assume so."

David shrugged. "All right. It's a gamble. But for a very small investment, you buy a world of possibilities."

"The investment being all your expenses and. . . ?"

"Half a million pounds. My permanent retirement."

"You couldn't drive a van of explosives up to this one," said Olshanskii. "Security will be tight and elaborate."

"I have a plan in mind," said David. "I've spent some time thinking about it. You are of course correct that I could not do it with a little blue van. That's not my idea. What I have in mind is to set off the charge inside the cathedral—a powerful charge, maybe enough actually to bring down the building."

"Notre Dame. . . ?"

"Does the idea trouble you?"

Olshanskii shook his head. "No, of course not. Not in the sense you seem to be suggesting. On the other hand, you are talking about killing perhaps hundreds of people. You've had scruples about that before. Think of the sustained outrage, all over the world."

"Hundreds died in the sinking of the *Belgrano*," said David. "World outrage lasted all of three days."

Olshanskii drew a deep breath. "All I can do is convey the idea to my superiors," he said. "I have no idea how they will react."

"There is not much time," said David. "I will have much work to do between now and October fifteenth."

"I can tell you one thing," said Olshanskii. "You won't be allowed to work alone on this one. Too much is involved. Too much risk. You will have to accept orders and discipline."

"I can endure six weeks of that. For the money."

"Your first order," said Olshanskii, "is not to contact me again. I will contact you. One way or the other."

"Will you have some money released to me?"

Olshanskii sighed. "A thousand pounds?"

David shook his head. "No, Josef. Money. Ten thousand pounds. Compensation for past work if the new project is not accepted. An advance on my half million if it is."

"Very well. The money will not come from Nina Stepanova, and she is not to know you have received it. She is not to know you have met with me. She is to be given no reason to think she has been overruled. You will treat her with respect, as your contact and superior. Those, too, are orders."

David smiled. "Do you want me to sleep with her?"

"The question will be if *she* wants to sleep with *you*, and I will leave that to her good judgment."

"How soon will I hear from you?"

"As you say, if the project is viable, you will have much work to do and not much time to do it. I expect I can have a response for you within a week."

"*Spasibo, Josef. Proshchaitye.*"

Olshanskii grinned. "*Do svidanya, David. Vsego horoshchego.*"

As the Russian walked away, the black Citroen began to move. David walked quickly across the access road and trotted into the heavy traffic on the Champs Elysées. Amid the honking of horns, the shrieking of brakes, and cursing, he managed to make his way across without being hit. Luck was with him. In the farthest lane he stepped into the path of a taxi. It stopped. He jerked open the door and threw himself inside.

"*Aéroport Charles De Gaulle, s'il vous plait,*" he said.

9

OLSHANSKII SMILED and raised a hand in a friendly gesture of farewell as he turned away from the immigration line. *"Passporte diplomatique,"* he said to the Frenchman who had sat beside him and chatted with him on the flight. *"Au revoir."*

He turned to the guarded door that opened directly into the main concourse of Sheremetyevo Airport. The guard inside the glass booth glanced at his passport, nodded, and pressed the button that unlocked the door.

A young KGB captain waited just outside the door. "Tovarishch Polkovnik Olshanskii?" he asked.

Comrade Colonel Olshanskii nodded.

"I have a car waiting for you, Comrade Colonel," the captain said. "My name is Filip Ivanovich Malik. Have you any bags? Would you wish to visit the toilets before we leave?"

"No bags," said Olshanskii. "I'm afraid I'll be taking a return flight in less than twenty-four hours."

"Then . . ." said the captain, gesturing toward the door.

Olshanskii savored the friendly Russian-ness of the scene around him as he walked through the airport with the captain—the Cyrillic lettering of signs, the familiar tones of spoken Russian in bits of conversation he overheard, the flat, simple faces of hurrying Russians, the plain, sturdy styles they wore.

"It's been more than three years since I last saw Moscow, Filip Ivanovich. I'm looking forward to it."

"I'm afraid you're not going to see it today, Comrade Colonel," said Captain Malik. "My orders are to take you directly to Zhukova."

"Zhukova. Ah. Well. Perhaps there will be time for a drive through Moscow tomorrow."

The driver of their black Volga sedan was another uniformed KGB man. He said nothing, and Malik said nothing to him; he knew where he was going. He turned west from the airport, away from Moscow, into the wooded hills that rise on both sides of the meandering Moscow River.

It was just as well that Captain Malik was taciturn. Olshanskii had slept only a few minutes now and then during the flight, and in the moving car he was overpowered by drowsiness. He dozed as the driver worked his way out of the tangled roads of the suburbs and settled to a steady speed on the highway that followed, generally, the westward course of the river. When the sedan rolled into the little village of Zhukhova, Olshanskii drew himself alert, ran his hand over his head to straighten his hair as best he could, and tugged at his suit to straighten a few of the more conspicuous wrinkles.

Except for the half dozen chauffered limousines usually seen on the paved parking lot at the extraordinarily large village store, Zhukova looks like any other rural village in that part of Russia. The Volgas, sitting with their engines running, chauffeurs leaning against their fenders, are the key. The ugly, concrete-block store stocks foreign luxuries for the privileged dignitaries who live in state dachas—country homes, summer homes—in Zhukova and the vicinage.

The store—the village, in fact—is on the right. Olshanskii's driver turned left. He headed the Volga into a narrow lane that led into cool green birch forest and uphill, across a railroad track and still deeper into the forest and higher above Zhukova and the highway. Olshanskii had never traveled this road before, but knew where they were going: to a secluded village above the river, known as

Zhukova-1, more often called Sovmin, meaning it is a village of the dachas of the Soviet Ministrov, the Council of State.

They reached a brick wall. Uniformed soldiers, with short automatic weapons cradled in their arms, guarded an iron gate. Passage was no trouble. They were expected.

Inside the wall, in Sovmin, the dachas are spread out through the forest: some relatively modest unpainted clapboard houses, in a traditional Russian style, others of yellow brick, more solid, more imposing, still others far more modern, with expanses of glass and great balconies on which their owners can stroll and enjoy the smell of the forest and a view of the river. Even here, the driver knew where he was going. He turned into a driveway and stopped the car before one of the more impressive of the modern houses.

Captain Malik led the way to the door. He was, apparently, someone's aide.

He was General Piritkin's. The general was at breakfast on his flagstone terrace behind the house, sitting in a pair of American blue jeans and a yellow knit shirt with a tiny crocodile stitched to the breast. He was alone. Over his breakfast he had been reading a stack of documents, which he turned face down as Captain Malik led Olshanskii out onto the terrace.

"Josef Vladimirovich," said General Piritkin. He stood and extended his hand. "Welcome home."

"Thank you, Comrade General."

"Sit down. Can I offer you breakfast? I suspect you had nothing appetizing on the flight from Paris."

"What Aeroflot provides," said Olshanskii. "Socialist simplicity."

"Filip Ivanovich," said the general. "Give the necessary orders in the kitchen. Breakfast for yourself, too, of course."

General Piritkin was old. Hard blue veins pulsed on the sides of his sunburned head. His hands were unsteady. Gold-rimmed eyeglasses lay on the table by his coffee cup. His secure grip on the powers of his office was convincingly established, however, by the simple evidence of this dacha. He was the subject of a myth that Olshanskii knew was not true: that Piritkin had personally shot Lavrenti Beria with a handgun. An equally untrue and totally vicious myth had it that he had poisoned Yuri Andropov. The rumor that probably did have some basis in truth was the one that he had played at least a minor role in ridding the country of Stalin.

"Now what is this?" asked General Piritkin as soon as Olshanskii was seated across the glass table. He tapped on the stack of papers, and Olshanskii assumed he meant the report transmitted from Paris two days ago.

"Do you refer to the Betancourt matter, Comrade General?"

"Is it at all possible?" asked the general. "Could this man Betancourt in fact carry out this project?"

"It is well within the realm of possibility, Comrade General," said Olshanskii solemnly. "Likelihood?" He shrugged. "No. But a realistic possibility."

"What is your judgment, Josef Vladimirovich, of the likely consequences if the project succeeds? The death of the Prince and Princess of Wales, plus that of the president of France . . . God knows who else. Do you see the same results that your man Betancourt promises? Isn't it just as likely that world public opinion would applaud an invasion of Ireland and the elimination of the IRA?"

"It could turn out either way, couldn't it?" said Olshanskii. "There can be no question, though, but that the Irish will fight. One way or the other, Britain becomes involved in a bloody war in Ireland that will occupy its forces and attention for months. England will be rendered essentially ineffective in world affairs. For a long time."

"What of the French, then? If their president dies. Probably some officials and officers, too. What will the French do?"

"What can they do?" Olshanskii asked rhetorically. "Applaud the British. Anyway, politicians are expendable. They are not the same as the prince and princess. Many Frenchmen will be glad to be rid of Mitterand."

"And the Americans . . . Do you see that the same way Betancourt does?"

"The influence of the so-called Irish American in American politics is beyond doubt, Comrade General. The Kennedys are not the only Irish immigrants in high places in America. A fight between Britain and Ireland will cause a violent row in Washington, at the very least. When American television viewers begin to see Irish corpses lying in the streets and fields, the administration might well be compelled to abandon all support for the British cause. Emotions will be very high, Comrade General."

"Your man Betancourt promises a great deal, Josef Vladimirovich."

"Let me point out carefully, Comrade General, that Betancourt does not promise those results, nor can I. He refers to the probability as being worth the investment."

"The investment is negligible for the possible results," said General Piritkin. "I am not concerned about the investment. What does concern me is the cover. What would happen if our sponsorship of this young man became known?"

"That would be a disaster, Comrade General."

"What contacts has he had, Josef Vladimirovich?"

"Besides myself, only Comrade Nina Stepanova Samusev and the Englishman, Malcolm Worth. I recruited him. He worked at first with Worth, and then, when he became somewhat difficult to handle, he was turned over to the woman."

"That is already too many. See to it there are no others."

"Yes, Comrade General."

"Possibly you follow my thoughts in this matter."

"I believe I do, Comrade General."

The general looked away from Olshanskii and the table, out over the river. The vista was of open country, showing no sign of agriculture or industry. It was difficult to believe that Moscow was less than twenty miles away.

"Have you been here before, Josef Vladimirovich?"

"In Zhukova, yes. Never . . . here," said Olshanskii cautiously, not sure if it were offensive to use the word Sovmin.

"Do you know how close the Germans came?" asked General Piritkin. "Did you know we dug trenches here? You can see them in the woods. Hitler was stopped only a few kilometers from here. Only a few kilometers from here." For a long moment the general seemed absorbed in that thought.

Captain Malik returned and sat down, facing the view.

"What do *you* think, Filip Ivanovich?" asked the general abruptly. "If Betancourt blew up Notre Dame and killed the Prince and Princess of Wales and the president of France, would any of the wild things he talks about really happen?"

"I believe some of them would, Comrade General," said Malik solemnly. "At least some of them."

"And this could be much more worthwhile than employing Betancourt in sending further messages to that beskirted Polish holy man in Rome."

"A pope is temporary, Comrade General," said Olshanskii. "Given a few years, we'll have another pope. In my judgment, anything that holds out a reasonable chance of imposing a severe strain on the Anglo-American alliance is far more important."

"The Irish connection is therefore essential," said the general.

"It is essential."

General Piritkin looked away again. "Of course," he mused, almost to himself, "the explosion will damage Notre Dame. That may shake the confidence of His Holiness a bit more."

"A worthwhile side effect, Comrade General."

The old general chuckled. "Yes. Yes . . . and beyond that, the excitement may create an opportunity for us to make some useful move, say in the Persian Gulf or East Africa. While the West howls over the death of the prince and princess and the president, or, let us hope, over a British military adventure against Ireland, we will have an unparalleled opportunity to make some useful practical move. That may be the most important effect, Josef Vladimirovich."

"The possibilities are endless, Comrade General."

"How will Betancourt recruit his Irish co-conspirators?"

"I don't know, Comrade General. He has demonstrated some facility for identifying and winning the adherence of a variety of lunatic fanatics."

The general laughed. "But surely that describes *all* the Irish, Josef Vladimirovich."

"So it does, Comrade General. We may have to assist Betancourt in sorting out his lunatics. Speaking seriously, it may be that he is the best man to do it. He has been in Ireland. He knows something of the Irish. He served with the British army there and killed an IRA man, though the Irish don't seem to know it. I would not be entirely surprised if he has his Irish fanatics already chosen."

A houseboy in a white coat came with a pot of coffee and cups. He poured steaming cups of what proved to be excellent Austrian coffee.

"Josef Vladimirovich," said General Piritkin, "we will go along with this idea. The responsibility will be yours. Keep it under close control at every stage. Be ready to stop it if you are not satisfied with any element. Let it be understood that we could tolerate failure but could not tolerate identification. Succeed or fail, it must never be known that Betancourt worked for us."

Olshanskii nodded. "I will give that first priority, Comrade General."

"Nina Stepanova doesn't know you, does she?" asked the general.

"No. Major Litvinko sees her. Vasili Ivanovich Litvinko."

"Let it continue so," said the general. "And, of course, Betancourt doesn't know Litvinko."

"No, Comrade General."

General Piritkin frowned deeply. "Nina Stepanova and Worth. It may be that, at some point, wisdom will suggest that we recall Comrade Nina Stepanova Samusev. She has served well in England and would perhaps like to come home. Do you follow my thought?"

"Exactly, Comrade General."

"Well, then. Here is your breakfast."

The houseboy put down a heavy tray, laden with platters of salmon, eggs, fried potatoes, and sliced tomatoes, a dish of black caviar, two loaves of bread, butter, buttermilk, and glasses of hot tea. He brought a bottle of Stolichnaya also, with three glasses.

General Piritkin poured vodka for himself, Olshanskii, and Captain Malik. He raised his glass in toast. "To our success, Josef Vladimirovich! May it be complete."

"To success, Comrade General!" exclaimed Olshanskii and Malik in unison.

"You have a seat on an afternoon flight to Paris, Josef Vladimirovich. You may be back at your office in time to contact Major Litvinko yet tonight. He should convey the new orders to Nina Stepanova no later than tomorrow."

"It will be done, Comrade General," said Olshanskii, uncertain if he were concealing his disappointment at returning to Paris without being allowed time even to see his parents in Moscow, much less the time to savor the city.

"And now, Josef," said the general, familiarly omitting the patronymic for the first time. "While you eat, tell Filip Ivanovich and me about Paris. Neither of us has ever been there. Tell us especially about the French girls. Tell us about their little tits. Tell us what they do in bed. Do they really know tricks that Russian girls never learn?"

"I obey my orders, David," said Nina. "Sometimes it's not easy."

"It would be worse if you didn't," he said.

She nodded. She reached forward with the bottle and poured Scotch into his glass. Then she offered the seltzer bottle, and he took it and squirted fizzy water over the whisky. Nina poured whisky for herself but took it straight. She lifted the glass in silent salute.

They were in her flat in Chelsea, in her cozy little living room crowded with bric-a-brac and books and heaps of magazines. She was wearing one of the cable-knit sweaters she favored and a pair of black slacks. She was smoking.

"My orders were to set you aside for the moment, to cut our ex-

penses with you. I don't know why, any more than I know why they
have changed their minds. In any event, I have a new project for you.
A big one. It's from a very high source."

"Am I to be paid this time?" he asked.

She drew a breath. "I am authorized to say that you will be gener-
ously compensated if you succeed."

"Good."

"This project must be carried out exactly according to specifications. There may be no shortfalls. What is more, you may not go off
and work this one by yourself. You must report to me almost every
day, to tell me exactly what you are doing and how you are doing it.
What you are doing will be reviewed, and you will receive orders
from time to time. This is an extremely important project, David."

"Are you ready to tell me what it is?"

She nodded, then paused to drink. "David. On the fifteenth of
October, the Prince and Princess of Wales will participate in the dedication of a monument in Notre Dame cathedral in Paris. You are to
get explosives into Notre Dame and set them off when the prince and
princess are there. They are to be killed."

David feigned astonishment. "In *Notre Dame?* My God, how many
people might be in there at the time?"

"A crowd, David. A large crowd. The president of France, certainly. Many officers. Television people. Reporters. Priests. You are to
set off enough explosives to be sure of the death of the prince and
princess. Many others will die. That has to be accepted."

"And the cathedral?"

"Damage to the cathedral is acceptable, too. But it is to be minimized, consistently with achieving your objective. In other words, we
do not want to destroy the building. Not totally. The purpose—Well,
I haven't told you the rest of it. The explosion must appear to be the
work of Irish fanatics, the worst of the IRA. We want to precipitate a
minor war between England and Ireland. It is not necessary or desir-
able to bring down Notre Dame. Damage it as much as you must—
but not more."

"My God, Nina! On October fifteenth? Everything has to be arranged by October fifteenth? How am I going to get explosives into Notre Dame? They will have to be carried *inside*."

"We will provide intelligence: the exact times for the events in the cathedral, as much as we can learn about the security arrangements, and so on. We will provide equipment. You may decide this time to go with something more powerful than your garage-door radios."

He shook his head. "It's a challenge."

"Yes. For both of us. I am to be directly involved, remember. The trading company will probably assign me to Paris for a while."

"It means retirement, Nina," he said. "After this one, I won't be able to work for you again. I won't be able to do it with two people, and I may not be able to eliminate everyone who can identify me. I may need help in arranging my future."

"Have you ever thought of living in the Soviet Union?" she asked. "You would be an honored guest there."

The fisherman wore a heavy gray turtleneck sweater, tan corduroy pants tucked into the tops of knee-high rubber boots, and a dark-blue wool watch cap. As David studied him from the quay, the man sucked hard on the dwindling butt of a cigarette, until it must have burned his thumb and finger before he flipped it impatiently into the dirty green water. He was six-feet-one or two, trim but thickly muscled. His long, grim face was deeply pockmarked.

"That's him," said the boy standing beside David. "Bobby Donegal."

David's eyes narrowed as he stared through the drizzle. He turned to ask the boy if the boat was Donegal's, but the boy was gone. David had given him a fiver to find Donegal and point him out, not to introduce him; that was the deal, and the boy had earned his money and disappeared.

Donegal's movements were those of a man accustomed to the work he was doing: practiced, yet rough, abrupt. He jerked on a rope, tightening a knot; he tossed a canvas over the boat's compass and engine gauges and began fastening it in place with snaps. He glanced angrily at a passing boat whose wake caused his boat to roll and slam against the tires hung from the dock for fenders, but he stood easily on the pitching deck and went on with his work.

David walked a little closer to the boat. PATTY K. it was called; and it was a working boat, scarred and worn and grimy. The hold was full of new-caught fish apparently; their smell was strong on the sullen morning air. Two men approached Donegal and began to talk with him. He was abrupt and emphatic in his responses to whatever they said, emphasizing his words with chopping movements of his hands. If David read the scene correctly, Donegal sold his catch to the two men. Another fisherman came around the cabin, greeted the two men, and grinned as he spoke.

The men walked away. Donegal spoke for a moment with the other man on board, then, finally, he jumped down to the stone quay.

"Donegal," said David.

Donegal turned, scowled, and did not reply.

David walked up to him. "Donegal," he said. "You're Bobby Donegal?"

Donegal shrugged. "It depends on who's askin'," he said. His voice was not friendly, nor yet unfriendly; his scowl distorted his face but was not threatening.

"I'm David Betancourt."

"English," said Donegal, and he turned and walked slowly along the quay, not abruptly or so fast that David could not readily keep up with him, yet not conceding the time of day.

"No," said David. "Argentine."

Donegal's glance came 'round, his brows rising—showing interest. "In Ireland?" he grunted.

"Where else will I find Irishmen?"

"Anywhere," said Donegal.

"True. Actually, I wasn't looking for Irishmen in general," said David. "I was looking for you."

Donegal stopped. He sighed noisily. "Argentine," he said. "Looking for Bobby Donegal." He shook his head. "Whatever you want, the answer is no."

"I want to talk to you about Jimmy."

Donegal's craggy face darkened. "Jimmy? What Jimmy?"

"Your late brother, Jimmy Donegal."

Donegal's scowl turned angry, and he resumed his purposeful stride along the quay.

David matched him. His own legs were as long as Donegal's, in fact longer, and he walked beside him. "I know who killed Jimmy," he said.

"Everybody knows who killed him."

"The man," said David. "Not just the Brits. Not just the unit. The man."

Donegal stopped again. His face was wet. So was David's beard. The rain ran off David's nylon jacket but collected in shiny drops on Donegal's rough wool sweater. Donegal ran his hand over his mouth. "What kind of game is this?" he asked quietly.

"I want to talk to you. I have a proposition," said David.

Donegal shook his head. "Who do you say killed Jimmy?" he asked.

"I did."

Donegal swung fast and hard, but David had expected that and easily sidestepped the bludgeon of his fist. Donegal spread his arms wide and charged. David chopped him sharply across the bridge of his nose. Stunned, blinking, Donegal stepped back.

"Take it easy, man," said David. "*Think.* Why would I come here, seek you out, and tell you I killed your brother?"

"Because you want to die."

"I can handle you. If I can't, I have a pistol inside my jacket. Now think, dammit!"

Donegal rubbed his nose. "My brother's name is sacred to me," he said. "As it is to many. He died a martyr."

"I will tell you how he died, if you want to know."

Donegal stood feet apart, his shoulders hunched, drawing breath between his lips. His eyes were hard with hostility; yet, there was in them an ambiguity; he was puzzled and curious. He nodded.

"I was with the Coldstreamers," said David. "An Argentine officer training with the Brits and assigned to the Coldstream Guards in Belfast to observe their counter-insurgency tactics. I was with the platoon that your brother and his friends decided to charge. I don't know what they had in mind. Maybe you do. They threw rocks first, then some bottles filled with gasoline, and there were big, smoky fires between us and them. Suddenly they came at us, leaping through the fire and smoke like a gang of madmen. The Coldstreamers fired. Their weapons were loaded with rubber bullets. One man came running at me, with a big club. Directly at me. I thought he was going to knock my brains out, and I'm not sure he wouldn't have. I shot him with my revolver. It was not loaded with rubber bullets. I killed him. I saw the funeral on the telly, and that's how I learned his name was Jimmy Donegal."

"The Brits kept it secret who killed him."

"Because I was a foreign officer. International incident, you know. I've made it a point to keep some track of you ever since."

Donegal turned and resumed once again his walk to some purpose at the far end of the quay.

David once more fell in step beside him. "That's how it happened. I pulled the trigger. My father himself pulled the trigger on the pistol that killed him. But both of them were really killed by the Brits— because they insist on keeping land that belongs to other people."

"My brother was in fact a fool," said Donegal.

"I was waiting for you to say it. I don't know what you're doing for your cause, but I imagine it's something a lot more effective. Do you bring in guns on that boat?"

Donegal glanced at him. "You're a fool, as well," he said.

They reached a low, scarred door. Donegal bent forward and passed through, into a dark, smoky barroom. David peered in, checked the Walther under his jacket, and followed.

A beamed ceiling. Cracked white plaster. A dirty wooden floor. To the left, a heavy old bar. Behind it, an aged bartender in a gray wool cap. Oak benches. Tables. Half a dozen men, all middle-aged or older, hunched over pints of beer, either at the tables or at the bar, already, this early. They smoked cigarettes and pipes.

Donegal stepped to the bar. The bartender drew him a beer and then looked expectantly at David. David nodded, and the bartender drew the same for him. Donegal walked to a bench and sat down, his back to the wall. David sat beside him.

"My father," said David, "shot himself after Argentina lost the war for the Malvinas. The Falklands."

Donegal nodded. "Admiral Betancourt," he said.

Startled, David nodded. "You know about that?"

Donegal looked at him. "We Irish can read, you know."

"Then you know why I hate them as much as you do."

Donegal shook his head. "I don't hate the Brits. Jimmy hated them. I just want them to get out of my country. We are fighting for liberty."

David smiled and shook his head. "No. You've got all the liberty you can use. What you really want is to run the country."

Donegal took a great swallow of beer. "So, what is it you want, Mr. Betancourt?"

"I want to do something that will make a real difference," said David.

"And what do you have in mind that would qualify?"

"The Prince and Princess of Wales."

Donegal cast him a glance of surprise and skepticism. "Oh, yes. And why not the Queen Mum while you're about it?"

"It's not a fantasy, Donegal. I can do it. I've got a plan, and I can do it. With you or without you, I'm going to do it."

"With. . . ? Without? You want *me*. . . ?"

"As I said before, Donegal—*think*. If it works, if it comes off, what do you think the Brits will do?" He glanced around and lowered his voice, aware that the old men at the bar were looking at him, idly curious for the first time. "What will they do?"

"Send troops, almost certain," said Donegal. "Not just a police force. A goddamn army."

David nodded, paused to let Donegal think it through.

"There'd be a bloody fight," said Donegal thoughtfully, softly. "A war."

David nodded. "And?"

"And what?" Donegal demanded, suddenly impatient. "What's your idea?"

David drew a deep breath. "I will very much regret the death of the prince and princess," he said. "He's a well-meaning sort of fellow, I suppose, and she's an innocent beauty. Killing them—" He shrugged. "Just killing them really won't hurt the U.K. After a lot of weeping and wailing, the country will survive quite nicely, as it did after the death of Mountbatten. Unless . . . Unless they lose their heads and invade Ireland—which you just said you think they will. Well, that's what I think, too. They'll send troops. Not just into the six counties. They'll go wherever they think they can find the IRA. Border counties. Maybe the whole country."

"We'd fight of course."

"As you haven't for a long time."

"What d'you mean by that?"

"A few of you are fighting. the rest . . . Well, you know. Your government in Dublin—"

"That's not *my* government."

"It's the government elected by the Irish people. It's all the government you've got. It calls you terrorists. It patrols the waters and seizes your arms shipments. It jails your leaders. And a lot of the Irish people applaud it."

"That would change," said Donegal. "Everybody would fight."

David nodded. "Exactly. A united Ireland. And not only that. Ireland united behind strong men."

Donegal smiled for the first time. "You're a devil, Betancourt," he said. "You've got a smooth tongue."

"Find the flaw in it," said David bluntly, lifting his beer to his mouth.

"You make free with other people's lives and fates," said Donegal. "What's your interest? And don't tell me you hate the British."

"Oh, I hate them," said David. "Superior . . . Arrogant . . . But, I'm like you. There is personal advantage for me. I will be paid. By people who will benefit from what we achieve."

"I will have to know who," said Donegal firmly.

David shook his head. "I am going to ask you to recruit, say, eight men. Ten at the most. I will have to see them and talk to them, but I don't want to know who they are. I will trust you not to tell them who I am. I'll be dealing with some other people, who will be giving us important help. They won't know who you are. Unfortunately, you and I know who each other are. That couldn't be helped. I have to place a great deal of trust in you, and you have to place as much in me."

"I don't know why I should trust you," said Donegal. "What do *you* propose to do, anyway? I mean, to earn your money. What's *your contribution* to this wild scheme?"

"I have the plan," said David. "I'll have information. I'll supply the necessary equipment. What's more, I'm an expert at what I do. To be very frank with you, Donegal, you can't do it without me."

Donegal grinned. "Confident of yourself, aren't you?"

"I have survived," said David.

"You've done the like before?"

"I am not new to this kind of work."

"Neither am I," said Donegal.

"I wouldn't have contacted you if I'd supposed you were just a rock-thrower," said David. "Or a speech-maker."

"How do you plan to do the thing?" Donegal asked. "With explosives?"

"Yes."

"When and where?"

"Very soon. I'll tell you where and how when you're committed."

"I want to talk to some people."

"Let's understand it," said David. "The date is fixed. I can't change that. The plan is settled, and I won't change it. I expect you will do whatever you have to do to maximize the political benefit to yourself, and I have nothing to do with that. But as to the project itself, I am the team leader. If I decide to abandon the project at any point, it is abandoned. If—"

"If *we* decide to abandon, because we think it too dangerous, *we* will abandon."

"Fair enough," said David. "I assume your people are tough-minded."

Donegal smiled. "How much experience have you had with true believers?" he asked.

"Not much. I'm reluctant to trust them. Let's not forget there's a secret to be kept."

"The police files are full of cases that remain unsolved because these people can keep secrets. Do I have to name any cases?"

David shook his head. "I take your point. It's eloquently made."

"I'll have to know the plan," said Donegal. "Sooner, rather than later."

"As soon as you're committed."

"We'll let you know, then."

"I don't have much time," said David.

"You'll have word tonight."

10

MONSIGNOR PÉRIGORD drove with pleasure and enthusiasm. The car had been lent to Major Glynbourne, but the monsignor had asked to be allowed to drive, at least on the country roads he knew, so now the major sat in the passenger seat. The car was a classic, a silver Lamborghini Miura, with a V-12 engine mounted transversely in the rear. The monsignor had left N 20 at la Ferté-St.-Aubin to take a twisting country highway that would be a more interesting road for car and driver, and the Lamborghini was meeting every element of its promise. It clung to the road as if its tires were cemented to the pavement, it shifted smoothly, the big engine gave it commanding acceleration, and the monsignor was enjoying every kilometer—enjoying it more than Major Glynbourne, who watched with the critical eye of a driving instructor.

The monsignor had telephoned Major Glynbourne yesterday, to suggest they meet at the airport since their flights would arrive within half an hour of each other. The major told him a French tennis player, with whom he had won a memorable doubles match two years ago, had given him the loan of a fine car for the weekend, so he was looking forward to the drive to Valençay. The monsignor had said he loved fine cars.

"I have a wealth of experience with this kind of driving, Major," said the monsignor. He pointed the car into a curve, accelerated slightly for better control and traction, and slipped through smoothly. Coming out, he floored the accelerator, and the Lamborghini roared ahead, accenting its gain in speed with a musical throb from the engine. He took the left lane and passed a Jaguar. "Years of experience."

"Glad to hear it," Glynbourne remarked dryly.

"Before I committed myself to the Church. Not many opportunities lately."

"We pursued the Stephanotis business," said the major, turning again to the topic of conversation he had interrupted by allowing the monsignor to see his concern about his driving. "We have a police-artist drawing, of course—though personally I place little confidence in them. I myself took it to the House of Floris in Jermyn Street. One of the counter girls actually, seriously believes she may have sold a flask of that perfume to the blond young man portrayed in the drawing."

"Fanciful," said the monsignor.

"Except that she thinks he comes in and buys it from time to time. She believes she has seen him more than once. She's promised to telephone if he comes in again."

"No idea of his name, I suppose?"

"No, he pays cash."

"How much importance do you place on it?" asked Monsignor Périgord.

"I am more and more convinced of the English connection," said Major Glynbourne.

"As am I," said the monsignor. "I read with interest your report as to how Oliver Cromwell contacted the Biharis in London. It stimulated my interest in a line of inquiry I was already pursuing, and I've followed that line to some profit."

"What line, if I may ask?"

"I've wondered," said the monsignor, "how Oliver Cromwell managed to enter Milan, we may assume as a stranger, and immediately make contact with an obscure little gang of anarchists called the Crociata Populare. You or I couldn't do it. And neither could he. He had help."

"Yes," said the major, nodding thoughtfully.

"The same thing had to be true in Perugia, for the Assisi bombing. It had to be true in Spain. Wherever Oliver Cromwell goes, someone is easing his way for him."

"Except in London," said Major Glynbourne. "He does seem to have found the Biharis himself."

"Yes. That is exactly why I think he's English. But who helped him in Italy and Spain? His employers, wouldn't you suppose? And who are they?"

"Some of my people think the KGB."

"Yes," said Monsignor Périgord. "Happily, we have some contacts among the Italian Communists. You know . . . Some whose consciences are troubled. That sort. I circulated an inquiry among our pet Communists in Milan. 'Did anyone, in the past six months, ask you a question to which the answer was: the People's Crusade?' One of the comrades told us—in confidence, of course—that such a question was asked about three weeks before the bombing of *The Last Supper*. What is more, the answer given was: contact Guido Messe— which, you will recall, is exactly what Cromwell did."

"Who asked the question?"

"Alfredo Peccioli. And there the line of inquiry ends. Peccioli is a hard-bitten, doctrinaire, faithful, lifelong Communist. We'll get no further information from him. But if he asked the question, it could very well be he was asking on behalf of a Soviet agent."

"Why would Peccioli ask about the Crusade? Wouldn't he already know?"

"No. He's a disciplined Communist, a respectable Communist, you might say. He would have nothing to do with fringe groups, little gangs of unorganized fanatics."

"But your informant did?"

"No. My informant overheard Peccioli asking the question of a member of the Red Brigade. He asked for a fringe group. He referred

to the kind of people he was looking for as *idiote*—idiots. The Brigade
man told Peccioli about the Crusade and told him the easiest way to
contact the group was through Messe."

"In Perugia?"

"We made the same inquiry but got no results."

"Peccioli's inquiry could be coincidence."

"Of course. But do you think it was?"

Major Glynbourne shook his head. "No."

Their destination was the chateau of Valençay. Monsignor Périgord
spoke of it as they covered the last few kilometers. "Part of it was built
in the sixteenth century, more of it in the seventeenth and eighteenth.
My famous ancestor acquired it in 1805. He was, as you remember,
an ordained priest, so of course he left no legitimate progeny. Happily, the family makes little of that distinction, and I have always been
welcomed at Valençay by the descendants of my ancestor's brother."

They would be met at the chateau by André Bonnac and Galeazzo
Castellano. Monsignor Périgord had suggested Valençay as an isolated
setting for their weekend meeting. They would not be disturbed there,
he said. Indeed, someone had taken care that they should not be. As
he drove the Lamborghini into the lane leading to the chateau, they
were stopped by two men in civilian clothes: agents of Sûreté.

The chateau was magnificent. Deer and llamas grazed in the sur-
rounding park. Peacocks roosted in the trees, and flamingoes stood in
one of the fountain pools. The house itself was everyone's dream of a
romantic chateau—a rambling stone building incorporating a variety
of architectural styles, a mansard roof, domed roofs on the corner
towers, conical roofs on lesser towers, chimneys, dormers, peaks; furnished inside with antiques and art from the chateau's great period,
the days of the illustrious Prince Talleyrand.

Bonnac and Castellano had already arrived and, except for servants
and some more security men, seemed to be the only people in residence. Each man was settled into an apartment of his own, in one of

the wings, and the monsignor suggested they all meet an hour before dinner and begin their work.

"I have something to show you," said André Bonnac immediately after they had assembled in a small, comfortably furnished, ground-floor room dominated by two faded tapestries that pictured posturing Roman warriors.

Bonnac handed to each of them a large yellow envelope. In each envelope was an enlargement of a slightly fuzzy photograph of two men sitting on an outdoor bench, one a bearded man wearing a tweed hat and eating an ice-cream cone, the other a grim-faced, long-jawed man dressed in a dark suit. "It is remotely possible the bearded one is Oliver Cromwell," said Bonnac.

"How is it possible?" asked Castellano.

"Do you recognize the other man?" asked Bonnac.

"I do," said Monsignor Périgord. "Olshanskii."

"Very good, Reverend Father," said Bonnac with a nod and a smile. "Josef Vladimirovich Olshanskii, counselor in the Soviet embassy in Paris. Almost inevitably he's a colonel in the KGB. Naturally, we keep an eye on him. A week ago he met the bearded man in the park by the Champs Elysées."

"Could be anyone," said Major Glynbourne.

"It could, of course," said Bonnac. "But when their conference was finished, the bearded one quickly and effectively eluded the men who attempted to follow him. It was no accident. He darted into the heavy traffic on the Champs Elysées, made his way across at risk to his life, and stopped a taxi where taxis are not supposed to stop."

"It could be anyone, just the same," Glynbourne insisted.

"Granted, once more," said Bonnac. "But here is something else." He handed to Glynbourne another photographic print. "We had an artist airbrush off the beard," he said. "And the hat and spectacles. Notice the resemblance to your police drawing?"

"Yes . . . Very good."

"It remains highly speculative," said Monsignor Périgord.

"Of course," said Bonnac. "But let's examine the facts. Olshanskii meets an unknown man in the park. They confer for some five minutes on a bench. The bearded man instantly identifies our observers and skillfully eludes them. What are we to suppose?"

"Are you saying Olshanskii didn't understand he was being watched?" asked Castellano.

"Olshanskii knows he is watched all the time. It doesn't trouble him."

"Why would he let you have a look at Oliver Cromwell?"

"I can think of two reasons—one, that Cromwell demanded a quick meeting, over which Olshanskii didn't have complete control, or, two, that he knew Cromwell was so well disguised behind a beard and spectacles and a funny hat that a picture of him wouldn't do us much good."

"Why didn't your men pick him up?"

"Why would they? This was routine surveillance. Olshanskii meets dozens of people every week. We photograph the ones we don't know and try to identify them. Most of them are nobody in particular. This one could have been a pimp. When the man so easily evaded our attempt to tail him, suspicion was raised to a different level, and I was notified for the first time."

"It is very interesting," said Monsignor Périgord, "but, as you say, of very limited value. If the man grows a beard, cuts off a beard, puts on a hat, takes off a hat—"

"I'd like to show this photograph about in London," said Major Glynbourne, tapping a finger on the airbrushed picture.

"Before you do," said the monsignor, "I would like to see it subjected to computer enhancement techniques."

"That's being done," said Bonnac. "The enhanced pictures may be delivered here before our meeting is over."

Their dinner conversation ranged over many subjects, and Monsignor Périgord was more satisfied with the education and intelligence of his colleagues than he was with any information they had so far produced—which was, in the final analysis, negligible. At the present rate of progress, he said to himself as he mounted the stairs toward the apartment always reserved for him at Valençay, Oliver Cromwell would blow up St. Peter's and the Washington Monument before they stopped him.

In his apartment on the second floor, overlooking the gardens, now moonlit, the monsignor slipped out of his cassock and loosened his body with a few knee bends. Under the cassock he wore black trousers and a white cotton T-shirt. He was a trim, muscular man, a little younger than his status in the Church suggested. His left shoulder was scarred. He had been grazed by a bullet some years ago, before he entered the seminary. Alone in his apartment, he finished his knee bends and knelt before a small table where a candle burned before a tiny fourteenth-century painted panel, showing the Virgin at prayer. For a few minutes, he prayed. Then, in an abrupt transition from the fourteenth century to the twentieth, he rose and sat down before a small computer.

Installed there that morning so that he might have access during the weekend to any information he might need, the computer was capable of communication with the electronic files of some of the world's principal security and investigative agencies—provided one had the complex, multilevel codes that access required.

He switched on the power. After a minute or so, during which the little computer checked its own circuits for any defect or error, it displayed a message declaring itself ready. (The computer communicated in English.) Monsignor Périgord inserted the communications program disk in the slot in the disk drive, and in a moment the screen asked for a telephone number.

He entered a number and waited. The communications program scrambled and unscrambled everything sent and received, so the protocol was a little jerky.

COMMUNICATION ESTABLISHED. YOU ARE?

He typed a number—ACD–1448–DD—2251.

PLEASE WAIT. The mainframe in Paris did some checking. First it compared his identification number to the invisible number the little computer had automatically transmitted. Access to the files was available only to a few listed mini-computers, which carried their own identification inside themselves, on a chip, and sent it to the mainframe without prompting. What was more, access through this mini-computer was available only to Monsignor Périgord. If his identification number came from any other mini-computer, or any other operator tried to gain access through this machine, the combination would not work.

INVALID IDENTIFICATION. INVALID IDENTIFICATION. INVALID IDENTIFICATION. SECURITY PROCEDURES ACTIVATED. CONTACT TERMINATED.

It was not terminated. He knew that. He pressed the keys. DD4–DD4–14TQ.

PASSWORD?

He typed: DOWN THE LINE. (That was personal. It meant, descended in direct line from Prince Talleyrand.)

INVALID. TRY AGAIN.

He typed: VALID.

FILE?

KGB.

QUERY?

OLSHANSKII AND PECCIOLI

PLEASE WAIT.

He waited. He knew so simple an inquiry would take only a quarter of a minute or so. He had told the computer to look in the file for any record that contained both names: Olshanskii and Peccioli.

2 DOCUMENTS SATISFY YOUR REQUEST. DISPLAY? PRINT?

He typed: FULL. It meant, display those documents in full text. The screen filled with the first document:

OLSHANSKII, JOSEF VLADIMIROVICH, COLONEL, KGB—KGB 114–3860–02. 1534 of 4176 documents. 06/02/84 Source: SISDE, Milan.

> Subject arrived Milan by air 01/02/84, Splendido
> Hotel, departed 03/02/84, air. Spent time in hotel room,
> departing only for meals, one walk around neigh-
> borhood. No telephone calls. Visits from 6 subjects, 5
> unidentified. 1 identified, 1-hour visit—Alfredo Peccioli
> (see COMPARTITAL 331–4444–96).

The second document retrieved by the search was the same report, filed under the name of Alfred Peccioli. Peccioli, in the COMPARTITAL file, had his own dossier. The monsignor did not bother to look into it. He had seen it before.

He tried another search—OLSHANSKII AND LONDON.

12 DOCUMENTS SATISFY YOUR REQUEST. DISPLAY? PRINT?

He typed DATES, and the computer displayed a list of the twelve reports in chronological order with their dates specified. Olshanskii had not been in London since November 1982. The monsignor called for the report of that visit.

> OLSHANSKII, JOSEF VLADIMIROVICH, COLONEL, KGB—KGB
> 114–3860–02. 232 of 4176 documents. 18/11/82
> Source: SIS, London.
> Subject arrived Paris to Heathrow via BEA 21.00 hrs
> 14/11/82, departed 16/11/82 8.30 hrs via BEA to Paris.
> Flemings Hotel. Eluded observers 9.45 hrs 15/11/82. At-
> tended diplomatic reception, Peruvian embassy, 20.00
> hrs 15/11/82. Observed in conversation with: Col. Julio
> Diego, military attaché, Mexico; Concepcion Valenzuela,
> Guatemalan consul; Anatoly Zhdravchev, Bulgarian am-
> bassador; Roger Trevelyan, correspondent, Manchester
> Guardian; David Betancourt, son of late Argentine Admi-
> ral Hector Betancourt; Lady Elizabeth Gladwyn; Dr. John
> Sedgewick, physician; Mrs. Barbara Sedgewick; Cecilia
> Maycourt, widow of Colonel Hamilton Maycourt; 2 un-
> identified. Eluded observers on departing embassy at

22.15 hrs. Returned hotel 1.35 hrs 16/11/82. No telephone calls to or from hotel. No observed contact with
any known Soviet agent.

Monsignor Périgord called up the immediately preceding document, a report of a visit by Olshanskii to London nine weeks before,
in September 1982. The pattern of the visit was the same—a room at
Fleming's, no visitors or calls, easy evasion of the bored and possibly
dull men assigned to tail him (consequently many unaccounted-for
hours), attendance at a Japanese embassy dinner at which he was observed talking to eight people (none of them on the November list),
return to Paris after less than forty-eight hours.

Another search disclosed that Olshanskii had never been in
Spain—at least that he had never been reported there. Still another
disclosed that he had never been in Italy before he came to Milan to
see Peccioli; thus, he had not been in Perugia or in Assisi before the
blast there—again, assuming the reports were correct.

Finally, the monsignor did searches on all the people Olshanskii
was reported to have talked to at the Peruvian and Japanese embassies.

The scant facts were intriguing. Monsignor Périgord lay awake for
hours trying to make sense of them.

Major Glynbourne had asked Bonnac for assistance in setting up a
telephone connection with London, and from his room he spoke first
with his office, then with his home. His daughter was well—weak but
wistfully optimistic. They talked for half an hour. Then he talked
twenty minutes with Katrina.

When the men gathered in the morning they found that each had
been busy after dinner, on the telephone or on a computer terminal—Bonnac, too, had brought one with him—seeking information
that might some way link Josef Olshanskii to Oliver Cromwell. Bonnac had seen the same reports Monsignor Périgord had seen, and both
of them brought printed copies to the meeting.

"I have already ordered increased surveillance of Olshanskii," said

Bonnac. "He has made a quick flight back to Moscow since we saw him in the park with the possible Cromwell."

Major Glynbourne reviewed the computer printouts of reports on the people Olshanskii had talked with at the embassy reception and dinner in London. "I know about some of these people," he said. "Trevelyan is a left-leaning journalist but perfectly loyal. The Betancourt lad, son of the admiral . . . We watched him for a while during the Falklands War and after, but he's clear as far as we're concerned. Lady Elizabeth Gladwyn is a fine old lady, almost eighty years old, I should think. She was a Communist in her day, but that day has long since passed. Doctor Sedgewick spent World War Two on the Archangel run and makes it a point to talk over old times in Russia with any Russian he can find. Cecilia Maycourt is a Soviet sympathizer. We keep an eye on her. The others, the ones he talked to at the Japanese dinner . . . An odd assortment, but nothing significant I think."

The report on David Betancourt read:

> BETANCOURT, DAVID TOMAS, CAPTAIN (DETACHED), ARMY OF REP. ARGENTINA, LATAM—225–8709–02. 2 of 2 documents. 22/10/82. Source: SIS, London.
>
> Captain William T. Fogg, DI5, approached subject at Mexican embassy reception as ordered, 18/10/82. Proposed subject consider connection DI5. Subject stated he did not intend to return to Argentina or to active service Argentine forces, would therefore be in no position to assist DI5. Expressed willingness to act in event circumstances placed him in such position.
>
> Surveillance, mail and telephone covers this subject terminated 22/10/82.

"The only Olshanskii contact significant to our investigation is the one with Peccioli," said Castellano.

"We have facts that are beginning to suggest the outlines of a pattern," said Monsignor Périgord. "One, Peccioli asked a member of the Red Brigade to identify a radical fringe group for him and was told about the People's Crusade. Two, Peccioli was told the way to contact the Crusaders was to talk to Guido Messe. Three, Oliver Cromwell did just that, talked to Guido Messe. Four, a member of the Crusade, Margherita Catania, delivered the bomb that destroyed *The Last Supper*. Five, Olshanskii came to Milan and met with Peccioli about the time when Peccioli asked his questions of the Red Brigade man." The monsignor shrugged. "Nothing is proved. But the combination of facts is suggestive."

"Did either of you," asked Galeazzo Castellano, "check for a connection between Olshanskii and Sergei Antonov?" Antonov was the Bulgarian arrested in Rome in 1982 and charged with complicity in the 1981 attempt to assassinate the pope. "I continue to relate Oliver Cromwell's activities to an assault on the Church."

"I had the same thought," said Bonnac. "There is nothing on file."

"The Holy Father," said Castellano, "visited Poland for the second time in June 1983. Shortly after that, the destruction of sacred places and objects began. I am convinced these crimes represent an attempt by the Eastern-bloc governments to intimidate the Holy Father, as the assassination attempt failed to do—to discourage him from continuing his role as a focus and inspiration to dissidents in the slave countries."

"Agca," said Monsignor Périgord—he referred to Mehmet Ali Agca, the Turk who attempted to assassinate the Pope—"insists he was trained by the KGB and that the KGB as well as the Bulgarian secret state police were behind the attack." The monsignor shook his head. "I've tended to be skeptical of that, but . . . it does add another bit to our pattern."

"Assuming," said Bonnac, "there is a connection between Olshanskii and Oliver Cromwell, I find Olshanskii's brief trip to Moscow ominous. Did he go to get another assignment?"

"Let us be careful," said Major Glynbourne, "not to build assumptions on assumptions."

"If we do not build something on something," said the monsignor, "we will stand by and watch Oliver Cromwell destroy another treasure that the world cherishes."

"At the risk of sounding racist," remarked Bonnac, "I will hope it is nothing more worthy than another Asian defence minister."

"The Abbey will be repaired," said Major Glynbourne. "The damage to the main fabric is superficial. What we lost is life."

"My point," said Bonnac, "was badly made. I am concerned that Oliver Cromwell is indeed, as we suspect, a KGB agent—"

"An independent working for them, I should rather suspect," said Monsignor Périgord.

Bonnac nodded. "Probably. In either event, I think the time has come for us to agree that we must proceed to what we once called 'extraordinary measures.' We must take no chances on his escaping to Moscow—to pop up again someday and start it all over. Once we know who he is, we must nullify him."

Three—Bonnac, Castellano, and the monsignor—looked to Major Glynbourne. "My instructions from the prime minister," he said quietly, "have been amended. I am authorized to agree to nullification. I cannot exaggerate, though, the importance of capturing him alive if we can. His interrogation—"

"But do you agree to nullification if the rest of us think it necessary?" Bonnac persisted.

Major Glynbourne drew a breath. He nodded. "I do."

Late Monday morning, Major Glynbourne and Monsignor Périgord left Valençay together. A telephone call had assured them that the loan of the Lamborghini continued as long as they might need it, for which they were grateful; and this time the major drove, avoiding the main routes as the monsignor had done and putting the car through its paces on a day-long drive, south and east, across the Rhone, into Provence, into the French Alps, and down over the forested hills to St. Tropez.

To find a hotel room at this season in the world-famous resort was impossible, but the monsignor and the major were welcomed in the rectory of the Church of St. Tropez, given rooms, and invited to share with the priests a pleasant meal with bottles of a good Côtes du

Rhone. Their rooms were small and spare, but Major Glynbourne was satisfied, was drowsy from the long drive and the wine, and slept gratefully and well.

Monsignor Périgord entered the candlelit church late that night and prayed before the bust of St. Tropez. (Tropez was the Christian martyr beheaded by Nero and set afloat, head beside his body in a small boat. He came ashore at what is now the village named for him, carrying his head, and there established the Christian community that still honors his name.) The monsignor prayed, not to St. Tropez, but to Christ, who, even if the legend of St. Tropez were false, inspired in men the ability to believe that saintly men could accomplish miracles and ordinary men and women could do good.

His prayer was for forgiveness for what he had come here to do.

In the sunny, misty morning, dressed, not in a cassock, but in the black clothes of a priest, with his pectoral cross the only evidence of his rank, Monsignor Périgord walked from the rectory into the bustling little town. Major Glynbourne, in his gray-tweed jacket and black trousers, though the morning was already warm and promised a hot day, walked beside him.

"I've heard of this town for years but never had the occasion to come here," said Major Glynbourne. "I suppose I expected something quite different."

"Topless girls," said Monsignor Périgord. "You will find them on the beaches or around the hotel pools. The town is . . . well, it's what you see. It has kept its character."

Housewives were on the streets, doing their early-morning shopping: on the quay for fresh-caught fish, and in the shops of the town, for chickens, beef, pork, vegetables, and bread—carrying their purchases in small net bags or in round baskets.

The fishing boats that, apart from tourism, were the life of St. Tropez, were back from their night on the Mediterranean. Trucks, refrigerated or loaded with ice, were filling with *fruits de mer* to rush to Paris, where tonight the prosperous would dine on what was taken from the sea before dawn this morning. A few fishermen spread their catch on the stones of the quay and waited for the women of St. Tropez to come to buy. Crewmen from the yachts backed to the quay ambled along the waterfront, buying the food that likely would be their dinners, or, less likely, the dinners of their masters.

The monsignor found the shop he wanted, one door off the Rue de la Citadelle. It was a tiny tobacconist's, operated by license. Behind the counter, already open, stood Lucien Trebonzi.

"*Lucien. Bon jour!*"

"*Ah? Père. . . ? Charles! Mon Dieu! Charles! Un prêtre!*"

Lucien Trebonzi was a man whose age would always remain a mystery. Monsignor Périgord knew he had a daughter, twenty-five years old. Lucien was, then, surely forty-five. But maybe he was only forty. Or maybe he was sixty. Those comprehensive files you could check by computer did not tell you how old Lucien Trebonzi might be. He was a Corsican, according to him, but no one had ever been able to find a record of his birth, either on Corsica or anywhere else. He had once had a Paraguayan passport.

"*Puis-je présenter Major Duncan Glynbourne, Lucien,*" said the monsignor.

Trebonzi's chin rose abruptly, and his eyes hardened. "Glynbourne . . ." he said. "*SIS, n'est-ce-pas? Sûreté Anglaise.*"

"*Oui, Lucien.* And, if you can, speak English. Major Glynbourne understands French well enough—but not always at the speed with which we speak it."

Trebonzi laughed. "We must be linguists in our business, eh, Charles? But never the English. No. They don't make that concession."

"*Je peux parler Français, Monsieur,*" said Major Glynbourne.

Trebonzi shrugged. "Speak what's comfortable for you, Major," he said. "It is immaterial to me. Anyway . . . To what do I owe the honor? My old friend Charles, now a priest. An officer from the English intelligence service. You didn't come to St. Tropez to look at the girls, I think. No. You came here to ask . . . You came to ask Lucien Trebonzi to kill someone. Eh? I knew it would come to this, Charles.

Who do you have in mind? The bomber? The man who destroyed *The Last Supper*? I am at your service."

The monsignor laughed. "Your retirement is not as complete as Paris supposes," he said.

Lucien Trebonzi raised his chin high and drew a deep breath through his wide nostrils. "You can make a man a prisoner, Charles. You cannot make him a fool."

"We speak in confidence," said the monsignor. "You have not lost your skills?"

Trebonzi's face widened in a grin. "You don't fly airplanes any longer, I suppose, Father Charles. Do you still drive racing cars? Or, more crudely asked, do you still drill holes in any virgin foolish enough to come within your reach? I suppose not. But have you lost the skills? I have not lost mine, either."

His face was tanned and deeply lined. His blue eyes were cold and narrow. His mouth was wide, his lips were white and hard, and his chin was sharp. His sandy hair was thin. His arms, bare in the short-sleeved shirt, looked as though wire cables ran beneath his skin; they were strong arms, yet not heavily muscled. He held a cigarette between his lips and let the smoke stream upward over his face.

"Can we talk?" asked Monsignor Périgord.

Trebonzi shrugged. "Why not? But I suppose you mean elsewhere. My daughter will be back in a few minutes, then she can watch the store. We can have coffee on the quay. Why not? No one will interrupt us."

The daughter, a dark beauty, returned as Trebonzi had said; and the three men walked a short distance to a restaurant on the waterfront. They sat at an outdoor table, their chairs facing one of the big yachts—this one a ketch with a black hull and white masts and spars—backed to the quay. As they talked, the monsignor watched the crew scrubbing the teak decks. Major Glynbourne stared at the girls—not topless but outlandishly and revealingly dressed, many of them—who strolled the quay.

"Now that I recall," said Trebonzi, "I read somewhere that you have become a monsignor, Charles. My congratulations. I am curious, though, as to why it is you who comes to me."

"We are old friends, Lucien."

Trebonzi smiled ironically with one side of his mouth. "Old enemies, Monsignor Charles."

"I did you an important service," said the monsignor.

"You did at that. I never expressed my gratitude. Consider it expressed now."

Monsignor Périgord nodded. "According to the records of the Sûreté, you have adhered meticulously to the conditions of your parole—"

"Until now, when you come to ask me to break them," said Trebonzi.

"You seem certain of that. You assume a good deal, Lucien."

"Why else would you come to see me?"

"I am authorized to offer you a full pardon," said Monsignor Périgord.

"And absolution, Monsignor?" Trebonzi asked with another lopsided smile.

"No. Both of us will have to seek that from higher authority."

Trebonzi leaned back as the waiter poured coffee into his cup. He watched the man pour for the monsignor and the major. "What is it you want me to do?" he asked when the waiter was gone.

"You guessed correctly," said Major Glynbourne. "The man who destroyed *The Last Supper*. We have given him a code name: Oliver Cromwell. He is also the man who destroyed the church of Santa Chiara in Assisi, set off the blast in the sacristy in Toledo, and damaged Westminster Abbey in London. There is reason to believe he is in the employ of the KGB."

"Isn't everyone?" asked Trebonzi with quiet irony.

"There may be a connection between him and the attempt on the life of the Holy Father in 1981," said Monsignor Périgord.

"Who *is* he?"

The monsignor shook his head. "We don't know."

"Then what can I do for you, gentlemen?"

"We will find him," said Major Glynbourne. "Then we will call on you. We will hope to take him alive, but if that involves an unacceptable risk of our losing him—"

Trebonzi nodded. "I understand," he said. He looked away from the monsignor, fixing his eyes on the distance, on the mole that guarded the harbor. "If I fail. If I am identified, maybe arrested . . . you will deny me. No?"

"If you catch the man in France or Italy, or maybe in England, we can protect you," said the monsignor. "Otherwise it may be difficult."

"The difficulty will be mine," said Trebonzi.

"We agreed to approach you for two reasons," said Monsignor Périgord solemnly. "First, because we know from experience that almost no one ever survived—"

"*No one,*" Trebonzi interrupted. "No one ever did. I completed every assignment I ever accepted."

The monsignor nodded. "And," he continued in a low voice, "because you would be . . . unofficial. There is a deep concern over the moral and juridical implications of arranging the extrajudicial execution of a criminal, no matter how despicable or dangerous."

"What big words you've learned to use, Charles!" said Trebonzi. "You are hiring me to murder someone, and it troubles your conscience."

"Yes, it does," said the monsignor.

"And it troubles mine, I may tell you," said Major Glynbourne.

Trebonzi sneered. "You always have nice consciences, your kind. Does it soothe them to hire me to do the job for you?"

Monsignor Périgord shook his head. "Not in the slightest," he said firmly. "Morally, I'd rather do it myself. Morally, I dislike the idea of sending you to do it. But—"

"But you *can't* do it," said Trebonzi. He grinned. "A priest. A monsignor. You can't. And an English policeman, you—"

"You understand," the monsignor interrupted curtly.

Trebonzi made a short nod. "You haven't escaped the world, have you, Charles?" he said quietly, sympathetically.

"I didn't become a priest to escape the world, Lucien."

"The world needs your special talents," said Trebonzi. "Even in a cassock and behind the cross, you are what you were."

"I acknowledge it is not what I expected," said the monsignor. "But I serve as I am called to serve. Believe me, it is different."

Trebonzi lifted his cup to his lips. "Forgive me. It is none of my business. Please don't think I'm scornful."

Monsignor Périgord lowered his eyes to his hands. "I am authorized to offer you expense money, payable today. Also, I am authorized to say we will pay two hundred thousand francs for the attempt, five hundred thousand for success. If you should . . . suffer some misfortune, the money will be paid to your daughter. It will, of course, be free of French taxes."

"Swiss francs," said Trebonzi. "No French paper."

The monsignor nodded. "The equivalent in Swiss francs."

"And French passports for me and my daughter. Free and clear. I want to go on living here. I'll keep the little tobacco shop." He paused, frowned. "It was *you* who arranged—"

Monsignor Périgord nodded. "Not the parole. They were giving you that anyway. You asked to be allowed to live in St. Tropez. I endorsed that request. I understand you've enjoyed it."

Trebonzi nodded. "With the money I'll buy a house. One of those outside of town that overlook the sea."

"The government of France will make certain that you get one."

Trebonzi smiled. "You don't speak for the Republic anymore, Charles. Who does?"

"Bonnac."

"Bonnac! Then why do you need me? Bonnac would kill his own parents."

"Maybe you misjudge him," said the monsignor. "Even if you are right, what if we locate Oliver Cromwell in, say, Denmark? Or, say, Greece?"

"What if you locate him in Russia? I can't go there. What if you locate him in Bulgaria?"

"We expect to find him in London, actually," said Major Glynbourne. "I am in a position to offer you the necessary assurances of my government."

Trebonzi frowned and began to speak in quiet, businesslike tones. "I foresee a job that has to be done very quietly, against a careful man, probably in circumstances where the unimaginative shot from long range won't be possible. Through a ring of protection, maybe."

The monsignor nodded. "That could be."

"I'll want Gossler," said Trebonzi. "You and Bonnac can arrange that. We won't have to pay him anything. Release from the German prison will be enough. But he'll need his shop. Bonnac can duplicate it, somewhere near here. Arrange something nice for him, Charles, as you did for me; and Gossler will make the weapon that will destroy Mr. Cromwell."

11

BOBBY DONEGAL'S boat rose on a high swell, slipped easily over the top, and seemed to slide down into the trough. It pitched crazily, and David marveled at his stomach's stability while at the same time wondering how long it would endure. Two smaller boats, one powered by an outboard engine, the other rowed, pulled away, disappearing behind the crests of swells, reappearing, and disappearing again. Their color and lines blurred in the drizzle.

Donegal advanced the throttle, and PATTY K. wallowed forward. He stood at the wheel, and David stood beside him, inside the cab. Donegal struck a match and lit a cigarette.

"Well, David. What d'you think?"

David nodded. "They're good people. We can carry it off."

Donegal raised his chin, narrowed his eyes, and glanced around—checking their position, David supposed, though he wondered if Donegal had any concern for the possibility of interference by a police patrol boat. The four men and the woman who had come aboard and met with them were all wanted, both by the Irish and British; two were escapees from British prisons.

"You said something the other day that we should keep in mind," said Donegal. "You said I don't want freedom, what I want is to run the country." He cast a cold look into David's eyes. "You're wrong but not by much. I don't owe you any explanation, any statement of

162

my motives or philosophy. You had better understand, though, that the case is very different with *them*." He turned to face David. "Never forget how men just like them starved themselves to death to become martyrs to the cause. My friends are fanatics."

"So I gathered," said David.

"You are a cynic, my new friend. And so am I. My patriotism—if we can dignify my motives with that word—is lightened by cynicism. It—"

"Why not call it realism?" said David. "A healthy admixture."

"Whatever we call it, they don't have it," said Donegal. "And you had better understand that. They are quite capable of killing you."

"I gathered that, too."

"Did you? Well, don't forget it. They're handsome lads and a pretty girl, but they are *believers*. They never think. They don't have to. They *know*."

David had sensed what Donegal was telling him. You could see it on their faces, hear it in their speech: absolute certainty, complete confidence that what they knew was the truth, self-evident, beyond discussion. That some of them had suffered the loss of a father or brother, that all of them had spent hard time in jails and prisons, had generated bitterness; but bitterness was something apart from their blinkered self-assurance. That was their special quality, by no means common to everyone with a cause.

They talked it. In their terms, half of Ireland was occupied by foreign troops. In the occupied part, there were of course some aliens and traitors—English profiteers and contemptible Protestants. That any part of Ireland should be enslaved by an occupying army on behalf of foreign exploiters and traitors to the race and faith was a crime against God and man. It was the duty of every Irish man and woman to fight for freedom and nationhood—whether the present cowardly government in Dublin was ready to lead or not. Because the English fought cruelly, so must the Irish. The world would understand and sympathize and ultimately come to their aid if necessary.

David had worked with fanatics before. They had been tame compared to these. They had been illogical, emotional. These were coldly logical. Everything they did and promised to do was reasonable, right, and inevitable—if only you accepted their premises.

"They suspect me of thinking," said Donegal. "They don't like it, but I've got credentials. You haven't got any."

"None they know about," said David. "But they accepted me."

"For the moment. They accepted the idea that you hate the English as much as they do. You were convincing on that point. You almost made me believe it."

"You *can* believe it," said David.

Donegal grinned and shook his head. He frowned into the drizzle and spun the wheel to adjust the boat's course.

David elected to change the subject. "Only Mary speaks French," he said. "Don't you have anyone else who can?"

"We'll work on that."

"I'll supply passports. I'll need passport photographs of each member of the team."

"What sort of passports?"

"British, mostly. Mary's accent isn't good, but we might set her up with a French identity card. Or . . . maybe a French Canadian passport. Oh, yes. Not just one passport photo for each. Several. I will have to arrange some other identity documents. I'll want physical descriptions to go with each set. I don't care about names. They'll get new names for the operation. Put everything in a package and send it to the Ritz Hotel in London, for Emily Bacon. Remember that, Emily Bacon. Get a shopkeeper to put some sort of label on it, to make it look like a gift from Dublin. I'll need all that within a few days."

Donegal nodded. "We won't need your plastique. We can supply it."

"No. I appreciate the gesture, but I will supply it. It has to be delivered in France, remember. My sources have it there already. I don't want to worry about your people being caught with it. I want your people to come into France clean. No weapons. No explosives. No contraband of any kind. In fact, I want your personal guarantee that every member of the team will be stripped starkers before they leave here and will come to England and France dressed in the clothes I supply, carrying nothing but what I give them, including watches, rings, money, cigarettes, candy, everything. Let's have no illusions about how well they could stand up to a police challenge to their new identities. Let's have nothing about them that will arouse suspicion at first glance."

"They'll obey orders. They're accustomed to it."

"What about yourself?" David asked. "Are you coming to Paris? Are you taking part?"

"Of course. With me, you've got six."

"Two or three more, then," said David. "A French speaker if you have one. Tourist French is good enough. Like Mary's. I'll come back in two or three weeks, and we'll begin rehearsals. And I mean rehearsals. Playacting is the biggest part of what they're going to do."

"We'll set up a rehearsal hall," said Donegal with a little smile. "In a barn, likely. In Galway, likely—somewhere isolated and away from the cities where our people are known."

"You know how to reach me, and I know how to reach you—for this time."

"I'll do my part, David," said Donegal soberly. "You can count on it."

David stared away into the drizzle. "It's a pleasure to work with a professional," he said.

"You know how he was," said Nina. "He was full of beer. Staggered off the platform, fell on the tracks. The tube train was coming fast." She shook her head. "So that was that."

They were sitting in Malcolm Worth's office, and she had just told David that Worth had been killed. What she had not told him was that she suspected the death was no accident. The police didn't seem to question it, but she entertained an uneasy suspicion that Malcolm Worth had been executed. The thought troubled her so much that she had made the mistake of mentioning the matter to Vasili

Ivanovich. That *had* been a mistake. He had reminded her coldly that it was none of her affair; if their superiors had wanted her to know, they would have told her. Anyway, he had said, the death of Malcolm Worth *was* an accident. He was not a convincing liar. Maybe he had not meant to be.

"So," said David. "Do you inherit his title here?"

"No. You do. Congratulations. You are now Vice-President for Continental Operations."

"Malcolm's retirement," said David.

"It improves your cover."

"Very well. I have no illusions, of course."

"No. I am still in charge, as I have always been. It will be necessary, however, for you to give some attention to the business of Trafalgar Trading. After October fifteenth, that is."

"In the meanwhile," said David, "I am going to need as many as ten forged passports. I can't arrange all that in the time I have."

"You have the photographs and descriptions?"

"I will have, in a few days."

"Including your own?"

"Yes. Assuming the work will be well done."

"I have little experience with that sort of thing. But I have the necessary contact. As to the quality of the work, I think you hardly need ask."

"As soon as I have the pictures and descriptions, I will give you names and other facts for each person," said David. "Additional documents should be supplied. Driving licenses, credit cards, union cards—that sort of thing."

"Understood," said Nina.

"The plan is as we discussed. Nothing is changed."

"The American girl. . . ?"

"Not tomorrow. But, yes. She will be with me. She knows nothing, of course."

"Be careful of her, David. I will suggest to you that you know little of her, either."

*   *   *

Leaving the offices of Trafalgar Trading Company, David went to the Garrick Street offices of a firm of solicitors who knew him as William Gascoigne and kept for him in a box in the firm vault an envelope of documents the firm supposed were title deeds to some Scottish land. Although the receptionist at the office was confused by his new beard, she accepted his key and signature as ample evidence of his identity and summoned an attendant to show him into the little vault. His box in fact contained, among other papers, three United Kingdom passports—all genuine, none forgeries. Selecting one, he tucked it into the inside breast pocket of his jacket and left the offices.

It had been easy enough to obtain the passports. Months ago he had had business cards engraved, bearing the name of a firm of Fetter Lane solicitors, with the false name of Wiggins as his own identity. A couple of hours' library research in 1950s newspapers had produced obituaries of male children who had been born within a year or so of his own birthdate and had either died as infants or within a few years of birth. Presenting his business card on different days to different clerks at the Registry Office, he had explained that his firm was looking for the heirs to an ancestor of each of the deceased children. The clerks had cooperatively issued to him copies of the certificates of the birth and death of each child. Within a week he had passports in each of the names.

The passport he carried in his jacket pocket was in the name of James William Cadogan, mortician, Saffron Walden, Cambridgeshire.

He returned to Emily at the Ritz. The package from Ireland had not yet arrived, and he exacted from her a renewed promise that she would not open it. He explained to her that he had accidentally mailed his gift to her to his office at Trafalgar Trading Company and a package of confidential import duty papers to her at the Ritz. He took her to dinner and slept with her that night, and in the morning his package was at the hotel desk. He delivered it to Nina.

*   *   *

Major Litvinko sat in the small living room of Nina Samusev's flat, smoking, drinking tea. They had opened the package of photographs from Ireland and had spread them on her coffee table.

"It's not simple, this kind of work," he said. "We should have had more time."

"I am under specific instructions never to establish contact with anyone so useful as a forger," she said. "Otherwise, I could probably have had the work done here in London."

"With a possibility of compromising your cover, Nina Stepanova," said Litvinko. "A local forger could become a blackmailer. No, this work will be done by our own people, in our own excellent facility, in Moscow."

So competent were the KGB forgers in Moscow that Major Vasili Ivanovich Litvinko traveled constantly back and forth between Paris and London, and between Paris and many other cities, on orders from Colonel Olshanskii, without acquiring for himself even a single entry in the computer files of the many security agencies that would have been intensely interested in him if they had had the least suspicion of his real identity.

He traveled as George Jean Lechevalier, sales representative of a French company called Ligature Mercader, manufacturer of surgical sutures and a small line of other medical equipment. Its headquarters and manufacturing facility was at Pontoise, just northeast of Paris, and he had lived there for more than twenty years. He was a bachelor, a churchgoer, a member of the local Rotary Club. In Pontoise, everyone but his employer, Mercader, thought he was from Marseilles. Mercader, by reason of an elaborate charade played out for him twenty years ago, actually believed his salesman Lechevalier was a French security agent. He didn't much care any longer, since Lechevalier invariably returned from his travels with orders for Ligature Mercader. Litvinko, as Lechevalier, was in fact known in every major surgical hospital in Europe.

SIS had never taken note of the occasional visit by George Jean

Lechevalier to the offices of Trafalgar Trading Company or to Nina Blankenship's flat. SIS knew of no reason to pay any attention to the French sutures salesman. Similarly, in France, DGSE—Direction Générale de Sécurité Extérieur—took no notice of the traveling representative of Ligature Mercader. It would have noted any contact between him and Josef Vladimirovich Olshanskii, but those contacts—as well as years of contacts between Litvinko and Olshanskii's predecessors—had always been carefully concealed.

Litvinko's telephone calls to his KGB superiors were made only to their offices at the Soviet embassy and always from public telephones in random locations. Conversation was in Russian and in code. Their infrequent meetings occurred only after Olshanskii and his predecessors were confident they had evaded the DGSE men assigned to them, and often the KGB colonels had failed to shake the tail and had failed to keep appointments. Such burdensome precautions had preserved Litvinko's Lechevalier identification since 1963.

At 8:13 P.M. on Thursday, September 6, Ambassador Svishchev's black limousine swung out of the Soviet embassy in the Faubourg St. Germain, bearing the ambassador to a diplomatic dinner at the Hôtel Meurice. The DGSE and DST cars that fell in behind it kept a discreet distance. When the limousine stopped before the hotel and the ambassador and his two bodyguards left it to enter the hotel, the French security men were so intent on watching the ambassador that they did not notice that a man remained in the back seat. The limousine pulled away to return to the embassy. The DGSE men stayed at the Meurice. The DST car followed the limousine only far enough to be sure that no one else was following it and that it attained anonymity in the heavy traffic circling the Place de la Concorde and entering the Concorde Bridge, then it dropped off. The man in the back seat ordered the driver to drive west on the Quai d'Orsay, recross the Seine on the Alma Bridge, and enter the Avenue Marceau. A short distance from the Champs Elysées, at the corner of the Rue Euler, the man in the back left the limousine and walked away into the night.

He was of course Colonel Olshanskii, wearing a double-breasted suit in the style of a French businessman, with tinted rimless eyeglasses—not a disguise, actually, but enough of a change in appearance to avoid casual recognition. He walked the three blocks to the Champs Elysées and descended into the George V Métro station. He rode the Métro only the short distance back to the Place de la Concorde, walked into the Rue Royale, and caught a taxi just before he reached the Place de la Madeleine. Deposited twenty minutes later at the edge of the Place du Tertre at the summit of Montmartre, he took the final precaution of shouldering his way into the midst of the tourist crowd and losing himself in the bustle before finally he entered La Mère Catherine, where Litvinko waited for him at one of the tables favored by generations of tourists.

"Monsieur Lechevalier, n'est ce pas?" he asked loudly enough to be heard by the waiter and perhaps by one or two of the conspicuously American tourists at the tables around.

"Oui. Monsieur Duclos?"

They spoke French. Although they kept their voices low enough to obscure the words, the tone might have been overheard, and it was French.

"This is a tour group," said Litvinko, inclining his head toward the nearby tables of Americans. "Automobile dealers from Ohio."

"I've brought the pictures and descriptions of the Irishmen. For the documentation," said Litvinko.

"Good. It will go in the pouch to Moscow in the morning. I hope we'll have the documents back by the end of next week."

"He picked a good-looking group of young people. They should be able to play their roles well," said Litvinko.

"I wish he'd sent the names, too. We'll send the photographs to the identification office, but the names would have been helpful."

"Donegal?" asked Litvinko.

"He's what he says he is."

"Emily Bacon?"

"An American. Daughter of a rich family in Boston. Educated

partly in England, at Cambridge. Married, divorced, no children. She's nobody."

Litvinko smiled as he nodded. "Nina Stepanova's concern reflects her own developing interest in Betancourt, I'm afraid. She'd like for the American to go home, to leave her a chance at the young man."

Olshanskii raised his brows and peered over his spectacles. "Let her not forget herself," he said firmly.

"Betancourt is concerned for his detonator," said Litvinko. "His door opener would be very risky for this operation. He can't use microwave. He's opposed to timers."

"Have Nina Stepanova tell him we will provide miniature radio receivers and a transmitter. American military equipment. Highly dependable."

Litvinko smiled. "Of course. That's what the Irish would have: American equipment. And, of course, if any of it is identified in the ruins . . ."

"Precisely."

There was no escape from the shooting. Nowhere, not for a mile in any direction. David sat in the Rose & Thistle, sipping from a pint, conscious of the sound, waiting for the end. The locals hunched over the bar seemed to ignore it. Maybe living near the shooting ground eventually deafened a man to the particular note of the booming shotguns.

He had cut off all his beard but the mustache, which by now was thick and covered his upper lip with a fat brush. He wore a tweed jacket, a sweater, corduroy slacks, a flat wool cap. Folded in his jacket pocket and sticking out to be seen by anyone who paid him any attention, he carried a program for today's shooting.

"You'll not know who wins," said a pretty girl with light brown hair. "Standin' here, drinkin' beer, you'll not see the final shooting."

David smiled at her. "I've lost interest," he said.

"So have I, now that Harry Wilton's lost." She sighed. "Ah, well. Are you driving to London, by any chance?"

He raised his pint of beer. "I wish I were," he said.

She walked away. Shortly the guns fell silent, and he finished his beer and stepped outside.

Already the traffic was lined up and crawling on the two-lane road leading out of Halley-Grinford. Maybe two thousand people had come to see the shooting, and it looked as if each one had come alone in his own car. David walked along the road to the entrance to the dusty field that had served for three days as a car-park, and there he ducked through the line of traffic and made his way among the moving cars toward the line where the shooters had just finished and a small group of men and women were gathered to award and receive trophies.

The sun beat down on the roiling dust, somehow not tempering the glare but augmenting the brightness. Dust on his sunglasses caught the light and further impeded vision. Squinting, he hurried toward the awards ceremony, arriving at the edge of the little crowd just in time to see the final silver cup handed to the overall winner.

"Marvelous, marvelous!" exclaimed a man distractedly, to David perhaps but more to the heavens, as he strode away.

They were the well-to-do, these people—dressed in tweeds and twills, tilting silver flasks to fortify themselves for the search for the car and the drive in traffic. They were pleased with what they had seen; most of them were smiling, chatting brightly, anticipating perhaps an after-shoot dinner at some inn between here and London. David knew them. He had traveled in this circle for a time.

The BBC cameramen began to disassemble their equipment. Two cameras had been mounted on the tops of vans, three were on the ground, and he counted two small portables. Men and women were dragging in cables now, loading equipment into the vans. They were hot and impatient and did a lot of shouting in harsh London accents.

David approached one of the vans. He had scouted the area before and knew which one he could disable without attracting attention. For a moment he stood behind it, staring as if fascinated by the equipment; then he slipped between the van and a Ford parked within two feet of it. Edging along the side of the van, he reached the cap to the petrol tank. With practiced movements that took less than a quarter of a minute, he unscrewed the cap, pulled four pellets the size of golf balls from his jacket pockets, dropped them into the tank, and re-screwed the cap.

The pellets were a simple device, akin to the nasty-little-boys' trick of pouring sugar into a petrol tank. They would dissolve slowly—faster when the van began to move and the petrol began to slosh about in the tank—contaminating the petrol with a combustible hy-drocarbon that would not only itself burn in the cylinders of the en-gine, but would interfere with efficient combustion. After a few miles' driving, the sparking plugs would be so thoroughly fouled that the engine would missfire on one cylinder after another and would shortly stop and be impossible to restart.

David returned to the Rose & Thistle, where he drank another pint of lager to wet his dust-parched throat. By the time he left, the traffic had thinned. He walked back to the car-park, started his rented car—this one a big, boxy Humber—and drove into the road toward Uckfield. Three miles on he found the BBC van. He stopped.

Luck was with him except for one thing. The rest of the crew, impatient to be back in London, had abandoned their one disabled vehicle. Unluckily, they had left a man with the van.

"Trouble? Can I help?"

The man, a long-haired young fellow with a splotchy beard, was sitting behind the wheel listening to rock music on the radio. "Thanks," he said. "But my mates are sending back help."

"What's the trouble?"

"Just stopped."

"I know something about engines. Unlatch the bonnet."

David stepped to the front of the van. The bonnet did not in fact unlatch from inside; it could be opened from the front of the van, as he knew. He reached under the bonnet, popped the latch, and the bonnet rose on its springs.

"Hey! Help's coming, mate. I don't need—"

David shot him. The sound suppressor on the Walther kept the noise down to an insignificant pop, but the 9mm slug tore through the young man's chest and made an ugly hole. He fell back, and David hurried to drag him away from the road, into the inadequate cover of the stand of cattails growing in the water that stood in the draining ditch between the pavement and the fence.

It was a bad place to work. Cars passed. The stopped Humber and van were perfectly visible. They could in fact be seen from houses in both directions on the road. He could not be certain someone had not seen him dragging the body of the BBC driver off the road. He stopped at the front of the van to wipe his fingerprints from the bonnet latch and again at the side to wipe off the cap to the petrol tank. With the cloth still in his hand, he opened the rear door.

There was what he wanted: a television camera—better still, two television cameras, one a handheld. He seized the bigger one and carried it to the Humber. Returning, he grabbed out the little one. Lying on the floor, carelessly tossed into the van, also lay something else he could use: half a dozen BBC identification badges. He took one, thrusting it into his pocket. Maybe there was more he could use, but he had taken too much risk already. He tossed the small camera into the back seat of the Humber, got in, and pulled out.

A mile and a half farther along the road he came on a road-service lorry, hurrying in the opposite direction. He had finished his work at the BBC van and made his escape with no more than two minutes to spare. He took the time to stop just the same, to load the two cameras into the boot. A few minutes later, a police car rushed past. He reached Highway A23 by five o'clock and turned north for London.

"Here?"

Nina backed away from the door of her flat. David, awkwardly burdened with the two BBC television cameras, now packed in boxes and wrapped in brown paper, stood in the hall, grinning.

"What better place?" he asked. "I have to work with them, see how they're wired, how far they can be disassembled and still function,

and all that. I can't take them home. My mother might see them—
and the story of how I come to have them is the number one story in
the news tonight."

She stepped out of the door and let him carry his two boxes into her
living room and deposit them on the floor. "I'll find you somewhere
else where you can work with them," she said.

"Fine. And until you do . . ."

He sat down wearily on her sofa.

"It wasn't well done, David," she sighed. "You took an immense
risk, the kind you've never taken before."

"Not as much as you might think," he said. "The risk was of
failure, not of being caught."

"Where is the pistol?"

He shrugged. "Not traceable. But, in any event, gone where it's not
likely to be found. In the Thames, off Vauxhall Bridge. In the current
and the mud—"

"And the car?"

"Rented for three days. Driven hard for half a day, to put so much
mileage on it that the agent will never suspect it was the black
Humber that went only as far as Halley-Grinford."

"They're not talking of a black Humber."

He raised his eyes. "So far. Anyway, it was not rented under my
name."

"God, David . . ."

"Aren't you going to offer me a drink, for Christ's sake? And something to eat?"

She went to her kitchen without a word and in a moment returned
with a glass and a bottle of whisky. He had begun to open the boxes,
and she returned to the kitchen.

"You'll have to take eggs," she called. "That's about all I can provide without notice."

"Scrambled," he replied.

When she brought out a tray a few minutes later, he was squatting
in the middle of her living room, with the bigger of the two television

cameras already partially disassembled. He had removed half of the sheet-metal case and was peering at the tangle of electronics inside.

"Already?"

He looked up. "You want these out of here? The quicker I finish what I have to do with them, the quicker they can go."

She sat down beside him on the floor, and while he ate from the tray she had brought him, she removed screws as he instructed her and pulled off the remaining plates of the case. The camera sat then in its chassis—lens and tube, racks of circuit boards, and what looked like a hundred yards of brightly colored wire, all exposed.

"Copy the numbers from that plate," he said to her, pointing to a number plate mounted on the inside of one of the access doors on the left wall of the case. "I've got to have the instruction manual for this camera. Notify your contact. I'm sure the KGB has a library of such material."

They spent the next two hours on the floor, meticulously measuring the vacant space inside the cases—folding pieces of paperboard into measured little boxes, sticking them to the cover plates and replacing the plates, crushing the paper boxes or not, moving the boxes around and retrying, until they knew the dimensions of every substantial nook and cranny where anything could be inserted in the camera.

As they worked together, contact between them was inevitable: their hands brushing, their shoulders touching, once his cheek touching her hair. Nina was quickly aroused and sought more contact. When the work was finished, she reached for his hand, tentatively, wistfully, and lifted it to her mouth.

He stayed. They slept together.

12

THE IRISH INSPECTOR glanced only for an instant at the two black cases in the boot of the old Austin.

"Embalming tools and chemicals," David had said, The cases were stenciled with CADOGAN MORTUARY, SAFFRON WALDEN, CAM.

He had crossed on the car ferry from Wales, landing at Rosslare, just south of Wexford. He was carrying the James William Cadogan passport, with a driving license in the same name; and his story, if anyone asked, was that he had been called to Kilkenny, where an old man from Saffron Walden was dying, to embalm the body and arrange for its shipment home—all according to the specific wishes of the family.

"You drive out of town, you'll come to Highway T8," said the inspector. "Take that road to Wexford, then T12 to New Ross and T20 to Kilkenny. Just follow the signs. You won't be returning with the body in this car?"

David smiled. "Oh, no. It will be shipped in its coffin—with the help of the mortician in Kilkenny."

He was not of course on his way to Kilkenny. He did not turn onto T20 at New Ross but onto T7 to Waterford, then onto T13 to Limerick. From Limerick he drove north, to Ennis, then on to Galway. It was a long, tiresome drive, under gray skies that sent down intermittent rain. It was a few minutes before five when finally he reached the

village of Ballinrobe and located the inn where Donegal had promised
to meet him.

"Best that I drive," said Donegal.

"I'm glad to be relieved of it," said David.

"You've brought the passports?"

"And a great deal besides."

Off the highways, Donegal drove on country roads and lanes, finally through a gate and into the mud of an unpaved track that
crossed what seemed to be an immense pasture, rolling land studded
with rocks, with only an occasional stand of trees to break the gray-
green monotony. A few cows here and there looked up from their
grazing to watch the car pass.

After half a mile or so, the land began to rise gradually toward a
ridge where trees in a line formed a kind of boundary. There, at the
top of the ridge, stood a low stone house and a larger stone barn, both
in disrepair from the look of them, but both apparently habitable. As
the car reached the crest of the ridge and they approached the house
and barn, David saw that the line of trees did in fact represent a
boundary, for the land beyond fell steeply away to the shoreline of a
body of gray water—one of the loughs or a small lake, he was not sure
which.

Eight people were waiting—six men and two women, five of them
the people he had met aboard Donegal's fishing boat. They were of
course the people whose photographs David had sent to Moscow.
Since he was carrying forged passports for all of them, their faces were
not new to him. They were young: none was over thirty-five. For the
most part, they were handsome, except that all shared the humorless
intensity of believers. Donegal introduced them by their first names
only, as he introduced David only as David.

He opened the boot of the Austin, and two of the men sprang
forward to take out his two black cases and carry them into the house.
One of the young women drove the car into the barn.

"I suppose this place is absolutely secure," David remarked as he followed Donegal and his two black cases through a low doorway and into the gloom of the old house.

"We've all got as much at stake in that as you," said one of the men.

The house was unheated except for a weak and smoky fire burning in a small stone fireplace in the living room and—as he would see later—a peat fire burning in a cast-iron stove in the kitchen. There was no furniture, none at least in the sense of a house furnished as a home. There were sturdy wooden tables and wooden benches, a couple of folding camp chairs, hissing petrol lanterns for light, and—he would learn—an assortment of bedrolls and sleeping bags.

As soon as he and Donegal were seated, one of the men brought them bowls of hot stew from the kitchen—a savory but unquestionably impromptu concoction of whatever had been available, put in water and boiled with salt and pepper. He was hungry, and, following Donegal's example, he drank from the bowl, then stabbed chunks of meat and vegetables with the blade of a pocket knife. Glasses poured half full of Irish whiskey were put before them, too.

"I've brought your passports and other documentation," David said when he had eaten and had drunk part of the whiskey. He opened the smaller of his two black cases and pulled out a large envelope. "Each one gives you a new identity. Naturally, it's essential that you study your documents and prepare to assume that identity. I know you'll all be proud to discover you are Englishmen—except for Mary, who's a French Canadian. Look carefully at your pictures. You have been changed a little; our forgers did some artwork on the photographs. That means you should change yourselves to match your pictures. It's a matter of hair coloring, mostly, or changing the way your hair is cut. Or putting on glasses. No new beards. We don't have time to grow them."

Donegal frowned over his passport. He shook his head. "I don't see how I can make myself into this Albert Mosley. I don't look like that at all."

"You're a special problem, Bobby," said David. "You're the subject of an Interpol green notice."

"Meaning what?"

"A red notice means 'Arrest on sight; hold for extradition.' A green notice means 'Report movements to all cooperating agencies.' You are considered a likely weapons dealer and smuggler. You can be sure that your face has been studied by every airport security officer in Europe and America. They're watching for you."

"And not for me?" asked one of the Irishmen, the one who was using the name Matthew. He was wanted for murder.

"It's considered unlikely you will leave Ireland," said David. "Unless you leave just to hide somewhere—in which case, the security forces that worry me are not particularly concerned about you."

"Still," said Donegal, tapping the passport. "What's going to make me look like this?"

"We'll manage," said David. "For one thing, we'll stuff your cheeks with putty and cotton, to puff you out and give you a broader-looking face. Some more putty, stuffed up your nostrils, will give you a wider nose. Colored contact lenses will give you brown eyes. The people who touched up the photo knew the limits of what we can do. It's not a question of making a different man of you. It's a matter of altering the points of reference that people use to recognize each other."

"I've never been in French Canada," said Mary. "What if someone asks questions?"

"The identifications you've been given," said David, "are to get you through the airports and into the hotels where some of you will be staying. If you are challenged—" He shook his head.

"We can handle ourselves," said the man using the name Richard.

David turned to Richard. "I don't know if you can or not," he said. "I won't try to judge. But I think there is something you had better understand. When you're arrested by the British, you are in the custody of people who, on the whole, will play by the rules. Oh, I know some of you have been knocked about while in custody, but I would guess none of you has been systematically tortured. If you are arrested by the French, and if they suspect why you are in France, you are going to fall, sooner or later, into the hands of a unit called GIGN—Groupe d'Intervention de la Gendarmerie Nationale. From that point"—he paused to shake his head—"from that point, you are dead. And there is no limit to what they may do with you before they kill you."

"There's a way to handle that," said the man using the name Paul.

"I know. But it's not for me to suggest," said David.

He glanced around the room, into the faces of people who had to be thinking of how they would kill themselves if they were arrested, and he saw no emotion. It was as though they were talking about the best roads to drive to travel from Galway to Kilarney.

David unlatched the bigger of his two black cases. He swung back the lid, reached in, and pulled out the BBC television camera.

Now he saw emotion. Even on the face of Donegal. More than that, he saw satisfaction.

"So," said Paul. "You've been busy. You must be the most wanted man in England, right now."

"No," said Donegal. "The man who blew off the west face of Westminster Abbey is the most wanted."

All the faces turned toward David. He glanced hard into the eyes of Donegal, then shrugged. "Inside the body of this camera," he said, "there is room for the receiver that will trigger the detonators, plus five kilograms of plastique. If we can get four cameras like this, not just into Notre Dame but up close to the ceremony, we can accomplish what we have in mind. Actually, we may be able to do better. These cameras have to be operable, have to be capable of transmitting a signal to the BBC—otherwise what we are doing will be tipped off instantly. The handheld cameras don't. We can pull all the electronics out of two handhelds and load them with five more kilos each."

"Detonated by timers?" asked the man who used the name Eric.

"No. By a remote radio signal."

"Sent by you," said Eric.

"Not necessarily. Sent by any of us. I don't care who does it, so long as it's done by someone who won't lose his nerve."

"Why not timers?"

"What if something goes wrong?" David asked. "Is someone to run to all the cameras and unhook the timers? Anyway, how would we know exactly what time to set them for?"

"What about your two Asians in London?" asked the woman who was calling herself Eileen. "They died in the blast. What's more, the Indian defence minister didn't."

"That *was* a timer," said David. "And that's why I won't use one for our purposes. The two Biharis were supposed to wait until they saw the limousine coming, then set the timer and walk away. They had three minutes to get far enough away—which should have been plenty of time. They set the timer too soon, then somehow failed to cover the two or three hundred yards they needed to be safe."

"I can think of a hundred ways in which this scheme can fail," said Paul.

"I can think of two hundred," said David. "That's why I insist on the final say as to whether we make the attempt. If at any point I judge the scheme has become impractical or too dangerous, I intend to cancel it. If that happens, I want no argument. I want agreement on that now."

"It's been agreed to," said Bobby Donegal. "By everyone."

David glanced about him, at all the faces. "All right?" he asked. They nodded.

"All right, then. We have work to do."

He discovered after dinner that there was no plumbing in the old farmhouse. Water was carried in from a well behind the house. A rickety wooden structure that he had taken for a tool shed or a roofed feed bin turned out to be the sanitary facility. It stank, and for the rest of his stay he avoided it as much as he could. Early in the morning after his arrival, prompted by his bladder, he shrugged himself out of the sleeping bag they had given him and walked outside, away from the house, to relieve himself at the edge of the bluff that fell away to the water.

The young woman called Eileen was squatting for the same purpose just over the crest. He turned away quickly, but she saw him and after a moment came up to him.

"Good morning, David."

"Another wet day."

She nodded. Eileen was in her late twenties, as he judged: a busty, rotund young woman with long dark-brown hair and hazel eyes. Donegal had told him she had spent fourteen months in jail in Londonderry but had been released and was not now a fugitive. He had not mentioned the crime for which she had been imprisoned.

"You came out for the same reason I did," said Eileen. "Go ahead. I won't stare."

He turned his back toward her and urinated into the wet grass.

"You're English," she said.

"No."

"I don't think you're Russian either, though Bobby says that's who you're working for. And you don't talk like an American. It makes no difference, I suppose. I . . . just wonder a little about why you are here."

"I'm a mercenary," he said. "I'm paid."

"I suppose that's good enough."

"I have as much at stake as you do."

"You mean your life. We have more."

David zipped up his trousers and turned around. "I envy you," he said. "It must be a source of satisfaction to have a cause."

"It is," she said.

He turned his eyes toward the fogged gray waters of the lough—if that was what those waters were—and focused on the spreading ripples from the point where a fish had broken the surface. A gentle wind swirled the fog. He was aware of it settling on his face, his hair, his clothes. He ran his hand over his cheeks, and his fingers came away wet.

Eileen stepped closer. "It's beautiful, isn't it?" she said.

He hadn't thought so. On his drive across Ireland, from Rosslare to Galway, he had looked for the fabled beauty of Ireland and had not found it. It was ordinary land—poor and peopled poor. The world was full of cold, rained-on pasture land, with thickset people trying to grub a living from it. He had seen enough of it.

She went on. "For centuries they've tried to take it from us, by any means they could devise. And we've fought. Others have written our history, David, so what we've done is not well known; but we're a fighting people, and we won't be robbed of what we know is ours."

"For the sake of discussion," he said, "what of the fact that the great majority of the people of the Six Counties are Protestant and want to retain their attachment to the United Kingdom?"

Eileen shook her head. "The English occupy Ireland the same as the Germans occupied France in the 1940s. And Holland and Norway and other countries. Those people fought the German occupation by every means they could. So do we. And when they had driven out the occupiers, they dealt with their collaborators. So will we."

"Collaborators . . ." he repeated.

She frowned and raised her chin. "You're not. . . ? *You're* not Protestant, are you?"

"Duly baptized in the Holy Roman Catholic and Apostolic Church," he said with a grin. "I suppose I'm an atheist, actually. Or maybe an agnostic."

"Well, many of us are that," she said. "But not Protestant atheists. We're none that."

David turned and began to trudge back toward the house.

Eileen fell in step beside him. "We are like the Resistance in France forty years ago. Maybe the majority would have gone along with the occupation, for the sake of peace, but the world remembers the Resistance fighters as heroes."

"The analogy has its limits," said David.

"The Czechs killed Heydrich," she said. "We killed Mountbatten."

David stopped. "Did you have a part in that?"

"I was in jail in Londonderry when our people got Mountbatten," she said. "I'd been there eight months, so I couldn't have had a part in it."

"The death of Mountbatten hardened attitudes in London," said David.

She moved on toward the house again, walking slowly. "When the news came, the Protestant matrons handcuffed me to the bars of a gate and beat me with a leather belt. I've got scars on my back. They kept me in handcuffs and leg irons for three weeks after that. Gestapo tactics."

"Did they think you knew something about the murder?"

"No. I couldn't have known anything. I'd been in jail too long. They did it because I laughed and cheered when I heard the news. It made them furious. The whipping hurt, but that day was still the best day I had while I was in jail. We'd won a victory." She sighed and looked up into David's face. "They made me say I was sorry, though. Eventually. To get the chains off my arms and legs. They hurt worse than the beating, and I . . . Well, you can imagine. I begged, in the end."

"It made you hate them."

"I hated them thoroughly well already."

He nodded. They had reached the back door of the house.

"You do work for the Russians, don't you?" Eileen asked. "For the KGB?"

"Let's don't worry about that."

"I want to know if it means de facto recognition," she said. "Yashir Arafat was invited to speak to the United Nations General Assembly. Why isn't someone asked to speak for us? Our cause is as good as the Palestinians'. Our land is held by foreigners, just as theirs is. Does the Soviet leadership understand this?"

"Bobby only speculates that the Soviet government is backing me," said David. "Certainly I haven't told him it is. Maybe my backing is from Irish-American millionaires."

"We should demand open acknowledgment."

"Then the project would be at an end."

"But the cause would not be. We will win, sooner or later. We will free our country, sooner or later. I suppose we should welcome the services of a mercenary for the time being, while we've got one. I'd rather we could do it all ourselves, without anyone's help. But I'm practical. I'm glad you're with us, David—even if it's only for a little while."

Major Glynbourne himself carried the computer-enhanced copies of the Paris photograph, first to the House of Floris in Jermyn Street.

The girl behind the counter obviously hoped she bore some slight resemblance to Princess Diana. She wore her hair like the princess, which was the only element of resemblance she in any way achieved. Just the same, she was blonde and pretty in her own way, and she was conspicuously anxious to please the major, whom she found a most interesting, handsome man. She held the first picture the major gave her in her hand and frowned over it. It was the photograph of the man with the beard, as he had been captured by the telephoto lens in the park by the Champs Elysées.

"Oh, it would be difficult, sir. There is a resemblance, I suppose. But—"

"You couldn't be sure."

"No, sir."

"Then what of this one?" the major asked, handing over the air-brushed photo, on which the artist had removed the beard, hat, and eyeglasses.

She nodded. "This could be the man who comes in and buys Stephanotis. Yes, it very definitely could be. This is much like the man."

"What would make it more like?" asked Major Glynbourne.

"Well . . . The hair," she said. "He wears it differently. It . . . I don't know how to describe it."

"Could you spend an hour at our offices, working with an artist who can give this picture some different hairstyles?"

"Certainly. When?"

"Now, please."

*   *   *

Her name was Rose. She sat nervously in a chair and watched the technician adjust the projector. On the screen lying flat on the table, the picture she had seen in the shop came into focus. As she watched, the upper third turned dimmer. Then a new, brighter image overpowered the dim third; and, as the technician adjusted the register and focus, a different forehead and head of hair appeared on the man in the picture.

"Umm?"

"Oh, no," she said, shaking her head, smiling, almost laughing.

"No, of course not," said the technician. "Just to show you the method. Now we'll look at some realistic possibilities."

A quarter of an hour later she was firm about the picture. The new upper third, superimposed on the picture from Paris, greatly improved the likeness. Still, it wasn't quite right, and she didn't know what was wrong. Major Glynbourne asked her to wait in another room.

Ahmed Yayah, proprietor of the New Lahore food shop, was brought in. He sat down, and the technician switched on the projector. The image that appeared on the screen was the eyes and nose, the central third of the picture, with the forehead and hair and the mouth and chin dimmed almost to obscurity.

"Could be," he said. "Yes, that could be Reitlinger."

The technician turned up the forehead and hair.

Ahmed Yayah nodded. "Yes. Very like."

The technician turned up the mouth and chin.

"No. Now it's not Reitlinger. No, that's not him. I don't know how to describe what is wrong."

"You don't have to describe," said the major. "We will show you a lot of different mouths and chins."

Within ten minutes, Ahmed Yayah had made his choice and swore the picture was now a true likeness of Friederich Reitlinger. The major called Rose in again. She was not satisfied. It was better, she said, but it was still not the man who came in to buy Stephanotis. They let the two work together then. Rose chose another mouth and chin.

Ahmed Yayah insisted her choice was wrong. She insisted his was. The major thanked them and summoned a car to take them back to their shops.

He had the picture made up both ways; and, accompanied by the sergeant major, he set out for Soho.

At the strip theater they showed the two pictures to the Jamaican girl who had been questioned by Policewoman Alice Stevenson.

"That's 'im!" said the black girl, unhesitatingly choosing the picture Rose had insisted on. "That's the one that hung around 'ere after Sohaila before she was killed. The one she called Fritz. That's 'im. No question."

Two other strippers were less confident—and less enthusiastic about cooperating—but chose Rose's picture over the Pakistani's as the one that best represented the man they had seen with Sohaila.

At Ricardo's the proprietor raised his brows and sighed over the two pictures. "You're asking if one of them is Reitlinger, of course. Either one could be. Then too, perhaps neither. These photographs are composites of some sort, aren't they? I think you are close, but you haven't quite achieved it. Of course, you remember, it has been a long time now since the man was in here."

Major Glynbourne turned the favored image over to Scotland Yard and suggested it be shown in Soho in the continuing investigation into the murder of Jawaharlal Sjarif. He sent copies to Monsignor Périgord, Bonnac, and Castellano. He secured a warrant for the arrest of Friederich Reitlinger and issued it to Interpol, to be circulated to all police agencies with a red notice—arrest on sight and hold for extradition. The photograph at least—though he had no fingerprints, no description, no record of past criminal activities, and no certain idea of the nationality of the subject—would be available in every police office in Europe.

More important, circulation began in every police and security office in the United Kingdom.

*   *   *

On a wooded hillside of the Maures Massif—specifically, above Highway D25, between Ste.-Maxime and le Muy—the old Action Service, Service 5 of SDECE, maintained a convenience house for some twenty years, until the Service was abolished. The lease continued, and the house was inherited in 1981 by GIGN. It is, to appearances, a very modest stone farmhouse, with an attached stone barn. In the barn, however, there are cells, where the agency can hold prisoners it would be inconvenient to lodge in a jail where their presence might become known outside the agency. The house is equipped with sophisticated communications gear. In a clearing a bit farther up the hill, small helicopters can land without attracting much attention in the vicinity. The farmers in the area have a rather accurate suspicion of what the house is, and they do not approach it. The nearer neighbors have been recruited to adjunct service with Sûreté Générale, have been given a cover story for the house, and are paid a small monthly stipend to lie and to report every inquiry or approach.

It was to this house that André Bonnac delivered the weapons maker, Karl Gossler, on the morning of September 11. Although released from the German prison where he had been serving a ten-year sentence for being accessory to a murder in Hamburg in 1982, Gossler was brought to the Massif as a shackled prisoner and lodged in one of the cells in the barn. He was assured by Bonnac that he would be released and allowed to live under supervision in France if he successfully carried out the work he had been brought here to do. Otherwise, he would be returned to the German prison. In fact, his release from Germany was final, a courtesy to France's ministre de la défense by the government of the Federal Republic.

Each time Lucien Trebonzi came up from St. Tropez, Gossler was brought from his cell to the comfortably furnished living room in the house, where Trebonzi was to suppose he was living. Gossler was not actually being badly treated; except for the barred and locked door, his cell was much like a small hotel room, and his meals were the same as the duty staff took, with ample wine. Bonnac did not want Trebonzi to know his old friend was a prisoner and ordered him not to mention it. Gossler played his role as required.

Bonnac had been present during the first meeting between Trebonzi and Gossler. They had spent their time talking about killing Oliver Cromwell. The first essential, Bonnac had said, was for the death to be certain and quick. It was possible that Trebonzi would get a long shot at him with a rifle—a method Trebonzi did not favor—and in anticipation of that possibility, Trebonzi would have to be supplied with a suitable rifle, with a telescopic sight and explosive bullets. It was more likely that Trebonzi would be able to approach closer to Cromwell. He did not kill with a knife. He liked small pistols, with silencers, which he could carry as he climbed to an encounter.

Trebonzi's speciality was climbing. He could scale any building except one with a smooth or slippery surface. Climbing, he was fearless. Glancing down from two hundred feet above the pavement, he was not chilled. His supple fingers sought tiny cracks, found handholds on sills and spouting, as fearlessly he worked his way upward. Even Bonnac did not know that during his supervised parole in St. Tropez, Trebonzi had kept himself strong by climbing trees and had in the night scaled the walls of the tallest buildings in the village.

"I have been thinking," Gossler told Trebonzi and Bonnac on their first meeting, "of a different kind of weapon. Is silence any consideration?"

"That is always a consideration," Trebonzi had said.

"Even silenced pistols make a pop," Gossler had said. "Anyone who has ever heard the sound knows it. It is, unfortunately, distinctive."

"There is a worse problem," Trebonzi had said. "A silenced pistol fires a small bullet, without maximum velocity. It can be made to explode, but if it hasn't penetrated first, the explosion only makes a mess. And the target begins to jump and run and yell." He had shaken his head. "The second shot may hit another rib. In this respect, the rifle is superior. The big, high-velocity bullet breaks through, and the explosion happens inside. It's a bigger explosion, too—because it's a bigger bullet."

"That's why I've been thinking of a different weapon," said Gossler. "A way to get a big projectile inside, where the explosion will do enough damage to make the thing sure."

"We have no time for experiment," Bonnac had said curtly.

"You have time," Gossler had said. "Bring me a good pistol: a revolver, not an automatic. I'll silence it for you. Bring me the ammunition, and I'll make you the exploding bullets. I'll need a machine shop. What you have here isn't adequate. I can silence the pistol and make the bullets in two days. And between now and the time when you'll need the weapon, I'll make you something different."

"Something good?" Trebonzi had asked.

"You can choose, after you've seen it."

Gossler had proceeded then to sketch a weapon and to explain his idea. Bonnac and Trebonzi had expressed enthusiasm for it, as a backup, in case the usual weapons did not suffice. It had been apparent, as well as a source of worry, to them both that Gossler was ingenuously enthusiastic about his new idea. It made them wonder if he would give the attention they needed to the conventional weapons Trebonzi expected to use.

On September 24, Major Glynbourne came to the house on the Maures Massif, flying from Nice in a helicopter with Bonnac. They had come for a demonstration of the weapon with which Karl Gossler proposed that Trebonzi should kill Oliver Cromwell.

Glynbourne had never met Gossler, though his name was familiar to him. Gossler had the reputation for being a genius in his specialty. Like the American, Pope, who had made incomparable rifles one hundred and fifty years before, Gossler was known, not just for the accuracy of his guns, but for the comfortable way they suited the man who used them. He was fifty years old, an overweight, florid German, who spoke only German—an advantage to Glynbourne, who was fluent.

"I am grateful," said Gossler to André Bonnac, "for the tools you have placed at my disposal. You may commend your staff. They secured everything I demanded—and my demands are not easy."

"*Grossartig*," said Bonnac dryly—wonderful.

Gossler showed them first his conventional weapons. The rifle was a modified hunting weapon, made originally by a custom gunmaker in Jermyn Street in London, now modified by Gossler with a removable and abbreviated stock and equipped with a fat telescope. He had loaded two dozen cartridges for it, six of which were explosive. The pistol was—to Trebonzi's and Bonnac's surprise—an American revolver, a Smith & Wesson .357 magnum six-shooter. Gossler had modified it so it was capable of firing only one shot—having removed the revolving chamber and replaced it with a silencing baffle—but it would fire that one silently, he assured them, and the immense powder charge behind an American .357 would drive the explosive bullet deep into a victim. It would serve if Trebonzi could approach within close range and get off one shot into the trunk of the body.

"Now," he said, "let me show you my new idea."

They walked away from the house, into the grove of cork oaks on the hillside behind. Gossler carried his new weapon in a hard-sided vinyl briefcase. Fifty meters from the house, he stopped and put the briefcase down on the ground. He knelt and opened it.

"A crossbow!" Bonnac sneered.

Packed in foam rubber inside the briefcase was indeed a finely machined miniature crossbow. It was all of steel: gleaming body, twelve-inch bow, wire bowstring. It had no stock. It was made to be fired like a pistol, gripped in one hand at arm's length, with perhaps the left hand clutching the right wrist to support it. Four bolts lay in their foam-rubber slots in the case. Only, they were not crossbow bolts. They were arrows, each ten inches long, and thin, with pointed heads and a set of thin steel stabilizers around the rear of the shafts.

Gossler removed the crossbow from its case. He fitted the steel bow in the body, settling it in a slot and securing it with a solid clip. He pressed the wire bowstring into a slot in a traveling slide and turned a small crank on the body to draw the wire back, bending the fine steel bow. He took one of the arrows from the case and laid it in a slot in the top of the crossbow body. The wire of the bowstring touched a slot in the rear of the arrow.

"*Fertig?*" he asked—ready?

Lucien Trebonzi nodded.

Gossler clutched his right wrist in his left hand and leveled the little weapon at the trunk of a cork oak some twenty meters distant. He steadied his aim, pulled the trigger, and the steel arrow flew. It flew straight, struck the tree, buried its point, and exploded. The trunk of the tree splintered, and the top fell over. The explosion had been half silent, a deep *chunk*, no more; but the tough wood of the tree was shattered.

"A round steel bearing held to the rear by a wafer of mica," Gossler explained. "The deceleration of the projectile hurls the bearing forward, it shatters the mica, and strikes the primer." He shrugged. "Simple enough. I've tried fifty shots since I was satisfied with it, and it has not failed once. Among the beauties of it is the fact that you can vary the charge. Big. Little. Almost any explosive you want to use. The charge is in the very tip of the arrow, so the explosion occurs inside the body of the subject. I think we should try it on some beef carcasses—and maybe on a living pig or dog. We can adjust the charge. Whatever you want. Small and quiet. Big and loud. Blow the son of a bitch to pieces, if that's what you want."

"Let me try it," said Glynbourne.

"The other arrows have no charges in them," said Gossler.

"Good." Glynbourne leveled the crossbow at another tree and loosed an arrow. It buried its point three centimeters in the hard oak and hung quivering on the trunk. Glynbourne moved back and loosed another arrow at forty meters, raising his aim to compensate for the greater distance. The arrow hit the tree only a little below the aiming point. "Marvellous," he said.

"Good for trees, beef carcasses, and pigs," said Bonnac. "But useless until we identify Oliver Cromwell and bring Monsieur Trebonzi within fifty meters of him."

13

THE FIRST detailed news announcement of the dedication of the BSC monument in Notre Dame was released on Monday, October 1. The memorial, dedicated to the memory of the members of British Security Coordination who had died in France from 1940 to 1944, would be a bronze book, hinged so that its bronze pages could be turned. It would stand in one of the chapels in the northeast corner of the ambulatory.

For thirty-five years after World War II, the names of many of the British agents who had died in France had been kept secret, under the prohibitions of the Official Secrets Act; but now most of them had been made public and could be engraved on the bronze pages. They had been, for the most part, men and women who had died under unspeakable tortures in Gestapo prisons. Their sacrifices, said the governments of Britain and France, had never been adequately memorialized, and this monument in Notre Dame would make up for the deficiency.

The monument would be dedicated by His Royal Highness Charles, Prince of Wales, representing the United Kingdom, and President François Mitterand, representing France. Among the celebrated guests who would witness the ceremony would be Her Royal Highness Diana, Princess of Wales. The ceremony, beginning at

11:00 A.M. on Monday, October 15, would be broadcast live over both French and British television.

It was on October 1, too, that David explained to his mother that he would have to be absent from London for perhaps as long as a month. He was going, he told her, on a business trip to Greece, where Trafalgar Trading did little business and was sending him to see if he could increase it. Because he would be as far away as Greece, he might not telephone. Also, if she did not receive letters, it would only be because he was going to be very busy and constantly moving.

His mother was not wholly deceived. She had long suspected he was involved in some sort of criminal activity. She cared about him, but the shock she had suffered in the loss of her husband and daughter had left her a prematurely aged woman with a complaisant personality. She only smiled, told him she would miss him, and asked him to be careful.

He booked a table for himself, his mother, and Emily for dinner that night at Wheeler's Sovereign in Mayfair, his mother's favorite restaurant; and late in the afternoon he stopped at House of Floris in Jermyn Street to buy her a small bottle of her favorite scent—Stephanotis.

He asked the young woman behind the counter if the girl who usually sold him Stephanotis was not in. She lied. She knew Rose was in the back, having tea, and she supposed Rose would not want to interrupt her break just to sell one bottle of scent. David bought the Stephanotis. The young woman asked him for his name and address, explaining that the shop would send him its Christmas catalogue. David disliked leaving his name and address about, even here, so he told her his name was Thomas N. Ryan and that he lived at 2 Wilton Crescent.

Rose returned from the back just as David left the shop. He saw that she recognized him, and he smiled at her and waved.

*   *   *

"And it's not his writing," said the major, looking at the slip the young woman offered him.

"No. I wrote it," said Sally. "His name and address so we can send him our Christmas catalogue. So maybe it's all right. You know where to find him."

Rose had given this information when she telephoned, and a squad had set out immediately for Wilton Crescent.

"The picture," said he. "Does he look like the picture?"

"Yes, sir. It's a good likeness."

Major Glynbourne took a description of the man's dress, mannerisms, and speech. Sally had not been particularly observant. As she kept saying, why should she have been? No one had suggested to her that the young man was a fugitive from the law. Yes, he was shaven. No, he had no beard. No mustache. He wore no spectacles, no hat. He was young. He was handsome. He was English.

She had no doubt of that: he was English, well educated, probably well placed. A Guards officer, she suggested.

Sergeant Major Tate telephoned while Glynbourne was still at House of Floris. No Ryan lived on Wilton Crescent. No one fitting the description of Oliver Cromwell was known in the neighborhood. He was leaving three men on the street, just in case. He would return to the office now.

Glynbourne put the picture into renewed distribution, with an Urgency One designation. He notified Monsignor Périgord, Bonnac, and Castellano that Oliver Cromwell had been seen and positively identified in London.

Emily was happy. David treated her like a new bride. He carried their tickets and passports to the counter at Heathrow and got a window and adjoining seat on BEA flight 30, London to Paris, 9:45 A.M., Tuesday, October 2. Wearing a gray cashmere cap he had bought in a shop in the Burlington Arcade just the day before, he grinned and laughed and capered like a teenager. In the duty-free shop, he bought a quart of Jack Daniels Tennessee Sour Mash Whiskey—a distinctly American liquor, in a gaudy box that he insisted on carrying under his arm.

She did not see that he presented her passport, an American one in the name of Emily Bacon, and his own, also American, in the name of Roger Duncan McConnell. It was the passport Nina had handed him, artfully forged in Moscow. In the false bottom of his vinyl Pan American flight bag he carried all the passports from the solicitors' offices, plus his own Argentine passport. Also, he had driving licences and other documentation, plus ten thousand pounds cash. He was prepared to travel as the developing situation might require.

He carried no weapon. He regretted the loss of the silenced Walther he had thrown into the Thames after he took the television cameras that afternoon in Kent. It remained in the river-bottom mud and would never be found. The cameras had been smashed into small pieces and dropped into the pit beneath the outhouse on the farm above Lough Mast, in Galway. He was confident no one would look for them there.

He did not know that his likeness, ingeniously created, had been studied that morning by every security agent in the London airports. In fact, half a dozen men were at Heathrow that morning, detailed to look for the man whose face they knew from the photograph produced by the combined efforts of André Bonnac's GIGN telephoto photographer, computer enhancement, and the SIS technician working with the shopgirl, Rose, and the food-shop operator, Ahmed Yayah. They knew the face of Oliver Cromwell, yet he passed by them unnoticed. His instinct for deception, the chance notion that he would pass more easily as a happy bridegroom or lover in the company of the striking American, was his salvation. He had asked Emily to accompany him for the very reason that he thought she might lend credence to his incognito. (The Pan Am flight bag and the bottle of American whiskey were additional elements.) Unconsciously—and despite their training and instruction—the security men were looking for a grim criminal. David went by as a lightheaded swain.

Again at Orly they passed through immigration and customs, unnoticed by any of the score of uniformed policemen and plainclothes officers who had, that very morning, studied the picture of Oliver Cromwell.

DST (Direction de la Surveillance du Territoire) duly noted the arrival of Roger Duncan McConnell and forwarded a record of his arrival to RG (Renseignments Généraux—General Information). When, an hour later, he checked into the hotel Emily favored and would pay for—the Royal Monceau on Avenue Hoche—his arrival there was reported to the Paris Préfecture de Police, which similarly forwarded a report to RG. Thus, within hours of his arrival in France, two sections of Sûreté had established a record—an American, Roger Duncan McConnell, was in France on a tourist visa and was staying at the Royal Monceau in Paris. The computer into which RG technicians fed such information was programmed to issue an alert if he overstayed his ninety-day visa. Otherwise, Mr. McConnell was welcome. Official France saw no reason to suspect him. It might be hoped he would spend a lot of dollars on his honeymoon.

Later that same day, when David and Emily were happily soaking together in the immense bath tub in their Royal Monceau suite, an English tour group arrived in Paris. In the group was Nina Blankenship, a secretary, making her first visit to Paris. She was to spend her two weeks in Paris in far more modest circumstances than David and Emily would. The little group was placed in Hotel Edouard VII, on Avenue de l'Opéra, where she would share a room with a late-middle-aged widow who had made her living as a hairdresser in Bristol. At dusk they were loaded aboard a bus for a Paris-by-Night tour that would include dinner at Mère Catherine on Montmartre.

Bobby Donegal, as Albert Mosler, arrived the next morning at Gare du Nord, having taken the night train from Victoria Station, the Channel ferry from Dover to Dunkirk, and the train on to Paris. He checked in at the Windsor Reynolds, a comfortable hotel a few blocks north of the Champs Elysées, where at last he could pull out of his mouth and nostrils the cotton and clay that had effectively changed the shape of his face but had nearly gagged him for twenty-four hours.

The rest of the Irish were scattered over Ireland. During the next ten days they would leave one by one, arrive in Paris by varying routes, and establish themselves in hotels and pensions. No two would travel together. No two would stay in the same accommodations. None, if they followed their orders, would know where any of the others were. They would be summoned when they were wanted and in the meantime were to act as tourists. Among the attractions they were to visit was Notre Dame. They were to familiarize themselves thoroughly with the nearby streets and bridges that would be their escape routes after the blast.

Roger Duncan McConnell rented a car, a small yellow Renault. Telling Emily he had to make some calls on customers, which he had warned her would take up much of his time during their stay in Paris, he left the Royal Monceau in mid-morning of their third day, saying he would return in time for dinner. Not knowing the city well, he drove east on the Champs Elysées to make his way to the Opéra Quarter and to a café on Rue de Caumartin, where Nina, sitting at a table just behind the glass that now sheltered the sidewalk tables, was sipping coffee and waiting. She came out, got in the car, and immediately unfolded a map.

Their destination was not easy to find. It would never be, even after they had driven there half a dozen times. The difficulty was that St. Denis, the soot-blackened industrial suburb that lay roughly between the two big northeast railroad stations and Le Bourget airport, was a tangle of streets, railroad tracks, canals, and plants and warehouses. When finally they located the place, it proved to be a dark and ugly brick building: an unused shop that had once been a printer's, with a narrow garage next to it and two poor flats on the floor above. It faced the doors of a string of warehouses on the opposite side of the brick street. It had in effect no neighbors, no one who would observe the comings and goings of the next ten days.

Nina had a key, and they entered. The ground-floor rooms were a tiny office with a business window that opened on the little foyer, two big rooms behind where the presses and other machinery had been, and a big storage room at the rear. There was a wide door at the rear, where supplies had been delivered and finished work loaded to be taken to customers. Except for a few wooden chairs, a dilapidated desk, and two long, solid tables, the rooms were unfurnished. Everything was covered with dust.

The flats upstairs shared one toilet in a dark little closet at the end of the hall. There was no bath. Each little kitchen had a sink and cold water. The rooms were not furnished, except that someone had left an assortment of aluminum-tubing-and-vinyl-webbing lawn chairs and a couple of folding cots of wood and canvas.

One of the little bedrooms was newly secured, with a strong padlock. Nina had a key for that, too. Stacked in neat packages inside was enough plastique to bring down the neighborhood. Still in wooden boxes, stenciled U.S. ARMY, were two powerful little radio transmitters and ten tiny receivers—radio equipment specifically manufactured to set off explosives from a distance. The detonators, packed in a paper carton, were American blasting caps.

David spent fifteen minutes examining the equipment, looking into the instruction manuals, comparing diagrams to equipment, pondering.

Nina leafed through one of the manuals. "I suggest you don't let the Irish see these," she said.

"Why not?"

"This is sophisticated equipment. You set the radio frequency to carry an audio frequency, which is what you've done before. But on this equipment the whole signal is pulsed by an adjustable oscillator circuit. The receiver must identify the incoming signal by radio frequency, audio frequency, and pulse interval. There's no chance of an accidental detonation. This equipment could be armed for hours before the time to send the signal, with no danger. How, then, are you going to get your Irish fanatics to stand by the cameras until they explode? They don't have to arm them at the last minute."

"They have to carry them in close," said David. "That's what they understand. Also, the cameras have to be feeding a signal to the BBC, or it would be understood something is wrong."

"You're confident they can maintain the deception long enough?"

"Nina, I've been planning this operation for months. Every time I've had a chance, I've stood near television cameras and watched how the technicians operate them. The directors and cameramen talk to each other on little two-way radio sets. I bought one so I could pick up their signals and listen to them. I've read a lot. And finally, I rehearsed those Irish idiots for five days. There's a risk. Of course there's a risk. But it is acceptable. The deception has to be good for ten minutes at the very most. Even after it fails, it will take the technicians outside some time to guess what's wrong inside the cathedral. And after they guess, they have to run to some security agent. By then . . . *Bang!*"

"You know our orders, David. Even if the operation fails, the secret must be secure. Absolutely."

"I'll be listening to the talk between our people at the cameras and the technicians outside. If the directors in the vans guess that their cameramen have been replaced, I'll be able to tell. They'll challenge. 'Hey, what the hell? You ain't Erich!' If I hear anything like that, Bang!"

He wanted to see one of the transmitter and receiver combinations work. Everything on the equipment was digital, and together he and Nina set in UHF and audio frequencies and a pulse interval. He carried one of the receivers downstairs and to the back of the building, in the old storage room. She pressed the button on the transmitter, and the relay in the receiver closed with a snap. They set in another combination and tried it one more time. Then they repacked everything, left the bedroom, and locked the door.

Outside, in the old living room with the lawn furniture, Nina abruptly dragged David into her arms and kissed him. She pulled him to one of the wood-and-canvas cots and began to undress. They could not lie side by side on the narrow cot, and it threatened to collapse beneath them; but, awkwardly, hazardously, they managed to couple. When they were finished, she remained lying on her back after he got up. David went to the window and looked down through the dirty glass at their car, still safely parked.

"Did you really have to bring the American with you?" Nina asked.

"She's perfect cover. We're taken for newlyweds."

"Is that why you brought her?"

"Besides, she pays the bills."

"David . . ."

"And she's an attractive young woman." He sighed and turned away from the window. "She's an innocent. Sometimes I wonder how she could be so naive."

"You think she suspects anything?"

"I'm sure she doesn't."

"Or maybe she's in love with you and doesn't care."

David nodded. "Yes. She is."

"When this is over, you'll never be safe anywhere in the West. Especially not in America. The CIA, the FBI . . . You know you can't go there."

"So I can go to Russia," he said.

"You'll be an honored guest of the Soviet state, with a nice flat in Moscow and a dacha in some lovely place. A generous pension. They'll bring your mother, if you want. You've never been in the Soviet Union, David. You have no idea how beautiful it is, how warm and friendly people are, how much respect will be given you."

"And you'll be coming, too?" he asked.

She had begun to dress. "I hope so. I'd love to go home."

"To be truthful, I haven't given enough thought to what I'll do afterward," he said.

Unnoticed by most tourists is the extensive cluster of antennas on the Eiffel Tower. The French national radio and television services broadcast from there. Every Parisian knows that. Less known is the fact that the tower is the site also of an array of specialized receiving antennas. Almost the entire radio spectrum is monitored constantly by one or another government agency in France, and the antennas for the security forces are clustered near the top of the tower.

At 11:10 an antenna cut and shaped to a specific band of UHF frequencies picked up two odd transmissions. Each was of three seconds' duration, on two different frequencies, carrying two different audio frequencies, and pulsing at two different intervals: a half second and a quarter second. The audio frequencies did not block the signals as they were meant to do—this receiving equipment had hundreds of frequency filters and simply sorted out the signals and passed them on through the appropriate circuits. The equipment then created a record: time, radio frequency, audio frequency, duration, pulse, direction, strength. Each record so created was digitalized and matched by computer to a file of signals specified to generate an alert. These signals matched alert profiles, and the alerts were immediately transmitted to the Préfecture de Police on the Ile de la Cité.

Though attached to DGSE, a military intelligence agency, André Bonnac was at heart a civilian and kept his office much like that of a professor of history in an old university: a tiny room, reeking with smoke, cluttered with files and loose papers, spartanly furnished. It differed from an academic's office only in the small computer terminal on the corner of his desk and in the three telephones with many buttons that filled the deep windowsill behind him.

"Significant? Probably not," he said, tossing the report of the odd radio signals to his assistant, Jacques Lépine. "And yet . . ." He heaved with a pronounced Gallic shrug. "Why would we pick up two radio signals that seem to have originated from one or more transmitters developed by the United States Army for the remote detonation of explosives?"

"Is it certain that this is what we are looking at?" asked Lépine, studying the report.

"Three-second signal, one of the ten UHF frequencies available on the transmitters, one of the ten audio frequencies they carry, pulsed at one of the four pulse options they offer . . . Persuasive, I'd say."

"Strong, too. A crisp, strong signal."

"Exactly what's needed for the purpose."

"From the northeast."

Bonnac nodded. "The strength of the signal suggests that it originated not more than twenty kilometers from the receiving antenna."

"Oliver Cromwell?"

Bonnac shrugged again. "He's been inactive for a while. He hasn't paid us the honor of a visit yet. He favors American equipment. What could he have in mind? Notre Dame? Chartres? Rheims? Amien? Sainte Chapelle? Or something secular—the Eiffel Tower, the Arch, the Louvre? What?"

"I hate the risk," said Lépine. "But I like the idea of having him where *we* get a chance at him."

"Send the proper notices to all sections," said Bonnac. "Notify my friends the monsignor, Glynbourne, and Castellano. I myself will call the Defense Intelligence Agency in Washington."

Within five minutes he was speaking to Captain Richard Sheridan, United States Navy, at the DIA in the Pentagon. Sheridan identified the radio signal as originating from an MV–2357, United States Army Detonator Transmitter, as defined in the classified specifications shared by the United States with selected national security agencies. Captain Sheridan insisted on the courtesy of speaking French to Bonnac. Unhappily, his French wasn't very good.

"I much appreciate your call, Major Bonnac. I see a problem for the United States as well as one for France. If the equipment is used in some sort of terrorist attack, there may be an effort to place blame on the United States. That equipment could well be on its way to the Middle East, for example."

"Is any of that equipment missing from inventory?" Bonnac asked.

"It will take a little time to find out. I'll notify you as soon as I know."

"Is there anything about the MV–2357 that we haven't been informed about? Any additional information?"

"I'll find out."

*   *   *

It is not in the nature of man to endure the fabled isolation of a spy for more than twenty years, cut off from the consolations of normal human contact. If the KGB supposed Vasili Ivanovich Litvinko had lived in such isolation for all that time, they read too many spy stories and misjudged, not only human nature, but also their man. Litvinko was a neighborly, sociable man to whom the simple pleasures of church membership (the fellowship, not religion, for he was an athe- ist) and weekly lunches with his brothers in Rotary were essential. On his travels, he visited Rotary clubs in many cities; indeed, the contacts he had so made over the years had contributed to his success as a salesman for Ligature Mercader.

Besides this, he longed for feminine companionship. He liked women. He liked their warmth, the non-competitive character of his relationships with them. If he had in fact been George Jean Lechevalier, he would have married; only the secret of his identity had discouraged him from it. As it was, he sought out women who were willing to be his friends without expecting marriage. He craved sexual contact, but he wanted their friendship more. Over the years he had enjoyed liaisons with half a dozen women. His superiors in the KGB did not know. If they had, they would have had cause for concern.

He lived in Pontoise, but he kept a small flat in Montparnasse. It would have been the usual thing if he had been a married man: a comfortable little apartment for the mistress who relieved the tedium of his marriage. In Litvinko's case, the flat was more modest than such establishments usually are; and the woman who lived in it was not the usual mistress.

Evelyne Clayeux was as careful about keeping a secret as was Lit- vinko. She was twenty-eight, a lifelong Parisienne, dark-haired, dark- eyed, chic, witty, intelligent. Litvinko believed she was a clerk in the Secrétariat d'Etat à la Condition Féminine. He was not confident she was in love with him, actually, but he believed she cared for him, enjoyed his company, enjoyed their intimacy, and was pleased to save rent by living in his small flat.

The truth was, Evelyne Clayeux was a prostitute. When Litvinko was not in Paris—which he was not four or five nights a week—she spent her evenings in the lobby of a bright and bustling tourist hotel in the Eighth Arrondissement, where by arrangement with the concierge she sat in a chair near the elevator and waited to be invited upstairs. It was a rare evening when she did not earn a thousand francs, and sometimes she earned two thousand—though of course she had to leave a part of each fee with the concierge and hand generous tips to the bellboys. Litvinko provided her quarters but did not otherwise support her, and this was how she made her living.

Evelyne Clayeux was well known to the police as something more than a prostitute. She had spent most of 1979 and all of 1980 in jail, while an examining magistrate conducted a meticulous investigation of a police charge that she was a seller of cocaine. The magistrate had found her guilty and recommended a two-year sentence, which was imposed by the Correctional Court. Released from prison in January 1983, she had become a prostitute for want of another immediate idea of how she was to live. She was the subject of a rather fat dossier in the computer files of the RG section of Sûreté, was kept under police surveillance (though somewhat casually), and the fact of her residence with a salesman named George Jean Lechevalier in a flat on Rue Boissonade was known.

As she well understood, it was to her advantage for it to be known. That she shared a flat with a middle-aged bachelor who was a traveling salesman and practiced prostitution only when he was away suggested to the prosaic *commissaires de police*, who from time to time reviewed her dossier, that she had settled into a more stable style of life and was less likely to involve herself again in the narcotics trade. Before she moved into the Montparnasse flat, Evelyne had been picked up regularly, questioned, and sometimes held overnight. After, she was left alone. The flat was a refuge for which she was grateful.

When she first moved in with Litvinko–Lechevalier, a check had been made to see if Lechevalier had any form of criminal record, particularly one involving drugs. He had proved to be clean. The police commissaire who looked into the question spent no more than a quarter hour on it and was amused. He established no dossier on George Jean Lechevalier. He did not even note the name in the Evelyne Clayeux record in such a way that a check for the name Lechevalier would call up the Clayeux dossier.

On the evening of October 4, Evelyne Clayeux was arrested as she arrived at the hotel to begin her evening's work. She was handcuffed and taken in a car to the Préfecture de Police, where in the cellar she was stripped, searched, given back her clothes, and locked in a tiny cell, behind a heavy, gray-painted steel door with a small barred window that let in all the light she was to see as long as she remained there. No one would speak to her. No one gave her any explanation as to why she was detained.

She spent a miserable night, sleeping little on the narrow bunk in the cell. She became confused about time, and when in mid-morning she was taken to an office for interrogation, she did not know what time of day it was.

The interrogation was brief and curt. The interrogating officer was Commissaire Claude Michelin, a gray-haired man who let the attractive young woman see no sign that he appreciated her beauty or felt the slightest sympathy for her. A lieutenant from DGSE watched and said nothing.

"This may be a very simple matter, Mademoiselle. All I want to know is, what is this?"

He pushed across the desk a small plastic cylinder. It looked like a bottle of aspirin tablets, but she knew it wasn't; she had seen it before. She knew it was no ordinary little bottle of pills. It was too heavy, in the first place; and, besides, the cap would not screw off.

"I don't know what it is, Monsieur."

"Have you ever seen it before?"

"Yes."

"When and where?"

Evelyne had a practiced instinct for lying. Besides, she knew she had a perfect answer. "You know what I do for a living," she said. "One of the gentlemen had that in his room. I had a headache, and when I went in the bathroom I saw that lying in his kit and supposed it was a bottle of aspirin tablets. I picked it up and tried to open it, to use one or two of the tablets. I couldn't get it open. Besides, it seemed very heavy. I put it back in his kit and of course said nothing about it."

"When did this happen?"

"It was . . . It was several months ago. As long ago as the spring, maybe. I am not certain."

"Describe the man."

"Oh, Monsieur . . ." She shook her head. "I can't. He was, uh . . . a tall man, I think. Middle-aged." She shook her head again, more emphatically. "You understand why I can't remember."

"You see too many," said the commissaire.

"Yes, Monsieur."

"And you insist you don't know what this thing is."

"I don't know what it is."

They released her. She had told the truth when she said she did not know what the object was. She had lied about where she had seen it before. The truth was she had seen it in circumstances not very different from those she had described, except that she had found it in Lechevalier's travel kit. He had been about to leave on a business trip to London and had brought his bag to their flat so he could spend the night with her before he went on to Orly Airport in the morning. She'd had the headache, as she said, and finding no aspirin in the bathroom had looked in his bag.

The object was a tiny radio transmitter. It was a bug. It was meant to be left in an office or perhaps in a bedroom, where its microphone would pick up conversation and transmit it to a receiver as far as three or four hundred meters away. It was of Russian manufacture, a KGB tool.

It had been found in the flat of the late Malcolm Worth by his sister, who had come to clear out the flat after his death. She could not believe her brother had walked drunk off an Underground platform, and in his flat she looked for anything that might suggest a motive anyone might have had for killing him. When she was unable to open the heavy little bottle, she concluded naively that it might contain smuggled gems or nuggets of gold. She turned it over to the police. In time it had reached MI5 and had been recognized. It had reopened and entirely changed the nature of the investigation into the death of Malcolm Worth.

When finally the incomplete and overlapping fingerprints on the little transmitter had been sorted out, three sets had been identified: Worth's, his sister's, and a third. That set had been transmitted to Interpol, which had a file on Evelyne Clayeux—name, criminal record, mug shots, and fingerprints—because of her narcotics conviction. Her arrest on the evening of October 4 was a matter of cooperation between MI5 and DGSE, and the arrest and interrogation were handled by Police Judiciaire so that she might not know—if she didn't already—that the matter was one of national security.

The lieutenant from DGSE telephoned London with a report of the interrogation of Evelyne Clayeux. Commissaire Michelin transferred her dossier to a more active status. Both of them noted that the man who allowed Evelyne Clayeux to live in his Montparnasse flat made frequent trips to England. For the first time since his arrival in France, more than twenty years before, Major Vasili Ivanovich Litvinko became the subject of official attention. A police dossier was established, and his travels would be observed and recorded.

Worse, for him, a file was opened by DGSE.

Evelyne Clayeux returned to the Montparnasse apartment. She bathed, ate, and began a search of the rooms. For an hour she searched, not knowing what she was looking for except that she had developed a strong suspicion that George Jean Lechevalier was not the simple salesman he claimed to be, and she thought she might find some evidence of what he really was. She was careful about her search. If he was what she suspected, and if he learned of her suspicion, he could turn hostile and dangerous.

She need not have bothered, either to search or be careful. Litvinko kept nothing in the flat that could incriminate him. Indeed, he kept nothing in his home in Pontoise. But for his one mistake in carrying with him to the flat a little piece of equipment that his mistress happened, by the remotest of chances, to touch, his incognito would have continued perfect.

She expected him that night. She dressed in tight blue-denim jeans and a white silk blouse—an unstylish but youthful costume for which George had expressed affection. She brushed her glossy dark hair and let it hang around her shoulders. When she heard him at the door, she also kicked her shoes under the sofa—he liked to see her barefoot.

He said he was tired from his trip. She said she was tired, too. In her case it was true; she had slept only fitfully in the cell last night. They sipped a bit of brandy, and she sat close to him on the sofa and put her head on his shoulder. He asked if she would mind relaxing him, which was his way of asking for oral sex. She put her brandy aside, slipped down, and did for him what he wanted. Neither of them undressed.

"George . . ."

"Mmm?"

"Someone telephoned a while ago," she said. It was not, of course, true. She was testing him. "A man. He wouldn't leave his name."

"Was there a message?"

"Yes. He said you should contact him, that you would know who he was."

Litvinko rose from the couch. "I'll have to go out."

"George! You only just got home. Can't you telephone him?"

Litvinko shook his head. "No. I have to go out."

He left the flat, walked to the Métro station, and caught the first train that arrived—it happened to be a northwest-bound train, which he rode all the way to the Trocadéro station. There he called

Olshanskii and learned that Olshanskii had not called him. He returned to the Montparnasse flat after an hour's absence.

He was a perceptive man. He saw that something was wrong. Evelyne was different. He did not guess what the problem was—that she suspected he was the agent of a foreign government, probably of the Soviet Union. The idea frightened her. What would the police do to her if they learned she lived with a KGB agent and suspected she gave him her cooperation?

14

THE BODIES of Louis XVI and Marie Antoinette were taken from the guillotine to a small burial ground not far away, on what is now Boulevard Haussmann. There they were buried among hundreds of other victims of the guillotine, until 1815, when they were removed and reinterred in the royal necropolis at St. Denis. The little cemetery remains, and in it stands a small church known to Parisians as Chappelle Expiatoire. It was to the Chappelle Expiatoire, rather than to the nearby Madeleine, that Monsignor Périgord came to pray, early on the morning of Friday, October 5. It would be quiet there, he knew. He spent an hour at prayer and then sat for another half hour in the cloister, talking with two young priests who had seen him in the chapel and had quietly waited for the opportunity to speak with him.

Afterward, as the city began its morning rush, he set out to walk to the Ministère de l'Intérieur. On his way he sat down in a small café and enjoyed a cup of coffee, taking the time to chat amiably with the fat proprietor. He had plenty of time. The meeting at the Ministère was scheduled for nine o'clock. All the while, the two security men who followed him—one of his own, one from GDSE—kept a discreet distance, talked quietly with each other, and were amused at the monsignor's leisurely pace.

The meeting had been called by Yves Laffont, ministre de l'intérieur, the cabinet minister to whom the heads of all French police agencies reported. He had invited the ministre de la défence, Jacques Balabaud, as a courtesy, knowing the ministre would send Général de Brigade Jean-Louis Bernard, chief of DGSE. Knowing, too, that Général Bernard would bring Major André Bonnac, the ministre had sent invitations to Monsignor Périgord in Rome, to Major Duncan Glynbourne in London, and to Galeazzo Castellano in Milan. Only Castellano had indicated he would not be present.

The conferees gathered in a chandeliered, silk-draped room with windows overlooking the Palais de l'Elysées, residence of the président de la république. Seated around the ministre de l'intérieur at the head of the table were Jean Marchal, directeur-général de Sûreté, Maurice Fournier, directeur de police judiciaire, and Gérard Parbot, préfet de police, Paris. Général Bernard sat at the other end of the table, flanked by Bonnac and Colonel Aaron Cau. Colonel Cau was Bonnac's superior, the chief of GIGN. Monsignor Périgord sat opposite Major Glynbourne at the middle of the table.

Laffont, ministre de l'intérieur, opened the meeting by saying that evidence had been adduced in the past several weeks suggesting strongly that the man called Oliver Cromwell might strike next in France. ("*Le chien enragé,*" he called him—the mad dog.) He was vague as to his evidence, but he spoke of the radio-detonator signals picked up on the Eiffel Tower, of the meeting between Cromwell and Olshanskii, and of Olshanskii's subsequent quick trip to Moscow. The photograph taken along the Champs Elysées had been definitively identified now as a picture of Cromwell meeting with Olshanskii— thanks to the work of Major Glynbourne and his longstanding suspicions about an English scent called Stephanotis. Whether or not Cromwell was about to strike in France, the ministre went on, it was incumbent on these conferees and the nations and agencies they represented to do everything they could to find this mad dog and effect his immediate nullification.

"Are we to understand, Monsieur le Ministre," asked Monsignor Périgord, "that the République will now commit additional resources to the effort?" He alone, among all the conferees, had the status to ask the question.

Laffont nodded emphatically. "Président Mitterand has directed the ministère de l'intérieur and the ministère de la défence to commit every available resource to this case."

"That is so," said Général Bernard. "Although, I must say, I am uncertain as to what additional resources may be helpful. Major Bonnac has long since been relieved of every other responsibility but to hunt down and nullify this man. So long as we have no idea who he is, I am not sure what anyone can do."

"The photograph has been circulated to every police agency in the world," said Directeur-Général Fournier. "It has been slapped under the eyes of every police agent at every airport, seaport, highway entry, and railroad station in France. It is difficult for me to believe Oliver Cromwell is in France."

"Unless," said Bonnac, "he was in France before the photograph was distributed. We know he was in France on the date of his meeting with Olshanskii. Are we certain he ever left?"

"Actually," said Major Glynbourne, "we are sure he did. He bought a bottle of scent in Jermyn Street in London on Monday. I am confident of that identification, gentlemen. On the other hand, I have little confidence in port-of-exit and port-of-entry surveillance. He could have slipped out of the United Kingdom, under our noses or otherwise, and he may have entered France. I do point out that we have a confirmed sighting of him only four days ago. It is the closest we have ever come to him."

"He could be anywhere by now," said Colonel Cau. "The vital question is identification. Until we know who he is, what can we do?"

"I should like," said Major Glynbourne, "to offer a suggestion as to how we might effect an identification."

"We will be grateful," said Directeur-Général Marchal.

The major nodded. "Oliver Cromwell," he said, "has been described by the two eyewitnesses we are certain have seen him. Those London shopgirls give him the character of an English guards officer.

As we have guessed before, it is highly unlikely that Oliver Cromwell slinks across international frontiers like a common criminal. It is far more probably, I would suggest, that he travels as a businessman, a tourist, perhaps even a government official—but, in any event, openly and in some style. Is it not likely, then, that he travels with a credit card? Indeed, today the traveler who pays all his charges in cash excites some notice. I suspect our man carries one or more credit cards."

"So?" asked Ministre Laffont.

"Credit-card companies maintain computerized records of the charges incurred by their cardholders," said Major Glynbourne. "Suppose we give the major card companies some dates: the day before the blast in Assisi last fall, the day before the blast in Toledo in February, and the day before the blast in Milan in June. Now, we ask them to make a computer match of dates and cities, using Perugia and maybe even Florence and Siena as well as Assisi. How many men will they find who have used a card in those three cities on or about those three dates? If they identify any, we will at least have a body of suspects: men we know were in those cities on those days."

"You omit London?" asked Ministre Laffont.

"I do," said Major Glynbourne. "I am strongly of the opinion that Oliver Cromwell lives in London. If I am right, he would not show London hotel charges; he would have been living at home when he set off the blast at Westminster Abbey. I suggest that any man for whom we have a date-and-city match for the other three is a suspect."

"I hope," said Monsignor Périgord, "that if ever I decide to become a criminal I will not have Major Glynbourne looking for me."

"But will the card companies cooperate?" asked Colonel Cau.

"It will not be without expense to them," said Major Glynbourne. "They do not maintain their records this way and will have to do special, and perhaps rather difficult, computer searches."

"Here in Paris," said Gérard Parbot, préfet de police, "a man can use one of the major credit cards to buy the services of a prostitute, to

purchase cocaine, and so on. If any of them deny their cooperation . . . Well, you follow my thought, I am sure."

"Even without pressure," said Directeur Fournier, "they will cooperate. I am confident of it."

"American Express," said Bonnac. "Carte Blanche. Diner's Club.
Barclay Card. Visa . . . How many? It should not be difficult."

"I do not propose," said Général Bernard, "that they take a month
to report. I think we should demand answers by Wednesday of next
week."

"That could be impossible," said Major Glynbourne.

"When you call them," said Ministre Laffont coldly, "advise them
that the French government will revoke the right to do business in
France of any company that does not report by Wednesday, October
tenth."

On that same Friday morning Vasili Ivanovich Litvinko, as George
Jean Lechevalier, sat down over coffee at a table in a small café on
Rue de la Huchette, in the St. Séverin Quarter. At the table with him
was a heavy, sallow-skinned woman known to him until this morning
as Madame Bello. He discovered just now, from her name on the
document she handed him, that her name was Jeanine Bello. She was
a rental agent, and the document was a lease on a studio flat.

"It is to be clearly understood, Monsieur," she said in the rasping
voice he had quickly learned to dislike, "that the premises are not to
be used for an illicit purpose."

"Quite so, Madame," he said.

"You see," she said, touching a paragraph in the lease with a short,
fat finger. "Specifically. The flat is not to be used as a house of prostitution."

"Most clearly understood," he said.

"Nor in any way involved in the narcotics trade," she went on.

"Absolutely not, Madame."

He signed the lease. Thrusting out her lower lip, Madame Bello watched through the bottoms of her bifocals as his pen traced his signature on two copies of the document.

"Your friend will have excellent light for painting," she said. "A north light, what artists most prize. And, if she cares, a fine view of Notre Dame."

"Yes, a fine view," he said. "I noticed that. From the roof, especially."

"The roof. Yes. It is cold there in winter. Hot in summer. But . . ." She shrugged. "In fine weather, an excellent place for an artist to work. But no nude models on the roof, Monsieur. You must remind your friend of that. After all, the fathers of St. Séverin . . ." She laughed. "It would be good for them, really. They would have to climb up in the tower to see them—which they'd do, I have no doubt, and the exercise would do them good. But . . ."

"The first month's rent, Madame," he said, shoving across the table the amount in cash. "Ensuing payments will be by check."

"Ah. Thank you, Monsieur," said Madame Bello. She gathered up the cash and separated the copies of the lease. "I hope your friend enjoys the studio and has good success with her art. The keys, Monsieur."

The studio, with rights to the roof, was one of four flats he could have rented. One was on the Ile de la Cité itself, in the Notre Dame Quarter just north of the cathedral. Three were in St. Séverin, with a view across the Seine to the cathedral. This one, the last he had found in St. Séverin, he had chosen as the best. It was leased in his name for a year, and he planned to close the flat in Montparnasse and move Evelyne here. He himself would enjoy the view of the cathedral—or what was left of it after the bombs went off.

He was confident there was no risk to him in renting the studio flat in the name George Jean Lechevalier. Betancourt need not be on the premises more than an hour. He would take his equipment with him when he left. Eventually every rooftop in Paris with a view of the cathedral would be checked, but what suspicion would be raised by a traveling salesman from Pontoise, leasing a flat for his mistress? Maybe Evelyne could even be encouraged actually to take up painting.

The young woman David had met on Bobby Donegal's boat had been introduced to him as Mary. At the farm above the lough he had called her Mary. Actually, her name was Margaret FitzGerald. She was one of three fugitives wanted for the murder of an Ulster constable in 1983. She had not, in fact, had anything to do with the murder and could probably have won acquittal on the charge, but she was unwilling to surrender, to go to jail pending trial, and face a jury. In her terms, she would be placing herself in the hands of the enemy, and she assumed they would rig a conviction. Anyway, she had played an important role in the importation of arms bought for the Irish patriots by their American friends, and the Brits probably knew it and would charge her with that if they got their hands on her.

Because she spoke a little tourist French, the KGB man—which is what she took David Betancourt to be—had secured for her a Canadian passport. They had given her the name Anne Laroche. She was supposed to be from Montreal, an office drudge of some sort, on holiday in Europe for the first time in her life. The passport was already stamped with an English visa, showing that she had entered the United Kingdom at Heathrow on October 2. She could not, therefore, cross from Ireland to England in any ordinary way but had been smuggled across by boat at night and put ashore on the Cornish coast. Met by friends on the beach, she had been driven to London, and from there was traveling by train to Dover where she was to catch the hovercraft to cross the Channel at Calais.

To make herself look like the Anne Laroche of the passport photo, she had had her hair cut short and bleached it. The bleaching was imperfect—streaked—but it was probably in character. She had submitted, too, to the requirement that she strip absolutely naked in the cottage at Hook Head and abandon everything of her own. She had nothing on or about her that could not have originated in Canada or the States—except the London tour books and a London newspaper she had bought during her few hours in the city. She was wearing a pair of American blue-denim jeans, a red sweatshirt, and a yellow-nylon hooded jacket with drawstrings that hung down her back. She wore American sneakers. She slept on the train. Americans probably did, too.

Detective Inspector Martin Ramsey—Scotland Yard, Special Branch—sat on one of the immigration officers' high stools and watched the passengers stream through the passport line. The immigration men were good enough fellows, but you would never train them to keep an effective watch for the people you wanted. Only this morning, once again, he had shown them the picture of Oliver Cromwell, reminded them of how despicable a criminal the man was, and urged them to look closely at every man who went through. They were looking. But not closely enough. It was the old perfunctory glance, doubled but not tripled.

He could sympathize with them. He had made their job more difficult—and only on the very remote chance that Cromwell would leave England through the port of Dover. It was his own belief that either Cromwell was long gone or that he would have the good sense to stay put in England and not risk drawing attention by trying to leave the country.

The fellows from SIS Group Four thought so, too. But you couldn't let him just walk out of the country; you had to make this effort. Hundreds of men were making it. Hundreds of men—and some women—were standing around airports and seaports, watching. They had been at it for days and would go on doing it for days. Let the writers of detective adventure shows for the telly try this duty one time . . .

Shortly after noon a little cluster of passengers came in. The train had arrived, and this group were hoping the Channel was smooth enough to let them go over on the hover. They would not be disappointed, Ramsey knew. The hovercraft was going.

No Oliver Cromwell in this crowd. No man under fifty, except a pair of Asians chattering away. No man could disguise himself well enough to look like one of that pair. Here's a good-looking gel, uh . . . Hello! Could it be? For God's sake!

"Excuse me. Wait just a moment, miss. Detective Inspector Ramsey, Scotland Yard. Margaret FitzGerald, as I live and breathe!"

"*Je ne comprend pas, Monsieur.*"

"I'm afraid you do, Miss FitzGerald. Give up on it, now. It didn't work. You didn't make it."

"*Je suis Canadienne, Monsieur. Voici mon passeport.*"

Ramsey grinned. "If I'm wrong, I'm going to be most embarrassed. But not half so embarrassed as I'd be if I let Margaret FitzGerald slip through my hands. Come along, now. You are under arrest."

"Lucky for her she was stopped on this side of the Channel," said Major Glynbourne. "If she'd been caught on the other side, the French would use methods of interrogation that would get an answer out of her soon enough."

"I'm sorry to have troubled you with it, Duncan," said Detective Chief Inspector Ross. "You have your hands full with the Oliver Cromwell thing, I know; but I thought you should be advised, on the remote chance it could have something to do with Cromwell. I know the French are convinced he's over there now."

"No, I'm pleased you brought it to me," said Glynbourne.

"The passport," said Ross. "It's a very good one. Canada disavows it. It's not even a stolen passport, altered to fit. No Canadian passport was ever issued with this number. But in the absence of a number check, it would be accepted anywhere."

"We could have done it ourselves, hey?" said Glynbourne wryly.

"We. Or the CIA. Or the KGB."

"She's not going to tell us anything, hmm?"

"Not under any method of interrogation allowed to us."

Glynbourne rubbed his fingertips together. "The people working on Irish problems will be interested, of course," he said. "And, as you suggest, I doubt it has anything to do with Cromwell. Yet . . . Bobby

Donegal is missing from his usual haunts. Has been for a week. Also Eileen Gavin. And Cromwell has always worked with fanatics. I'll transmit their pictures and so on to Bonnac."

"I'll order more intense port surveillance for them."

"Yes, of course. Unlikely, I'm afraid, we'll have another bit of luck like we had with Margaret FitzGerald. Convey my compliments to your man Ramsey."

When Chief Inspector Ross left the office, Major Glynbourne remained at his desk, looking out over a cold and rainy Sunday night. He picked up and turned over in his fingers, for perhaps the fiftieth time, a tiny scrap of metal. After almost two months of patient— probably highly impatient, actually—sifting of tons of debris and rubble from the west front of the Abbey, someone had come up with this little scrap of machined steel. The laboratory at Croydon had worked with it for forty-eight hours and submitted a report that surprised Glynbourne by its boldness. He suspected the technicians had gone out on a limb in saying this tiny fragment was almost certainly a part of the barrel of a Potopava Karandash.

What connection? Any? Another Russian detonator. A passport forged so cleverly that it very likely came from the workshops of a major national intelligence agency—perhaps the KGB. The woman carrying the passport, on her way to France. The photograph of Oliver Cromwell meeting with Colonel Olshanskii in Paris. Yet, Oliver Cromwell had been in London on Monday, buying a bottle of scent, the same scent Margherita Catania had been carrying when she died in the blast in Milan.

He was already hours late for his Sunday-evening dinner. He telephoned his daughter to apologize and promise her he would be home within the hour. Then he placed two more calls: one to Bonnac in Paris, the other to Monsignor Périgord in Rome. He wanted to review all these facts with them, to see if they could make a connection different from the one he was beginning to fit together. Neither was available so late on Sunday evening.

It was after ten o'clock when he called for a car and driver to take him home to his flat in Kensington.

That same Sunday evening David Betancourt and Emily Bacon dined at Tour d'Argent, at a table overlooking the Cathedral of Notre Dame, gleaming under the municipal spotlights in the pouring autumn rain. It was the finest restaurant in a city of fine restaurants, and Emily had insisted on it. The wine alone, David noted from the prices printed on his menu and not hers, would cost more than he had ever paid for a dinner in his life. It would be Emily, though, who would present the American Express card.

"Once you've experienced it," she said, "you can live the rest of your life, really, without experiencing it again." She was speaking of the restaurant, the food. "I must confess something you'll probably think is very American. On the ordinary day, really, I can enjoy a McDonald's burger very nicely, or one from a chain we call Wendy's. I'm glad I'm introducing you to the Tour d'Argent, but I'd like to introduce you to Wendy's, too."

"What else is there in the Wild West?" he asked.

"No Tour d'Argent, you can be sure. Wendy's and McDonald's. And lots of steak houses. Americans love their beefsteak."

"Could one . . . live there? I mean, in Wyoming or some such place? Denver. I've heard much of Denver."

"Do you want to go there, David?" she asked somberly.

He nodded. "Maybe."

"I have friends in California."

"That's something else. But not to live there. I understand it's not a good place to live."

Emily laughed. "'There's no *there* there,'" she quoted Gertrude Stein.

David smiled. He stared moodily across the Seine at the spotlighted cathedral.

"We've talked of going to the States," she said. "Can't you spare the time?"

He put his hand on hers. "What would you say, Emily, if I told you I might want to go to the States sometime, not as David Betancourt, but under an assumed name."

Emily shook her head. "I wouldn't be surprised," she said. "What is Trafalgar Trading, anyway?"

"Well, we're not in narcotics or anything like that. But we do transfer goods across international boundaries without paying the taxes."

"You want out? You want to start over?"

He nodded. "Something like that. I may not have a choice."

"Well, I suggest we get out of France before anything happens," she said. "It wouldn't be a good place to be caught."

"Do you want to go home accompanied by a criminal, a fugitive from the law, using an assumed name?"

"I'm in love with you," she said simply.

"I won't be poor," he said.

"I don't care about that. We can buy a home in Wyoming, if that's what would be safe for you. A ranch. We don't have to travel or see anybody much until the heat is off."

David nodded.

"Soon?" she asked.

"Probably."

"Do you love me, too?"

"I've trusted you with my life," he said.

On Monday morning, Detective Chief Superintendent William Dole, Scotland Yard, Special Branch, arrived at Orly. He was met by Commissaire Jean Trillat, chief of GSPR—Groupe de la Sécurité pour le Président de la République—the police section charged with the protection of the president. Dole was accompanied by two inspectors from Special Branch. Trillat was accompanied by two of his men. They drove in two cars to Notre Dame.

Their joint task was to establish security for the visit of the Prince and Princess of Wales. The schedule was for the royal couple to arrive at Orly at eight-thirty. They would be met at the airport only by the

British ambassador and a protocol officer, who would give them, in the car on the way into the city, their final briefing about the dedication ceremony. Their first official function was a brief private meeting with Président François Mitterand at the Elysées Palace, followed by a breakfast that would be attended by survivors of the BSC and of the Résistance. At 10:45 the official party would leave the palace in a group of cars and would be driven to Notre Dame. They would be greeted at the portals of the cathedral by Jean-Marie Cardinal Lustiger, Archbishop of Paris, who would conduct them into the cathedral for the ceremony. The ceremony should require no more than twenty minutes, after which the official party would return to the Elysées Palace for lunch and a diplomatic reception. The prince and princess would return to Orly by midafternoon and would be back in London for a concert they were scheduled to attend at seven-thirty.

Security for the Prince and Princess of Wales was to be tight, but it was not considered that the royal couple were likely to be the targets of any terrorist fanatics likely to be found in France. Only ordinary security would be afforded them at Orly and on the drive to the Elysées Palace. While they were in the company of Président Mitterand, who was considered a target, security would be much tighter. The route the official cars would take from the palace to the cathedral would not be announced, and obviously a number of routes could be taken. Which of the black Citroens actually carried Président Mitterand and the prince and princess would not be apparent to those who saw the procession. Only on the parvis before the cathedral and within the cathedral itself would security be particularly tight.

As soon as the early morning masses had been said, the cathedral would be closed, and no one who could not be positively identified would be permitted to enter. The cathedral would have been thoroughly searched during the night by scores of specialists and by dogs trained to detect explosives. The curator of the cathedral had been working with the GSPR for two weeks, showing the agents every obscure nook where a man or a bomb could be hidden. Doors had been sealed. Microphones had been hidden, to listen for entry into places where no one had any business being. After the morning masses on Monday October 15, a hundred men, with dogs, metal detectors, and electronic scanners would sweep the cathedral one final time.

Everyone admitted to the ceremony would be put through a metal detector. Special passes were being issued for all visitors.

Every window overlooking the Place du Parvis would either be sealed or occupied by a policeman. Since the square was faced on two sides by the Hotel Dieu and the Préfecture de Police, and the other two sides by the cathedral itself and the narrow park and the river, securing the windows would be easy. Rooftops, too, would be either sealed off, occupied by police, or both.

"I am concerned, Commissaire, about the television personnel and the other news reporters," said Superintendent Dole.

"We are using the special badges," said Commissaire Trillat.

"Special badges?"

"Yes. Identification badges. Each one bears the photograph of the person to whom issued. Those photographs, together with complete identification of each person involved, are given to us three days in advance. We issue them only when they are needed—in this case, an hour or so before the ceremony begins. We issue them in a different color for each event. No one will know before the morning of the ceremony if the badges are to be green, red, yellow, or what. Furthermore, the badges contain an invisible magnetic code. Before a badge holder is admitted to the cathedral, a sensor will be passed over the badge. Even if someone managed to guess the color and forge a badge, the forged badge will not carry the correct code, which will have been imposed on it in a police van just before it is issued. We feel confident of this system, Superintendent Dole."

Dole nodded. "Identification materials for BBC personnel will be in your hands by Friday. They will want to park three equipment vans on the Place du Parvis. Only the camera operators and microphone technicians, plus maybe an assistant or two, need enter the cathedral."

"An announcer?"

"He will speak from inside one of the vans, where he will be sitting before monitors and can see everything at once. The director will be beside him."

"And your newspaper and wire reporters will obtain identification from us in the usual way," said the commissaire.

"Yes. Accredited journalists. If you have questions about any of them, you can inquire of me."

Superintendent Dole stood for a long moment in the curve of the ambulatory, staring around him and above, at the ancient stones of Notre Dame. The monument to the men and women who had served British Security Coordination and had died for civilization was already in place between the tombs of two of the archbishops of Paris. The monument was covered with a purple silk shroud. People, tourists mostly, strolled through the nave and transept, into the ambulatory, and around the chancel into the nave again. Few of them, obviously, paused to consider where they were, what they were seeing; the tour buses awaited outside. For himself, the superintendent could wish he had more time.

By coincidence, David, peering at the Place du Parvis through a powerful telescope mounted on a tripod on the St. Séverin rooftop, saw the British and French security officers leave the cathedral—although of course he had no idea who they were or why they were there.

"As I told you," said Nina.

For her it was a second visit to the studio flat Litvinko had leased. He had brought her here on Sunday and given her a key.

From the roof David had a clear view of the Place du Parvis and the west front of Notre Dame. The Quai St. Michel and the Quai de Montebello, on this side of the narrow Seine, were hidden behind rooftops, as was the river itself. It was an ideal place for his command post.

A view was not, of course, necessary. He would listen to the radio

transmissions between the BBC cameramen—*his* BBC cameramen—
and their control van on the Place du Parvis. What he heard would
tell him if their incognito had been penetrated, if they were in trouble. What he heard would tell him, too, the exact moment at which
to send the signal that would detonate the plastique that would be
hidden in each of their cameras. But he would see how much damage
was done. He would see the southeast corner of the cathedral blown
out and the tons of stone and masonry and wood and copper falling
into the ambulatory and chancel. He would know if he had achieved
what he had promised Colonel Olshanskii.

"It is essential," said Nina, "that nothing be left here that could
identify this roof as the place from which the signal was sent. You will
have plenty of time to gather up everything and leave. It will be a long
time before the police think to look at these rooftops."

"I understand," he said distractedly. He was fascinated by the clarity of his view through the telescope and was paying her little attention.

"I can be here with you, David," she said. "We can do this thing
together."

"No," he said. "I can carry everything I need. I work alone, Nina. I
always have."

They opened the door and descended through the narrow stairwell
into the flat. "An artist's studio," she said. "They have painted here,
for generations."

"Generations of bad paintings of the cathedral," he said, peering
through the broad window at the intricate stone tracery of the rose
window on the south wall of the transept.

He wondered if the great rose windows of the transept—this one of
Christ and His angels and the older one to the north of Old Testa-
ment figures and the Virgin—would survive the pressures of the huge
blast. He wondered in fact if the entire structure might not collapse.
He had a reasonably accurate idea of how much power his explosives
would unleash. What he was unsure of was the strength of the building. He would regret bringing it down. His purpose would be accom-

plished if the Prince and Princess of Wales and the president of France were killed. Olshanskii wanted major damage to Notre Dame. The Russians were barbarians.

"David . . . A model, eh?"

He turned around. Nina had removed her clothes and stood naked on the little platform where the north light from the window kindly modeled her planes and curves. Although she was twelve or fifteen years older than he was, he had learned to appreciate her body. It was thicker than Emily's; her breasts were heavier, her hips broader. Still, she was solid, not flabby, and her skin was taut. Her apparently ungovernable blond hair fell over her brows and the bridge of her nose. Her calm eyes were fixed on him, expectant and yet defiant.

"Could I have done this for a living, do you think? Model in the nude?"

"I have no doubt of it," said David. "Though it's a poor living."

She flipped her hair away from her eyes. "I have something to tell you, David," she said. "I am being ordered home. When our work is finished here, I won't even go back to London for my possessions. I am to fly directly to Moscow."

"Are you in trouble?"

"Not at all. I will be promoted. I am to be a teacher, in the school where I was trained before I went to England. It will be a good job, David. It will bring honor and a comfortable living."

"I am glad for you, Nina."

She jammed her hands to her hips. Her chin rose. "Are you coming with me?"

"Why not?"

Emily smiled happily as she emerged from the American Embassy on the northeast corner of the Place de la Concorde. She had used her family's political influence subtly, had offended none of the cautious bureaucrats of the diplomatic service, but had gotten what she wanted. She and David would be guests in Notre Dame Cathedral on the Monday morning of next week, when the Prince and Princess of

Wales and the president of France would dedicate a monument. Only a few people were being admitted, and the number of tickets allotted to the American embassy had been few indeed. She had never seen the prince and princess and was determined to get a look at them. Her name, and David's, had been put on the list. Their tickets would be delivered to their hotel. She hoped David would be as pleased and excited as she was.

15

BOBBY DONEGAL, lodged in what he considered a luxurious hotel and supplied with what he considered a generous allowance of spending money, enjoyed Paris. He spent his days wandering the streets of the city, discovering some of its sights by chance, since he had only a vague idea of what he might want to see. Finding whisky expensive, he acquired a taste for Calvados, the strongest, cheapest spirit available; and, the first few nights, he stumbled into his room by midnight, happily drunk and at peace with the world, ready to throw himself gratefully on his bed and sleep in his clothes. Then he discovered he could arrange for attractive young women to visit his room. After that he postponed some of his drinking until after his nightly exercise. Only when the girl had left his room did he open his bottle and bring another day to an end.

On the morning of Tuesday, the seventh of October, he was wakened earlier than he wished by the ringing of his telephone. The concierge, who knew by now that the Irishman in Room 409 spoke no French, told him in English that two people were in the lobby to see him. Without asking who they were, Bobby told the concierge to send them up.

"Who the hell are you?" he asked the young man and young woman who faced him when he opened the door of his room.

"From Dublin," said the young man. "Call me Pat. You can call her Kathy."

"Pat and Kathy," sighed Donegal. "Oh, yes. A fine Irish lad and lassy, hey? What kind of passports are you carrying? How did you get into France?"

The couple walked past him into the room. They looked around distastefully.

"Hmm?" Donegal prompted them. "How? And what are your real names, anyway?"

"Never mind," said the one who wanted to be called Pat. "She's my wife. You don't need to know any more."

Donegal grabbed the young man by the lapels of his coat and lifted him off the floor. "Don't tell me what I need to know," he grunted. "*I'll* decide what I need to know." He glanced at the young woman, who held a small Browning automatic pointed at him. "Put away the popgun, little sister," he said, letting the young man down. "Do you have any idea what the French security services would do to you if you shot me and they wanted to know why? Time in a Brit jail, if you ever did any, would glow in your memory like a vision of a sunny day on the beach, after you spent a few hours in a lockup here."

"We didn't come here to have trouble with you," said Pat.

"Then tell me who you are and why you're here, sonny."

Pat sat down on the sofa, and his wife sat beside him. He took a moment to adjust his tweed jacket and to tuck his shirt tail back into his trousers. "You're here to do something dangerous," he said. "And you may get caught. As you just said, a person doesn't keep any secrets from the French police."

"Point taken," said Donegal. "You're Pat and Kathy. I'm not happy you know who I am and where to find me."

"It won't make any difference," said Pat. "We entered France under our own names and with our own valid Irish passports. We're not wanted anywhere."

Donegal picked up his nearly empty bottle of Calvados and tipped it for a swig. "God, a man's mouth tastes foul in the morning!" he complained, shaking his head. "How'd you know where to find me?"

"There is only one way we could know, isn't there?" asked Kathy.

"They told you."

"Yes. Your friends in Dublin are our friends," she said. "Do you want names?"

"Yes."

"Morris," she said solemnly. "Dunmore."

Donegal sighed heavily. "And why did they send you?"

"To bring you a warning," said Pat.

"Mmm. A warning."

He disliked the solemnity of these two young people. Nothing leavened it. They were a handsome couple. Indeed, she was a beautiful girl: honey blonde, pink, full-figured. He wondered if she ever thought of anything but The Cause.

"The man," said Pat. "The man you suppose is from the KGB. He isn't. He's English."

"You're half right," said Donegal.

"Do you know who he is?"

Donegal nodded.

"He set off the explosion at Westminster Abbey last summer," said Kathy.

"Yes."

"The two people who carried the bomb to the Abbey died in the explosion."

"Yes, little girl. We know that."

"It is very, very likely," she said, "that he is also the man who set off the bomb that destroyed *The Last Supper*."

"That's possible."

"The people who delivered that bomb died in the explosion."

Donegal nodded.

"There was an explosion at Assisi about a year ago," said Kathy. "The same thing. And at Toledo, in Spain, last winter. The woman who carried in the bomb was killed when it went off."

Donegal nodded again. "We know."

"Well?"

"Do Morris and Dunmore think I'm a fool? Do you?"

"Well . . . No. No, of course not."

"Then go back and tell them I know what I'm doing."

"One more thing," said Pat. "You're short-handed. Margaret FitzGerald was taken by the Brits at Dover. She's in jail in London. Morris and Dunmore suggested we stay. Why not have someone here that your man doesn't know?"

"If you stay, you take orders from me. Without hesitation or question."

"Agreed."

"Not because you agree. Because I outrank you. And Morris. And Dunmore."

"Understood."

"You're carrying a gun, little sister. Get rid of it. If either of you have any others, or anything else you shouldn't have in France, get rid of it. For right now, go down to the breakfast room and order us eggs and ham and potatoes and lots of coffee. I'll be down in ten minutes. We have some work to do."

Josef Vladimirovich Olshanskii glowered over a package that had been delivered to him five minutes before at the Soviet Embassy. He had torn off the brown-paper wrapping and found a book inside. It was in English, a well-worn volume, some twelve years old—*Cromwell: Our Chief of Men* by Antonia Fraser, published by Weidenfeld & Nicolson, London. Inside the front cover, a sticker identified the book as having come from a shop in Rue St. Vincent. On the sticker, someone had made a mark in pencil—*4.00*—which could of course have meant that the used book was for sale for four francs. Olshanskii understood it meant he was to meet Oliver Cromwell at the book shop at four o'clock that afternoon.

He was furious.

He checked his map of Paris. Rue St. Vincent was one of the narrow streets on the steep northern slope of Montmartre. To avoid the surveillance that had become much more determined in the past few days, he left the embassy two hours early, riding in a car that was taking a member of the embassy staff to her regular weekly visit to St. Louis Hospital, where she would receive another injection in the course of treatments that was desensitizing her to an allergic reaction to fall foliage. Turning through the short streets leading into the Boulevard de Sébastopol, the embassy car made a quick stop. Olshanskii jumped out and ducked between parked cars and into a *patisserie.* Using taxis and the Métro, he began the circuitous course that took him to Rue St. Vincent and brought him there, in spite of his meanderings, forty-five minutes early.

Having nothing else to do, Olshanskii walked to the Montmartre Cemetery and wandered through the lanes, stopping momentarily at the graves of such men as Emile Zola, Alexandre Dumas, Edgar Degas, and Hector Berlioz. On the streets again, he walked up and down the steps, his annoyance growing. He stopped for coffee, bought a newspaper. At four he was outside the book shop.

"Pardon, Monsieur. Voulez-vous me dire où se trouve un pissoir?"

Olshanskii turned to the shabby, bent, cane-carrying old man who had approached him. "You are without discipline," he said.

David continued to bob his head, and he kept his shoulders hunched high. "Are you sure you were not followed?"

"Absolutely."

"Then . . ." He nodded in the direction of a nearby wineshop. "Buy your old father a glass of wine."

They sat at a table in the tiny, tile-floored wine shop, and Olshanskii went to the bar to buy and bring back two glasses of *vin rouge ordinaire.*

"I have no problems," said David when he had taken a sip of the wine. "So far as I can see, everything is going to come off as planned. Your people have done their part."

Olshanskii studied the simple, yet effective, disguise David had contrived. He was shabbily dressed in an ill-fitting gray suit, and a dark-blue beret was jammed down on his head. His hair was dusted with powder. His complexion . . . On close examination, Olshanskii decided he had simply rubbed his face and hands with street grime. Likely he wore other clothes under the shabby suit; its bulk suggested as much. Given a moment in a public toilet, he could come out as David Betancourt.

"I want to make certain of something," said David.

"The money."

David nodded.

"Half a million English pounds. I will meet you here. What could be better? Two hours after the explosion."

"What assurance do I have?"

"We've trusted each other. You know my identity."

"Good."

Olshanskii lifted his glass and stared critically at his wine. "You have a reserved place on next Monday's Aeroflot flight to Moscow."

"What time does it leave?"

"In the evening."

David shook his head. "Too risky. Much too risky. They'll be watching that flight. If I come to the Soviet Union, I'll come my own way."

"But will you come? Will you come at all?"

"What is your advice, Josef?"

"It is the only place in the world where you will be safe, the only place where you will be able to live a normal life. Everywhere else . . . They'll never give up. Not in this century or the next."

"And you can never acknowledge me."

"Immaterial. We'll give you a comfortable life. Nina Stepanova is smitten with you. A man could do worse."

"She'd like to turn me into a house pet."

"A man with your background need not be idle," said Olshanskii. "You can teach languages. Every year we bring bright country boys and girls into Moscow and put them through intensive training to enable them to live in the West without looking and acting like Russian bumpkins. I can think of no one better equipped to play an important role in that training. You can turn them into proper Englishmen."

"Even so, trying to board a flight out of Paris Monday night—especially on Aeroflot—will involve a risk I don't want to take."

"It will be available to you if you change your mind."

"*Doe ponyedyelnik,* Josef Ivanovich." Until Monday.

André Bonnac slept late on Tuesday morning. He had been exhausted when finally he allowed himself to be driven away from the ministère de la défence and dropped at his flat in the Palais-Royal Quarter. He shared a small, modern flat with a young woman who performed nude at the Crazy Horse Saloon, under the name Violette. (Her name was Marie-Luise.) Fortunately, their hours regularly coincided. They had made coffee at 4:00 A.M. and had gone to bed only after they had drunk it and had subdued its foul taste with little sips of brandy. When the telephone rang at 10:30 they were still in bed, he with her slender, boyish body clasped close to his for her warmth, both of them sound asleep.

"*Allô.*"

"*Qui est à l'appareil?*"

"*Ici Violette.*"

"*Je voudrais parler à Monsieur Bonnac, s'il vous plait.*"

Violette yawned and regarded the sleeping André. "*Il n'est pas ici. Puis-je lui communiquer un message?*"

"*A quelle heure sera-t-il de retour?*"

"*A midi, peut-être.*"

"*Dites-lui que Colonel Cau a téléphoné.*"

"*Colonel Cau. Oui. Bonjour, Monsieur.*"

André rolled over and opened his eyes. "*Colonel Cau?*"

She nodded. "Colonel Cau."

Colonel Aaron Cau was Bonnac's chief, the only officer who outranked him at GIGN. Together, so far as he was concerned, they ran Groupe d'Intervention de la Gendarmerie Nationale: the colonel in

command for military functions, himself in command for police matters. Three quarters of an hour later he was in the colonel's office.

"PJ has come up with something very interesting," the colonel said.
"You recall that Scotland Yard found the fingerprints of an Eighth-
Arrondissement whore on a KGB transmitter turned over to them in
London? You remember that she lives with a middle-aged salesman in
a flat in Montparnasse?"

"Yes, of course."

"The salesman's name is George Jean Lechevalier. His passport
application, filed more than twenty years ago, indicated he was born
in Marseilles and lived there, on Rue de Panier, until he moved to
Pontoise and went to work for Ligature Mercader. It is false. George
Jean Lechevalier was born in Marseilles in 1939 and did indeed live
on Rue de Panier, but he was a seaman and jumped ship in Rio de
Janeiro in 1961. I would guess our new George Jean Lechevalier
knows something we don't know: that the original George Jean
Lechevalier is dead. He has some reason, anyway, for his obvious
confidence that the original will not return. The identity has been
most useful to him."

"And he is the man who makes frequent trips to London," said
Bonnac.

"And elsewhere. To Italy. To Spain."

"Oliver Cromwell?"

Colonel Cau shrugged. "Why not? Maybe the man who met with
Olshanskii and was photographed was someone else."

Bonnac sighed. "Major Glynbourne is convinced that Cromwell
bought a bottle of perfume in London only last week. His shopgirl
positively identified her customer as the man we photographed meeting with Olshanskii here in Paris."

"The English have been wrong many times before."

"Where is Lechevalier now?"

"In Pontoise, at the offices of Ligature Mercader."

"I suggest we don't arrest him," said Bonnac. "I'd rather have him
watched."

"He does not seem to suspect he is being watched. Unless he is extremely clever . . ."

"Let's get fingerprints," said Bonnac. "Run him through the Interpol files. He's clean in ours, I suppose?"

"Utterly."

"Then watch him. See where he leads us. If he's not Cromwell, or involved with him, then what is he? Someone important, I'd guess. Twenty years . . . God knows what he's done to us!"

Brigadier Alan Fulham, his tall thin body settled wearily in the chair at the head of the table, ran his fingers through his fine gray hair and nodded welcome to Major Glynbourne. He did not rise. He seemed thinner than ever, if it were possible for the man to stretch even less flesh over his skeletal frame. Glynbourne wondered if the chief of Group Four were ill—he looked so pale and weak as compared to his appearance only two months ago when they had met with the prime minister.

They were in one of the secure conference rooms, a place constantly swept for any form of electronic device, elaborately soundproofed, one of the rooms where taking notes was forbidden, where no paper could be brought in or carried out. Besides the brigadier and Glynbourne, Colonel Harcourt of Group Four and Detective Chief Inspector Ross of Scotland Yard, Special Branch, sat around the small conference table.

"Detective Chief Inspector Ross has something for us," said the brigadier, drawing himself up a bit more nearly erect as he opened the meeting. "It's unlikely to have any bearing on the Cromwell thing, I imagine; but I called you in for the few minutes his report will take, Duncan, in the thought that there is a possibility."

"I am interested in any possibility, sir," said Glynbourne. "At the moment, we are living on possibility."

The brigadier nodded at Ross, who began his report: "As you all know, a highly sophisticated tiny listening device with radio transmitter, positively identified as a bit of KGB equipment, was found in

London last week. It was in a flat that had been occupied by one
Malcolm Worth, late vice-president for continental operations of
Trafalgar Trading Company. In consequence we began looking into
the history and operations of that company and of its vice-president
for continental operations. The first thing that struck us was that Malcolm Worth had died rather suddenly and in rather odd circumstances. He was drunk apparently and stumbled off a station platform,
into the path of an oncoming train. The autopsy established that he
had been drinking heavily, and the incident was treated by Metro-
politan Police as a simple accident. If, however, Mr. Worth was in
some mysterious way involved in KGB activities, the simple accident
may well have been murder."

Interrupted by a knock on the door, Chief Inspector Ross paused
while a secretary brought in a tray with teapot and cups.

"We began to look at his business associates," Ross continued when
the door was securely closed behind the departing secretary.
"Trafalgar Trading is a legitimate enterprise, for all we can tell. Its
other officers are a variety of types. It employs two score people and
does a thriving business in the export-import trade. It would be difficult to say we found anything particularly mysterious about any aspect
of the operation."

"It would be a service to us, Chief Inspector," said the brigadier, "if
you told us what *is* mysterious, instead of what's not."

"Very well. We've concentrated on the question of how Worth happened to be in possession of a piece of KGB equipment. According to
the personnel at Trafalgar Trading, Worth had not been out of the
country during the past year. We must suppose, then, that someone
brought it to him. If so, who? Are not the company's salesmen as
likely suspects as any? In the absence of others, we looked at those
salesmen. A number of them travel extensively. Five, in fact, do. Of
those five, two are here in London now. We've checked them rather
thoroughly and interrogated them. Three are away. One, Galbraith,
is in Germany. Another, O'Carnahan, is in Spain. They've been in

frequent contact with the London office. The company knows where they are, what hotels; it can telephone them or send them mail."

"The third one, then," the Brigadier interrupted.

"As to the third one," said the chief inspector, "he is a young man named Betancourt. He is supposed to be in Greece. The company thinks he is. His mother thinks he is. But he isn't. The Greek government insists no David Betancourt has entered the country. What is more, none of the airlines that fly from London to Greece carried a David Betancourt there in the past two weeks."

"Betancourt . . ." repeated the brigadier. "The name is somehow familiar."

"Yes, sir. He's an Argentine, the son of the Argentine admiral who committed suicide after the Falklands War. He was granted permanent residence in the United Kingdom. One of your men, Fogg, contacted him two years ago and asked him to consider doing some work for MI5. Betancourt declined. It's on record, of course. The point is, it would appear that at the moment this chap Betancourt is missing."

"Young man, hmm?" asked Glynbourne.

"Yes, sir. Twenty-eight. Good-looking young fellow, according to the secretaries at Trafalgar Trading. And something more. The gossip in the office is that he has enjoyed an intimate relationship with the secretary who served the late Malcolm Worth. Nina Blankenship. Miss Blankenship, it seems, is out of town, too. She is in Paris on a holiday tour. It's her first trip abroad, so far as anyone knows. It occurred to us that maybe Betancourt was in Paris with her. But he hasn't entered France either."

"Have you spoken with his mother?"

"We had a policewoman call, without identifying herself as such, and ask for David. Mrs. Betancourt said her son is on a business trip to Greece. She had not heard from him, she said, and didn't have an address for him."

"Señora Betancourt . . ." mused Colonel Harcourt.

"Perhaps," said Ross. "But she is English, of a Kentish family. She has spent relatively little time in the Argentine, actually—I mean, considering that she was married to an Argentine admiral."

"Do you have a photograph of David Betancourt?" asked Major Glynbourne.

"Two," said Chief Inspector Ross. "Both rather old, I'm afraid."

"I shall want to see them," said Glynbourne.

"Since we bring nothing into this conference room, I—" The chief inspector shrugged. "But I have them in my office, and of course you are welcome to them."

"What of Miss Blankenship?" asked the brigadier. "What do we know of her?"

"Very little," said the chief inspector. "She's from Leeds, apparently. We are making inquiry there, for her family, her education, and so on."

"I should like to be informed of everything you learn, as quickly as you learn it," said Glynbourne.

"Relevant, you think, Duncan?" asked the brigadier.

"I'll know more when I've seen the pictures of Betancourt. Also, Brigadier, have you looked in the computer files yet? When you do, you'll see that this young man had a contact with a known KGB agent some two years ago. I've known that for some time, but this gives the fact a new significance."

When Major Glynbourne emerged from the meeting, a secretary gave him a message that he should see Sergeant Major Tate immediately on an urgent matter. He returned to his own office to find the sergeant major waiting.

"The French have been on the line twice. They're asking you to be in Paris for an evening meeting. Monsignor Périgord endorses their request. I've taken the liberty of arranging transport. A small RAF jet is ready to fly you to Le Bourget."

"Can you come with me, Sergeant Major?"

"I've taken the liberty of packing kits for both of us, sir. Also of telephoning Miss Glynbourne to advise her you will not be at home for dinner. I believe there is time, sir, for a stop by your flat on our way to the airport."

The meeting, opening at six o'clock, was held in a small conference room at the Préfecture de Police. Present were Colonel Aaron Cau, Major André Bonnac, and Bonnac's assistant Jacques Lépine, for GIGN; Maurice Fournier, directeur de police judiciaire; Monsignor Périgord; Major Duncan Glynbourne and Sergeant Major Bryan Tate; Galeazzo Castellano; and Theodorus Companjen from Interpol. Monsignor Périgord was asked to take the seat at the head of the table and preside over the meeting.

"We followed through on your suggestion, Major Glynbourne," said the monsignor, "and reports have begun to come in from the credit-card companies. Enough have arrived that we have something to work with. It is urgent, I suggest, that we set to work on the names these reports contain. I will ask Interpol to check its files on each of these names, and I will ask that we have a report within two hours after we adjourn this meeting."

"You will have it," said Companjen. "Assuming, that is, there are not too many names . . ."

Monsignor Périgord continued. "We asked all of you to be present because we hope one or more of these names may mean something to you—something more than we can learn from a simple computer check."

He paused to open a file folder.

"These are the reports, copies for each of you. Note, please, what they contain. So far, American Express, Barclay, and MasterCard have given us reports from searches in their central files. We are advised that others will be reporting during the night and in the morning. I might say that the cooperation these companies have given us has been most gratifying."

The conferees frowned over their copies of the reports.

"Look at Barclay first," said the monsignor. "They did an excellent

job. Their computers first isolated all charges incurred by their cardholders in the cities of Assisi and Perugia from October 1 to November 15, 1983, then all from Toledo in February 1984, then all from
Milan in May and June 1984, then all from London in August 1984.
This created four lists of accounts, each containing thousands of
numbers. Then they used their computers to match those lists. What
they have given us is exactly what we asked for—a list of their cardholders who used their cards in any three of the designated cities during the designated time frames. As you can see, the list contains only
twenty-three names, all but six of them English."

"I recognize none of these," said Major Glynbourne.

"Very well," said Monsignor Périgord. "Turn to American Express."

Major Glynbourne began to run his finger down the list of eighty-
one names provided by American Express.

ABBOT, CHARLES G.—New York City
ALEXANDER, WILLIAM F.—Denver, Colorado
ANTZ, EUGEN W.—Munich
ARTIZZIO, G. J.—Milan
BARTLETT, DONALD A.—Marietta, Ohio
BETANCOURT, DAVID T.—London

"Allow me to interrupt," said Major Glynbourne. "I should like to
ask another question of American Express. I'd like an answer as
quickly as possible. This name—" He tapped his finger on the list.
"David Betancourt. You remember the name? He's one of the people
who were observed talking to Colonel Olshanskii at the Mexican Embassy in October 1982. I'd like to know where and when he last used
his American Express card."

"Your memory is astounding, Major," said Bonnac. "Anyway, you
want someone to telephone now?"

"Yes, please," said Glynbourne. "What is more, I am going to ask
Sergeant Major Tate to telephone London and arrange for some pho-

tographs to be transmitted by wireless. Can someone assist him with that?"

"Yes, of course," said Bonnac. "Jacques . . ."

Sergeant Major Tate and Jacques Lépine left the room. The others went on scanning the lists.

"Finally," continued Directeur Fournier, "we have a list of eighteen names from MasterCard."

"While we waited for you to arrive from London, Major Glynbourne, and for you to arrive from Milan, Signor Castellano," said Monsignor Périgord, "we proceeded to run all these names through the computerized files of Sûreté and through the shared files. Several of these credit-card holders produce hits in the computer files. Your Mr. Betancourt"—he paused and nodded to Glynbourne—"is the subject of two entries, as you recall. They are ones we have already seen. We thought them not very suggestive when we looked at them before, but now . . ."

"We should perhaps revise our judgment," said Major Glynbourne.

Bonnac nodded and went on. "The others, six men, three women, are the subjects of entries not much more suggestive. One of them, the Australian Grenville, has been in a Belgian prison since July. The Swiss woman on the American Express list—Corinne Levander—is the bed partner of the Egyptian minister of the interior whenever he visits Europe; otherwise there would be no reason for a dossier on her. And so on. We have activated all the dossiers and are investigating the present whereabouts of all these people."

"I can relieve you of the necessity of investigating one," said Galeazzo Castellano. "Cesare Santellini is dead. Shot his veins full of his own merchandise and expired of the overdose."

"*Quel dommage,*" remarked Directeur Fournier.

"I am going to ask you to do something more, Directeur," said Major Glynbourne. "An English subject named Nina Blankenship is supposed to be in Paris. Traveling as part of a tour group. I should like to know if she is indeed in Paris."

The directeur nodded. He picked up a telephone and gave the necessary order.

"Some pieces are beginning to fit together," said Glynbourne to Monsignor Périgord.

"Betancourt?"

Major Glynbourne nodded.

Two hours later, after a break for dinner—a modest meal served to them at their conference table—they concluded that David Betancourt was Oliver Cromwell.

The pictures were not the most convincing evidence. The handsome young face in the photographs transmitted by microwave facsimile equipment from London did not match the airbrush-debearded and computer-enhanced photograph they had been using for Oliver Cromwell since DGSE photographed a man meeting with Olshanskii in the park along the Champs Elysées. The pictures transmitted from London were a passport photo and a picture published by a London newspaper at the time of Admiral Betancourt's suicide—Captain David Betancourt escorting Lady Lynda Bedillion to an Argentine embassy ball.

"American Express says the last activity on the David Betancourt card was a charge of ninety-five pounds for dinner at Wheelers Sovereign, a Mayfair restaurant, on October first," Sergeant Major Tate reported. "No charges have come through since then."

"The day he bought the Stephanotis at House of Floris," said Major Glynbourne. "He was supposed to have left for Greece on October second."

"I took the liberty," said the sergeant major, "of initiating a further inquiry whilst on the telephone to London. Fortunately, our people there had begun already, without my initiating it. I can give you some interesting additional information about Mr. David Betancourt."

"By all means do," said Monsignor Périgord. He spoke English to the sergeant major, who had demonstrated total incapacity for French.

"Very well, sir. Though the young man is an Argentine citizen, he is the son of an Englishwoman and was educated in English schools in the Argentine and then at Cambridge. As an Argentine army captain, he was allowed to study at Sandhurst for a time and after that was attached to the Coldstream Guards for training in counter-insurgency tactics. His training particularly included"—the sergeant major paused for effect—"instruction in the use of explosives by insurgents and terrorists."

"My God, we taught him ourselves," said Glynbourne.

"I'm afraid we did," said Sergeant Major Tate. "During his service with the Coldstream Guards, Mr. Betancourt was involved in something of a dustup on a street in Belfast. It seems some IRA thugs charged a squad of soldiers, and Mr. Betancourt drew his service revolver and killed one of them."

"You kept that secret well," said Monsignor Périgord to Major Glynbourne.

"This is the first I heard of it," said Glynbourne.

"Continuing," said the sergeant major, "Mr. Betancourt is known to be fluent in French as well as in English and Spanish. He speaks passable German and Italian as well. He has been employed by Trafalgar Trading Company for somewhat less than two years, during which time he has traveled extensively for the company on the Continent and in Great Britain. It is the company who obtained the credit card for him."

"His business travel could account for his having been in Toledo, Assisi, and Milan at the significant times," said Galeazzo Castellano. "We must keep an open mind, consider all alternatives."

"Coincidence—" said Major Glynbourne.

Bonnac interrupted. "No. Not coincidence," he said in a surly tone. "American Express was good enough, not only to report as we asked, but to list the charges. Betancourt checked out of his hotel in Perugia the very day of the blast at Assisi. He ate at Scoffone Bottega in Milan the night before the destruction of *The Last Supper*. Not coincidence. Not coincidence, Major."

"Can you guess whether he dined alone or with a guest?" asked the monsignor.

"The bill was enough to have covered dinner for Margherita Catania," said Bonnac.

"Cheeky bastard," muttered Glynbourne.

"He was confident of his incognito," said the monsignor.

"And totally amoral," said Glynbourne. "Dinner for the girl he was about to kill."

"Actually," said the monsignor, "we don't know that."

"We know it of Sohaila Mohmand," said Glynbourne. "And of her father. He treated them to pleasant dinners shortly before he killed them. He's a cold-blooded professional killer."

"And at large," said Directeur Fournier. "We have increased security at some of our most cherished religious monuments—Sainte Chappelle, Notre Dame, Chartres, Rheims—and at secular ones as well. But—"

"Fanatics," Bonnac interrupted. "Terrorists. I need hardly confess to this group that we have infiltrated virtually every terrorist organization that tries to function in France. Our operatives are being pressed to report any hint they get that Oliver Cromwell has contacted anyone in any of these organizations. So far—" He shrugged. "Nothing."

"It is by no means certain he will strike next in France," said Galeazzo Castellano. "We have suffered him twice in Italy already, but we have plenty of other monuments he might choose to destroy."

"Let us remember," said Monsignor Périgord, "that his last target, in London, was a *man*, not a monument. He is capable of political assassination as well as attacks on great monuments of civilization."

"Our chances of finding him are much improved by knowing who he is," said Major Glynbourne.

"If we have not erred," said Directeur Fournier.

"The photographs of David Betancourt are being carried this evening to the shopgirls from the House of Floris," said Sergeant Major Tate. "Also, to Soho. If any question remains, it should be settled within hours."

"Still," insisted Directeur Fournier, "we do not know where he is and what he plans to do *next*. I find it most ominous that he has disappeared. It could mean many things, but most likely it indicates that he is about to perpetrate another outrage."

"I must agree," said Monsignor Périgord. "One shudders to think what it might be."

"Unless we find him first," muttered Bonnac.

"*Merde!*" grunted Bonnac as soon as the door had closed and the three of them—himself, Colonel Cau, and Lépine—were inside the colonel's office. He slammed a fist down on the colonel's desk. "Betancourt! Damn!"

Colonel Cau took a flask of brandy from his desk and poured a swallow into each of three small glasses. "The files?" he asked calmly as he took a sip.

"There's nothing in the files," said Bonnac. "I cleaned the files a long time ago—what little mention there was. Nothing recent has been mentioned, of course."

"Jacques," said the colonel to Lépine. "Do you know what we're talking about?"

Lépine shook his head.

The colonel nodded at Bonnac. "Perhaps the time has come to tell Jacques our little secret," he said.

Bonnac sighed and nodded. "I need hardly tell you that Monsieur le Président de la République—the *temporary* head of our government, let us hope—places his socialist philosophy ahead of every consideration of national security. If he'd had his way, we would have disbanded all our security forces and relied on fraternal solidarity between the French socialists and the Russian communists to restrain the KGB. As it was, we were reduced, reorganized, and deprived of money."

Colonel Cau stroked his black mustache with the index finger of his right hand. "Specifically and less emotionally stated, Monsieur Mitterand deprived us of the secret funds we have always used to—"

"Corrupt people," said Lépine blandly, tossing back his brandy.

The colonel's brows rose indignantly, then settled. He nodded. "Something like that," he agreed. "In short, we've always had a fund we could use to buy whatever we thought was necessary—without, of course, ever having to report what we spent it for."

"I suppose," said Bonnac with a faint, wry smile, "we have bought a ton of heroin since I've been involved—plus a regiment of whores."

"Or, more to the point, file clerks, telephone operators, messengers, merchants, teachers, priests, physicians . . ." chuckled Colonel Cau.

"And that fool Mitterand—"

"Expects us to account for every sou we spend," said the colonel, pushing the flask across his desk to offer more brandy. "Democracy. Accountability."

"And Betancourt . . ." said Lépine. "What does it have to do with him?"

Bonnac sighed. "Exocets," he said. "Betancourt's father was a political admiral of the Argentine navy. Not much of a military man, but smart enough to know that Exocet missiles were his navy's only chance against the British fleet. They almost defeated the British, too. I mean, the Exocets did—not the Argentines."

"I see," said Lépine. "The problem was to sell Exocets to the Argentines without the British—or, probably more important, the Americans—knowing about it. Export licenses . . . transport . . . Oh, I can see a thousand problems."

"Including corruption," said the colonel. "Remember, we were dealing with a Latin American government. But it was in the national interest to sell the Exocets. Naturally, our group became involved. We are"—he paused to let a little smile curl his pursed lips—"the experts in solving problems."

"It was a complicated deal," said Bonnac. "In the end, forty million francs—in gold, let me emphasize—were deposited in Geneva. In other words, Argentina paid forty million francs more than the normal price of the Exocets. And that money, or most of it, is the money we use in place of the fund that Monsieur le Président de la

République denies us. None of it has gone into our pockets, you understand. It is how we are able to—"

"Yes," said Lépine briskly. "I understand."

"But there is a problem," said Colonel Cau. "Admiral Betancourt was neither an honest man nor a fool. Ten percent of all such money was to be his. He wanted it kept with ours, in Switzerland, and made available to him through us. A fine cover for him, of course. He anticipated trouble in Argentina and specified that his son should be able to draw on the fund in the event he himself was prevented from doing so. David Betancourt has drawn on it twice: once shortly after his father's death, to the extent of one hundred thousand francs, and once recently, for another hundred thousand."

"Why hasn't he taken out his whole four million?" asked Lépine.

"Apparently his father didn't tell him how much there is, only that he could call on us for financial help if he needed it," said Bonnac. "One suspects the admiral didn't trust his son entirely."

"The fact is," said Colonel Cau, "his father didn't know how much there was. It was a complex deal, and he died without finding out just how much more than the price of the missiles his government had paid. Anyway, this makes the son—"

"A blackmailer," said Lépine. "In the circumstances, it would be difficult to resist his demand for even more than his father's share."

"Exactly," said Colonel Cau. "We had decided to regard him as a blackmailer if ever he asked for a third payment. And then . . ."

"We would have nullified him," said Bonnac.

"But if he is Oliver Cromwell—"

"The necessity is absolute," said Bonnac coldly. "And urgent. The Englishman and the priest talk about taking him alive." He shook his head. "If he were taken alive and talked—and Président Mitterand learned about the fund in Geneva . . . Well, I need hardly tell you. It is not to be contemplated. Betancourt must not be taken alive."

Lépine allowed himself to grin. "If one had the slightest conscience about the matter, the fact that he is Oliver Cromwell—"

"Eliminates any ambiguity," said Colonel Cau.

16

DETECTIVE CHIEF SUPERINTENDENT William Dole placed great stock in punctuality, to the point, actually, that many people considered him something of a bore on the subject. To be absolutely certain of being on time for his appointment at Kensington Palace, he had left Scotland Yard a quarter of an hour before anyone else would have. He was, of course, early, as he very often was. He offered to sit and wait, but the equerry insisted on sending up word that he had arrived, and shortly the Prince of Wales entered the room and reached for his hand.

"Good morning, sir," said the chief superintendent. "I hope I've not inconvenienced you by showing up early."

"Not in the least, Chief Superintendent," said the prince with a warm smile. He wore a dark-gray double-breasted suit, slender of cut, with narrow lapels. He was thin. He looked as if he had lost a couple of stone of weight in the past two or three months. He sat down in a brocaded armchair and suggested by a gesture that the chief superintendent sit on the sofa. "I've long since learned to knot my necktie in five seconds and skip down the stairs four at a time. Goes with the job."

Charles, Prince of Wales, invariably surprised Chief Superintendent Dole—though he had seen him countless times and had conferred with him on a score of other occasions—not just by his

251

affability but also his sharp sense of humor. The chief superintendent carried in mind an image of a Prince of Wales, and when the reality did not coincide with his image, it muddled him for an instant. He blushed, and his lips fluttered.

"I've ordered coffee brought. I trust you'll join me in some?"

"With pleasure, sir."

"Good. But let us go ahead. What have you come to tell me?"

"I spent half a day with Commissaire Trillat in Paris," said Chief Superintendent Dole. "The security arrangements are quite elaborate. I think we have little to be concerned about."

The prince nodded. "My only question is whether or not the princess should go with me," he said.

"I have two concerns," said the chief superintendent. "One is that we must leave principal responsibility for your security to the French."

"Is that indeed a concern?" the prince asked. "The French police have powers we deny ours."

"It is the lesser of my two concerns, sir. The other is that you will be with the president of France. It is unlikely anyone would try to harm you. On the other hand, there are terrorists about who think they have good cause to assassinate the president of France."

"Which means, Chief Superintendent, that the French security will be exceptionally tight."

"Yes, sir. It means that."

"So factors balance out, do they not, on the side of our going forward with the announced plans?"

"That is Special Branch's recommendation, sir."

"Unless, then, you learn of some defect in their procedures, or some special threat arises, we will go to France on Monday morning, my wife and I. Agreed?"

"Agreed, sir."

"Then let us enjoy our coffee, which should arrive in a moment. Tell me, Chief Superintendent, is there any new development in the matter of this fellow Oliver Cromwell?"

*   *   *

David and Donegal sat on the lawn chairs in one of the flats above the former print shop in St. Denis. The rest of the Irish leaned on the windowsills or sat on the floor.

"Let me explain how this is going to work," said David. "The BBC will have three vans on the Place du Parvis, just outside the west façade of the cathedral. One van, the biggest, will be their command center, with the directors' consoles inside. One of the two smaller ones carries their microwave transmitter, which will send audio and video transmissions to a relay antenna on top of the Eiffel Tower. You can distinguish that van by the dish antenna on top. The third van carries the cameramen and their equipment. That's the one we're interested in.

"The crew," he went on, "will arrive on Saturday morning. They have two advance men in town now, staying at the Hotel Suède. The rest will come over on the ferry, bringing the vans. They will stay outside of Paris, at Varennes. Bobby . . . I'll leave it up to you to assign your people. Every member of that crew must be watched from the time they arrive. They will come in and do a run-through, meet with the French security men, check the spots where their cameras are to be. It is important for us to watch that as closely as we can, but I need hardly tell you what a disaster it would be if they were to discover they are being watched. Aside from that, it is essential for us to know if any member of the crew has any conspicuous physical attribute the French security men might notice and might be looking for on Monday morning. Is anyone obese, bald, or in any way crippled? How many wear beards?"

"How many are women," suggested Eileen.

"Exactly," said David. He grinned at the young men. "One or more of you may have to dress as a girl on Monday morning."

"Paul can handle that," said Bobby.

"Notice what they wear," David went on. "Do any of them seem to dress in any eccentric way? You can carry no weapons. You will have to pass through metal detectors on your way into the cathedral."

"What about the cameras?" asked Paul. "Can we be certain they won't open them up and look inside?"

"We don't really care," said David. "The way the plastique will be packed in the cameras, no one will detect it unless he's a technician. So far as explosives-sniffing dogs are concerned, the charges will be sealed in vinyl packages, and the packages will have been smeared with garlic just before we leave for Notre Dame. What is more, no one who is to go into the cathedral will have touched any plastique. I am the only one who is going to touch it. When you get your hands on the cameras, you can load the charges and detonators into the cases—as we rehearsed back in Ireland—without touching even the vinyl packages."

"The radio-triggered detonators," said Bobby Donegal. "Show us how they work."

David nodded. "Okay. These are American, as I told you they would be. They are powerful and highly sophisticated. They transmit a pulsed signal that can be set to pulse at one-eighth-second, quarter-second, half-second, or full-second intervals. There are ten possible UHF radio frequencies, ten possible audio frequencies. We set the receivers to a pulse interval, a UHF frequency, and an audio frequency. They are precisely filtered. Once they are set, no other combination will activate them. You need have no concern about an accidental detonation. The transmitter will be set to the same combination. It will send the only signal to which the receiver will react. Look, I'll demonstrate . . ."

"There it is again," said Lépine. "Three different combinations this time."

"From the same direction? Northeast?" asked Bonnac.

"Yes. If we had other receivers equipped to accept so large a variety of combinations, we could easily triangulate. Unfortunately . . ."

"Unfortunately, the United States manufactured more than four hundred of these transmitters and more than two thousand receivers for them. Unfortunately, too, they have lost at least twenty of them here and there in Lebanon and Central America."

"Twenty," said Lépine. "Only twenty?"

"Yes," said Bonnac. "And you are thinking, if someone has one of them, he must be a pretty important fellow."

"What I was wondering, actually, is whether or not Betancourt was shown one of them when he was taking his counter-insurgency training with the British army."

"Find out, will you? Call Glynbourne. Also, call Captain Sheridan at the Pentagon. Tell him we've picked up three more signals from an MV–2357. See what he has to say."

"In the morning," said Major Glynbourne to his daughter. "Very early in the morning, in fact. And I shall be gone through the weekend. Back in time for dinner Monday evening, I should think. In the meantime, I shall be stopping at the Paris Hilton of all places. Not my choice of hotels, but it's what they got me."

"Poor man," she said. "Luxury can be a burden, I suppose."

They were at dinner in their flat in Kensington: the major, his daughter Betty, his father and mother, and Katrina.

"A weekend in Paris," his father grumbled good-naturedly. "At the cost of the rate-payers. When you come back, you can tell us about all the naked girls."

"I shall be spending all my time conferring with French policemen," said the major. "Struggling to understand their English or to think of some way to express myself in French. And they do smell like garlic. They really do."

"We shall see more of you when you've settled this Oliver Cromwell business," said Betty. "That's my personal reason for wanting him captured. That and being able to see you finish a dinner without being summoned urgently to your office and leaving the food on the table."

"I'm sure the Queen would want you to finish your dinners, Duncan," his mother said with a small grin and a twinkle in her eye. "You can't, after all, carry on Her Majesty's business very effectively on an empty stomach."

He was able to finish this dinner. He had left word at the office that he would return by eight and that he was not to be called except in emergency. Captain Fenwick and Sergeant Major Tate were waiting for him.

"It's beginning to fall together," said Fenwick. "I think we've happened upon a KGB operation. A small one, apparently, and already broken up, very likely. Nevertheless—"

"Trafalgar Trading?" asked Glynbourne.

"Yes. Nina Blankenship is the name of a child born in Leeds in 1946. Died in 1948. Almost certainly the woman we know as Nina Blankenship assumed her identity. It's the usual thing—not difficult, as we know. For the moment we have no idea, of course, who the false Nina Blankenship is. She's in Paris. I'm not prepared to assume she's KGB, or indeed anything else; but we do know one thing for certain—she is not Nina Blankenship."

"Have you notified Bonnac?"

"Not yet," said Captain Fenwick. "Sergeant Major . . ."

"We've found out something else," said Sergeant Major Tate. "I took the photographs of George Jean Lechevalier to the Trafalgar Trading Company offices this afternoon. The personnel there identified him as a man who called at the office from time to time. He called on Malcolm Worth, but he also visited Nina Blankenship. In fact, it was noticed that sometimes Nina Blankenship met with Lechevalier in Worth's office, in Worth's absence. Miss Blankenship, it seems, has been the subject of a great deal of gossip: that she enjoyed a meretricious relationship with Malcolm Worth, with David Betancourt, and with George Jean Lechevalier."

"And that may be all it was," said Major Glynbourne. "A little funny business on the office couch."

"Except for her false identity," said Captain Fenwick.

"Yes. Except for that."

"We had a quick audit run on some of the books of account of Trafalgar Trading," said Captain Fenwick. "It seems that David Betancourt was paid commissions on sales he did not make. For example, he was credited in July with having sold thirty-five hundred pounds worth of wines and spirits to the Albany Hotel in Birmingham, twenty-three hundred pounds worth to the Leofric in Coventry, and twelve hundred pounds worth to the Falcon in Stratford. Three telephone calls proved he sold none of these orders. I'm sure further inquiry will extend the pattern."

"And there is no question now but that David Betancourt is Oliver Cromwell," said Glynbourne.

"None whatever," said the sergeant major. "The photographs of David Betancourt—all we could find, the old passport photos and some more recent ones—were shown to the shopgirls at House of Floris and to the various people in Soho. David Betancourt was Friederich Reitlinger. He was also the purchaser of Stephanotis."

"Stephanotis," mused Glynbourne. "I wonder who it was for."

"I suspect his mother, sir," said Sergeant Major Tate.

"Indeed . . ."

"She is English," said the sergeant major quickly. "English ladies favor the scent."

"Has anyone spoken with the lady?" asked Glynbourne.

"Not directly," said Captain Fenwick. "We are advised she is a highly respectable lady, of a fine Kentish family. We also are given to understand that the shock of her husband's suicide—after he had murdered her daughter and her son's fiancée—reduced the lady to something of a cipher. She takes long walks, sits in the parks and feeds the pigeons, and plays endless games of cards with widowed ladies older than herself. On the indirect contact we did make, she said her son is in Greece. It is most likely she believes it."

"Very well. Leave it at that for the moment. I think I had best have a telephone conversation with Bonnac. Let's see if we can raise him."

*   *   *

On Wednesday night, October 10, there occurred one of those co-
incidences that so often happen in human affairs, which might have
been of immense significance but as it turned out was not. Evelyne
Clayeux, having spent the evening in her usual hotel and having
earned only one fee, left about eleven and walked two blocks to the
Windsor Reynolds. There, she nodded to the concierge and sat down
in a chair near the old cage elevator—where, a few minutes later, she
was seen by a guest from the fourth floor: Monsieur Albert Mosler,
Bobby Donegal. He called down a few minutes later and asked the
concierge to send her up. Evelyne went up and spent an hour with
him. She earned five hundred francs. It was a forgettable experience
for both of them—he was satisfied, no more, with the pretty, unimaginative, French girl who stank faintly of sweat; she was pleased with
her money and glad to leave the room of the big, muscular, half-
drunk Irishman. The police agent who was watching her saw no significance in her visit to Albert Mosler.

André Bonnac had chosen Wednesday for an evening away from
his office. He dined with Marie-Luise—Violette—in an Italian restaurant in the Palais-Royal Quarter and then accompanied her to the
Crazy Horse to see the first show. He drank two whiskies and watched
Marie-Luise perform as a member of the chorus, wearing nothing but
a pair of hip-high black-vinyl boots and a wild wig—to the whistling,
shouting approval of the tourists who made up almost all of the club's
clientèle.

At midnight he checked with his office and found that Major Glynbourne had tried several times during the evening to reach him by
telephone and, failing that, had sent a long cable, which was waiting
on his desk. He went to the office to read it.

THE FOLLOWING ESTABLISHED BY FIRM EVIDENCE—
    ONE. NINA BLANKENSHIP IS AN ASSUMED IDENTITY. TRUE
IDENTITY NOT KNOWN. SHE IS IN PARIS AS PART OF TOUR
GROUP STAYING AT HOTEL EDOUARD VII.

TWO. GEORGE JEAN LECHEVALIER HAS BEEN PERIODIC VIS-
ITOR AT OFFICES OF TRAFALGAR TRADING, DURING WHICH VIS-
ITS HE HAS HAD PRIVATE MEETINGS WITH NINA BLANKENSHIP.
  THREE. DAVID BETANCOURT CONFIRMED AS OLIVER CROM-
WELL BY SEVERAL INDEPENDENT WITNESSES. ADDITIONAL
PHOTOS WIRED TONIGHT. TRAFALGAR HAS PAID BETANCOURT
COMMISSIONS ON SALES NEVER MADE, SUGGESTING HIS SER-
VICES TO TRAFALGAR WERE FOR OTHER DUTIES.
  FOUR. BETANCOURT NOT INTRODUCED TO AMERICAN RADIO
DETONATOR DURING GUARDS TRAINING.
  WILL TRY TO REACH YOU BY TELEPHONE IN MORNING FROM
PARIS HILTON WHERE I WILL BE STAYING UNTIL AFTER 15TH.
                                                 GLYNBOURNE

"I do not want that woman arrested," Bonnac said into the telephone, speaking to the night duty officer at DGSE. "On the other
hand, she is not to be allowed to elude surveillance. Put as many
people on her as you need. Photograph anyone she talks to. Be sure
everyone who follows her has studied the pictures of David Betancourt. If she leads anyone to him, he is to be captured if possible,
killed if not. Is that clear? If Betancourt is identified, he is not to be
allowed, in any circumstances, to get away."

"Understood, sir," said the crisp voice on the other end of the line.

"Something more. Get in touch with Lieutenant Sagan. Lucien
Trebonzi is to be brought to Paris tomorrow."

On Thursday morning Nina Stepanova Samusev left the Hotel
Edouard VII at nine-thirty and boarded a tour bus that was to take her
group to Versailles. Dressed in black slacks, a gray silk blouse, and a
loose, bulky cableknit cardigan, she impressed the three DGSE
agents, two men and a woman, assigned to follow her, as an interesting, attractive woman. She carried a Kodak disc camera on a nylon
cord around her neck and a fat leather purse on a strap over her
shoulder. As she boarded the bus, she chatted gaily with some of her
fellow tourists. To the DGSE agents she seemed an unlikely threat to
the national security of France.

What they failed to reckon with was that Nina Stepanova Samusev had been trained in Moscow, not just to speak flawless working-class English and to blend into the London scene as a dutiful secretary in an export-import firm, but also—among many other things—to spot and elude surveillance. She was alert here in Paris as the day approached for the blast at Notre Dame. The tour stopped first at the Malmaison Château, to allow the English tourists to see the one-time home of Napoleon and Josephine. Before they left Malmaison, she had decided that the three French people who followed the tour but were not of it were police agents. At Versailles she eluded them. For someone else it would have been difficult. For her it was not. The crowds were her ally.

She did something very dangerous. She went to the Royal Monceau, the hotel where David and Emily were staying. He was out, so she sat in the lobby and waited. He came in, alone, at four-thirty. Their eyes met. She got up and left. He followed her at a distance, looking for someone else following her. No one was. She went into a wine bar and took a table. He went in and sat with her.

"I am being followed, David," she told him. "I am reasonably sure of it. I have escaped them this time, but I won't be able to always. You must regard me as no longer a part of the operation. I can't make any further contact with you."

"This one was dangerous enough," he said.

"No. I made sure. But now that they know I can do it, they will be much more careful."

"What will you do?"

"What can I do? I'll play my role as English tourist. I'll go back to London. But I want you to do something for me."

He nodded.

"My contact," she said. "I want him to know what's happened. He will have to be your contact from now on. I want him to send the word back, so they will arrange my escape."

"Of course."

"His name is Vasili Ivanovich Litvinko, known in the West as

George Jean Lechevalier. I've written down two addresses and two telephone numbers. You must memorize those and destroy my note before we leave here. Let him take over for me. His cover is perfect. It has not been penetrated."

"But you think yours has been?"

"I don't know why they are following me, David. It has to be because something has gone wrong in London. Malcolm Worth did not die accidentally, you know. I suppose you guessed that. Probably I made a mistake in leaving London so soon after Malcolm's death. Maybe they think I had something to do with his death and have come to Paris to escape. Perhaps they think I am here spending money I took from him."

"Then maybe they think I had something to do with it," said David. "I worked for him, too. It was damn clumsy of them to kill him just before we—"

"David."

"What, Nina?"

"Are you coming to the Soviet Union?"

"I'm beginning to wonder if either of us is going to make it to the Soviet Union."

"But will you try to come?"

David drew a breath. He nodded. "Yes, Nina. I will try."

"I haven't talked to you about living in a socialist state. It's a much better life than anyone has in the West. And Russia is so beautiful. Besides . . . I love you, David."

"I am honored by that, Nina. I will see you in Moscow if it's any way possible."

He walked to the Franklin D. Roosevelt Métro station and placed his call from a public telephone. The Soviet embassy said Counsellor Olshanskii was unavailable, but he told the curt man on the line to tell the counselor his bookseller was calling.

"Are you insane?" Olshanskii demanded. "This line—"

"Sam is being followed," said David. "Sam is no longer a part of things."

Olshanskii was silent for a moment. "Understood. Do you want to cancel?"

"Cancel Sam," said David.

"Understood. We'll take care of it."

As soon as Olshanskii put down the telephone, he pressed a button on his desk and a young woman entered his office—a solid young woman in a tight black skirt and a white-satin blouse. She was followed by a stern young man—another Russian, with bristly short hair and a pallid, pock-marked face. Their names were Irina Mikhailova Narishkina and Pavel Alekseivich Zotov.

"Nina Stepanova Samusev has been compromised," Olshanskii said to them. "She is being followed by French security agents."

"Then we will have to do what is necessary, Comrade Colonel."

"Succinctly put, Irina Mikhailova. But how? None of us dare go near her."

"We have but little time, I suppose," said the young man, Zotov.

"Very little, Pavel Alekseivich. Very little."

"I visited the hotel where she is staying, as you ordered, Comrade Colonel," said the young woman. "She sleeps in a third-floor room with an Englishwoman. If I were a security agent and wanted to be certain she did not leave the hotel during the night, I would have only to cover the lift and stairways. Unless she jumps out the window, she is not coming down otherwise. If their purpose is to keep her under surveillance, and not to protect her—"

"They would cover only the lift and stairways," said Olshanskii.

"Yes. And they won't care who goes up. Unless it's Betancourt."

"We dare not risk—"

"Comrade Colonel," interrupted Zotov. "I think I know how we can do it. A French addict. I have been keeping him on a string for some time, in the thought he might one day be useful. A vicious bastard. He's killed for his heroin before. If he is caught . . ." The

young man shrugged. "It is immaterial. He has no idea who I am. He
will do the job, and I will pay him with heroin. Only this heroin—"

"Will kill him."

Zotov nodded.

"What of the other woman in the room?" asked the young woman,
Narishkina.

"He'll have to kill them both to be sure he's killed the right one,"
said Zotov.

"Is there any way," asked Narishkina, "that your man could be
encouraged to spill a small amount of heroin in the room, so it would
appear he killed for that?"

"It is possible, Irina Mikhailova," said Zotov.

"'Sam' . . ." Bonnac repeated. "'Cancel Sam.' Who the devil were
they talking about?"

He was reading the transcript of the DGSE intercept of the telephone conversation between David Betancourt and Josef
Vladimirovich Olshanskii. As Olshanskii had tried to warn David, the
ordinary voice lines into the Soviet Embassy were tapped and constantly monitored.

"The voice, Major, was one we have heard only once before," said
Captain Max Guyonnet, the officer in charge of electronic surveillance of the embassy. "We took a voice print, digitalized it, and
put in on the computer. Olshanskii has received one other call from
this man, on September third."

"September—The day we photographed him talking with Oliver
Cromwell!"

Captain Guyonnet had not worked on the Cromwell problem and
did not understand the reference. "In the call on September third,"
he said, "we recorded the same voice, saying, 'Leonard must talk with
you. Under the chestnut trees.' Apparently Olshanskii knew the
meaning of that message."

"Now he calls himself 'the bookseller' and apparently asks

Olshanskii to kill someone. 'Sam' . . . Someone we are following. Someone we have just begun to follow . . ."

"Nina Blankenship," said Jacques Lépine.

"Yes," said Bonnac. "Entirely possible. Where is she now?"

Lépine glanced at his watch. "Boarding a bus about now, to go with her tour group to dinner. Our people are following."

"If they don't lose her again, like this morning's idiots."

"They've learned her skill in eluding surveillance," said Lépine. "I don't think they'll lose her."

"I'm tired of the game," said Bonnac. "Pick her up. Bring her in."

Just after midnight, Olshanskii's young man, Zotov, met the heroin addict in the Bois de Boulogne. He had waited there for an hour, coldly patient. He had hidden his packet of heroin in a crotch of a shrub, so it would not be found on him in the event a policeman came along and asked why he was loitering in the park at this hour. Separately, he had hidden a pocket-sized automatic. He didn't want that found on him either.

Over a period of several months he had become the addict's chief supplier. Usually he had sold the heroin to the man, taking the known Paris street price. The addict was chronically short of money, and twice the Russian had encouraged him to steal: once a Japanese ivory carving from a shop just off the Place Vendôme, another time a cashmere coat from a shop on Rue de Rivoli. These had been tests, of the man's willingness to commit crimes for his heroin, also of his ability to commit them. What was more, these tests fortified the Russian's incognito. The addict truly hadn't the slightest inkling that his supplier was anyone but a French dealer. He would have been astounded to learn that his heroin arrived in Paris in a diplomatic pouch.

He had given his name as Jean, and it was that name that the addict spoke as he approached in the darkness of the woods.

"Did you do it?"

"Yes. But there was only one woman in the room."

"Describe her."

"Tall. Thin. Wore eyeglasses. Uh, black hair."

The Russian drew a deep breath. "You are certain."

"Yes. There were clothes for another woman in the room, but only the one was there. I left the good stuff in the bathroom, as you said. Now. . ."

"There. In the bush."

The addict groped for his packet and found it. "Next week?" he asked.

"Yes. Next week."

It was after one when Zotov roused Olshanskii and told him the addict had killed the wrong woman.

"Where, then, was Nina Stepanova?"

Zotov shook his head.

"Arrested, very likely," said Olshanskii.

"Very likely."

"And under interrogation," said Olshanskii. "Which means that within a matter of hours, Betancourt will be compromised. And that in turn means we have no choice but to eliminate Betancourt."

"If we can find him in time," said Zotov.

Olshanskii nodded. "Only Nina Stepanova knew where to contact him."

"Litvinko?"

"Possibly. Initiate a contact with him."

Bonnac began with what he liked to call the easy interrogation. It was carried out in a large room not far from his office. The drama was craftily staged. The psychology had been carefully studied.

The room was in fact a busy office, with six desks where shifts of junior officers of DGSE worked twenty-four hours a day—writing reports, studying dossiers, talking endlessly on the telephones, and, at this hour, drinking coffee and munching wearily on whatever some clerk had fetched for them from the canteen. Clerks and secretaries moved through the room constantly. The air was heavy with cigarette smoke. Blackened, flickering fluorescent tubes shed a cold, shadowless light.

On the east side of the room, one of the desks faced a small wooden platform perhaps twenty centimeters high—not unlike the model's stand in an artist's studio. On that platform, in the glare of two floodlamps on flimsy stands, stood Nina: naked, flushed, and perspiring.

By the time Bonnac and Glynbourne arrived, she had stood there ten minutes. For ten minutes a young officer sitting at the desk had played a charade of preliminary interrogation, asking her name, age, place of birth, place of residence, nationality, reason for being in France, and so on—allowing himself to be interrupted by frequent telephone calls, during which he turned away and seemed to ignore her. Others in the room cooperated in the charade by making a show of working intently, yet being constantly distracted by the sight of the naked woman on the platform.

She was under no physical restraint. She could have stepped down from the platform, out of the bright light. But in the years Bonnac had used this technique, only one subject—that one a woman, too—had ever defied the order to stand there.

Bonnac strolled into the room, carrying a cup of coffee. He glanced at Nina, stopped to exchange words with a woman at a desk, then made his way across the room to the desk facing the platform. He picked up the paper on which the officer had been writing her answers to his questions and leaned casually against the desk, glancing back and forth between the paper and Nina as if he had to refresh his memory as to who she was and why she was here.

Glynbourne, his face grim, put his coffee down nearby and stared hard at the naked woman's face, trying to remember if he had ever seen her before. He could not recall that he ever had.

Bonnac spoke English. "Well. Miss Blankenship. Won't it be embarrassing if we've picked up the wrong lady?"

"You have," she said. Her voice was thin, from a dry throat and mouth. She stood hunched forward, holding her left hand over her crotch, her right arm across her breasts. "I am English."

"All right. We can be finished with this matter very quickly, if you will answer just one question." He put aside his cup of coffee and raised his chin to look directly into her face. "Where is David Betancourt?"

"I don't know anyone by that name."

"Oh, come now, Miss Blankenship. You are a secretary to the vice-president for continental operations of Trafalgar Trading Company, in London. David Betancourt is one of the principal salesmen for that company's continental sales branch. Of course you know him."

She closed her eyes and shook her head. "Oh. Yes. Of course I know him. I . . . was confused."

"That's understandable. But you did lie just then, didn't you?"

She nodded.

"You will get yourself in a lot of trouble that way. So let's start again. Where is David Betancourt?"

"I don't know."

"He left London on October second, on a business trip for the company. Where did he say he was going?"

"He didn't tell me. I didn't talk to him."

"What is your real name, Miss Blankenship?"

She shook her head. "I don't know what you mean. My name is Nina Blankenship."

Glynbourne's instinctive sympathy diminished with her every lie. "From Leeds," he said, stepping closer to the platform. "I'm afraid not," he said coldly. "Scotland Yard has checked that. A child named Nina Blankenship was born in 1946 and died in 1948. You assumed her identity in 1969. Why? What is your real name?"

She looked down and seemed to notice him for the first time: an Englishman, conspicuously an Englishman; and her eyes seemed to appeal to him. "Scotland Yard is wrong," she said tearfully. "I am Nina Blankenship."

"Who ordered the murder of Malcolm Worth?" asked Glynbourne.

"I don't know. He wasn't murdered. He died in an accident."

"He worked for the KGB," said Glynbourne firmly. "Scotland Yard found a KGB radio transmitter in his flat after he died. Did *you* order his death?"

"No. I know nothing of all this."

"David Betancourt set off the blast at Westminster Abbey in August," said Glynbourne. "A couple of months before, he destroyed *The Last Supper*. We're going to find him before he commits another such outrage. Does that suggest to you that we *will*, one way or another, have your answer to the question of where he is now?"

"I don't know. I swear to you, I don't know."

It had been a mistake to come to France. She had been told, years ago during her training, that she was fortunate in being sent to England, because if things went wrong there the worst the English would ever do to you was lock you away in a squalid prison. On the Continent, particularly in France, it would be different. She wondered, though. This Englishman in the handsome gray-tweed jacket and black trousers, though he was pale and sweating and evidently uncomfortable with what the Frenchman was probably going to do to her, was a cold, determined man, morally outraged by the things David had done, and in some ways more threatening than the Frenchman.

They took her to the cellar now. Weak and sick with fear, she stumbled between the guards who marched her naked through the corridors and took her down in the lift.

The brightly-lit room had something of the aspects of an operating theater. (Although she didn't know it, a doctor would in fact be present throughout the rest of her interrogation, and he had available the necessary equipment to monitor her vital functions, plus the oxygen and other materials he might need to revive her in the event she lost consciousness or suffered heart failure.) When she saw the frame on which she was to suffer, her knees buckled and her two guards had to grab her to keep her from falling.

It was a huge, braced wooden X, made of heavy oak fastened together with thick bolts and hung with the straps with which she would be fastened to it. It was suspended from the ceiling on chains that ran through pulleys, so it could be raised and lowered, hung vertically or horizontally or at an angle.

The frame hung vertically now, and they backed her against it and lowered it a little so that the crossing point of the X was at the level of her waist. They buckled a heavy leather belt around her waist, pinning her tightly to the frame. With other straps they bound her wrists and ankles to the four points of the X, then secured her even more tightly with straps around her elbows and knees. Finally, pulling on the chains, they raised the frame to a horizontal position.

She had been trained to expect them to use electricity, so it was no surprise when they began to attach wires to her body, screwing little clamps on her toes and on her fingers, pinching the flesh of her left nostril with the sharp teeth of a spring battery clamp, then, as she writhed from the pain, pinching two larger battery clamps on the tender flesh of her labia. Finally, as she had been told to expect, and had dreaded, they pushed two cold metal probes into her body, one into her anus and one into her vagina. She moaned, and she felt streams of sweat running on her skin.

They slanted the frame then, setting it on a forty-five-degree angle, so that she faced the electrical switching panel: half a dozen knife switches and two big black knobs. The two guards left the room, leaving her with the female attendant, who walked around her, checking the tightness of her straps, adjusting the clamps. Another man came in to attach additional wires to her body with sticky tape. (She did not guess that these were the electrodes for an electrocardiograph.)

With everything ready, they let her wait a few minutes. This, too, she had anticipated; she had been taught something of the psychology of interrogation and knew she would be forced to wait, thinking about the agony that was coming. The pain was bad already, from hanging in the tight straps.

At last they arrived: the Frenchman and the Englishman.

"I believe I forgot to introduce myself before," the Frenchman said. "My name is André Bonnac. Have you heard the name?"

She shook her head.

"I may tell you," he said, "that a few subjects have decided to cooperate just on hearing the name. I have some little reputation for what I am about to do to you."

He was difficult to judge. His eyes were half hidden behind the gleaming reflections in his rimless octagonal eyeglasses. His voice was soft but cold. He lit a cigarette with calm, steady hands.

"Major Duncan Glynbourne accepts no responsibility for this element of your interrogation," said the Frenchman with a measured, chilling little smile. "The English don't do this sort of thing. Major Glynbourne has entered a protest. In writing, even. He will, however, you note, stand by and watch—and he will accept and use whatever we learn from you."

The Englishman stood apart, as if by separating himself by two paces from the frame where she hung he could in fact insulate himself from the inhumanity of the process that was about to begin. He was pale, and he kept his hands in his pockets, probably so Bonnac would not see them tremble; but it was plain to her that he would stand and watch them torture her and would not interfere. It was very English of him to have made formal protest.

"You may understand what is coming," the Frenchman went on. "You chose not to answer our questions upstairs, so now I will force the answers from you. You *will* answer, you know. The pain will be severe, I warn you. We won't let you lose consciousness. We won't let you die. We can continue to administer unbearable pain for some considerable period of time, days if we have to. Or we can employ drugs. Personally, I dislike using drugs. I have seldom found them necessary."

He stepped away from her, to the switching panel. While she

watched, he turned one of the big black rheostat knobs to fix the
voltage and closed two knife switches to select the places where it
would enter her body. He put his hand then on the red-handled
switch.

"This will be just a little demonstration," he said. He jammed the
switch shut, jerked it open, jammed it shut, and opened it again.

Her body stiffened against the straps and jerked wildly in agonizing
spasms. Her vision failed in a burst of white light, and her breath
spilled from her in a wild, animal yell. She heard her guttural shriek
as if it were from a distance, yet she knew it was from her own throat.
The pain stopped, then it came again, worse than before. It stopped
again, and her body hung slack in its straps, urine running down her
legs. An ache remained, and she choked and sobbed.

"You see," said the Frenchman. "That's just a little. You can't endure much of that. Think about it."

"Don't be a fool, woman," grunted the English major.

Closing her eyes, she thought first of David. They would do this to
him, too, and then kill him. He would confess, and they would
trumpet his confession, and hers, to the world. The whole world
would know the Soviet Union had used David as their agent to destroy *The Last Supper*. The whole world would know the KGB had
used him as chief actor in a plot to murder the Prince and Princess of
Wales and the president of France and to destroy the great Notre
Dame Cathedral. It would be a tragedy for the Soviet Union.

She could not endure the pain that was coming. She would confess
everything. She would name Litvinko. He, arrested too and tortured,
would name his contact, someone higher up. Before the chain
stopped, a dozen valuable agents might be compromised, and the line
might be followed all the way to Moscow. The effects of the spreading
disaster would be felt for years.

But it did not have to be so. She had the means to prevent it.

Fifteen years ago in Moscow, over her protest, a KGB dentist had
extracted from her mouth a perfectly healthy upper right molar. He
had fitted her with two bridges, each with a false tooth to fill the gap.

One—the one she had worn every day since—filled the gap with a gutta percha tooth, the kind commonly used in the West. The tooth in the second bridge was hollow. It was filled with a powerful compound of cyanide. She had always carried that second bridge with her; and yesterday, when she became aware she was being followed, she had inserted it for the first time. Whenever she had to, she could break the hollow tooth.

She could die any time, but she was possessed of an overpowering instinct for life.

Major Glynbourne was astonished at how much pain the woman could take. Though it sickened him to see her suffer—and to see Bonnac coolly torture her—the woman's suffering won from him little sympathy, not even grudging admiration for her courage. He had seen suffering and death before, and what she endured without talking only convinced him she was indeed a trained agent. Bonnac puffed on one cigarette after another, littering the floor with their butts, and administered the torture without visible emotion.

After the third shock, the woman's body had turned pink. It had begun to swell. Her face was swollen, and Glynbourne had to peer into it to see evidence that she was conscious: her eyes following Bonnac as he moved back and forth from the switching panel. She had spat vomit with her screams, and she kept urinating. Bonnac had had the female attendant hose her down once. Now she was urinating again. The hot, stinking yellow fluid ran down her legs, dripped off her feet, and ran across the tiled floor to the drain.

And each time Bonnac asked her where David Betancourt was, she only clenched her eyes tightly closed and seemed to hold her breath.

"Am I supposed to think you're brave?" Bonnac said to her. "Well, I don't. I think you're a fool." He sighed. "You seem to enjoy it most when I send it up into your guts, up your backside. Let's see how you like two full seconds there."

She groaned and shook her head. "No . . ."

Bonnac could not safely increase the voltage, Glynbourne guessed.

Only the time. He switched to the probe in her anus. He shoved down the switch and Glynbourne could see his lips move as he counted the time to himself—*un mille et un, un mille et deux.*

She could not scream as loudly anymore. She had torn her throat, almost certainly. She whipped her head from side to side—the only part of her body she could really move; and a low, vomit-choked moan erupted from deep in her chest. When Bonnac opened the switch, her head lolled back and forth, and she seemed to slip out of consciousness.

And damn! Her bowels had let go. The stench was nauseating.

"Hose her down, Corinne!" Bonnac snapped, and he bolted from the room.

Outside Bonnac lit still another cigarette. "Soon she will begin to babble," he said to Glynbourne, who had followed him. "She'll tell us everything she can think of, everything we want to know and much besides."

Glynbourne shook his head. "I hope so," he said quietly. "I'm afraid she'll die before she talks. Besides, I . . . I'm not sure I can witness much more. It's making me sick. I don't deny it. Do you really think—"

"Trust me," said Bonnac crisply. "I have experience."

Glynbourne's eyes narrowed. He wouldn't trust him. The last thing in the world he would ever again do, he knew now, was trust Major André Bonnac. Bonnac would be sorry when the woman began to babble. He was not perhaps a sadist, exactly; but it was plain to see that he took some satisfaction in what he was doing. He thought he did it well, and was quietly proud of it. He had utterly no sense of what that made him.

"Major Bonnac!"
They rushed back.
"Major Bonnac!" the doctor shouted. Already he was over her, pounding her chest. He reached for the syringe handed him by Cor-

inne, and he jabbed it into the recumbent woman's chest. "Major! Come here! Sniff!"

Bonnac bent over the woman's face. The odor was distinctive. Bitter almonds. The woman who knew where to find David Betancourt was dead.

"Imbécile!" Bonnac screamed at the doctor. *"Vous avez—"*

"You're the imbecile, Major," growled Glynbourne between clenched teeth. "Our one chance to lay hands on Betancourt . . . You goddamned fool!"

17

VASILI IVANOVICH LITVINKO was wakened by the ringing of the telephone in his flat on Rue Boissonade, Montparnasse, at eight o'clock on Friday morning.

"Monsieur Lechevalier?"

"Yes."

"One moment. Doctor Roure calling."

Litvinko blinked and tried to focus his eyes on the clock, which was on the other side of the sleeping Evelyne. He could not recall the name Doctor Roure.

"Monsieur Lechevalier?" A male voice. Unfamiliar. "This is Doctor Roure. I am calling to tell you we are having a most unsatisfactory experience with the last shipment of ligatures we have received from your company. I should appreciate it if you would investigate the matter at your factory, then report to us as to why we should be having such problems."

"Uh . . . the nature of the problem, Doctor?"

"They break, Monsieur. Under tension, they break. That creates a critical danger. Need I explain further? I hope I may count on you to investigate the matter fully, immediately, and advise us as to what the problem may be. We will, of course, look to you for replacement of the entire shipment. That is secondary, however, to the hazard to our patients. Understood?"

"Yes . . . yes, of course, Doctor. You will hear from me before the day is over."

André Bonnac had been too long without sleep and was tired and angry. He knew at least that he had not tortured to death an innocent English secretary, the victim of a dreadful misunderstanding. Innocent women did not wear dental work fitted with cyanide capsules. She had been an agent of the KGB. That was certain. But he was heavily burdened by the knowledge that he had clumsily botched the interrogation. It had been the doctor's responsibility to check her mouth but his own to be sure the doctor had done it. It was a stupid mistake, which he would have to mention in his report even if the Englishman did not whine about it to everyone who would listen. Though Bonnac did not rationalize his own error by telling himself he wouldn't have made it if Glynbourne had not been there distracting him, all squeamish and every minute on the verge of vomiting, it had been a mistake to let him witness the interrogation.

There are few things in this world more infuriating than to have your own failure pointed out to you—unless it might be to have it pointed out by the typical middle-class Englishman: they of the smooth nasal voices and practiced air of superior civilization. What made it doubly infuriating was that Glynbourne was so damned right; the woman had *known* where Betancourt was and had died without telling. Bonnac would not confide in the Englishman again.

"You arrested her too soon," said Colonel Cau. "It would have been better to have kept her under surveillance."

"The woman with whom she shared a room in the Edouard VII Hotel was murdered during the night," said Lépine. "Our surveillance might have come to an abrupt end."

"What sort of surveillance did we maintain that allowed an assassin to go to our subject's room in the hotel?" asked the colonel.

Bonnac sighed. "The orders were to watch the woman, not to let her leave the hotel unobserved. No one suggested that our people should check every person who went upstairs in the hotel during the night." He drank coffee and puffed tensely on a cigarette. "The surveillance could hardly have been kept a secret if our people had been stationed in the hallway outside the women's room."

"Now this," said Colonel Cau, tapping his finger on the transcript of the Lechevalier telephone tap. "What do you make of this?"

"They're signaling each other," said Bonnac. "And not being very careful about it. They know we arrested the woman. They don't know she died. I'd say they're thoroughly frightened."

"Lechevalier. What are your plans for him?"

"We have his telephone tapped, as you can see. We are following him."

"Is there any way we can use his woman?" asked Lépine.

Bonnac nodded. "Yes. I'm not yet sure how. Let's don't forget her, though. She may become our hidden advantage."

Litvinko left his flat an hour after he received the mysterious telephone call. The voices were unknown to him. He had never spoken with Irina Narishkina or Pavel Zotov. He had little doubt, though, that the call was really from Colonel Olshanskii and was an emphatic order to contact him. That it had been communicated to his flat and in such peculiar terms could only mean the colonel suspected the telephone line to the flat was being listened to. It was a simple matter to place a call on a clear line; one only had to go to a telephone kiosk. The problem therefore was not with the taps on the embassy lines; it had to be at his end. Coming out on the street, Litvinko glanced around at a sunshiny autumn morning. For the first time in years, he was fearfully alert.

And there they were: three of them, a team set up to follow him. He walked to the end of Rue Boissonade and turned toward the Raspail Métro station. An attractive young woman in a short, tight, red skirt followed him. The older man had gotten into a car, driven out of the street, and turned toward the station. The younger man had for the moment disappeared, but Litvinko had no doubt he was

around somewhere. His stomach hardened and burned. In twenty
years in France, he had never been followed before.

If he did something clever to evade them—a quick switch from one
train to another, something like that—it would only confirm whatever
suspicion they had that led them to put him under surveillance. He
saw no option but to mime a normal business day, let them follow
him, and see if they stayed with him. That meant he would have no
chance to call Colonel Olshanskii.

David told Emily he had a late-morning business appointment,
preceded by a brief meeting at a hotel on Avenue de l'Opéra, and he
invited her to accompany him to the hotel, where they would have
breakfast together while he waited for the man who was to deliver him
an envelope of documents. He donned a floppy Irish-tweed walking
hat and a pair of sunglasses, and he carried a folded *Herald-Tribune*.
Emily never looked like anything but an American, and he told himself he was not a bad simulacrum of one himself. She was the best
element of his incognito as he walked boldly into the Hotel Edouard
VII.

They sat in the breakfast room of the hotel and ate—he ordering
bacon and eggs, toast and coffee for them both. It required little
shrewdness of observation to see that something horrible had happened in the hotel during the night. He divided the *Herald-Tribune*
with Emily, so she would be silent a few minutes while she read; and,
staring blindly at his own half while he listened intently, he shortly
overheard enough to tell him what he wanted to know: that an Englishwoman, one of the tour group from London, had been murdered
in her room during the night.

They finished breakfast. He told Emily that his courier had apparently chosen not to appear. He asked for his bill, paid it, and left,
passing four French security officers of various agencies in the lobby.
None of them looked at him. If he had listened to the breakfast-room
talk a little longer, he would have heard that another Englishwoman

was missing—the one who had shared the room in which the murder had occurred.

In the afternoon he drove to St. Denis and spent two hours fitting the tiny radio receivers and the plastique into the carefully shaped and measured packages that would fit into the BBC television cameras. He inserted the detonators and wired them to batteries and the little receivers. He set the pulse rate and frequencies.

He had another bomb to make, the one that would be set off by the second of the American detonator transmitters. He wired that one and set the receiver and transmitter to a different pulse rate and frequencies.

He was not without feeling for Nina. As he worked in the room where they had made love so awkwardly on the cot, his throat tightened and he shuddered. He had condemned her to death by his call to Olshanskii, and the KGB killers had reached her within hours. If in fact he went to Moscow, he would miss her there. She had been sincere about her offers to him, and she would have been a help and comfort to him.

When he left the former print shop and flats in St. Denis, he packed everything into his rented car. He had turned in the Renault and had a Citroen now, with a copious boot into which he packed everything, so it would not be necessary to return. He had intended to leave the explosives in the print shop, but on impulse he decided he did not want to return there. Maybe it was instinct, maybe it was the memory of Nina; but something irrational in him said that he did not want to see the St. Denis rooms again.

On his way back to the center of the city, he stopped at a grocer's to buy two dozen large cloves of garlic and at a hardware for several pairs of rubber gloves. On the street not far from the hardware he donned gloves, sliced two of the cloves, and rubbed garlic over everything in the boot of the car. Back in the city center, he parked the Citroen in an underground garage not far from the Place Charles de Gaulle.

*   *   *

The two young people who had told Bobby Donegal their names
were Pat and Kathy were in fact Patrick and Kathleen McCarthy, and
they were in fact married, as they had said. They were children of
prosperous Dublin families, were students at the Sorbonne, spoke
flawless French, and were associated with a Marxist student organization. They were almost as interested in a social revolution as they
were in the unification of Ireland. They had been photographed at a
number of Marxist meetings and rallies, and each of them was the
subject of a tagged dossier in the RG files of Sûreté. The next time
they went home to Ireland and tried to return, they would probably be
denied reentry as undesirables.

On Friday evening, October 12, they ate with Bobby Donegal in an
undistinguished tourist café on the Champs Elysées.

"He loaded his car," said Kathy. "I couldn't see what he was putting in the boot, but he carried down several loads. It looked like all
the material—but that's of course only a guess."

"Where did he go with it?" asked Donegal.

"He stopped twice and went into two stores, a grocer and a hardware. I have no idea what he bought, but he put it in the boot with
everything else and spent some time bent over the boot."

"But where did he go? Where is the stuff now?"

"I don't know. I lost him. He drives in Paris traffic like he's been
doing it all his life."

"We've got to find out, you know."

Pat sighed and shook his head. "We'll pick him up tomorrow morning again. I'd like to know the significance of the breakfast at the
Hotel Edouard VII this morning. He seems to have disguised himself
a bit, as if he thought someone there might recognize him. I mean,
he wore a funny hat and sunglasses."

"Well, he had to have breakfast somewhere," suggested Bobby.

"But why there? Why go to the Hotel Edouard VII, that far from
the Royal Monceau, just to eat bacon and eggs?"

"You have got to find out where he will be on Monday morning," said Bobby, impatient to change the subject. "That is absolutely vital. We can't depend on following him that morning."

"It has been impossible to stay with him at all times," said Pat, "but when we've been with him he hasn't gone near the Ile de la Cité or near the quays that overlook the cathedral."

"Who does he see, besides the American woman?"

"No one. He has taken her to night clubs. They went to the Crazy Horse the other night. They have been to the Louvre together, and to Les Invalides. Other than that, he has twice watched a French television news crew covering an event in the city. Also, he has twice visited an industrial-supply house in Gennevilliers. We couldn't find out what he does there."

"We are meeting him at the place in St. Denis tomorrow morning at eight," said Bobby. "Pick him up and follow him from there. Rent another car. You'll do it better if both of you are following him."

Returning to his room later, Bobby found a message:

"Meeting in St. Denis cancelled. Bring your people to the Holiday Inn in Varennes at eight. D."

He was unable to reach the McCarthys to tell them.

It was easy to understand why the BBC television crew had chosen the American-style hotel in Varennes: for the ample above-ground parking it would afford for the three vans. David drove the Citroen there on Saturday morning. The presence of thirty kilograms of plastique in the boot did not trouble him. He was confident it would explode only under the impact of the fiery shock of the detonators. Even so, when a big blue lorry bore down on him, its brakes screeching as its driver fought to stop it short of hitting the Citroen from the rear, he knew a moment of cold fear.

His Irish people were early and waiting for him. They assembled around his car and listened. He wore a bright-red nylon jacket that morning, over a black cashmere sweater. It was cool, and he plunged his hands in his pockets for warmth as he spoke.

"This is where they will be staying," he said to them. "The vans will be parked in this car park. We have discussed and rehearsed everything you have to do. I will see Bobby on Monday morning, but this is the last time I will see the rest of you. There is an element of luck in the whole thing. I wish you the very best of it. You and I were brought up in the Church. If you are inclined to pray, this weekend would be a good time."

Except for Bobby Donegal, the Irish—seven men and one woman now—dispersed, some of them into the Holiday Inn for breakfast. Donegal remained with David.

"Why not St. Denis?" Bobby asked immediately.

David drew a deep breath. "Where do you suppose the plastique came from? The American radios? The—"

"From the KGB," said Bobby.

David blew out the breath. "Whatever you want to believe," he said. "But obviously, there are others besides you and me and your young people. The French began to follow one of the others yesterday. A woman. We work at levels, you understand. She did not know what we plan. She did, however, know about the place in St. Denis. We won't go near it again."

"Where is the plastique? The radios?"

"In the car."

Donegal glanced at the Citroen. "All. . . ?"

David smiled. "All of it. You're leaning on it."

"My special equipment?"

"It's here. I'll give it to you now."

David opened the boot. He took out one of the American transmitters and the special bomb he had assembled and set to match its pulse rate and frequencies. Both were contained in a brown-paper bag that might have held a beef roast or a medium-sized chicken.

"One thing more," said Donegal. "I don't know where you will be. Don't you think I should know where you are on Monday morning?"

"Of course," said David. "A measure of trust, shall we say? I will be on a rooftop at eighteen Rue de la Huchette. From there I will be able to see the Place du Parvis, and I will be able to hear the radio chatter between the BBC directors' van and the cameramen. You can speak to me if you have to. Just as if you were talking to the television director."

Donegal nodded. "Good." He extended his hand. "Until Monday morning, then."

"Monday morning," said David.

The BBC vans arrived as expected, before noon. By then the Irish had scattered. Two of them—a young man called Michael and the girl called Eileen, the one who had talked with David that misty morning above the lough north of Galway—had taken a room in the Holiday Inn. Bobby Donegal had walked around the area and then installed himself in the bar, where he was nursing tiny glasses of Calvados and trying not to drink too much. The others were around, in the lobby reading newspapers, drinking coffee in the restaurant, walking in the car park.

There was nothing conspicuous in staring at the BBC vans. Many others were doing it, too. Two of them in the car park strolled boldly up to the van that had brought the cameras and stared inside when the rear doors were opened. They counted four full-sized cameras and one handheld. Also, there was a microphone in a parabolic reflector, to pick up voices from a distance. That equipment would require six people. There might be two factotums to drag wires and so on. That made a crew of eight, which matched the number of Irish available to replace them—since the loss of Mary at Dover, they were eight.

There was a problem, however. If indeed eight people were going inside the cathedral, which eight were they, of the thirteen English who had come in the three vans? It made a difference, because there were ten men and three women among the English and only one woman among the Irish. If two or three of the crew who went inside the cathedral were women, the Irish were short one or two women. It could be noticed.

"We can't guess about it," said Bobby Donegal to Eileen. "And we can't take a chance."

"Bring in Kathy McCarthy," said Eileen.

"Still, that would only be one. Anyway, I have another job for her and Pat. No. What we've got to do between now and Monday is create two women and get their pictures taken."

"But what if—"

"Paul," said Donegal decisively. "And Frank. We've got to set it up so they can be men or women, as necessary. They've got to work it out this afternoon and get their pictures taken. Monday, they've got to show up with alternative pictures and clothes and wigs. Set them to it, Eileen. They're resourceful boys. This is one bit that David can't do for them."

Olshanskii alone could decode his messages. A coded transmission from Moscow arrived at 1:00 p.m., Paris time, and he closed himself in his office and decoded it:

COMRADE GENERAL PIRITKIN HAS DIRECTED ME TO REMIND YOU THAT IDENTIFICATION OF THE BETANCOURT OPERATION WITH THE USSR WOULD BE A LONG-RANGE AND WHOLLY UN-ACCEPTABLE DISASTER. THE ARREST OF COMRADE SAMUSEV RAISES THE QUESTION OF WHETHER OR NOT THE WHOLE OP-ERATION SHOULD BE TERMINATED. FROM THIS POINT IT IS YOUR CHIEF RESPONSIBILITY TO PREVENT IDENTIFICATION BY WHATEVER MEANS MAY BE NECESSARY. THIS RESPONSIBILITY TAKES PRECEDENCE OVER ACCOMPLISHMENT OF ALL OTHER GOALS OF THE OPERATION. SUGGEST YOUR MOST EFFECTIVE COURSE MAY BE TO TERMINATE BETANCOURT IMMEDIATELY.
                                          CAPTAIN FILIP MALIK

He summoned Pavel Zotov and Irina Narishkina. "Find him. Go to Litvinko. That's a risk we now have to take."

For the second day, Litvinko was unable to shake his tail. Unwilling to do anything professional, for fear of confirming their obvious suspicions and compromising himself irretrievably, he spent Saturday morning miming a man shopping for a new suit. He took the Métro to the Madeleine station and began visiting men's clothing stores in the fashionable and expensive neighborhood. Each time he came out of a store, his faithful dogs were waiting. There were at least three of them, maybe four or five, and he had observed yesterday and today that the personnel changed. It was no casual operation. His fear intensified, and he considered evading them and fleeing—out of the country, back home. That, too, would confirm their suspicions and would constitute a betrayal. He continued wandering, waiting for an opportunity to call Olshanskii.

Evelyne was at home, in their flat in Montparnasse. She had failed to detect the fear and tension in the man she knew as George Jean Lechevalier. Yesterday morning's call had not alerted her. She pulled on the tight blue jeans that George liked, and a loose white-silk blouse; and, half an hour after George left, she was playing a game of solitaire in the living room when two woman agents of the DGSE came and arrested her.

She was taken to the Préfecture de Police as before, but this time she was not strip-searched or locked in a cell. She was taken directly to a small, severe office, where an interrogator sat behind a small desk, occupying the one chair in the room. She stood facing him. A dossier lay open on the desk.

"You are Evelyne Clayeux?"

"Yes, Monsieur."

"My name is Major André Bonnac. I am an officer of Direction Général de Sécurité Extèrieur. You have heard of it?"

"Yes, Monsieur."

"You are a prostitute, I believe?"

"Yes, Monsieur."

"And former dealer in cocaine. You spent, uh, forty-six months in the women's prison at Fleury-Mérogis, I believe—twenty-two months preventive during the investigation and twenty-four under sentence."

"Yes, Monsieur."

"And now . . . And now we find your fingerprints on a piece of KGB espionage equipment."

"I explained that before, Monsieur. I swear I touched it only by accident."

"Yes, of course—in a hotel room in the Eighth Arrondissement. Isn't that what you said?"

"I—"

"Actually, you touched it in your flat in Montparnasse, where it was brought by George Jean Lechevalier."

She drew breath. "Yes, Monsieur."

"So you lied to Commissaire Michelin."

"Yes, Monsieur."

Bonnac sighed and leaned back in his chair. "Very well, Mademoiselle," he said wearily. "Whether or not you are yourself a KGB spy, you impeded a national-security investigation by your lie to Commissaire Michelin. I see no choice but to return you to Fleury-Mérogis. You will be confined there pending the completion of the investigation, after which you may expect a sentence. It will be a long one this time, Mademoiselle."

Her face turned deep red, and she put a trembling hand to her mouth. "*Monsieur, please! I swear—*"

He stopped her with a curt gesture. "What you swear is of no interest to us. You've confessed your lie." He rose and pushed his chair back so abruptly it slammed against the wall. "Duplessis!"

A uniformed police matron, Duplessis, entered. She pulled a pair of handcuffs from the pocket of her jacket.

Evelyne Clayeux wept. "Please, Monsieur . . ."

Bonnac raised his arm, and the policewoman quietly slipped out and closed the door.

The charade had been effective. Half an hour later, Evelyne Clayeux left Bonnac, swearing to him, and re-swearing, that she would carry out his instructions faithfully.

A woman driving an unmarked yellow car dropped her at the Port-Royal station and let her walk the last few blocks to the flat on Rue

Boissonade. She arrived about two o'clock. She carried a scrap of paper torn from a small notebook—and, for verisimilitude, the notebook itself. Written with a fountain pen on the scrap of paper was a note in a strange script she could not read.

The words were:

Gdye B? Bydy edat vashchego zvonka. O.
Where is B? I expect you to telephone me. O.

She placed the scrap of paper on the table beside the door and tucked the little notebook in her purse. Sitting down in the kitchen over a glass of wine, she began to rehearse the description of the man she was to say had come to the door and written the note.

Returning to the Royal Monceau from an afternoon at the Pompidou Center, Emily Bacon stopped at the desk to pick up her key and mail. There was an envelope from the United States Embassy. It contained passes that would admit Emily Bacon, an American citizen, and David Tomas Betancourt, a citizen of the Republic of Argentina, to Notre Dame Cathedral on the morning of Monday, October 15, to witness the ceremonies attending the dedication of the monument to the members of British Security Coordination who had given their lives, 1939–1944, in the underground struggle against Nazi tyranny. To be admitted to the cathedral, said an accompanying letter, holders of passes would have to present their passports as well, for purposes of positive identification, and would have to expect to pass through metal detectors and perhaps submit to searches. No cameras, radios, or sound recorders could be carried into the cathedral.

Smiling happily over the passes and the letter, she carried them up in the lift, expecting to hand them to David. Instead, she found a note from him in the room. He had been there during the afternoon, had changed his clothes and packed a kit, and he was off to Rheims. He would return, his note said, in time for dinner tomorrow evening.

The fact was, he would not return. His extra passports and money had been hidden in his airline bags, which were in their room, and he had come to the hotel only to retrieve them. He had telephoned to be sure Emily was not there, and he had hurried in and out of the Royal Monceau as quickly as possible. He had begun to sense that elements of his plan were beginning to unravel, and the Royal Monceau, where he had stayed for almost two weeks, was not the place to be in the event he had somehow been identified.

His plan for escape did not involve Emily, however much he wished it could. Sooner or later she would discover, or guess, why he had come to Paris. If Nina had been compromised, then almost certainly the whole Trafalgar Trading operation had been compromised, and the name David Betancourt was as much involved in it as the name Nina Blankenship. Shortly, David would be one of the most wanted men in Europe—if, in fact, he wasn't already. After the blast, his name would be broadcast. Then, for sure, Emily would know everything. She loved him, but he doubted her love would survive the knowledge that he had murdered the Prince and Princess of Wales and destroyed much of Notre Dame. He would be a fool to trust her.

It was his plan to remain in Paris for several weeks at least. Their border security would be fanatically tight for a while; France was in effect a huge prison, with an overblown security system that documented every living person in it—at least in theory. Even so thorough, regimented, and computerized a system, however, fell short of checking the passport number of every visitor who registered at every hotel in France. He carried in the false bottom of his Pan Am bag still another United Kingdom passport, this one in the name of William Gentry Hodges, and he had carefully forged in it a Sûreté stamp indicating he had entered France from Italy at Menton on October 9. The passport photo was of himself with a thin mustache and close-cropped hair. He would check into a modest hotel somewhere away from the places he had frequented the past two weeks, show the Hodges passport, and live quietly until he judged it safe to leave France.

What he would do after that, he was not sure. He did not rule out presenting himself to the KGB officer of some Soviet embassy and accepting Olshanskii's offer of political asylum in the USSR. That had the attraction that he could probably arrange sooner or later for his mother to join him. Another possibility was Italy. Still another was to return to France. He loved France. He doubted he would ever see the States, and certainly he had no intention of returning to Argentina.

The truth was, he had not thought as carefully about his life after October 15 as he had about the means of accomplishing what he meant to do. In a real sense, it was not as important. The operation had a momentum and justification of its own.

Monsignor Périgord returned to Paris on Saturday evening. Lucien Trebonzi arrived at almost the same hour, in a car driven from St. Tropez by a DGSE agent. His special weapons were in the boot. The DGSE placed him in a convenient small hotel on the Boulevard St. Germain. Monsignor Périgord dined with Jean-Marie Cardinal Lustiger, Archbishop of Paris. He reported to him that it seemed quite likely that Oliver Cromwell, now identified as a young former Argentine army captain named David Tomas Betancourt, was in Paris and might be plotting some new outrage against the Church. The monsignor urged the cardinal archbishop to extend every possible cooperation to Sûreté and the DGSE, who were engaged in a desperate effort to find Betancourt before he destroyed another treasure of civilization.

Major Glynbourne's Saturday lunch at the Hilton was made dismal by the oral report of a psychiatrist the brigadier had insisted must be flown over from London to offer him the conclusions a team of doctors had reached about the mind of David Betancourt.

"There can be no question, utterly no question, that the lad's mind was unsettled, utterly unsettled, by his father's murdering his fiancée and his sister, then commiting suicide," said the psychiatrist. "That would unhinge the best of us, wouldn't it? Let alone an emotional Latin."

Sergeant Major Tate drank Alsatian beer and waited impatiently to deliver a more factual report. "Two detectives went up to Cambridge," he said when he got a chance. "They returned with the name John Sedgwick. Sedgwick's a don. Says he encountered David Betancourt on Trumpington Street in August. He had another name for us. He says Betancourt was escorting a beautiful American gel named Emily Bacon. She was once a student at Cambridge, too."

The psychiatrist had lit his pipe while the sergeant major was speaking—producing a huge cloud of thick, perfumy smoke. "Of course there was the incident in Ulster. I mean, when he shot the man. That leaves something behind in a man's psyche."

"Special Branch nudged Immigration," said the sergeant major, forcefully ignoring the psychiatrist. "Emily Bacon entered the United Kingdom through Heathrow Airport on July eighteenth. She left Heathrow on October second on a flight to Paris. Her UK Immigration entry card indicated her London address would be the Ritz Hotel—which the Ritz confirms. The American young lady was a guest from July eighteenth to October second. Photographs of David Betancourt produced a positive reaction from the hall porter and half a dozen of the hotel staff. Yes, indeed. They remembered him well. He slept with her now and again."

The psychiatrist dragged hard on his pipe, producing a loud sucking noise. "He leads a vig'rous sex life, apparently," he said. "You're looking for a man very ordinary in the great majority of his habits and drives and reactions. He—"

"He's probably with this Bacon gel now," said the sergeant major. "Look for *her*, we'll find *him*."

Having with some difficulty convinced Major Glynbourne that his presence would contribute nothing and that he could best serve by waiting at the Hilton, André Bonnac personally led the team of police agents who entered the Royal Monceau Hotel shortly before midnight. The night concierge confirmed the presence in the hotel of an American woman by the name Emily Bacon. He studied the photograph of David Betancourt and said, yes, that was the man who shared her room. But the name was not Monsieur Betancourt; it was Monsieur

McConnell. The room had been booked by Mademoiselle Bacon, for
two people, and Monsieur McConnell had arrived with her. His passport had been examined and the report duly made to the Préfecture.

Who was in the room now? Mademoiselle Bacon, the concierge
believed. She had dined alone in the hotel and had gone alone to her
room. Monsieur McConnell . . . The concierge had not seen him
tonight.

Bonnac considered for a moment. "Ring her room," he said to the
concierge. "And hand me the telephone."

She answered on the third ring.

"*Pardon, Mademoiselle.* A telephone call for Monsieur McConnell."

"You are calling the wrong room. There is no Monsieur McConnell here."

"*Ah, pardon, Mademoiselle.* The call is for Monsieur Betancourt."

"He is out of the city for the night. I expect him tomorrow evening."

"*Merci, Mademoiselle.*"

Her readiness to acknowledge the name Betancourt was evidence to
Bonnac that she was telling the truth. He decided not to intrude on
her. He assigned four men to the hotel, two in the hallway outside
her room, two in the lobby. The maid who entered the room in the
morning would be a police agent. If David Betancourt was there, it
was as good as having him in custody. He would not get out.

Bonnac returned to his office. Marie-Luise would be on stage for
her second show now, and he could not expect her home for at least
two more hours. A message was waiting for him: telephone the Préfecture.

"Ah, Bonnac. You won't believe the temerity of your man Betancourt. He applied at the American Embassy for a pass to be admitted
to the dedicatory ceremony at Notre Dame on Monday. What's more,
he got it!"

Notre Dame! My God! Bonnac began making calls.

18

GEORGE HAD TURNED the little note over and over in his hands, repeatedly, as they ate, later as they watched a classic film on television—*Le Cuirassé Potemkine*, an old story of the rebellion of the sailors on a Russian battleship during the Russo-Japanese war. He stared at the note as though he expected to find something more on the paper, something but the words written by an aide for Major Bonnac, in the Russian script that was illegible to Evelyne but immediately, easily legible to him. This confirmed Bonnac's accusation. George Jean Lechevalier was a Russian. Maybe that much information would satisfy Bonnac. She hoped so.

She was afraid of George now. If he entertained the least suspicion she was cooperating with the police, he would kill her; she had no doubt. (Her four years in the central French prison for women had totally revised her perception of the possibility of becoming a victim.) He had questioned her intently about the man who had come to the door and, finding him not at home, had left the note. She had used the description Bonnac had given her. It seemed only to increase George's suspicion. She had played the innocent as intently as she could. She had given him sex while he stared sullenly at the film on television, to relax him, to direct his suspicion away from her. Still he was cool, and it was apparent that one of the possibilities turning in his mind was that she was lying.

"I've got to go out," he said abruptly.

"George! On Saturday night?"

"Yes. I may be late. In fact, I may be gone all night. Don't wait up for me."

She watched at the window. When he was almost out of sight, she picked up the telephone and called the number Bonnac had given her.

Litvinko had never doubted his ability to elude the French security team assigned to follow him. That he had not done so until now was a measure only of his forlorn hope of saving his long-time incognito. Obviously that was gone now—sacrificed to the insane bombing scheme endorsed by the latest ambitious fool Moscow had sent to Paris. The time had come to show the French that they maintained surveillance over a trained and experienced officer of the KGB only as long as he chose to play their game.

It was quite simple. He stopped for coffee and brandy at a small café-bar on the Champs Elysées. One of them came in and took a nearby table. Two others guarded the street. After a few minutes, he asked for directions to the WC, walked to the back, and, instead of entering the door to the toilets, strolled casually through the kitchen and out the rear door. It was one of scores of places in the city where he knew his way out the back. He had long prepared for a night like this. He could have done it in London or Frankfurt just as well.

Back on the Champs Elysées, he walked into the Georges V Métro station, took a train only to the Clemenceau station, and there used a public telephone. He dialed a line in the embassy, let it ring three times, then hung up. He waited one minute, then dialed again. He let it ring four times, then hung up. He walked from the station to the small Italian restaurant on the Place André Malraux. He knew it would be some time before Olshanskii would arrive.

He was eating a platter of pasta and sipping from a carafe of quite respectable *vin de table* when Olshanskii entered and came immediately to his table, obviously confident that Litvinko would not be there if there were any question of his having been followed.

"I have important things to tell you," said Olshanskii curtly.

"You took an immense risk, Comrade Colonel," said Litvinko.

"In what?"

"In coming to my flat, leaving the note."

"Vasili Ivanovich, I have never ventured near your flat."

Litvinko's face darkened. "Then neither shall I, ever again," he said.

"How did they know where to find you?" Olshanskii demanded.

"I don't know."

"Nina Samusev?"

"She did not know where I live."

Olshanskii gestured distractedly at Litvinko's plate, suggesting to the waiter that he would have the same. "How much did she know?" he asked. "Where to find Betancourt?"

"Yes. She could contact him."

"And you?"

Litvinko shook his head.

"Do you have any idea where he is? We must find him."

"She did not tell me where to contact Betancourt, and I assume she didn't tell him where to contact me—any more than I identified you to her or told her how to contact you."

"Nina Samusev has been arrested," said Olshanskii ominously. "We have to assume she has been tortured. We must assume that anything she knew is now known by the DGSE."

"She knew about the place in St. Denis. She knew what we provided for him there. She knew about the studio in Rue de la Huchette."

"Even I don't know about that. Is that where Betancourt will be on Monday morning?"

"Yes. At 298 Rue de la Huchette. On the roof."

"Vasili Ivanovich," said Olshanskii. "We must find Betancourt. The arrest of Nina Samusev creates an unacceptable risk in the Wales operation. It must be stopped, and Betancourt silenced. It will be difficult for them to publicize any statement they force from Nina Stepanova; it would be the statement of a woman tortured out of her wits. But if they move in on Betancourt's Irish fanatics and take the explosives from their hands on Monday morning, and capture him with the detonator radios . . ." He stopped and shook his head. "The consequences to the Soviet Union are not to be contemplated."

"The project was foolishly dangerous from the beginning, Comrade Colonel," said Litvinko.

"You did not say so before."

"Would you use such words to describe orders from Comrade General Piritkin?" asked Litvinko. "No. And neither would I about my orders from you. But it is time, perhaps, to express our thoughts."

"You mention the comrade general," said Olshanskii coldly. "He gave his express approval to this project."

"I have done my best, Comrade Colonel. Our secrecy was not compromised by me."

"Then why is your telephone tapped? Why were you sent a false message purporting to be from me?"

"I have to look to Nina Samusev," said Litvinko. "Maybe she knew more than I thought."

"It's immaterial," said Olshanskii. "The point now is to find Betancourt. I want you to go to the studio you rented for him and wait for him there. If we don't find him sooner, at least you can kill him when he arrives."

Litvinko nodded.

"When it is over, Comrade," said Olshanskii, smoothing the edge off his voice, "make your escape from France. I assume you have a route prepared? Use it. Do you need funds?"

"I have what I need, Comrade Colonel."

Olshanskii rose. "Tell the waiter I became ill," he said.

Litvinko remained at his table. He finished his pasta and wine before he left, and he paid his bill with cash.

It was a cool night in Paris. He had worn his black topcoat and a black hat. He stood for a moment outside the restaurant, looking thoughtfully across the street at the fountains playing before the Comédie Française. Then he turned north and west, into the Rue d'Argenteuil, into the dark away from the lighted façade of the theater and the fountains.

"Vasili Ivanovich."

He turned, not to respond to the thin, threatening voice, but simply to fire one shot from the 9-mm Beretta he had carried in his right hand, withdrawn into his sleeve, ever since he left the restaurant. His pistol was not silenced, and the explosion from its short barrel rang through the street. A machine pistol fell from the other man's hand and clattered on the pavement.

Litvinko stripped the plastic film from the trigger, grip, and barrel of the Beretta, leaving it clean of fingerprints, and tossed it on the pavement. He paused long enough, before he walked away, to look down at the face of the young man he had killed. He did not recognize him. He had never met Pavel Zotov. "If you live long enough," he muttered, "ask Colonel Olshanskii if he really supposed I am as big a fool as he is."

He walked back the way he had come, into the square before the Comédie Française, where he joined the small crowd around the entrance to the theater. Shortly he walked the few paces along the Rue de Rohan into the Rue de Rivoli and down into the Palais-Royal station. In minutes he was on a train. His escape, with his new identity, was better established than Olshanskii could have imagined. Within an hour, he was well on his way out of Paris on the road to the Swiss frontier. He guessed it could be twenty years before he would need to change identities again, and he was probably right.

In his room at the Windsor Reynolds, Bobby Donegal pried open a shaving-soap can he had carried into France in his luggage. The can was nearly filled with keys. He poured them out on his bed, selected half a dozen, then put the rest back in the can and pressed the top on again. He picked up the brown paper bag David had given him in the morning. He took out the transmitter and hid it in the pocket of a jacket hanging in his closet. Carrying the small bomb David had built, along with a roll of tape, a screwdriver, a pair of pliers, and a tiny electric torch, he left the hotel a little before midnight, walked to the Étoile station, and caught one of the last RER trains for the night on the St. Germain-en-Laye line.

It was 1:00 A.M. when he reached the Holiday Inn in Varennes.

He was distressed immediately to see how much light there was in the car park. What was worse, the BBC camera van sat directly under one of the light poles. The hotel was quiet. Nearly all the rooms were dark. He knew, though, that a watchman patrolled the premises all night; in the morning he had noticed the little red clock stations where the man had to turn a key at intervals. So far as his quick inspection of the premises had suggested, the watchman patrolled inside only. Even so, he could not be sure he would not appear in the car park, and he could not approach the van until he knew where the watchman was.

Fortunately, the doors at the ends of the corridors were of glass. From a point outside, behind the building, he could see the length of one of the long corridors, all the way to the far door that led into the lobby. Donegal walked boldly across the car park, as if confidently on his way to a car. As soon as he was out of the brightest light, he vaulted over the low fence that bordered the lot and entered the dark, narrow alley beyond. There he settled to wait.

He waited ten minutes. The watchman appeared. He ambled the length of the long corridor, turned his key in the red clock, and started to walk casually back to the lobby. As soon as his back was turned, Donegal jumped over the fence and trotted to the BBC van.

One of his keys fit, as he had expected it would. He opened the rear doors and entered the van.

For a while he crouched in the darkness inside the van, waiting to see if he had been noticed, if anyone would come to check. He had learned patience, and he waited perhaps another ten minutes before he set to work. Once he was at work, his task was a matter of a few minutes only.

The van was fitted with seats for the crew as well as with racks for the equipment. With his screwdriver, he removed the self-tapping screws that attached one of the seats to the floor of the van. He tipped the seat forward. He removed his little bomb from the brown paper bag and installed it between two of the springs toward the front of the seat and in the middle, securing it tightly with tape. He refastened the seat, slipped out the back doors, relocked the van, and hopped the fence once again.

He circled the car park, entered the lobby of the hotel, and asked the clerk if he could call a taxi for him—he wanted to be driven to the Champs Elysées.

Bonnac arrived on Rue d'Argenteuil within five minutes after the first officers on the scene identified the dead man as Pavel Alekseivich Zotov, a French-and-English interpreter at the Soviet Embassy.

"The shot was fired from a nine-millimeter Beretta," said the investigating detective. "It was lying on the sidewalk. No fingerprints. It had been wrapped. A professional killing, one would say. And look at this thing." The detective pointed at an oddly shaped firearm lying on the sidewalk beside the dead man. "An ugly weapon. What the hell is it?"

"It's called a Skorpion," said Bonnac. "Czech machine pistol. Silenced. Fires little 7.65 bullets, but twelve a second. A burst would cut a man in two."

"Too big to pull and shoot quick," said the detective. "Awkward. What happened here must have been like a Wild-West shootout, eh? Someone was too fast for him."

"What witnesses?" asked Bonnac.

"Oh, plenty of witnesses, all very positive that the killer was a man in a black topcoat, or a man in a leather jacket, or a workman in blues, and that he ran west or walked south or escaped through a doorway—all depending on who you want to believe. In any event, he is gone, and we have no reliable description, certainly none of his face."

"Have you notified the Soviet Embassy?"

"Not yet. We wanted to consult with you first."

"I will notify them," said Bonnac.

He returned to his office and made the call, and he was surprised when, half an hour later, Josef Olshanskii arrived. When he received word that Olshanskii had come to see him, he was on the telephone talking to Evelyne Clayeux. Lechevalier had not returned, she said. It was now almost 1:00 A.M. What more could she do? He told her she was doing well and to keep doing it. He left his office and received Olshanskii in a small conference room.

He closed the door. "Can I offer you coffee, Monsieur Olshanskii?" he asked, trying to study the Russian's face without being obvious about it. The Russian was a more handsome man than his photographs suggested. "At this hour . . ."

"No, thank you. I should like to arrange for the earliest possible release of the young man's body. It must be shipped home. His family will want to arrange a funeral."

"An autopsy is being performed," said Bonnac. "After that, I see no reason why the body may not be released to you."

"I shall be grateful."

"Can you offer us any suggestion as to a line of investigation, Monsieur Olshanskii? Do you know why this young man was on Rue d'Argenteuil or why someone might have wanted to kill him?"

Olshanskii shrugged. "An affair of the heart, possibly. Jealousy—"

"Which would hardly explain why the young man was carrying a Czech-made machine pistol fitted with a sound suppressor," said Bonnac curtly.

"That could have been placed on him by his killer," said Olshanskii evenly, "to confuse the investigation."

"Which would hardly be expected of a jealous lover," said Bonnac.

"Also, the young man's fingerprints were found not only on the trigger and grips but also on the magazine and even on the cartridges."

Olshanskii drew a breath, then sighed. "Are we heading into an international incident, Major Bonnac?"

"Let us hope not, *Colonel* Olshanskii. It is not impossible that the interests of the KGB and of GIGN may coincide for a moment. Can we talk frankly?"

Olshanskii hesitated briefly, then allowed himself a fleeting smile. "Is your coffee good, Major Bonnac?" he asked.

Bonnac picked up the telephone and ordered a pot of coffee, to be freshly made. "The prey proved too deadly for the hunter, is my guess," he said as soon as he put down the phone. "I'm wondering who is important enough for you to have sent out a hunter, at some risk. I'm wondering if it's someone I'm looking for, too."

"I'm afraid you will have to be more specific, Major."

"Let me guess who killed your man Zotov," said Bonnac. "Betancourt."

"I have never heard the name."

"Lechevalier had."

Olshanskii shook his head. "I have never heard that name either."

Bonnac smiled. "It was I who sent Lechevalier the note signed with your name. He found it when he returned to his flat in Montparnasse this afternoon. He contacted you tonight, didn't he? Three hours ago? Four? He is a clever agent. He slipped away from a skilled and experienced team I had assigned to follow him."

Olshanskii shrugged. "As do I from time to time."

"Was it then Lechevalier who killed Pavel Zotov?" asked Bonnac, conscious that his voice was betraying his enthusiasm for an idea that had just occurred to him. "Were you compelled to loose the hunter on him, once he told you he was compromised, to be sure he would not fall into my hands and tell me too much about David Betancourt?"

"Your speculations are becoming offensive, Major. Maybe all we have to discuss after all is the release of the body of Pavel Zotov."

"Lechevalier has operated in France for more than twenty years," Bonnac continued. "Your woman who operated in London under the name Nina Blankenship managed to work for you under cover for fifteen years. I can trace a connection between each of them and David Betancourt, and you've lost both of them: two valuable agents. Betancourt has become a very big liability."

"Allow *me* to speculate," said Olshanskii slowly, holding his words until his thoughts formed. "The woman you call Nina Blankenship is dead. Otherwise, you would not be speculating."

"May all of us find in ourselves the kind of courage that woman had, if ever we need it," said Bonnac solemnly. "But now that you acknowledge her, you in effect acknowledge Betancourt. She worked with Lechevalier, and Betancourt worked with both of them. And because of Betancourt, you have lost both of them. Even if some of my speculation is wrong, Betancourt has become a costly and risky association."

"You assume a great deal, Major Bonnac. But tell me where you think our interests might coincide."

"In the death of David Betancourt," said Bonnac in a quiet, matter-of-fact voice, pausing to light a cigarette. "Kill him for me, Colonel Olshanskii. Hand me his body."

"Well, that's . . . specific," said Olshanskii. "That's blunt. But *why?* Assuming there is anything behind your speculations—which I do not, of course, for a moment admit—why should *I* want to kill Betancourt?"

Bonnac clenched his cigarette tightly between his lips and drew smoke deep into his lungs. Then he put it aside. "The death of Betancourt," he said, letting out smoke with his words, "will put a major impediment in the way of anyone's ever fixing responsibility for him. It may make it impossible, in fact. I need hardly tell you that the most persistent security agencies in Europe want to know who has been behind the man they've called Oliver Cromwell, who supplied him explosives and detonators, who was paying him? If anyone captures him alive and interrogates him, we may find out. That's a reasonably strong motive for you, isn't it?"

Olshanskii tossed his shoulders in a little shrug. "Even if your speculations are correct, I am in no position to kill the man for you. I have no more idea where he is than you do."

"But you have an advantage over me, Colonel," said Bonnac, reaching for his cigarette. "You know why he is in Paris. You know what he is here to do and probably when he means to do it."

Olshanskii shook his head and smiled faintly. "You have your own special reasons for wanting him dead," he said. "I'd like to know what those reasons are."

"They are not as good as yours," said Bonnac coldly. "Anyway, I make you a proposition, Colonel Olshanskii. I will free you of surveillance. I'll make it possible for you to move freely in Paris, unobserved. Armed. Betancourt will contact you sooner or later, if only to be paid. When we learn of his death, the investigation will be quite perfunctory, I can also assure you."

Irina Narishkina was waiting in the embassy car. Olshanskii entered the rear seat and sat beside her.

"Let us go for a little drive through the city, Nikolai Vladimirovich," he said to the chauffeur. "Be watchful. I want to see if the French are following us."

"They photographed me," said Irina Narishkina. "Even as I sat here in a diplomatic vehicle."

"They want the identity of any woman they suspect I might be sleeping with, Irina Mikhailova." He laughed.

"I regard it as a misfortune that I don't, Comrade Colonel," she said blandly.

"Indeed? Well, I should not want you to suffer misfortune, Irina Mikhailova. Perhaps we can remedy the situation later."

She was looking behind. "They're not following," she said. "Or if they are, they're being very subtle about it."

"I was promised they wouldn't. We'll drive about for a while, until we are certain. Then I want to see something."

The street was deserted and quiet, after 2:00 A.M., when they arrived at 298 Rue de la Huchette, the number on the glass door of a print-seller's shop. It was one of three establishments on the ground floor of a nineteenth-century brick building—the other two being a dealer in antique silver to the east, at 297, and a seller of coffees and teas, biscuits, candies, and dried fruits, to the west, at 299. Each shop had one show window. The three doors, at 297, 298, 299, were wide, glassed, and welcoming. But there were three more doors: narrower, solid, and forbidding. These, Olshanskii guessed, opened on narrow stairways that led to flats above the ground-floor establishments. The building had three floors. He had to suppose that Betancourt's observation post and control center would be the top-floor flat. Only from there, he guessed, would one have a clear view across the quay and the river to the cathedral.

The lock on the narrow door was heavy and complex. He tried several keys the driver carried, but none of them would turn in the lock.

"It is possible," he said to Irina Nirishkina, "that he is up there now, asleep."

David was not there. He understood that Nina had not rented the studio herself; someone had arranged it and handed her the keys. That meant someone else knew about the studio. Even going there on Monday morning involved a risk. It was a risk he was willing to take, but he meant to be in the studio—on its roof, actually—no more than half an hour.

He was asleep in a hotel called Lyon-Panthéon, on Rue de Lyon between Place de la Bastille and the big Lyon railroad station. He had checked in with the passport indicating his name was William Gentry Hodges. The Citroen, filled with explosives, was in an underground garage a short distance away. He had eaten well in the dining room of the hotel, in the company of a very few traveling businessmen, the few who remained dolefully in the hotel on Saturday-Sunday night. That evening, he had discovered a minor problem with his Monday-morning plan. In the morning he would go out and find what he needed to solve it. Buying what he needed on Sunday would present some difficulty, he anticipated; but he was sure he could overcome it.

19

SUNDAY, OCTOBER 14, was a beautiful autumn day in Paris. The air was crisp and stirred by a breeze that drove dry leaves across the parks and along the streets. Tall, billowing white clouds rode across the city. The bookstalls were open on the quays as were the stalls that sold flowers and caged birds, and the usual morning streams of tourists mingled with other streams, of Parisians, who seemed invariably to be streaming in the opposite direction. The *bateaux mouches* headed into the Seine, carrying colorful crowds bundled against the cold in bright caps and jackets. Crowds flocked into Notre Dame for the morning masses.

Kathy McCarthy wakened Bobby Donegal at 10:00 A.M. on Sunday, knocking insistently on his door at the Windsor-Reynolds Hotel. He was wearing nothing but his undershorts when he let her in, and she mimed an indignant effort not to look at him until he pulled on his pants.

"We've been to number eighteen Rue de la Huchette," she said. "You remember? The address he gave you for his rooftop, where he'll listen to the radios and set off the bomb when our people are all clear. You remember?"

Donegal was unshaven, his hair tumbled over his forehead, and his

305

eyes focused only intermittently; but he nodded. "Yaas, yaas. Eighteen Rue de . . . whatever."

"If that's his rooftop, he'll have to hang by ropes. That roof is *steep*." She formed an angle with her hands. "He lied. Pat's looking for other buildings, ones with flat roofs and a view of the river and the cathedral. In the St. Séverin quarter. But maybe David's not even going to be in the St. Séverin quarter. *"He lies."*

Donegal stumbled into the bathroom. "Are you surprised? I'm not." He began to urinate noisily. "Of course he lies. Don't *we?*"

"How can we work with a man we can't trust?" she asked.

"We don't stake our lives on trust, Kathy. That's why *you'll* have a radio to talk to us, too; and that's why we won't give David the word we're leaving until we've left. It's also why we won't carry his bombs into the cathedral at all if you can't find him and get in place to watch him tomorrow morning. Trust has nothing to do with it."

He came out of the bathroom. She was sitting on his windowsill, slack-shouldered, chin down. She was wearing a black skirt, a white blouse, and a London Fog raincoat.

"Kathy," he said. He caressed her cheek, instantly conscious that he was touching her for the first time. Then he rested his hands lightly on her shoulders, looking down into her face. "What did you expect?"

She shrugged and sighed. "Why did we have to use a man like him? Couldn't we have done it without him?"

He closed his hands on her shoulders. "What the hell are you, an idealist?" he asked gruffly.

"Of course I am! And aren't you, in spite of the way you talk?"

"What are we doing tomorrow morning, Kathy? Have you forgot? We're going to *kill* a lot of people! Have you put that out of your mind somehow? Here's where the talky posturing stops and you—"

"It's for the cause!"

He slumped, dropped his hands. "The cause . . . Yes. Excuse me. I forgot."

"I wouldn't be doing it otherwise. Would you? But *he* would, for money. He's just a killer. An animal."

Donegal nodded. "He's different from us, hmm?"

"Well, isn't he?"

Donegal nodded. "Yes. I suppose so. But we couldn't have done it without him. He's smart and resourceful, and he arranged help for us that I don't know how we could have managed without. He has his own reasons, different from ours, for doing what he's doing. But we joined forces with him. And that was for the cause, too."

She shook her head. "Cynical . . ." she whispered.

He touched her cheek again. "The cause isn't pure and clean, Kathy. It's been dirtied for a long time."

A small, wry smile came to her face. "So is everything, I suppose. Marxism. Christianity, for that matter."

"Kathy. We can still let you out. I can send someone else—"

"No. I am not a child, Bobby Donegal."

He slipped his hand down from her cheek and lightly explored her breasts. "No. No, you're not, are you? I had noticed."

She stiffened and sucked in a loud, angry breath. "Another facet of the famous Bobby Donegal," she said scornfully.

He moved his hand on down, across her belly, down her leg. "Survive tomorrow, Kathy," he said. "And after. Be careful. Be cynical enough to be careful. I don't want to have to mourn you, too."

Kathy put up her hand and touched his rough, bearded face. She closed her eyes and shook her head.

He kissed her on the forehead, then on the nose, finally on the mouth. When he began to unbutton her blouse, she did not protest or resist.

"You make me think you like it."

Frank Milligan, one of the two young Irish men ordered by Bobby Donegal to establish disguises as women, stood in the bathroom of the Hotel Championnet on the north slope of Montmartre. Paul O'Brien

sat in shallow, soapy water in the tub, shaving the hair from his body
with a wet razor.

"Question: Do *you* like it, Frank?" O'Brien laughed. He ran his
hand over his newly smooth legs. "Does it make you horny?"

Milligan turned away. "I think it's goddamn sickening, if you want
to know what I think."

O'Brien lifted his penis out of the water. "Here's the only problem," he said.

"No one's going to look at that," said Milligan.

"Nevertheless," said O'Brien firmly, "we're going to dress, and
we're going out. We're going to get our pictures taken. Remember?"

They had bought the clothes they needed, and the wigs and
makeup, on Saturday afternoon—from half a dozen stores, not just
one, in an excess of caution. Last night, Saturday night, they had
tried on everything, in their hotel room. This morning, O'Brien had
insisted they must shave their bodies.

Donegal had chosen Paul O'Brien, not because there was anything
effeminate about him, but because of the young men in the group he
was the slightest. Though he was wiry, he was small, and the muscles
of his arms and legs were not prominent. He was the son of a Londonderry schoolmaster long imprisoned for arson and had been a dedicated soldier of the IRA since he was fourteen. Frank Milligan was a
farmer's son from Cork, ostensibly a student in Dublin. Taller than
O'Brien, he had been chosen by Donegal because he tended to fat, to
softness, and could probably be more readily taken for a self-indulgent
young woman.

"I am an hairy man." Paul laughed. "You . . . well, whatever. But
I am a twentieth-century Esau, and I'm shaving off a pound and a
half of hair."

Milligan had been in the tub first and had scraped a bit of light hair
from his legs and arms. Standing at the bathroom mirror now, he was
gingerly applying lipstick and a touch of blush to his cheeks.

"Not too elaborate," said O'Brien. "We'll have to make the change,
if it must be made, in less than five minutes."

"Practice," said Milligan.

They left the hotel in mid-morning, to return to the shop they had identified yesterday afternoon, where passport photos would be taken on Sunday. Milligan wore blue-denim jeans, a bulky gray sweater, sneakers, a light-brown wig styled short. O'Brien had gone further. He wore women's clothing from the skin out: panties, a brassiere stuffed with tissues, a garter belt holding up nylon stockings, high-heeled shoes, a dark-blue linen dress, a cream-white corduroy jacket, a dark wig with hair hanging to his shoulders. On the street they walked without attracting any special notice.

They had their passport photos taken in a shop where the old photographer said their pictures would be ready in two hours.

On the street again, they walked apart, first one walking ahead and the other observing from behind, then reversing, so they could appraise each other's gait and posture. Walking north with no particular objective in mind, they came by chance on the busy flea market at the Porte de Clignancourt. They walked among the booths where merchandise was displayed on open-air tables, into a jostling crowd of shopping families.

It was Milligan who was propositioned first—"*Cinq cent francs, Mademoiselle?*"—by a middle-aged working-class man with the stub of a cigarette in his dark face. Then O'Brien was offered six hundred francs by a tall businessman in a gray suit and rimless spectacles. Since neither of them spoke French, they did not know how much had been offered, though they knew from the tone and expressions that they had received propositions.

A young man walked up to them. He wore a vinyl jacket meant to have the appearance of leather, with gold chains and pendants hanging over his chest. "*Jolie robe!*" he said to O'Brien. "*Jolis souliers! Savez-vous Chez Charles? A bientôt, cheri!*"

O'Brien and Milligan exchanged mystified glances. They failed to understand that the young man had seen through O'Brien's disguise, had taken him for a transvestite, had greeted him with compliments on his dress and shoes, and had suggested he would see him later at a nearby homosexuals' bar.

The security conference opened at noon in the grand conference room at the ministère de l' interieur, at the long table under the great chandeliers. Presiding again, as he had at the last conference, on October 5, was Yves Laffont, ministre de l'intérieur. Clustered around him at his end of the table, as before, were Jean Marchal, directeur-général de Sûreté, Maurice Fournier, directeur de police judiciaire, and Gérard Parbot, préfet de police, Paris. At the other end sat Général Jean-Louis Bernard, chief of Direction Général de Sécurité Extérieur, and the three representatives of Groupe d'Intervention de la Gendarmerie Nationale: Colonel Aaron Cau, Major André Bonnac, and Jacques Lépine.

Once again, Monsignor Périgord was present, sitting at the middle of the table. Galeazzo Castellano sat beside him. Facing the monsignor from across the table was Major Duncan Glynbourne, with Sergeant Major Bryan Tate beside him.

Two new characters had joined the cast: Commissaire Jean Trillat, chief of GSPR—Groupe de le Sécurité pour le Président de la République—and Detective Chief Superintendent William Dole of Scotland Yard, Special Branch. They were the two men principally responsible for security during the dedicatory ceremony at Notre Dame tomorrow morning.

"I assume no consideration is to be given to cancelling the ceremony," said Général Bernard. He spoke English, as did all the others who could, for the benefit of their English colleagues. *"N'est-ce pas?"*

"Absolutely none," said Ministre Laffont. "The president is determined it shall not be cancelled. After all, if the forces represented here cannot protect the president of France and the Prince and Princess of Wales from terrorist attack at a specified hour and at a specified place, whom can we protect? And what?"

"I reviewed the security measures with the président," said Commissaire Trillat. "He is prepared to place his trust in them."

"But the prince and princess?" asked Général Bernard.

"The matter is being presented this afternoon," said Superintendent Dole."

"Personally," said Directeur-Général Marchal, "I take the significance of Betancourt's application to be admitted to the cathedral tomorrow morning to be a diversion." He shrugged. "That is, if it has any significance at all and does not represent a . . . How is it the Americans say? A foul-up."

"You have not arrested the American woman? Or questioned her?" asked Trillat.

"I still entertain a faint hope he will return to the Royal Monceau this evening," said Bonnac. "She says he will, and she impresses me as an innocent."

"How so?" asked the ministre.

"She doesn't know he registered at the hotel as McConnell, with a passport in the name McConnell. When I asked for McConnell on the telephone, she said there was no one there by that name. When I asked for Betancourt, she said he was away for the night but would return this evening. I propose to leave her alone. She's been his mistress for some time, and he may well try to contact her. If he does, we'll have him."

"I don't understand her," said Colonel Cau. "It is inconceivably stupid that she would use his name at the United States Embassy and have the embassy ask for—"

"Except on one theory," Bonnac interrupted. "That she doesn't know he's a criminal."

"Well, of course. On that theory . . ."

"I propose to let her enter the cathedral," said Bonnac. "Carrying nothing, of course—no bag, nothing that could contain a bomb. We'll watch her every moment."

"Would he be sending *her* in with a bomb?" asked Castellano. "She wouldn't be the first woman he's blown up."

"She will be carrying nothing," said Bonnac firmly.

"I am satisfied with every element of the security arrangements," said Superintendent Dole. "Except for one. I would like to review again the precautions you are taking about the television people."

"They will be the same for RDF and for the BBC," said Commissaire Trillac. "The bridges at the east end of the Ile de la Cité will be closed. All traffic coming onto the island tomorrow morning will have to cross one of three bridges: Pont St. Michel, Pont au Change, or Pont Neuf. No vehicles will be allowed east of Boulevard du Palais except by way of Quai du Marché Neuf. The quay will be barricaded beside the Préfecture. The television vans will be stopped, all personnel will be required to get out, and only then will they receive the identification badges that will admit them to the cathedral."

"The badges will bear—"

"Their photographs," said the commissaire. "The photographs provided by RDF and the BBC, of men and women whose names and faces have been subjected to a careful security check. Our men will compare the faces and the photographs and issue badges only to individuals who match their pictures. The badges have not been laminated yet. Two things remain. I have yet to choose the color, and I have not as yet specified the code that will be imposed on the magnetic strip inside each badge. That I will do no more than an hour before the badges are to be issued."

"This magnetic code of which you speak," said Glynbourne. "How is it checked?"

"By a sensitive probe in the hands of one of our men at the door where they will enter the cathedral," said Commissaire Trillat. "They will check the photographs on the badges and touch the probe to the magnetic strip."

"The vans? They will be searched?"

"Examined. In any event, they will be parked at the west end of the Place du Parvis, a hundred meters from the west doors of the cathedral."

"Has anyone anything further to suggest as to the security for the ceremony tomorrow morning?" asked Ministre Laffont. "That is, after all, our immediate reason for meeting."

"I have no suggestion," said Monsignor Périgord, "but I should like to explain that the cardinal archbishop has asked me to act as his representative with respect to all matters involving his own security and that of the cathedral and its treasures. I shall be present at the ceremony. Several young priests from Rome will be with me." He paused and looked around the table. "Each of them is knowledgeable and well trained. I ask you to regard them as the Church's own security force—for that is what they are."

Olshanskii was satisfied that Bonnac was keeping his word about relaxing surveillance for a few days. He drove away from the Soviet Embassy before noon; and, although he took the precaution of driving about for a while to be sure he was not followed, it was quickly apparent that he was in the clear.

Irina accompanied him. He was short of personnel. He had specialists at his command, but the loss of Zotov at the hands of Litvinko had left him without a man immediately available to hunt for Betancourt. He cast a sideways glance at the solid young blonde sitting beside him in the Renault. She was dedicated and capable, but inexperienced. What was more, she was a little too conspicuously glad for her new opportunity. It was almost as if she regarded the death of Zotov as a stroke of luck.

He had wired a report to Moscow. He doubted Litvinko would try to undermine him by sending back an accusatory report of his own, but it was a possibility that had to be covered. He had wired that Litvinko, who had apparently compromised the Betancourt operation by some blunder, had defected from the service and had murdered Pavel Alekseivich Zotov. He had wired also that two of his agents, presently on loan from Paris to Geneva and Zurich, should be returned to him as soon as possible. He had omitted from his wire the fact that he had not the remotest idea where to find David Betancourt.

He parked some distance away, on Rue Lagrange, and sent Irina ahead of him, to check the building on Rue de la Huchette before he himself entered the street. He could not risk being seen there by Betancourt. But Betancourt had never seen Irina Narishkina.

The girl walked up to the door to the upstairs flats and pressed the bell button. Olshanskii, standing across the street and some distance to the east, watched as she rang again and again. She turned and looked at him.

He strode boldly across the street then, pulling a key ring from his pocket as he came. Last night they had taken the name from the lock, and this morning a specialist at the embassy had machined a set of keys, one of which, he assured them, would open almost any lock of that manufacture. Olshanskii began trying these keys, one by one. The second key turned the lock, and he opened the door and stepped inside, beckoning Irina to follow him.

The street door opened as he had expected on a narrow stairway, dimly lighted by a small window at the top of the first flight. He pulled his pistol and tucked it in the waistband of his trousers, instantly accessible to his right hand. With a toss of his head he ordered Irina to follow him up the stairs.

The first flight ended at a dark-varnished solid door. From there the second flight of stairs ascended in the opposite direction, back toward the front of the building. Olshanskii kept climbing. At the top of the second flight he came to another door, much the same. He stood aside, pistol drawn, and Irina knocked.

She shook her head. She put her ear to the door. Again she shook her head.

Olshanskii took out his key ring again. Peering at the lock, he was encouraged to see the same name stamped in the dull brass. The first key fit this one. He unlocked the door and pushed it back.

He almost gasped at what he saw. The big window at the far end of the long room faced the Seine and on the other side, no more than two hundred fifty meters away, from left to right, the grim façade of the Préfecture de Police, the Place du Parvis de Notre Dame, and the exquisite beauty of the cathedral itself. He walked across the room and stepped onto the model's platform before the window. Irina followed him.

Olshanskii shook his head.

"To bring it down would be a blow from which the imperialists would stagger," said Irina.

"It *is* beautiful, you will admit."

"Of course."

"Fortunately," he said, "we are not going to bring it down. Our orders now are to prevent Betancourt from setting off the blast."

"To kill him," she said.

"Yes."

He looked around. The studio flat was simple. To the left of the model's platform was a bed, which could be shut off from the rest of the flat by drawing a curtain around it. On the wall to the right was a little old gas range, a sink, a small water heater, a cupboard. Beyond that was a toilet enclosed in a little closet. There was a table. There were three chairs. An open stairway to the roof went up along the right wall.

He climbed the stairs and opened the door that led out onto the roof. From there the view was even more fascinating: of the Seine and the whole Ile de la Cité. The roof was much wider than the studio flat. The center flat was apparently the only one with access to the roof. It was flat, studded with vent pipes and six small brick chimneys. To the south it offered a view of the churches of St. Séverin and St. Julien le Pauvre and beyond, over the rooftops, the Hôtel and Musée de Cluny.

Litvinko had found the perfect place. From here Betancourt would be unobserved and would have a clear view of the cathedral. From here he could listen on his radios, hear the BBC people and his own people, and set off his blast at the right moment.

Standing on the roof, staring across the river at the cathedral, Olshanskii wondered if maybe he couldn't let him do it, after all. Just how badly *was* the operation compromised? What a triumph it would be to be able to carry it off in spite of everything! With Betancourt dead, would. . . ? He put the question firmly out of mind. For now. He would think about it later.

The brick wall of the building rose about a meter above the level of the flat roof. It was pierced at intervals with small pipes that allowed the rainwater to run off into the spouting. The roof of the next building was identical. The walls of the two were separated only a little more than a meter. He looked down between the two old buildings. A brick-paved passageway sloped downward, from Rue de la Huchette toward the Quai St. Michel.

"You see?" he asked Irina.

"Yes. I will be with you."

"No. You will wait on the street. If anything goes wrong, you will kill him when he comes out."

Prime Minister Thatcher arrived at Kensington Palace at three. The Prince and Princess of Wales received her with cordial smiles and offered tea or whisky. She accepted a small whisky.

She reviewed with them all the information that had come back from France.

"The question, of course," said the prince, "is, What will President Mitterand do? Does he wish to cancel?"

"We cannot allow that to govern our decision, sir," said the prime minister firmly.

"Our own people are satisfied?"

"Detective Chief Superintendent Dole says the security precautions are extraordinary. In addition, Major Glynbourne is in Paris, and he is satisfied as well. On the other hand, we must remember that Oliver Cromwell committed the outrage at the Abbey in August as well as the one in Milan in June, and others. He is an exceedingly clever man."

"There was, as I understand it," said the princess, "no particular security at the Church of Santa Maria delle Grazie, because the crime was in no way expected."

"On the other hand," said Mrs. Thatcher, "we had mounted rather tight security around the Indian minister of defence."

"Not very good, I think, if you will forgive me, Prime Minister," said the prince. "In any event, General Sekhar survived."

"As did I, at Brighton," said the prime minister, "but I would not want you, sir, or the princess to have to undergo the experience."

"If the president of France is taking the risk, then so must we," said the prince. "I can't think it's very great, in view of the measures that are being taken in specific anticipation of an attack by Oliver Cromwell. In any event, we cannot allow ourselves to be driven from public view. What are we to do, Prime Minister?—retreat within the walls of Windsor Castle and cringe there in constant fear?"

"I shall convey your decision to Paris, sir," said the prime minister. "At least in Paris we need not, I should suppose, fear anything from the Irish."

David needed an electrical converter, a device capable of powering a 220-volt hot press from the alternator of an automobile or van. He had specified a heater that could be operated in a vehicle, but apparently the supply house had assumed he meant with 220 volts from a converter and assumed he had one. Anyway, the hot press was useless without the converter, and finding one in Paris on Sunday was proving difficult. He drove the Citroen into the quarters where he thought it most likely he would find an open store, but stores that carried such equipment were not open. By mid-afternoon he was tired and angry. The converter was essential.

It was four o'clock when finally he settled on the store that would provide what he had to have. It was in Clichy, on a street of stores that sold automobile parts, tires, paint, hardware, fixtures, and light industrial tools and supplies. Through the glass door bearing a painted sign—PICARD ELECTRIQUE—he could see shelves of electrical equipment, including almost certainly the converter he needed. He rang the store's telephone number from a nearby kiosk, but of course no one answered—it was Sunday. He would have to return.

*   *   *

Evelyne Clayeux watched impassively as three detectives searched
the flat in Montparnasse. They went through everything, everything
that was hers as well as what George had kept here. He had kept
relatively little, actually; he had another home somewhere—she was
not certain where—and had never moved even a full set of his clothes
into the flat.

"For a time I supposed he had a wife somewhere," she said to one
of the detectives. "He insisted he didn't."

She would have to move out now, as soon as the period of the rent
ran out. Her earnings were sufficient to keep the flat, probably, but
she doubted the owner of the building would allow her to stay if he
entertained any suspicion at all that she was a prostitute. Anyway,
Montparnasse was a long way from the Eighth Arrondissement.

The detectives were thorough but surprisingly conciliatory. They
replaced everything. One could readily tell they had been here, but
nothing was damaged.

"Mademoiselle," said the tallest of them, a young man with the
long mournful face of the young Charles De Gaulle. "What is the
purpose of this key?"

She shook her head. She had seen it in the drawer in the bedroom,
and she too had wondered what it was. "I don't know, Monsieur," she
said. "He brought it here not long ago. At least, I never noticed it
until the past week or so."

"We will take it," said the detective. "it may be nothing more than
the key to his home in Pontoise."

"I have never seen his home in Pontoise, Monsieur."

"You will call us if you hear from him."

"Of course, Monsieur. I am beginning to believe I never will."

"We are rather certain you never will."

The BBC television crew gathered for dinner in the restaurant of
the Holiday Inn, and Eileen and Michael sat at a nearby table and
studied them one last time. They had been gone all afternoon, and

Eileen had guessed they had been to the cathedral to work out the placement of their cameras. She and Michael had watched them go and return. They seemed to dress much the same all the time: in corduroy slacks or blue-denim jeans, open-neck shirts, sweaters, jackets. Someone must watch them leave in the morning. It would be a disaster if they all dressed in suits for the ceremony in the cathedral.

"That one is you, Michael," she said, nodding at one of the young Englishmen who had become a little giddy on successive glasses of red wine.

"Yes," said Michael. Yesterday he had allowed her to cut his hair so he would look more like the Englishman. "Ugly brute."

She laughed. "Think of me," she said. "Which of *those* shall I have to stand in for?" She cast her eyes toward the three women of the crew, none of them, unfortunately, very attractive. "The one with the teeth?"

"Listen to their voices," said Michael. "Can we do those?"

"We'll have to talk mostly in grunts."

Michael lifted his beer and shoved the mug to his mouth. It covered half his face. "Uhh," he muttered through his mouthful of foamy beer, nodding toward the door.

Bobby Donegal had come in.

"All quiet?" he asked when he was seated at their table.

"Entirely," said Eileen. "They took the camera van as their crew bus when they left here today—and returned it. Look at them. Fat, dumb, and happy, as the cliché goes."

"Be a little less obvious in staring at them, if you please," said Bobby. "I've come to review things one last time. We've got two problems at this point."

"I would have supposed a thousand," said Michael.

"Two that require a final review," said Donegal. "First is that we don't know, even at this hour, where David will go after he leaves us tomorrow morning. Everything—too much, indeed—depends on Pat and Kathy being able to follow him."

"I would have assigned someone we know better to do that," said Eileen.

"Which would be someone *he* knows," said Donegal. "Our advantage is that David does not know Pat and Kathy. More than that, he does not know we have two extra people. Anyway, they're tough kids. They're smart. The girl especially."

"The question is, what if they lose him?"

"We go back to Ireland," said Donegal. "Alive. We abandon the cameras and his bombs and absent ourselves from the Ile de la Cité as fast as possible."

"It will have to be fast," said Eileen. "Once they see those cameras abandoned, they'll be into them in minutes."

"Pat and Kathy will be using the same radio frequency as the BBC directors," said Donegal. "They can listen to everything the directors say to us and everything we say to them, but whatever they say to us will be heard by the directors, too. Everyone must know the significant phrases."

"Once again . . ." said Michael.

"If they lose him, their word to us is plain: 'He's lost. Scatter.' When they are in place to observe him, they'll say, 'Number five is clear.' Remember, *he'll* be listening. He's to take that as word from the directors' van to us. When the prince and princess and the president are in place, and the cameras are in place, my word to all of you and to Pat and Kathy is, 'Check four. Check four.' Remember, I'll say it twice. On that word, we move out of the cathedral. And finally, when I'm sure we're all out, my word to David is, 'Let 'er go, my boy. For Saint Pat and liberty.' When he hears that—*boom.*"

"God save us all," murmured Eileen.

"And there is my second problem," said Donegal. "If we succeed tomorrow, most of us will die, just as if we had let David blow us up in the cathedral. Does everyone understand? If we succeed tomorrow, our part of the world will never be the same. We're starting a war, and we'll only be the first to die in it. God give us victory!"

"God give us victory," Eileen whispered.

*   *   *

David was unhappy. It was stupid to be on a Clichy street on this Sunday night, compelled to break into a store and steal a vital piece of equipment that he would have gladly bought if only somewhere a single French electrical-equipment merchant had made himself available on Sunday. It was a final risk his carefully planned operation emphatically did not need.

One thing was right, at least. The KGB favored fine weapons. He had regretted the Walther he had dropped off Vauxhall Bridge; and Nina, in her womanly kindness, had appropriated a fine Browning automatic for him, from her contacts here in Paris. The weight of it, resting on his left hip, under his jacket but within easy reach, augmented his confidence.

He had parked the Citroen two blocks away and walked along the street toward the store where he expected to find the converter. He wore black pants, a black jacket, even a black beret. He supposed he looked something like a Paris street hoodlum. He was carrying also a small steel crowbar and an electric torch. He had been able to buy those in a department store in Montparnasse.

He judged arrogant boldness would give him his best chance—that and speed. He stepped up to the door and tried the bell again, on the long chance that someone was inside and that he could at last buy the converter. He heard the bell ringing inside, but it roused no one. He glanced around. No one was on the street. He pushed the wedge of the crowbar into the crack between the door and frame, pounded it with his hand to drive it securely into place, then wrenched. The wooden door and frame splintered, half a handful of wood falling away. He jammed the bar in again and wrenched again. More wood fell away. He had made an opening into which he could jam the bar now and break away the wood that held the lock. He wrenched. The door cracked.

An alarm sounded. A big bell on the face of the building, above the door, clanged frantically, echoing through the street.

David smashed the glass with the bar and jumped into the store.

Lighting his electric torch, he began to scan the words stenciled on cartons of equipment. In a moment he saw what he wanted—TRANS-FORMATEUR/CONVERTISSEUR—12v. À 220v. He grabbed the carton and bolted for the shattered door.

The street was no longer deserted. Lights were on in the windows of flats above the stores. Two men were crossing the street toward him. A car had stopped. David pulled the Browning and fired a shot downward, to hit the pavement at an angle. The hard crack of the pistol broke the quiet of the night, but it was probably the terrifying whine of the richocheting bullet that stopped the two men and turned them. They backed away, then ran.

He walked south and turned left at the corner. His idea was to get off the street where the excitement was, to follow the parallel street two blocks south, and then to return to the first street and his car.

"Halt!"

He spun around. A uniformed policeman ran toward him. David could see him unsnapping his holster, drawing his automatic. David fired the Browning. The policeman fell. David ran back, past the writhing figure. He aimed and fired at another man who was running toward him. That man fell.

For a moment, he was alone on the street. He trotted south again. No one followed. He reached the Citroen. He dropped the converter on the seat and started the car. Making a shrieking U-turn, he sped south.

20

GRAY CLOUDS hung over Paris on Monday morning. The fore-casters already chattering on the radio were promising that the clouds would break over Western Europe during the morning and that open skies, now over the Atlantic but moving east, would reach the Irish coast by daybreak, London by mid-morning, and Paris by noon. In the meantime, the day would be chilly, with a brisk wind from the west; everyone venturing out was advised to wear sweaters and coats. The temperature at 7:00 A.M. was nine degrees centigrade.

Among events in Paris for the day was the dedication of a monu-ment in Notre Dame, by the president of France and the Prince and Princess of Wales. The few who were interested in the monument had decided they would go to see it tomorrow, the next day, next week, or next month—when access to the cathedral was not limited by the security forces that would dominate it this morning. Anyway, what was it about? English agents who had come to Paris during the Oc-cupation? Something like that. Another piece of sculpture, commem-orating something that had happened a long time ago.

At 7:45 the RAF jet bearing the Prince and Princess of Wales took off from Heathrow, en route to Orly. It was slotted smoothly into the air traffic over the south of England; only two 747s coming in from the States and a Viscount arriving from Frankfurt had to enter holding patterns to accommodate the special departure, and each made only one circuit of its holding fix. The RAF jet climbed out of the overcast at nine thousand feet and turned southeast.

At that hour, Monsignor Périgord was already in Notre Dame, at prayer in a chapel in the ambulatory. Commissaire Trillat and Superintendent Dole were also in the cathedral. Fourteen agents of GSPR, together with forty-odd policemen, were at work, subjecting the cathedral to still another search. A dozen dogs sniffed through the ancient building, checking yet again for hidden explosives.

Outside, the bridges to the east end of the Ile de la Cité were closed. Vehicles that remained on the quays and Place du Parvis were being searched—or, better, moved if their owners could be found.

Policemen were moving into place in the shops and flats along the Rue du Cloitre. Men with high-powered telescopes were taking positions on the roofs of the Hôtel Dieu and the Préfecture and in the towers of the cathedral.

In a room in the cellar of the Préfecture de Police, Agent Robert Borge frowned over the ranks of identification badges laid out on a long table. Commissaire Trillat still had not given the word as to the background color or the code to be imposed on the magnetic strips, and the badges could not be laminated until he did.

Across the river and only a short distance south—only a few blocks south, in fact, of Rue de la Huchette—Pat and Kathy McCarthy drank tea and ate a light breakfast in their flat on Rue du Sommerard. Shortly they would leave. They had agreed that Kathy would go to the Ile de la Cité, observe David's final meeting with Bobby Donegal, and try to follow him, while Pat would take a post in a café at the corner of Rue de la Huchette and Place Michel, to watch for the black Citroen. David had to leave the Ile de la Cité by way of Pont Michel, they had decided, and there were not many ways he could go. Unless they were entirely wrong and he was staying on the Ile de la Cité, his choices were limited, and their chances of finding him were good.

At 7:45, Major Duncan Glynbourne was at breakfast in the Hilton, with Sergeant Major Tate. They knew the plane carrying the prince and princess was in the air, and they ate sparingly, nervously.

At 7:45 André Bonnac was still asleep with Violette. As usual, he had not gone to bed until well after 3:00 A.M.

Josef Olshanskii was asleep in his quarters at the Soviet Embassy.

Bobby Donegal was awake. He had decided to walk from his hotel to his meeting with David, to clear his head in the cold morning air.

Eileen and Michael were on their way in from Varennes, on an early train.

Paul O'Brien and Frank Milligan were on a bus, on their way to the Place de la Concorde, from where they would walk to Notre Dame. They carried their alternative clothing in paper bags.

David was asleep. He had set his alarm for 8:30.

At 8:32 the RAF jet broke out of the overcast at 2,100 feet and was established on a right base leg for Runway 24 at Orly. This course brought it over Sacré-Coeur, then over the Grands Boulevards, on over Bois de Vincennes, across the Marne, and finally into a right turn to the runway heading.

The airplane landed, roared to the far end of the runway, turned, and entered a taxiway. Shortly it stopped, at some distance from the terminal, and was surrounded by police and diplomatic cars.

Stairs were drawn up. The door opened. The Prince and Princess of Wales stepped from the airplane and paused at the top of the steps to smile and wave to the politely applauding personnel on the ground. The prince was wearing his Royal Navy uniform. The princess wore a dark-blue full-skirted silk dress, a tiny dark-blue hat, and a sable jacket. They moved briskly down the steps to receive the welcome of the ministre des affaires étrangères and the British ambassador to France.

By 9:10 the motorcade of three cars, escorted by half a dozen motorcycles, was on the Autoroute de Soleil, speeding north toward the intersection with the Périphérique, where it would turn east and take a non-standard and presumably unexpected route to the Elysées Palace.

At 9:10, in the post office at Pontoise, Agent Lebey began his examination of mail addressed to George Jean Lechevalier. There were only four items, and of those only one seemed to require any investigation. He slit the envelope and read the letter:

My dear Monsieur Lechevalier—It was a great pleasure to have had the opportunity to do business with you. I very much hope your friend will enjoy the studio flat. Your rental for the month of October is paid. Please remit for November and ensuing months by check payable to me. Once more, thank you for your kindness in doing business with us, and should we be able to assist you in any further way, please call on us.

Jeanine Bello
Rentals Agent

Lebey telephoned Bonnac. He had not yet arrived at his office, so Lebey, suspecting the matter might be important, left word that Major Bonnac should call him at the Pontoise post office as soon as he arrived. Agent Levey would wait there until he heard from him.

At 9:15, Agent Borge at last had his orders about the color and the magnetic code for the identification badges. He was at work on two machines: one that imposed the code on the strips, one that laminated the badges. Commissaire Trillat had chosen orange as the color for the badges.

David was in the garage where he had parked the black Citroen. He was not sure if it had been seen last night in Clichy, but he intended to abandon it now, and he worked on it with a cloth, wiping its surfaces clean of fingerprints. Fortunately he had rented it under the name of McConnell and had been careful not to touch it without gloves except on the steering wheel, brake lever and other controls, and on the door handles. He knew of course that the name McConnell would shortly be identified as an alias for Betancourt. The only name he wanted to protect now was William Gentry Hodges. Even so, he felt compelled, perhaps irrationally, to clean his fingerprints from a car that had been used in a burglary that had resulted in the shooting of a policeman.

He had already disposed of the Browning automatic. He had thrown it into the Seine from a bridge southwest of the city, as he circled on the Périphérique, returning from Clichy last night. He would go to this morning's work unarmed, but that was better than taking any risk at all of being arrested carrying a pistol that had been used to wound a policeman.

He wore gloves as he drove out of the garage at 9:10, on his way to his rendezvous with Bobby Donegal.

At 9:20, Olshanskii left the Soviet Embassy in a staff car driven by a chauffeur. Irina Narishkina was with him. As the driver maneuvered through the heavy morning traffic, taking a circuitous route toward the St. Séverin Quarter to be sure they were not being followed, Olshanskii examined their weapons.

He had issued to Irina a tiny Czech automatic she could carry in her purse. To kill with it, she would have to approach to within a few feet of her man. He had warned her, too, that it would take more than one shot. She should empty the magazine into Betancourt if she were the one who had to kill him.

For himself, he carried under his coat a Skorpion, the same kind of silenced machine pistol that Pavel Alekseivich Zotov had carried. It was heavy and bulky, but it could be set to fire single shots or bursts from its twenty-round magazine, and it was accurate at the range from which he might have to shoot.

Irina studied once more the pictures of David Betancourt. She would get a look at him in person if things developed as they planned. She would see him enter the building at 298 Rue de la Huchette. After that, she would station herself near the door. He was not to be allowed to leave.

*   *   *

At 9:30 David stopped the car on the narrow Rue de Venise, having been unable to find space for it anywhere around the Pompidou Centre or its plaza. No matter. Bobby Donegal had seen him, had saluted, and had followed him as he turned into Rue de Venise.

"Don't touch it!" David warned as the young man with Bobby Donegal reached for the door handle of the Citroen. "Fingerprints . . ."

The young man was called Steve. David had met him at the farmhouse in Ireland. He was a big man, heavy and muscular, with a solemn, vaguely threatening face. David glanced back and forth between him and Bobby. Donegal looked like a tourist, if you accepted the idea that nearly anyone could look like a tourist. Steve looked as if he did not know how to enjoy himself.

"The stuff is not heavy," David told them. "And it's perfectly safe to carry. Here's what I want you to do. Steve . . . Carry this bag open. Let anybody look into it who wants to—so long as they don't touch it. See, it looks like a bag of books. All you're carrying is the bindings, though. I've got the empty bindings glued to the top of two bombs. Swing it around all you want to. They're fastened down tight. Look careless with it, okay?"

"What's this?" Donegal asked, shoving aside a wrapped loaf of bread and pointing at the heater and converter.

"I'll explain as we walk," said David. "What we're going to do is walk to the Pont Neuf and cross to the island. Then we'll break up and head for the Place du Parvis on different streets. We'll meet again by the Hôtel Dieu. I'll turn over what I'm carrying, except for what I have to take with me; and from there I'll go across to my rooftop on the Rue de la Huchette."

"We're walking?" Steve asked. He glanced at the Citroen.

"This is the end for the car," said David. "It stays here."

"Well, if we're walking, we had better move," said Donegal.

Five minutes later, at the corner of Boulevard de Sebastopol and Rue de Rivoli, David and Donegal and Steve watched a motorcade pass by. They guessed it was the one taking the Prince and Princess of Wales to the Elysées Palace.

Ten minutes later the abandoned Citroen, which all but blocked the Rue de Venise, was the subject of a telephone conversation between a uniformed officer on the street and the Mairie of the Fourth Arrondissement. The car was immediately identified as one rented by one Roger Duncan McConnell, who had entered France under a false passport and was wanted by the DGSE. It was perhaps a coincidence, but a black Citroen had been involved in a burglary and the shooting of a policeman last night in Clichy. The Mairie notified the DGSE and the Préfecture.

Word reached André Bonnac at 9:51: a car rented under the name McConnell, with the same passport number used by McConnell at the Hotel Royal Monceau, had been found, apparently abandoned, in the Fourth Arrondissement. Security forces were being rushed to the Palais du Louvre, Sainte-Chapelle, and the Centre Georges Pompidou. Maximum security was already in force around Notre Dame.

Bonnac put down the telephone and had time to give his attention to a telephone message from Pontoise. He called the post office there. Lebey read him the letter from Jeanine Bello to George Jean Lechevalier.

Bonnac telephoned the offices of Bello et Cie, Agents Immobilières. Madame Bello was expected shortly. She would return the call to Major Bonnac immediately when she arrived.

Colonel Cau urged Bonnac to send men to arrest Emily Bacon. Bonnac checked with his team at the Hotel Royal Monceau. Mademoiselle Bacon had left the hotel. She was on her way to Notre Dame. She was being followed.

Olshanskii arrived at 298 Rue de la Huchette at 10:03. He admitted himself with his keys and climbed to the studio flat. From the window he could see evidence of the security in force around Notre Dame. The eastern bridges were closed. A crowd had begun to assemble on the Place du Parvis de Notre Dame. Though they could not be admitted to the cathedral, thousands of people, apparently, would congregate for a glimpse of the Prince and Princess of Wales. (The popular standing of President François Mitterand was at the moment so low that he would not, probably, have drawn a crowd of fifty.) Policemen by the hundreds were evident.

Olshanskii scanned the studio flat. There was no sign that anyone had visited there since his own last visit yesterday. He climbed the last flight of stairs and emerged on the roof.

Irina was below. At the edge of the roof, he raised a hand to her, and she, standing on the Rue de la Huchette below, lifted a hand in return. He stepped to the east side of the roof, put one foot on the top of the brick wall where it rose a meter above the roof, put up the other foot, for an instant stood poised above the long drop to the passageway between the buildings, and then jumped across. On the roof of the next building to the east he could crouch, hidden from the roof of 298 Rue de la Huchette, and watch.

At the Elysées Palace, François Mitterand, président de la république, beamed as he introduced his royal guests to the members of his cabinet, leaders of the Assemblée Nationale, and diplomats. With smiles bravely fixed, the prince and princess received them all, with as personal a word as they could manage for each.

David, Donegal, and Steve walked along the Quai du Louvre, under the trees where a few leaves still clung, beside the bookstalls just beginning to open for an unpromising chilly day, and turned left onto the Pont Neuf. Reaching the Ile de la Cité, they separated, Steve walking to the south side of the island and turning east, David and Donegal walking along the walls of La Conciergerie, where Marie Antoinette had been only one of the hundreds imprisoned and later carried north over the Seine in tumbrils to the guillotine. They walked on east to the Marché aux Fleurs, then on the Rue de la Cité to the Place du Parvis de Notre Dame.

"Thank God for idiots," muttered Bobby Donegal as they walked into the midst of the gathering crowd.

"He made many of them," said David.

The crowd was their cover. Even if one of the scores of policemen patrolling the big square, the Place du Parvis de Notre Dame, had known their faces, his chances of spotting them would have been minimized. People were there from every nation, many of them undoubtedly uncertain as to what they would see if they remained, but drawn by the evidence of extraordinary security and determined to stay and find out.

Kathy had identified Eileen and had followed her, unsure if Eileen had seen her or would want to acknowledge her if she did. Bobby had told her where he would bring David, but she was reassured by being able to follow Eileen. Kathy wore old and faded blue jeans: soft and tight and comfortable. She looked fresh and young, and no one would have suspected she was carrying a loaded pistol in the pocket of her suede jacket. She glanced up at the gray sky, where the overcast seemed to be lowering as if it would settle over the big square and the milling crowd. She looked across the river, at the jumble of rooftops between the quay and the tower of the Church of St.-Séverin. She hoped they weren't wrong, that David really was going to one of those rooftops.

And now she saw Bobby Donegal. She was glad she was alone when she saw him, for she knew her cheeks burned. He was so handsome. She wished she had appreciated him sooner. There he was, with David. Women probably thought David was more handsome. Kathy wondered what they would think if they knew what she knew about Bobby Donegal.

David handed over a big paper bag to Bobby. For a moment they stood and talked—David, Bobby, Eileen, and a young man she did not recognize—and then abruptly David turned and walked away, carrying now only a nylon airline bag. She trotted after him, closing the distance between them as he strode off the square and onto the

Quai de Marche Neuf, toward the Pont St. Michel. She checked her watch. It was 10:24.

Bonnac moved his headquarters to the Préfecture de Police, to be closer to where the possibility of an encounter with David Betancourt was likely to develop. Sitting beside the driver in his speeding car, talking on the radiotelephone, he passed David walking on the Pont St. Michel—then Kathy McCarthy hurrying to keep up.

He had sent a car to bring Lucien Trebonzi from his hotel. Trebonzi, with his weapons in neat vinyl cases, was waiting for him—a little too casual, a bit too philosophical to suit Bonnac.

Major Glynbourne and Sergeant Major Tate were at the Préfecture, too. So far as Bonnac was concerned, they were only in the way. This was *his* operation, with more at stake than the honest Englishman imagined, and he wanted no interference.

At 10:20 the BBC television vans arrived from Varennes. they crossed Pont St. Michel, turned right onto Quai du Marché Neuf, and stopped at the vehicle barricade.

The police inspectors waved the directors' van and the transmitter van through with little formality. No one in those vans was going inside the cathedral. Their orders were to check the crew van most carefully. They asked all the personnel to step outside and ordered them to stand in line beside the van. Without asking their names, they identified each of the BBC camera crew from the pictures on their orange-colored identification badges and handed the badges over to them. The crew entered the van again, and the driver moved it forward, through the lane created for it by policemen holding the crowds back, to the Place du Parvis de Notre Dame.

Bobby Donegal stood a few meters from the directors' van, encouraged to see that the two men and the woman inside were intent on their equipment and giving no attention to the camera van as it moved up and parked next to it. He stood with his hand inside one of the big brown-paper bags from the boot of the Citroen. His hand was on a switch on one of the American detonator transmitters. When the camera van stopped, he flipped the switch.

Inside the camera van the bomb under the seat exploded with a small but violent puff, instantly filling the inside of the van with gas. There were eight BBC people inside. Five of them died. Three would survive.

Donegal stepped to the back of the van and pulled open the doors. He put a cloth to his face and crushed the glass phial of antidote hidden inside. For a moment he stood and breathed in the antidote—nauseating though it was—and then he climbed into the van, still clutching the cloth to his face and breathing through it. Other members of his team opened both doors. He reached over the slumping driver and switched on the van's ventilating system.

The BBC crew sat as they had been when the gas surrounded them. None of them had struggled. Only the driver was visible from outside, and Donegal dragged him around his seat and into the enclosed body of the van.

Paul O'Brien was the next in—he, too, breathing through a hand-kerchief clutched to his face and half nauseated by the stench of the antidote to the poisonous gas. He looked at the unconscious—and dead—British. Two of them were women. He gestured to Donegal. Donegal nodded. O'Brien would have to go into the cathedral as a woman.

They kept the doors opened and let the fan blow, and in two or three minutes the smell of the poison was gone from the van. Even so, each of their people who now climbed into the van crushed a phial of antidote and sucked deep breaths of its sickening stench.

Donegal restarted the engine. He moved the van along the square just far enough from the other two vans that their occupants could not glance in by chance and see that the people in the van were not the ones who had driven it there.

Kathy's spirits rose. She was excited. David crossed the Place St. Michel to the left and turned into the Rue de la Huchette. She caught Pat's attention as she followed David past the café where Pat had been watching for the Citroen; and he hurried out and fell in step beside her.

"Number eighteen," he said as they passed it. "He's not going in there, for sure."

They kept to the opposite side of the narrow street from David and followed him as he strolled with a confident, jaunty air to the east. He came to the door of Number 298. He opened it with a key and went in. All they had to do now was find some way to enter after him.

It would not be easy. Inside the door, David stopped. He took wedges from his little equipment bag and pounded them under the door and into the crack between the frame and the door, all the way around.

In the cathedral, Monsignor Périgord watched the French television crew placing lights. Their thick cables lay on the floor of the ambulatory all the way to the transept and through St. Stephen's portal to a diesel generator running on the quay outside. These huge glaring lights would light the ceremony for all the television cameras, the French and British. The harsh, bluish glare was jarring, intrusive; it seemed a shame to have television cameras inside Notre Dame.

A rope bounded the area that was to be kept clear. Behind it the guests were gathering now. A metal detector had been set up just inside the Portal to the Virgin, and the guests coming in off the parvis were met by a team of policemen who were checking their identification, examining the contents of their bags, and guiding them into the metal detector.

One of those guests was Emily Bacon. She was worried about David. He had not returned. He had not called. She had left a note in their room, telling him where she was going. She had left his pass, so he could catch up with her here if he returned this morning. She had no idea that an agent of DGSE had entered her room and read her note shortly after she left the hotel, that she had been followed here, or that she was being closely watched now.

As soon as she was inside Notre Dame she was the subject of a call to Major Bonnac at the Préfecture.

Major Glynbourne overheard Bonnac taking the call, and his French was good enough that he understood. "That might ease our anxieties a bit," he said. "From what we know of Betancourt's relationship with Emily Bacon, it's hard to believe he'd set off an explosion in the cathedral with her there."

"It doesn't ease *my* anxieties in the least," said Colonel Cau testily. "Maybe he understands that the ceremony in Notre Dame this morning ties up a large element of the available security forces for several hours—making it easier for him to commit an outrage elsewhere."

Lépine picked up the ringing telephone. After a moment he handed it over to Bonnac. "Madame Bello," he said.

"You inquired," said the woman immediately, "about a rental to Monsieur George Jean Lechevalier. Yes. I rented a studio flat to him. It is at 298 Rue de la Huchette."

"Rue de la Huchette . . ." Bonnac repeated. "A flat with a view of . . ."

"Notre Dame, Monsieur. The Ile de la Cité and Notre Dame. The gentleman indicated he would not occupy the flat himself; it was for his sister, he said."

"Is there access to the roof?"

"Exclusively. The studio includes the roof, though with the limitation that nude models are not to be posed there."

"Have you a key?"

"Yes, Monsieur. I retain—"

"Give the key to the officer who calls for it, Madame."

"Rue de la Huchette?" Glynbourne asked as soon as Bonnac hung up. "On the roof?" He had understood more of Bonnac's end of the conversation than Bonnac had supposed.

Bonnac shrugged. "A minor possibility," he said. "Are you going into the cathedral? I will see you there in a few minutes. A few more calls . . ."

"Yes, of course," said Major Glynbourne. "Sergeant Major and I will go on, and we'll see you there in a few minutes."

The two Englishmen left the Préfecture. Just outside, on the curb on Rue de la Cité, Glynbourne stopped. "Rue de la Huchette," he said to the sergeant major. "A rooftop overlooking the cathedral. 'A minor possibility,' hey?" He glanced around. "Where's Rue de la Huchette, do you suppose? And how do I get there?"

Sergeant Major Tate strode off toward a police van a few paces away. "Gentlemen!" he yelled. "Uh . . . Messieurs!"

Glynbourne caught up. "Major Duncan Glynbourne," he said to a surprised French policeman. He pulled out his identification card. "*Service d'intelligence d'Angleterre. Il faut que je vais au rue de la Huchette. Vite. Pouvez-vous m'aider?*"

A huddle formed. An officer scanned a paper and found the name Glynbourne. "*Oui, Monsieur,*" he said briskly. "*Cette voiture là.*"

As Glynbourne trotted toward the car he turned and called back to the sergeant major, "You go on to the cathedral. And be damn careful, man!"

In the camera van, Donegal and the others were completing their preparations for moving into the cathedral. Paul O'Brien was dressed as a woman and was touching his face with light makeup. Donegal was changing the identification badges.

If the Irish had entertained doubts—and certainly some of them had—about the value of the man most of them knew only as David, what he had done about the badges won their admiration and respect. As they watched, Donegal first glued their own photographs to the plastic faces of the badges the French police had issued only minutes ago—covering the British faces and replacing them with those of the eight Irish men and women. (In the case of O'Brien, he used the picture of him dressed as a woman, which had been taken only Saturday.) Then he laid a thin sheet of plastic over the face of each badge and applied the heat from the small hot press David had provided. A converter let them use the electrical power from the van to power the hot press. Each badge was, thus, relaminated. When the excess plastic was trimmed away from the edges, the only evidence that the badge had been tampered with was its slight additional thickness.

Eileen, Michael, and Steve were opening the cameras and installing the bombs. This they had rehearsed, and they were efficient. The plastique and the little radio receivers fit precisely into the spaces they had been made for. Donegal was not finished with the badges when all the bombs were installed.

One of the handy-talkies squawked. "Better be on your way, mates. Their RHs will be here shortly."

Paul spoke into the little radio. "Right," he grunted. "On our way."

They did what they could to conceal the bodies of the British crew—noticing that three of them were still faintly breathing. They laid them out on the floor between the seats and put tool boxes and a spare hand camera over them. They had to hope that attention would focus on the arrival of the celebrities and not on a BBC camera van.

They opened the rear doors and got out. Moving on the side of the van away from the directors' and transmitter van, they made their way into the crowd as quickly as they could. Donegal remained for a moment to lock the van doors securely, then he trotted after them, carrying a handheld camera.

On the roof at 298 Rue de la Huchette, David watched the Place du Parvis de Notre Dame through a small but powerful telescope. He held his little radio to his ear and had heard the director's exhortation to the crew to get moving, which he had thought highly appropriate. Peering through the telescope, with a good view, he could see people on the square before the cathedral almost well enough to recognize faces. He saw the cameras. He watched the Irish move up to the parvis. Here would be a test. Would their relaminated badges work? They would be beyond his view when they confronted the police who would check their badges. Only when he heard more radio chatter would he know if they had passed that inspection.

On the roof across the narrow gap, Olshanskii raised his head enough to see what David was doing. As David peered through the telescope, Olshanskii watched him.

Lying behind the low wall, waiting in the cold, Olshanskii had analyzed the situation once more. He was under no orders to cancel the operation, only to be certain its secrecy was not compromised. Of those who could betray the secret of the connection between David Betancourt and the KGB, Nina Stepanova Samusev was dead, Litvinko had fled into hiding, the Irish (who might or might not know) were in the cathedral with the bombs, and David was here, within easy gunshot. If he let Betancourt kill the Irish and then he himself killed Betancourt, who could prove the connection between the Soviet Union and the bomb blast in Notre Dame? Except for the death of Nina Samusev and the defection of Litvinko, everything had worked out exactly as planned. In a sense, the plot had come round in a circle and was as valid again as it had been before it had seemed to be compromised.

And the triumph would still be there.

Bobby Donegal was the first to step up to the four policemen who would check the BBC camera crew's badges.

"Monsieur Brockington?"

Donegal nodded. The big policeman, whose breath stank from the cigarette he had smoked just before he took up his post, glanced up and down, between Donegal's face and the photograph on the badge. He nodded and gestured to the man with the probe. It was like a small plastic microphone, and the second man touched it to the face of the badge. This was something David had not anticipated, Donegal knew; and he tensed. The probe was attached to a wire that ran to a box on a table. The officer bent over the box and frowned.

"*Passez.*"

Donegal stepped through the portal, into the cathedral. He paused and watched as the rest of his group came through. His only real concern, now that he had passed through successfully, was with

O'Brien. He would have much preferred that Paul had chosen jeans and maybe a sweatshirt to wear with his wig and his makeup, so he would be as casually dressed as the real BBC crew had been and as the rest of this group was; but Paul had for some reason chosen to garb himself in a dark-blue dress, a white jacket, high-heeled shoes, and stockings. He was conspicuous in this crowd. Even so, the two policemen passed him through, into the cathedral.

His next problem was that he had had no word from Kathy or Pat. If he didn't hear the signal—"Number five is clear"—within a very few minutes, he would have to give the order to abandon the operation.

21

PAT AND KATHY had stepped into the antique-silver shop at 297 Rue de la Huchette, and just inside they paused to pull stockings over their heads. The elderly man in the back saw them do this, and he reached for the telephone. Kathy drew her pistol.

"I have little of value here," said the old man in a thin, frightened voice. "But you may take it without violence."

Pat pulled down the blind on the door, to indicate the shop was closed, and he turned the knob on the latch.

"We're not going to rob you or hurt you, Monsieur," said Kathy. "Let me explain. There is a man on the roof of the building. We must go up there and prevent him from doing what he is there to do—which is to commit murder. You must show us the way to the roof."

The old man's blue eyes were weak and wet. His razor had not reached the gray stubble of whiskers in his deep wrinkles. His mustache was stained yellow by cigarette smoke—he was smoking a short butt now. "There is no way to the roof from here," he said. He inclined his head to the left. "The door at 298—"

"It is locked," she said. "We must go up by another way."

"But there is no other way, Mademoiselle. There is an artist's studio up there, and the artist has access to the roof, where he paints and

340

sculpts. No one else in the building has access to the roof. When the artist rents the studio, he gets the roof."

"There are three shops," said Pat. "There are six flats?"

"No, Monsieur. Four. The flats under the roof are tiny: only one room each, really. But, on the floor above the shops there is just one flat: three times as big."

"How can we go up there?"

The old man sighed. "It is mine. I can take you up there."

"We do not want to hurt you, Monsieur," said Kathy. "We don't want to damage your home or take anything that is yours. Help us to prevent the man on the roof from killing our friends."

The old man nodded in resignation. He led them out of the shop onto the street, turned to the big oak door beside his shop, and unlocked it. He glanced up into their faces for a moment—they had pulled off the stocking masks before going out on the street—and nodded thoughtfully. They followed him through the door and up the stairs, pulling the masks on again as they climbed.

The old man unlocked another door and admitted them to a comfortable flat furnished with antiques. The place smelled musty: of old furniture and draperies and of the accumulated oily grease of decades of cigarette smoke.

"I live alone here," the old man said. "You may kill me if you wish."

"We will not kill you, Monsieur," said Kathy.

Pat explored the flat, moving anxiously from the parlor to the bedroom, then to the kitchen. The north windows opened on a magnificent view of the Seine and of Notre Dame. But as for access to the floor above, there was none.

Sitting in the parlor, facing the old man slumped in an overstuffed chair, Kathy listened to the radio that was tuned to the BBC command frequency. She could hear the directors in the van telling the Irish to move the cameras this way and that, to check angles and distances. Quite obviously, the BBC directors had not yet guessed they were not dealing with their regular crew. She checked her watch. Ten minutes until eleven. She and Pat had no more than ten minutes, at the most, to find a way to the roof above.

President Mitterand escorted the Prince and Princess of Wales from the Elysées Palace to the waiting limousines. They would go to the cathedral in separate cars, the president in the first car in the little motorcade, the prince and princess in the third. The middle car, undistinguishable from the other two, carried only agents of GSPR. The president had himself explained to the prince that they would not drive to Notre Dame by the most direct route but would, for security reasons, go a slightly roundabout way.

Led and followed by motorcycle policemen, the limousines sped west on Rue du Faubourg St. Honoré. They would turn south on Avenue Franklin D. Roosevelt, cross the Seine on Pont des Invalides, turn east on the Quai d'Orsay, then follow the quays to Pont Michel, where they would cross to the Ile de la Cité. The motorcade would probably arrive at Notre Dame a few minutes late—but only a few minutes.

Inside the cathedral, an agent of GSPR informed Monsignor Périgord that the motorcade was on its way. The monsignor noticed that the agent did not then go to Sergeant Major Tate and tell him, so he himself hurried to the sergeant major's side.

"Where is Major Glynbourne?" he asked.

"Pursuing a possibility," said the sergeant major. "The gel in green is Emily Bacon," he said, letting only his eyes move to indicate where Monsignor Périgord should look.

The monsignor glanced at the tall young woman standing behind the rope that kept the crowd back. "A beauty," he said.

"Yes. A rare beauty. However . . . I've been studying every face," said the sergeant major. "I don't see anyone who could possibly be Betancourt, even cleverly disguised."

"The television crews," said the monsignor. "The right age. The right sort, generally. Check them."

                                    *   *   *

The rental office of Madame Bello and her associates was on Rue Danton. Bonnac's assistant, Lépine, went there to obtain the keys to the studio flat at 298 Rue de la Huchette. Madame had gone out, leaving a secretary no more than seventeen years old to locate the keys and hand them over to the policeman she had been told to expect. The keys were in a big wooden box, identified with paper tags on strings and the secretary did not try to find the ones to the studio flat until Lépine arrived and asked for them. Then she began to sort through a hundred keys, staring myopically at the cryptic numbers on the paper tags, explaining repeatedly that Madame Bello kept these things to herself and that she, the secretary, had never looked for a key before.

Irina Narishkina pressed herself back into a doorway, trying to remain unnoticed. A police car had dropped a man on the street. Now he walked up and down, alone: an intent, handsome man in a salt-and-pepper tweed jacket, black slacks, and a floppy tweed hat peering up at the roofs. Rue de la Huchette was a short street, and the man had walked the length of it. As he walked past her a second time, he noticed her, and she smiled at him—she hoped seductively; maybe she could make him think she was a prostitute. He walked on. She stared up at the roof where Olshanskii was watching Betancourt. She wanted desperately to warn him there was a man on the street—almost certainly a French agent, although dressed oddly for one—but she couldn't think of a way to get Olshanskii's attention.

And now, suddenly, more cars arrived. One carried agents with machine pistols under their arms. Another carried an angry Frenchman, who leaped from his car and strode up to the man she took for a police agent.

"So, Major," sneered Bonnac. "Not at the cathedral? Afraid to risk the blast that may go off there?"

"If so, we seem to share that emotion," said Glynbourne dryly.

Lucien Trebonzi got out of the car, carrying his kit of special weapons. A police van pulled up, carrying six uniformed men with rifles and riot guns.

"Is he up there?" Glynbourne asked Bonnac, glancing up at the nearest roof.

"Possibly," snapped Bonnac curtly.

"'A minor possibility,' eh? Well . . . if he's up there, he must think he has his explosives in place inside the cathedral. It's still not too late to call off the ceremony, Major. It's still not too late."

"You know what security we have in place," said Bonnac through clenched teeth. "It is *impossible* that there is a bomb inside the cathedral."

"Not impossible," said Glynbourne. "Nothing is impossible."

"I refuse to send the warning that would stop the ceremony," said Bonnac. "We would look like fools."

"You have more confidence than I have," said Glynbourne. "But"—he glanced at Bonnac's car, where a burly, uniformed driver sat behind the wheel—"you are the one with radio communication to the necessary authorities. I can't send the warning. Allow me to remind you, though. The president of France will be in the cathedral, too."

"I am confident there is no bomb in the cathedral," said Bonnac. "And you are right: only I can send a warning."

"That means, then, that there is no need to kill the man up there," said Glynbourne. "We bring him down alive, don't we? For interrogation. Even your own special style of interrogation, Major Bonnac. We'll find out who he's been working for."

Bonnac nodded. "Yes. Who funded him."

As his driver tried the locked door at Number 298, Bonnac communicated by radio with the Préfecture. The motorcade bearing the president and the English royalty was turning into Quai d'Orsay and was no more than five minutes from the Ile de la Cité.

           *   *   *

"What is this, Monsieur?" Pat McCarthy demanded of the old man. He was in the water closet and was pointing to a trapdoor in the ceiling.

"Access to the pipes," said the old man. "To repair what's above, when necessary."

Pat dragged a chair into the closet and stood on it. He slid back the thin bolt on the trapdoor and pushed up. A puff of black dust fell on his head, but the door was open, revealing a dark crawl space between the ceiling of the old man's flat and the three flats above. Pat was slender and muscular, and he was able to lift himself up, through the hole, into the space between the ceiling below and the floor above.

When his eyes adjusted to the gloom of the dry and dusty place, he could see that it was not entirely dark. Where the pipes passed through the floor, the floorboards had never been closely trimmed to fit and close the holes. Small shafts of light entered around the pipes.

He oriented himself. He could judge the pipes. Water pipes were the smallest. Next larger were the drain pipes. Biggest were those that carried waste from the toilet fixtures. He could see three of those, and of course the center one had to be the one that entered the studio flat, the middle one of the three flats. He crawled to that pipe.

He returned.

"Do something with the old man," he said to Kathy. "Then come up here."

She led the old man to his bedroom and, as gently as possible, consistent with his not escaping, she tied his wrists and ankles to the head and foot of his great brass bed, tearing his sheets into broad strips for the bonds. Then she went back to the water closet, and Pat helped her wriggle up into the crawl space.

Together they pushed on the boards around the fat waste pipe coming down from the toilet above. The boards yielded, the rusty old nails pulling out with shrill squeaks. In two minutes they pushed up enough floorboards to give them entry to the water closet in the studio flat. Half a minute later they emerged cautiously into the flat itself, their clothes and stocking masks black with dusty grime.

The layout was simple enough. The stairway to the roof was obvious. Pat trotted across the room, slipped as quietly as possible up those stairs, and cautiously poked his head out the open door. In a second he turned to Kathy, and she whispered the signal into the little transmitter:

"Number five is clear. Number five is clear."

"What's that mean? Don't chatter on the frequency, mates. We need it to give you your orders. Now, Number Three camera, you are still too far to the left. Slip to the right. I don't want those idiot-face priests in the background of your shot. Move over to where you get the stone saint for your background. Got that?"

"Got it," muttered Steve, who was working one of the big cameras.

"Right. Now, Betty, I can't hear from shit. Point that dish at somebody's conversation, so we can hear what we hear."

That was for O'Brien, who was manipulating the tripod-mounted dish microphone, which was supposed to pick up the words spoken by the participants in the ceremony. He brushed the shoulder-length hair of his wig away from his face and tried to point the microphone at a church official and a big man with a bristling mustache, who was talking with him. He turned the knob to increase the volume.

"What I'd like to know," O'Brien heard in his earphones, "is where Bonnac has got to. Isn't he supposed to be here?"—"No, I think he's got another problem."—"He's got none as big as he'll have if something goes wrong here."—"Good enough, Betty darlin'. I can hear them two."—"At least we're here."—"Plus the Groupe pour la Sécurité du Président. I've got a good deal of confidence in them."—"Turn 'em off, hon. I can't hear nothin' but."

A small procession came along, circling the ambulatory, which was roped off to make the passage through the crowd of two hundred or so that had been admitted to witness the ceremony. Led by French and British army officers in uniform, a few gray and hunched people walked slowly—one was pushed in a wheelchair—to a group of wooden chairs placed to the side of the veiled monument. They were survivors of British Security Coordination, the colleagues of the men and women the monument honored.

French television was on the air. The French cameramen swung their lenses toward the faintly smiling, fragile veterans: four men and a woman. The Irish crew turned their cameras toward them, too, though the BBC still had not begun to feed a signal.

"Two minutes," said a voice in all the earphones. It was 10:58, and the BBC broadcast would go on the air at 11:00 A.M.

David heard the words. He had put his telescope aside. He might look again when the motorcade reached the Place du Parvis, but for now he only listened to the BBC directors. He had checked his transmitter one final time. It was activated by a thumb switch that snapped from left to right. The switch was covered with a red cylinder threaded into a collar on the top of the transmitter. He had screwed it off, then screwed it only halfway back on, to be sure it was loose.

It was cold sitting on the roof. He had been there half an hour, almost, and the way the chill penetrated his clothing was a factor he had not planned for. He sat on the dark, dusty surface of the roof, with his arms folded, listening to the BBC command frequency. He would not have much longer to wait.

It would take him no more than a minute to descend through the building, to reach the street. He would walk out of Rue de la Huchette, onto Boulevard St. Michel, and there, in the first restaurant he saw, he would sit down for lunch. There he would hear the terrible news from the cathedral, with all the others having an early lunch; and, like them, he would go on eating, and drink some wine, and an hour after the blast, he would walk into the Sorbonne quarter and find a taxi to take him to his appointment with Josef Olshanskii at the bookshop on the north slope of Montmartre.

He would not go there, actually. He didn't trust Olshanskii. The Russian might send a KGB killer. So David would not go to the bookshop; he would telephone. If Olshanskii—in response to a call for

"Monsieur Cromwell"—did not come on the line, David would know he was not there. If he did come on the line, David would call on him to meet on the Place du Tertre, among all the would-be artists and gawking tourists: too public a place for a KGB killing. Finally, when he met with Olshanskii, he would tell him he had written a detailed account of everything he had done for the KGB and had put the document with a firm of French lawyers. His instructions to the lawyers, he would say, were to deliver copies of the document to newspapers and the Sûreté if ever forty-eight hours went by when they did not receive a telephone call from him. Olshanskii was no fool. He would be highly skeptical of that story. But he would pay over the half million pounds, as insurance against its being true; and he would defer any plan he had to have David killed.

The radio chatter continued. The BBC went on the air at 11:00, and the director was now calmly, but with a note of urgency in his voice, ordering the movement of his cameras and microphone. It seemed to be going well.

David had deep regrets—his mother and Emily.

But he had concluded two years ago, brutal though the decision had seemed at the time, that he could not limit his life to what would please an addled late-middle-aged lady whose mind was occupied almost exclusively with bridge and canasta.

As for Emily, if she had returned to London eighteen months earlier, divorced and anxious to fall in love, she would have offered an alternative to the course he had chosen. On the other hand, what sort of life would it have been, to be married to a complaisant American heiress, living probably in America, doubtless with his mother nearby—fattening, stagnating, aging?

He was making a mark on the world! He would figure in the history of the twentieth century! How would the London headlines read?

ARGIE ADMIRAL'S SON BLOWS AWAY CHARLIE, DI!

David rose to his knees and pressed the telescope to his eye. Where was the goddamn motorcade?

The motorcycles turned right off the Pont St. Michel and sped a little ahead of the limousines. The police lowered the barricades, the motorcycles sped east on the Quai du Marché Neuf and into the Place du Parvis de Notre Dame, and the limousines followed, sweeping majestically into the square. Two hundred uniformed officers faced the crowd behind the sawhorse barricades and stiffened to full alert.

The doors of the first limousine opened, and François Mitterand emerged. He acknowledged the scattered applause of the crowd on the Place du Parvis and walked to the approaching third limousine. He extended his hand to Princess Diana as she emerged. The applause roared across the square, echoing off the Hôtel Dieu and the Préfecture de Police. The prince emerged. The applause did not grow, but it continued, sustained. Prince Charles smiled and waved to the crowd. Archbishop Cardinal Lustiger stepped from the Portal to the Virgin and stood ready to welcome the president and the prince and princess.

Agents of the GSPR urged the president to enter the cathedral, so the president pressed gently on the princess's elbow and led her toward the cardinal and the Portal. The prince fell in step. For a moment they were delayed just at the Portal, as the cardinal spoke his welcome; then he turned and led them inside.

Sergeant Major Tate was distracted by the applause that began to clatter through the cathedral. He turned to see the cardinal archbishop leading the president and the prince and princess through the nave. They would turn left in the transept and walk all around the ambulatory: an indirect route that allowed the guests in the cathedral to crowd the south aisle east of the transept. The party paused in the middle of the nave, to be joined by the French and British officers, who would also take part in the dedication ceremony. After that pause they continued east and passed beyond the sergeant major's sight, beyond the chancel.

They had distracted him from his concern with one of the BBC personnel. The young woman who was handling the dish microphone

had a peculiar habit that had impressed him as oddly unfeminine—
she persisted in stroking her chin between her thumb and index finger, as a man might, testing his shave. Also, she stood behind her
tripod with her feet well apart, her legs spread. She was an odd young
woman, at the very least.

Still, she had passed through the tightest imaginable identification
check before they let her in here. He turned his attention to the BBC
cameramen.

Kathy crouched on the steps leading to the roof, listening intently
to the commands from the BBC directors' van. Pat was just above her,
in the open doorway, from where he could take quick looks at David.
She reached up and touched him on the leg.

"The royals are inside the cathedral," she whispered.

Pat nodded. Now was the dangerous time. If David meant to detonate the plastique too soon, before the Irish were out of the cathedral,
he might do it in the next minute. Pat pulled out his pistol, and Kathy
pulled hers.

On the street below, Lépine had arrived with the key to the door at
Number 298. Bonnac pushed it into the lock and turned it. He
shoved on the unlocked door. It would not open. David's wedges held
it. Bonnac and Lépine put their shoulders to the door.

Lépine glanced at his watch. "If he's planning on doing something to the cathedral with the president and the Prince and Princess
of Wales inside, we have no time left," he said. "It's eleven-oh-
five."

"*Merde!*" grunted Bonnac. "Bring up the bars. We'll break it open."

A uniformed policeman trotted across the street to one of the cars,
to get the crowbars they would use to open the door. Major Glynbourne seized one of the heavy bars and began to pound on the door.

Trebonzi beckoned to Bonnac to step aside. "There is another way
up," he said quietly.

"Yes!" said Bonnac. "Go! And if you see him, kill him! Shoot!
Don't try to capture him."

Trebonzi opened the case in which he had been carrying the little crossbow and the silenced pistol. He jammed the pistol under his belt, hung the crossbow over his shoulder on a strap he had devised for the purpose, and pushed two extra darts into the waistband of his pants, beside the pistol.

"Trebonzi!" shouted Major Glynbourne. He handed the bar over to a policeman and strode toward Trebonzi. "We don't have to kill him. Capture him. Wound him. But . . . Unless he's about to send a detonator signal, try to capture him alive. It's important. We'll want to question him."

Trebonzi nodded. He trotted to the east corner of the building and grabbed the downspout.

Bonnac had followed. "*I* am paying you," he said quietly. "Not the English. You are to kill the man. And when you come back down, tell the English major anything you want. Tell him Betancourt had his thumb on the detonator button."

Trebonzi began to climb. He was a wiry, agile man, and he climbed quickly, finding handholds in the rough brick face of the building as well as on the rickety piping, which tore loose as he climbed. The spouting fell away, but not before it had given him the purchases he needed to move upward. He climbed with confidence born of experience.

"Three in," said the director. Kathy listened and waited for the word that the Irish were on their way out of the cathedral. "One, get the face of the princess. Get in close." Another voice: "Check four. Check four." That was the signal. The Irish would now move out.

The young woman abandoned her dish microphone. Abruptly, she turned away from it and walked purposefully toward the crowd behind the ropes. Reaching the ropes, she squatted and rose again, on the crowd's side; she began to shoulder her way through, away from the ceremony, toward the transept.

Sergeant Major Tate strode after her. Someone raised the rope for him, and the crowd parted to let him through. He caught up with the dark-haired girl in the north aisle of the nave.

"Just a minute, young lady."

She turned quickly and struck. Her fist caught him on the chin. He staggered backward into a pillar, but he recovered instantly and lunged after her. Grabbing her by both shoulders, he turned her and chopped her across the throat. As she dropped, her wig fell off.

The president of France spoke of the courage of the members of British Security Coordination who had served in Paris during the German occupation. The prince and princess listened attentively. The princess noticed that the BBC cameramen had abandoned their equipment. She glanced around. They were all walking away, every one of them. But it was her duty to listen to President Mitterand, and she focused on him.

"What the hell's with you people? You aren't doing a damn thing you're told."

David understood. His Irish were running away. He reached for the detonator transmitter and began to unscrew the cap that covered the switch.

Pat McCarthy pulled back the hammer of his pistol. It had been less than a minute since Donegal had given the signal—"Check four, check four"—and that was not time enough to let the Irish escape the blast. He stepped out and aimed at David's back.

The crossbow dart flew with a thin whisper, struck David a little higher than Trebonzi had intended—between the shoulders just at the nape of the neck—and exploded inside his body with a muffled crack. David puffed out grotesquely. Blood flew from his mouth and nostrils. He toppled to the side, a broken, misshapen corpse.

Trebonzi walked to the front of the building and waved to Bonnac on the street below. Bonnac acknowledged his signal and pointed at the broken door. Trebonzi understood. Bonnac meant the English major was on his way up.

Trebonzi returned to the body of the Argentinian and knelt beside it. He did not notice Pat McCarthy or Kathy, who had stepped out onto the roof, too. He picked up the detonator transmitter. He looked across at Notre Dame, then down at the transmitter. He lifted off the red cap that David had almost finished unscrewing.

"No!" yelled Kathy. Aiming her little automatic with both hands, she fired into Trebonzi's back.

Donegal was a realist. He had given his people two-and-a-half minutes to clear out of the cathedral. If they weren't out then, he would send the signal anyway. He couldn't wait for them to assemble to be counted. The cameras were unattended. The director was screaming on the command frequency. At any moment, the security people might figure out what was happening and try to rush the president and the royals out.

He did not know that in the nave Paul O'Brien lay on his face on the stone floor, his hands cuffed behind his back, his bare buttocks and his scrotum exposed below his pulled-up skirt and pulled-down panties. Two DSPR agents had assured themselves about his sex in the most direct way possible. Now they were pounding his face with their fists as he failed to respond to their questions. Because he understood almost no French, he did not know what they were asking him.

Eileen was a witness to this. There was nothing she could do. She hurried toward the door.

Sergeant Major Tate pushed his way back through the crowd. ("You could make up your mind, for the love of Christ!" an American woman hissed. "In or out?") He grabbed the arm of Commissaire Trillat, who was standing just east of the door to the treasury.

"The cameras!" he whispered to Commissaire Trillat. "They may be full of explosives!"

Commissaire Trillat spoke quickly into a little hand radio, then turned to three assistants standing nearby and snapped orders at them. "So," he said then to the sergeant major. "The BBC—"

"We must cut short the ceremony," said the sergeant major urgently. "Get the people out as quickly—"

"No," said Commissaire Trillat calmly. "We need not worry about your man Betancourt. He won't be sending a signal to set off any explosives. I just heard from Major Bonnac, by radio. The Corsican has killed Betancourt."

Kathy shuddered as she knelt between the torn and bloody corpse of David and the still-breathing body of the man who had killed him. She picked up the detonator transmitter.

"Listen!" yelled Pat. "They're breaking through the doors downstairs. We've got to go! We've still got a chance if we go back down through the water closet, the way we came. Set off the explosion! Our people have had time."

Kathy keyed the BBC command handy-talky. "Bobby," she said. "Everything's gone to hell. But we can still do it. Give me the word. We may as well do it, so it won't all have been for nothing. Bobby! Do you hear me?"

All she heard was the voice of the BBC director: "Wha' th' hell's going on, mates? Have all of you lost your minds?"

Glynbourne had reached the door to the studio flat. Still carrying one of the bars they had used to shatter the door downstairs, he began to beat on this one. The uniformed police were pounding up the stairs behind him. The door broke.

It was all too plain to Olshanskii. He had crawled along the roof to the south edge and had looked over. Rue de la Huchette was crowded with police and police vehicles. They were breaking down the doors and would be on the roof over there in half a minute. They had sent a professional climber up the spouting and the rough façade of the building to kill Betancourt before he could set off the explosion. Somehow they knew the whole plot.

Who were these two children who had come out from somewhere and shot the climber? Olshanskii didn't have time to guess. The girl had the transmitter in her hands and obviously meant to detonate the plastique in the cathedral. She too was listening to a radio. She was only waiting for some kind of signal.

Olshanskii had no choice. He stood, leveled the Skorpion at the girl's back, steadied his aim, and fired a burst. The pretty girl was thrown forward by the shock of half a dozen bullets, dropping the detonator transmitter as she fell. The boy swung around. Olshanskii fired a second burst. The boy fell across the girl's legs.

Major Glynbourne ran up the last flight of stairs and onto the roof. Horrified, he dropped to his knees beside the girl. A dozen uniformed men and then Lépine ran out and surrounded him. None of them heard Olshanskii kick in the door to the stairway from his own roof-top. None of them saw him disappear down the stairs.

Donegal had heard Kathy. He couldn't respond just then; he had been walking past two cold-eyed policemen. Now he was outside. The bridges remained blocked. Police were everywhere: hundreds of them. They were letting no one off the island. Kathy was right. Everything had gone to hell, but it shouldn't all have been for nothing. He put the transmitter to his mouth and gave the order: "Let 'er go, Kathy honey. For Saint Pat and liberty. Let 'er go!"

He was at the end of the Pont au Double, facing the cathedral and waiting for the shock of the blast, when a big man with a mustache ran from St. Stephen's Portal, followed by two uniformed policemen. The man pointed at him. He threw up his hands, but it made no difference. One of the policemen raised a short ugly submachine gun and fired.

On the pavement before 298 Rue de la Huchette, Bonnac and Olshanskii watched impassively as the bearers carried Trebonzi to the ambulance. He had a .25-caliber slug in his right lung, but the doctor said he would recover. David Betancourt and a young man and young woman as yet unidentified were dead. Major Glynbourne and Lépine were up there, examining the bodies, searching through their clothes.

Bonnac looked away from Trebonzi. "There is an evening flight from Paris to Moscow, I believe," he said to Olshanskii. "Aeroflot. Be on it, Colonel Olshanskii."

Olshanskii nodded.

"Oh, your girl," said Bonnac. "Irina Narishkina. She'll stay with us for a while.

"Be more careful with her than you were with Nina Stepanova Samusev, Major. She's an innocent, actually. You haven't much of a catch in her."

"She'll fill in the gaps in the investigation, Colonel."

"I'd like to see your report," said Olshanksii. "I wish someone could fill in some of them for me."

The Prince and Princess of Wales walked out onto the Place du Parvis de Notre Dame to find that during their quarter hour in the cathedral the skies had cleared. They stood in the warm sunshine, between President Mitterand and Archbishop Cardinal Lustiger, and waved to the lustily cheering crowd.

"Your Royal Highnesses," said the archbishop. "Before you go, allow me to present Monsignor Charles Maurice de Périgord. He has borne a large share of the responsibility for security during your visit. Happily, it seems to have been unnecessary."

"To the contrary, Your Eminence," said the prince. "I suspect the job only seems unnecessary because it was so well done. Please convey our thanks to your colleagues, Monsignor."

A few minutes later, Emily Bacon came out through the same door, just in time to see the motorcade leaving the square. She was happy and thrilled. She had stood not twelve feet from the Prince and Princess of Wales. She had heard everything that was said. She had seen the princess wipe a speck—or had it been one small tear?—from the corner of her eye with a gloved finger. She had seen the prince let his cap fall from his lap and snatch it up before anyone could reach it for him. She had seen everything. She was annoyed with David. He had missed an historic event—a once-in-a-lifetime opportunity.